HYPERBOLE

RYAN PARMENTER

HYPERBOLE

Printed in the United States of America

First Printing, 2013

ISBN: 978-0-9911070-0-1

Published by: Rype

Cover designed by Ryan Parmenter
Edited by Valerie Valentine

www.ryanparmenter.com

Please visit www.ryanparmenter.com to contact the publisher regarding distribution and other works by the author. Thank you for respecting the hard work of this author.

CONTENTS

1 FALL

Nothing happens all the time. This pale blue fuzz comes and goes, translucent, cast over cubicles, copiers, ferns. I hear a lot of static, a few key words slipping through. Whatever has gotten me here, I don't understand how to course-correct at this late stage.

I pull myself as far as the tiered stainless three-pot coffee station that reminds me of an Olympic tableaux. I hastily tip the bronze-level carafe into my sheepdog mug. A speck of brown liquid stains the dress shirt I purchased at 65 percent off. I feel a stiffness against my neck, lift up a pale blue flap of my collar, and find a piece of structural plastic meant to retain the collar's shape. I failed to fully dissect the package.

Pulled back to the worn-in swivel chair, I hear the buzzing intensify. Roy looks at me, waiting for a reply. Roy buzzes, steam coming out of his ears, his shirt catching on fire. Roy explodes. I smell someone's toaster pastry. I tell Roy what he needs to hear and he looks appeased enough and slinks away.

I have eleven new emails. I delete four of them at random. The seven left, I read them in reverse-alphabetical order by sender. Someone with the last name Zorro writes:

"Harland, we need to discuss the future of the USA."

"We sure do," I say to no one. I click the DELETE button.

I turn up at Orange Bamboo at 5:41 p.m. Rena has just ended her shift, and she's walking out of the swinging doors of the kitchen when I catch her and lean in. I kiss Rena on the neck as she cranes to make it difficult for me, and she smells like ginger and sweat and a little bit of perfume. Her black hair is tied up with too many things and spurts from all directions of her head like peacock feathers.

"My day?" she says. "My day sucked. How was your day?"

"Yeah, OK."

"The fuck is up with your shirt? How did you shit your front?"

"I spilled coffee on it. How did you see that? It's dim in here."

"Your eyes adjust, retard," she says, smiling for the first time. She sits as little as possible at the edge of a booth and starts counting bills. I slip into a chair on the opposite side of the table, because it's only a half booth. Because a full booth would have been too much to ask. So I'm in some fraying wicker chair. Rena's nostrils flare and she looks at a two-dollar bill like it just died in her hand.

"These are still in circulation?" She doesn't look up; maybe she's talking to the money. "It's like the only way to show a stripper you care is to slip her a two-dollar-bill."

"I like that. You should put that in your act."

She looks up at me. "It's a two-dollar bill."

"OK, never mind. I'm not here." Rena looks back down. We're not really together anymore, I'm realizing, but neither of us has said anything yet. Her hair is pulled tight by an orange scrunchy, a few stray strands flailing.

My hands rest on the half-booth table, and I notice the ragged cuticle on my left thumb. I used to suck my left thumb. In first grade, my mom put lemon juice on it to get me to stop. I complained that the lemon juice would burn my hands to smithereens. Somehow, back then, I knew the word "smithereens."

Rena looks nothing like my mother. My mother was fairly nondescript. My mother occupied, in sequence, a desk, a bed, a wheelchair, a hospital bed, and a casket, all before her sixtieth birthday.

Rena takes up space in the booth, in the restaurant, on the surface of the planet, and so do I. Time passes, and Rena gets her currency in order, and I stare at a flaking gold-painted dragon with ruby red eyes. My blood sugar drops down to nothing, and Rena doesn't ask if I require any caloric intake or anything, even though I'm sure that I must look like a beer-bellied skeleton. She looks down instead of looking at me.

She gets up without saying anything else and goes back into the kitchen, and a waft of fried whatever pours all over me, and I might as well be boiled in oil. No washing machine is going to unstench my business clothes now. Some mother of grease just gave birth to me, and the midwife is too excited to rinse me.

At Skizzers Bar, on one of the all-news channels, a probably computer-animated news reporter explains that the definition of democracy must be decided upon democratically. Half the bar yells for the game to be turned back on. The bartender apologizes, saying so that only I can hear that he accidentally slipped on a lemon wedge and fell onto the remote. I'm sure we'll see that in the history books.

Last year, terrorists destroyed Washington, DC, and it was scary for a few days, but then things sorted themselves out, as they tend to do because nothing is ever actually as horrible as the scenarios we imagine. The new permanent elections have been postponed again until the week before Thanksgiving, because the people who care are in disagreement over the technicalities, since this is a new situation, according to them.

Like many across the country, Rena had cried and cried and said all kinds of racist things, but then she calmed down and drank a lot, and Ollie came over and we got high, and then we watched a non-widescreen DVD of a crappy alien invasion movie, and Rena really did not like the scene with the aliens blowing up the White House, but Ollie and I just kind of stared in amazement and said, "Well, that makes sense, then."

Rena drinks cranberry vodka from a tall glass. She also smokes, which was against the law for a while in bars and restaurants, but then after what the news robots dubbed The Buffet Massacre, it was made legal again. Rena has short nails the color of her drink, a bit chewed and flaked away. I have a passing thought that my love for Rena is a bit chewed and flaked away. I remember the excitement of the early weeks of our relationship, but lately I find it a bit hard to truly feel love so much as think it. I remember it clearly, but the connection between heart and brain collapsed like the Golden Gate Bridge. I like drinking, though, and sitting on my sturdy wooden high-chair at the bar, I alternate between a Hefeweizen and sips of something that supposedly has deer blood in it. Rena's cigarette is giving me multiple simultaneous headaches. I wish I had a lollipop or just a straw to chew on.

Some jock is giving the bartender shit. I half wonder what it would take for me to want to help anyone.

Out in the car, I try to decide whether I am too drunk to drive. I'm about halfway home when I realize I shouldn't be driving. Rena follows me, sort of. She likes to take her own way home. So I see her car behind mine only about half the time, as it slips in and out of my rearview mirror at odd intervals. I pull into the driveway, knocking over some garbage cans as I course-correct.

Rena doesn't show up for twenty more minutes, and I'm trying to calculate if she had time to go to someone's house and have sex with him in that amount of time—not jealous, especially, just scientifically curious. I'm in the lightless backyard of the rental house on the porch swing, hating the coldness of the air I keep inhaling through my mouth. There is no spring or autumn anymore. It's October now, meaning it's essentially winter, and winter will outstay its welcome.

A coffee can on the cement slab-as-back-porch is full of cigarette stubs, boiled over, spilled, smeared, stained. A baby cries down the block. The light from a bulb dangling off a neighbor's garage faintly illuminates my breath, unless that's just interference.

I hear Rena slam her car door and start to unlock the side door and I stage whisper, "Hey."

She drops her keys, gasping. She picks up the keys and comes around the corner, tilting at me, saying, "What the fuck. You scared the shit out of me. I thought you were inside."

I'm almost completely in shadow. I say, "I wanted to let you know I was out here so you didn't get scared, but I scared you, so ..."

"You scared the fucking shit out of me." She repeats this presumably for someone's benefit.

"You're all backlit like a monster in a horror movie," I say.

"I'll be inside," she says. She's walking back around the corner.

"OK."

Her silhouette comes back into view. "What?"

"I said, 'OK.'"

"Oh." She disappears again. Keys jingle, screen and wooden doors creak and slam. Broken spring on the screen door, no pneumatics to slow down the velocity before it hits the frame. Some dog barks, and the baby is still crying. I have the urge to grow to thirty feet tall and walk through the neighborhood, one step in each yard, find the dog and feed the baby to it.

4

Or vice versa.

I walk around to the side door, and out of the corner of my eye, I notice my next-door neighbor's still got an American flag at half-mast. It's been that way for about fifteen months.

I wake up at 7:59 a.m. I'm supposed to be at work in one minute. I have sort of an erection. Rena's gone to her Tuesday/Thursday job. (It's Tuesday.) I wonder how much time it will take to masturbate, and whether that would significantly impact how late I'll arrive at work. Fifteen-minute increments on the time clock, not that I bother to punch in very frequently. Do I try to shower and just do it in there? Or do I just do it in the car on the way, like I tried one morning last month? It's best to find one-lane side roads instead of the crowded, slow freeway.

I cut myself shaving and decide to stop. I decide to turn this into a game where I will keep track of how many people seem to notice that only my left side is shaven. I make sure that I'm otherwise very presentable. By the time I'm dressed, my desire to masturbate has evaporated. My attention span has been hijacked.

When I was twelve years old, I captured a grasshopper in an upturned clear plastic cup slammed onto the sidewalk pavement next to where I'd drawn my initials. There's this suffocating grasshopper, and there's HUG in stone for the eternity until the city came around again to pulverize and pour. A couple days later, I made the grasshopper's husk into the jewel in a paperclip necklace that I presented to my mom. She politely declined.

The windshield of my two-door front-wheel-drive automobile amplifies sunlight by three and I'm more or less blind, once in a while breaking to a whiplash halt when I see the ghost of some SUV less than two car-lengths ahead of me.

I get to my desk by 8:41. No one acknowledges having seen me strolling in, but gossip doesn't spontaneously snap into being, which means the jokes I half-hear sometimes about the "late shift" are about me and whoever else straddles that limbo between obedience and utter anarchy. Once upon a time, I had a grasp of concepts like "motivation" and "investment" and "progress." I am not even sure now that those are words.

I log on, and I realize that I have not in fact shown up today. Though my body arrived late, my mind has yet to arrive, and I cannot rightly expect it to. My computer desktop shows a Möbius strip being marched by tiny stickmen. This is superimposed over the corporate logo, which is a stylized infinity sign. (I guess this is technically redundant, but I like my Möbius strip and its tiny voyagers, digital enhancements I added using pirated software.) So far, no one has said anything, which probably means that they haven't noticed, in the same way that they don't notice me coming in late or stealing whole boxes of pens, or falling asleep in the bathroom stall, or sometimes taking a lunch that lasts until the next morning. I want to kill a vagrant and put him at my desk in a nice dress shirt with a small coffee stain and see how long it takes for someone to notice the smell.

Cindy uses the kitchenette toaster to heat up banana peach breakfast pastries that smell like farts mixed with air freshener. Cindy is on a diet.

I see how long I can hold down the "Z" key on a word processing document before someone comes over to ask me a question. Apparently, the word processing program has a page limit of 32,767.

Roy comes by after lunch, and I comment that I thought he had exploded. Roy eventually goes away, and later I hear him talking to Gerald about *the game*. Someone won *the game*. And it sounds like someone lost *the game*. Quite a game, from the sound of it. The static is about average today. On the way to a non-smoking smoke break, I think I see Dolph do a double take at my partial shave. Score one.

My cellular phone vibrates in my pocket, where it rests sixteen hours a day, presumably giving me testicular cancer.

It's just a text message, and through the blue static, I see a few words: "fair sat smoke"

Ollie. He wants to go to the fair on Saturday. Because we have no consequence, we might as well go to the fair.

Three towns south, in the parking lot outside the apartment building where Terry lives, this random guy starts trying to wash my car with a rag pulled from gray water in a bucket he's holding. Terry yells at the guy that he's got the wrong car. The guy looks emotionally injured. There's a lot of subtext that I don't feel like I can get into. Terry, looking like a vulture in the way that a lot of rockers eventually do, sells me a baggie of what he says is a quarter ounce of Smoldering Mall, and I don't have the know-how to measure or tell good from bad before I smoke it, so I give him the cash (fifty dollars of it from Rena's reserve pile in the shoebox in the front closet, since I didn't have enough cash and didn't want to stop at an ATM).

Terry was Ollie's dealer until a few months ago, when I decided that I had to stop using Ollie as a middleman, because using Ollie for anything feels like taking advantage of a child. Terry starts telling me a story that sounds an awful lot like the plot of a movie that was always on television on Saturdays when I was a kid, and which I maybe never watched all the way through because I couldn't handle the used car commercials that broke up the story every eight minutes. I jokingly tell him, "I have to get to an AA meeting."

And he says, "Yeah, sure, no problem."

As I get in the car, I see the attempted car washer again in my rearview mirror, and for a moment, I think he looks like my dad. I scroll through several albums by G bands on my obsolete mp3 player (… Gel, Gimper, Goebbels …) before I find a Gwyrr cover of the theme from a popular children's program. The brisk air through cracked windows feels pretty good, considering how genocide and online banking have impacted modern conceptions of goodness.

Driving to the bar, I see this girl on Rollerblades that looks just like this girl I never got to date when I was in eighth grade. She has pigtails, knee-high yellow-and-white striped socks, and shiny black soccer shorts. I want to be twenty years younger and fuck her gently on a bearskin rug on a holiday. The light turns yellow, and I fear what will become of the remainder of my life if I stop, so I plow through the intersection.

Old Fuck tells us he was a war hero. He went to war when he was eighteen and didn't escape the service until he was thirty-two. Good and bad; he now lives large on government funds. The self-proclaimed "military millionaire" still appears, moment to moment, like he's just escaped the battlefield. He invested most of his post-service pay in social networking (before the collapse) and cashed out at the peak. Now he's in his forties, claims to have a personal driver, and can sing and entertain us whenever he wants. He looks and sounds eighty.

"And then this tall drink of A-rab …" (the story is almost over, because he's slowing down and getting louder) "… kicks in the door and says, in better English than I ever spoke, 'We are on the same side!' Well, the next thing I see is a turban that looks like a piñata bursting with A-rab brains, and my M4 is lighting up like Christmas Eve at the Vatican, and I say, 'Not if I have anything to do with it, Akmed!' And that's how I got this medal here."

Old Fuck pokes himself through a blank section of his brown leather jacket. If there was a medal, it's not there. But we're all too excited by the story, and it's sort of the perfect ending, and we cheer. Old Fuck looks down at his own chest like he grew tits all of a sudden—he's definitely surprised by the lack of medal. "Screw," he grumbles. He looks up, shrugging. "What are you goddamned civilians drinking?"

I drink a whiskey from the tray when it comes around. Rena's over at the end of the bar submitting her keno form. I thank Old Fuck for the drink, and he tells me the exact words he could say that would extricate him from any murder charge . Unfortunately, I sort of zone out, only catching the last three words: "you Jew shit." Through the mix of emotions and scents, it occurs to me that I did not in fact shower this morning.

Old Fuck tells me how the Catholic priests got away with raping children for so many years: "They didn't worry about getting caught."

Old Fuck tells me the best way to have a taco salad: "Eat the taco, and give the salad to some faggot."

Old Fuck tells me when is the right time to make a move on a lady: "When your dick is hard."

Ollie shows up wearing some kind of tiara with two silver balls sprouting from springs. I make a comment. His response: "Mars doesn't have a New Year's."

Ollie squeezes into the crowd by the bar, puts his hand on my shoulder, and says, "I got a job."

"Congrats," I say. "How'd that happen?"

"It's for a charity."

"Oh shit." I look around for secret cops, intelligent life, hope. I look back at Ollie.

"It's a military charity. It was founded by the provisional government. Half the profits go to the charity of your choice: burned children, nuns, or whatever. And then the military gets the rest of the profits."

"I don't think they're called 'profits' if it's a charity."

"Well, that's what they called them in orientation." He just looks at me. "Aren't you going to congratulate me?"

"Congrats … again," I say. "Did you get those at the orientation?" I ask, pointing at the silver balls dangling above his brow.

"No," he says.

After a second, I raise my eyebrows and say, "Sorry I asked."

"What do you mean? Oh, these?" Ollie's eyes roll up. "I found these outside."

"Gross. When do you start?"

"Tonight. I make my own hours. It's mostly telemarketing."

"You call people at night?"

"I make my own hours. So sometimes it'll be at night, and sometimes it'll be during the day."

"And do you expect anyone awakened by a telemarketer after midnight to donate to your war charity?"

"I would," he says, hurt.

"OK, sorry," I say. Ollie orders a beer and a shot. Rena is losing another round of keno and filling out her next form. Ollie drinks the whiskey and takes a big gulp of his beer before he'll talk to me again.

"You remember my dad had that sandwich shop?"

"Yeah," I say, sort of remembering. "He sold … sandwiches."

"Yeah." Ollie is distracted by a pinball machine's animated sequence leading into a multiball. "I worked there for a few months? Remember?"

I remember a sign and the taste of a cold Italian sub, sitting out by the curb. "It was near the community college?"

"Sort of. That was my first job."

"Wow," I say. Things start to get a little blue and statical. It makes me sad. I want to care about Ollie. I try really hard to think of a follow-up question. Now I'm watching the meatneck fucking up the multiball and wishing I could play instead. I finally think of something to say. "Did you like that job?"

"I don't think so," he says. "My dad sucks. So it seems like I wouldn't like it. But I don't really remember. I just remember that I worked there, and I got a paycheck every two weeks. I remember learning what a pain it was to get a check, and to have to go to the bank and deposit the check, and you better sign it or they won't give you money for it. How does that work? My signature is worth sixty-five dollars?"

I ponder his point.

"Well, the charity has direct deposit."

"Oh, good. That's good." I hate direct deposit. I hate auto bill pay. I never see the money. If I went away, what would change? "It's convenient."

I hate lying to Ollie, but he doesn't know how to take the truth. Or I always mess it up. I want to pull a reversal, but I've paused too long. It would seem fake.

"I like cash, but I'll just hit the cash machine. Go on the Internet to get a few more PIN numbers ..."

The last bit alludes to an e-commerce scam that Ollie successfully got underway. Ollie phished with great efficiency and captured the full details of at least three senior citizens, was able to anonymously withdraw a total of six hundred dollars into a dummy account, and had five hundred seventy of it wire-transferred to the copy center/hair salon near my house. (Thirty was deducted as the transfer fee.)

Then he spilled way too much barbeque sauce for it to have been wholly an accident on his old laptop. He next declared that he no longer wanted anything to do with computers. A week later, I showed up at his apartment, and he was using a new laptop. No explanation.

"Where's Rena?" he asks, looking almost directly at her. I direct his focus to her, now sitting at a table by the jukebox, next to the frighteningly blond Janet.

"They're keno-ing," I say.

"That game is worse than cocaine."

"Except on your sinuses."

"What?"

"Nothing." I want to explain all my jokes with a chalkboard and a pointer and a laugh track. I want to explain to Einstein why relativity is irrelevant.

"I miss Madonna." Ollie is still looking away from me as he talks, watching the lights over the electronic plastic dartboard.

"That old rat?"

"She was a mole."

"Moles aren't domestic animals. You knew what you were in for."

"Madonna liked living with me." Ollie says, finally looking my way. "She burrowed in my covers."

"That's bestiality."

"It's cuddling."

"How can you be sure you never accidentally stuck it in? Like in your sleep? Because that's definitely bestiality."

"I'm gonna put a dollar in the jukebox." Ollie gets up. The silver balls on his tiara dance as he wades through people.

At a loss for anything besides morphing into a rhinoceros and stampeding until I'm covered in blood, I step out of my bar seat and follow Ollie, without really following him, over to Rena and Janet.

"What's uuuup?" Janet says, her hair a shoulder-length intense pale yellow like nothing in nature. Her eyes are a little too wide apart, but other than that—and her personality—she's exactly my type.

"I was talking to the mole fucker," I say, straight-faced.

"Whaaaat?" says Janet, her teeth bigger than my fingernails. She makes that half-smile that people with no sense of humor make when they hear a joke.

"Don't be a dick," says Rena. Rena's wearing glasses for show, pointy horn-rimmed librarian glasses that she doesn't need. Her eyes look small behind them. "When does fuckface want to leave for the fair on Saturday?"

"I didn't ask him. So let's say two."

Janet hovers her left hand palm-down over the table. "Notice anything different?"

I look at her pale, slightly freckly hand. She has thinner fingers than Rena. "No, sorry. You grew another one?"

"No, stupid," Janet says, "the ring?"

"Oh, cool, you got a ring."

"She got engaged," says Rena.

"So?" I say.

Rena gives me the shit-eye.

"Congrats," I say. "I didn't know you were seeing anybody."

"You've met Brad!" Janet yells playfully. "You met him at the bowling alley."

"Oh, yeah, cool," I say. I have never met someone named Brad. "Well done."

"Janet and Brad are going to get married in DC."

"Oh, that's very brave," I say unflinchingly. "What a noble gesture. The time for healing is now. If we don't come together as one, then we are forever separate ..."

"Stop it," says Rena. "Janet's brother died in DC."

"Oh," I say. "Sorry."

"No, it's fine," Janet says. "I know that a lot of people can only deal with such a horrible tragedy by making light. It's hard to process. But I can live knowing that my brother died as part of a grander cause, for liberty."

I hold back the laughter as much as I can, and then (knowing that I look like I'm about to shit myself), I step backward, saying, "Beer time."

Rena is visibly pissed in my periphery. Janet looks up and away, upper teeth biting lower lip, no smile left in her eyes. I'm about to leave. I stop. I turn back, looking down at Janet.

"Look, over a half million people died. Fucking everybody knows someone, or knows someone who knows someone, who died. You're not special. You're not even lucky to still be alive. You're a fucking fluke, like anything else." In the tiny reflections from Rena's glasses, I look like a gnat. "Congratulations on your engagement. I'm sure you'll be happy."

Rena mouths "ass hole" (two separate words) at me. As I head to the bar, I see Ollie staring at the poster of the Grim Reaper drinking Canker Cola.

In line at the Provisional Secretary of State branch, I see a guy who looks like me if I were black. And skinny. And a bit shorter. I marvel at Black Me, staring with such intensity that when the line moves two feet, the troll woman behind me taps my shoulder and says, "The line moved."

To the woman, I say: "Whew. That was a close one. Thank you."

She doesn't know how to respond, but tries. "I didn't know if you saw—"

"OK, OK."

Black Me is next, and he approaches the counter. I peer over shoulders to see if he's also renewing a license. Sure enough, he's escorted over to the photo backdrop, and he smiles, and goddamn, it's just like me but with darker skin and curlier hair. I am really excited. Normally I don't engage black people, not because of racism, but just because I'm shy and I don't really engage anyone I don't know, and where I live there aren't a lot of black people, and any other excuses I can throw on the pile. But today feels different, and I have a very strong sense that I'm supposed to say hello to Black Me.

When he's done, he's smiling broadly and thanking the clerk, and I'm third from the front of the line, and I half-wave to get his attention. "Hey," I say. Then a little louder, "Hey!"

He stops, almost to the glass door, and turns to me.

"Hey," I say, as casually as I can. "Hey, what's up?"

He sort of looks around, and other people look back and forth between us. "Hey," he says. "I'm sorry, have we met?"

I'm sweating like never before. I feel like an astronaut. I feel like I have ripped abs and awesome hair. I come out with: "Do you know Skizzers Bar? Used to be Sober House?"

"Uh, yeah?"

Everyone is staring at us. The PSoS clerks have almost completely stopped working.

"Yeah, I've been to Skizzers some. Do you work there?"

"No," I say. "Nah. I work somewhere else."

Every second is taking about a minute.

"Cool, well …" Black Me trails off.

"You should go up there for Thursday wings, man." Now I'm just talking. Talking to hear myself talk. Talking because everyone in the place expects me to be talking. All progress has halted for this exchange. "The wings are fucking … like, out of this world. Maybe I'll see you up there."

"Yeah, OK," says Black Me. "Take it easy." He exits.

Way too slowly, a locomotive starting up, progress inside the Provisional Secretary of State branch resumes. I become convinced that Black Me has the same birthday as I do. I hold and foster this theory all the way to the clerk's desk, and I get the same clerk that served Black Me.

"This is going to sound weird," I say to the clerk, a plain woman with a dark bob of hair and clear plastic-framed glasses. "That gentleman who you helped a few minutes ago … The one I was talking to? Did he have the same birthday as me?"

Her brow furrows, and she looks down at my nearly expired license to read the date. She looks up at me in open-mouthed fake awe and says, "That's private information. And the next time you come here, don't harass anyone."

I score thirty-seven out of forty on the multiple-choice driver exam. The clerk condescends to explain the ones I got wrong before issuing my new license. When I get out to the parking lot, it's cold and I don't see Black Me anywhere. A four-piece oompah band hogs the nearest corner, coffee cans covered in yellow construction paper near their feet. They honk away, begging for a cause. I stroll over, low brass rumbling my chest, and I drop my expired driver's license into the nearest can.

Rena sucks my dick next to the dumpster behind Skizzers. This is how we make up. I'm literally humming the song the oompah band was playing, which was like a day and a half ago. I can't finish, and I tap her on the hair.

She says, "You gonna?"

My quiet face tells her all she needs to know. She stands up, dragging her forearm over her lips.

"Nice," she says.

"It was amazing, Rena," I say. "I'm just …" What am I? "I'm starving."

She looks up toward the sliver of moon surrounded by blue-gray clouds, in turn framed by two brick buildings, one of them the rear of Skizzers.

"I love you," I say. "You know that."

"Love you too," she says, still looking up.

"We should stay in tomorrow," I say.

She sighs until her lungs fall out of her face.

"I saw a homeless guy who looked like my dad," I say.

"Sure it wasn't your dad?"

"Good one." The wind chills my still-damp penis through two layers. "You wanna go back in?"

She walks down the alley, still wasted, but now angry, too. I feel an energy well up inside my thighs and upper arms that's about to blast me high into the sky, but it sublimates to a jaw-rattling shiver. I smell the wings inside, and that's why I don't make a break for it.

With fists the size of beanbag chairs, I keep punching my mom in the face. She rocks backward and rolls forward again, one pivot point, an inflated punching-balloon clown. The see-saw movement warbles, indicating a bottom-heavy shifting of sand. I punch and punch, and mom keeps rocking back, rolling forward. This goes on for some time. It's not real, but I feel it. My fists hurt at this size, swollen like they're irreparably wounded and tied off for amputation. Bam. Sorry, mom. Bam. Sorry, mom. I'm already annoyed that I'm going to have to catalog and dissect this later. Bam.

Ollie snores, slumped on my couch, covered in cheese corn. I can't feel my hands. Rena is in the bedroom. The light from outside is afternoon light—even through burgundy drapes, it's not delicate enough to be a decent hour. Somehow, I'm holding a can with about a third of its contents—a chocolate diet shake—intact. I can smell my pits. Must have been a good sleep.

I take the evidence of a 4 a.m. chocolate craving to the kitchen sink, dump it, and rinse the can. I throw it in the stolen postal service crate that we use as an in-house recycling bin. Then on Tuesday nights I dump the bin into the trashcan. It's all going to the same place anyway.

In the bathroom mirror, I get a moment of zone-out reflection time. The first one awake, I get to ponder what would happen if no one wakes up. I'm the last moron on Earth. Sorry, civilization: You shall not be restored.

The stubble on my face is longer on one side than the other. My eyes look old, recognize themselves as old; more philosophy to tear apart. I stick out my tongue, and it's a gradient from gray to beige. My teeth feel gritty with, undoubtedly, crystallized sugar from the SlimFast. The small, old scar on my temple looks like a newborn centipede. I haven't been rafting since my seventeenth birthday.

I pretend to have a palsy, shaking my head crazily. When I stop, my chin takes an extra second to halt. The beginning of goddamn jowls. I fart and like the smell. I pull my white gym socks off just to feel the cold tile on the bottom of my feet. I smell the socks, and I also like the smell. I bite my left thumbnail, and I almost wish there were a bit of lemon on it. I'm confiding in my reflection, who is just a little uglier than I'd like him.

When I suck the coated toothbrush into my mouth, which stings a bit, I slip back to the spelling bee I lost in fourth grade. I misspelled a word, in part due to my mom's presence. The word was "condemn," "to declare to be reprehensible." I knew the word. I knew how to spell it. I was one of three left standing. I stepped to the microphone and said, "Condemn: C … O … N … D … E … M …" The judges paused, waiting to see if I had the final "N" in me. I did, but I didn't say it, because all I could keep thinking was, "I just spelled 'condom' in front of my mom." Which I hadn't, but almost. So I choked, and after a long enough pause, the gray-haired woman in the tweed coat leaned into her silver microphone and said, "I'm sorry, that's not correct." The Asian student from another elementary school nailed it as I walked back to my mom to get my coat and go for a consolation dinner at a horrible buffet restaurant.

I spit out brown toothpaste foam.

I hear a groggy, "What … the … ?" from the other room, and I know that Ollie has discovered the cheese corn disaster.

I get on the scale and I'm disappointed, though not pissed off. I could bust through the wall and climb the tallest building and wave my arms, but no plane would try to shoot me down.

"Are you in there, Harland?" Ollie asks through the door.

"No," I say. "You're in there."

There's a beat, and he states the facts.

"I gotta take a poop."

"OK," I say. "I'll be right out." I open the cloudy glass window. I place the air freshener prominently on top of the toilet tank. One last glance in the mirror before I leave allows me to see the art on the tee shirt that I got for three dollars from the resale shop. A curly pink font reads: DADDY'S LITTLE HOMO.

I open the door, and Ollie's hand has some blood on it.

"Your hand is all bloody, dude," I say.

"Oh crap," says Ollie. "My scab must have come off."

Rena, taking a quick break from her watercolor painting, inhales deeply from the tapered tip of Ollie's glass kangaroo dick. She holds it in and sits on the windowsill and I hear the clock ticking. Glancing beyond her, I see a bunny hop by. Rays of sunlight cut through reddening leaves. A nearby marching band tunes up for a homecoming parade, warbling winds and arpeggiating low brass. Ollie picks his nose with his left ring finger. Rena exhales through the open window. A butterfly flaps through the quickly dispersing smoke.

I take the kangaroo dick to my lips and after four strikes light the bowl with my flint striker. I inhale deeply, tapping my lemon thumb on the shotgun (Ollie laughs when I call it the nostril) to get bursts into my lungs. Outside, a raven comes to rest on a birch branch. Through the smoke, I can distinctly smell a neighbor's fresh batch of chocolate chip cookies. Heat lightning rumbles, and I worry that the fair will be rained out as I puff out music note-shaped clouds of blue-gray smoke.

Ollie waits politely to see that I have finished my turn, and gently takes his kangaroo dick, the pink glass almost the same hue as his already-stoned face. He grabs a glowing tea light from the felt-matted top of the hutch and tilts it forty-five degrees, spilling a dollop of wax on his brown corduroys that quickly turns opaque. He brings the bowl up to the flame, the tapered tip on his slightly chapped lips. The proximity of the glass tip to his cold sore makes me nervous until I picture the cold sore saying, "Nah, don't sweat it. It's cool."

Ollie sucks in bursts and holds it in. Through a neighbor's window, Bert and Ernie tilt their heads in tandem. On occasions like this, the clarity of high-definition television scares the shit out of me. Wind chimes jingle. A breeze creeps up my tee-shirt sleeves and Ollie exhales a flowing scroll, listing the names of everyone who ever died in battle, which soon dissipates into wormlike wisps.

A family of raccoons dines at a small picnic table on the stump of a sequoia. Rena flicks out her tongue as she paints. She points at certain spots on the canvas, declaring names for the raccoons, after the kids she's babysat over the years. The yellow stuff that the raccoons are scooping up with big spoons is potato salad, says Rena.

"Raccoons like potato salad because it reminds them of Idaho. Raccoons originally came from Idaho."

"Yeah," says Ollie.

Rena bites her lower lip, scrunching her face and coughing a bit, and continues. "But the Antelope, you know. The Antelope said, 'No way.' The Antelope weren't having Any of that. And that's Why the Raccoons had to go." Rena makes it very clear by enunciation which words are capitalized. "They had to leave their Home, and they can never go Back. It was like the Exodus of the Chosen people. The Raccoons were Chosen, and they Had to Leave. But at the same Time, they were Freed. You know? They were Freed. Because they didn't have to Worry about the Antelopes anymore. Never Again."

"Yeah," says Ollie. "I heard about that. And it's like DC. You know, the people, the politicians, got blown up. But really, they were freed."

"We should have been freed," I say. "Why weren't we?"

There's no question that the local fair is underfunded. Everything tries so hard, the amateur efforts failing hilariously, and I love it all. The old lacrosse field finally serves a purpose. It's amazing because it's not great, but people tried really hard to make it good. It's a spectrum of attempts, a triumph of understood-but-not-actualized possibilities. I wouldn't have it any other way.

The food trailers feature airbrushed elephants blowing water from their trunks and leotard-clad woman twirling fire-tipped batons. A male in a leotard holds semi-cupped hands forward, either releasing a dove, or having just rendered it into existence. Curved streaks framing the dove's form indicate flapping. Rena pensively points at the silvery airbrushed bird, tilts her head, and names it after the first boy she ever kissed. A seven-year-old version of myself is momentarily jealous of Jason the Dove.

The game booths and stables offer: beanbag cornholes, bowling ball suspended from wire to knock down pins on adjacent table, squirt gun fight (I can't tell how the winner is determined), ring toss onto beer bottles, "Recycle Activity" featuring plastic milk jugs collected by soccer moms, blindfolded clothespin-on-nose walk (which implies impaired smelling and vision), crazy mirror black light closet, mouse race, tabletop skee ball, Chinese handcuffs tug o' war, plastic cups-and-string telephone game, coin toss (betting on heads or tails), rubber ducks with winning or non-winning numbers on the underside of said ducks, hopscotch challenge, broom-between-the-legs race (like witches, I guess, or wizards), arm-wrestle the psychic, cap gun Russian roulette, and blackjack for charity.

Ollie runs over to an animatronic clown. "I saw this with my third eye before we even got here!" he yells happily. Sprouting from the frozen-expression clown's mouth is a red balloon cyclically inflating and deflating. Ollie collects clown figurines. His apartment walls are accented by a surprisingly diverse array of clown-themed paint-by-numbers, all unpainted. Rena won't go to Ollie's apartment. I can think of reasons besides clowns not to go to Ollie's apartment, most of them olfactory, but clowns are Rena's chosen reason. Rena faces the opposite direction from the clown, grasps my arm, and states with a restrained urgency without looking at me, "Lead me away."

I am starting to feel it, big time. The rush has permeated every pore.

The main theme starts to be overalls. Near one of the art booths, I see a guy wearing overalls, a yellow tee shirt and a straw hat. I immediately want overalls and am sad that I'm not wearing them. I get pretty infantile about it right away. I turn to Rena:

"That's guy's overalls, I mean …"

Ollie nods, because he loves me. Rena looks at a gray sculpture of the old Capitol building. I tug on her sleeve.

"Did you hear what I said?"

"No, Harland." Rena finally turns to face me. "What did you say?"

"Um, I …" This takes some effort, which strikes me as very funny, and I start laughing. "I just wanted to say something. So, like, hold on …"

Ollie grins at me, then he takes a big lick from an orange sherbet pop that he has somehow attained. Now his tongue and lips are bright orange.

"Look out, Rena," I say. "Ollie's a clown now. Ollie has clown mouth." I'm giggling. "Ollie has clown mouth, Ollie has clown mouth." I start to sway my hips in rhythm and Ollie starts hinting at doing a breakdance, and Rena stands nonplussed, waiting for this moment to pass.

Ollie and I clap a cool syncopated rhythm and when we happen to stomp our left feet at the same time, it's absolutely thrilling. "Ollie has clown mouth!" We try to get a crowd chanting. "Ollie has clown mouth!"

The crowd, I soon realize, is three teenagers who might be more high than us, and a rent-a-cop, who, I stage-whisper to Rena, is "clearly formulating a plan for how to capture all of us in one fell swoop."

Ollie sings, dancing like a marionette: "One fell swoop! One fell swoop! Ollie has clown mouth! One fell swoop!"

Rena escorts us to the lemonade stand. She orders a very large pretzel suffering from a serious acne of salt and a thick-plastic souvenir cup of lemonade. She pulls random cash from her pocket, plucks a ten from the middle, and says something I can't make out to the cashier (the cashier looks like my dad), and drags us over by a couple of large disembodied tires.

"Have some lemonade, lemonhead," says Rena.

"It's lemon thumb," I say. "Thank you."

I take the cup and suck a big gulp through the straw. Ice cold and very watered-down, it's delicious. The cup is way too heavy, which makes me suspicious. I peel the lid back, and I find two mostly-gutted halves of a lemon atop the ice.

"There's a whole lemon in here," I say. "That's redundant."

Ollie tries to make a beat out of "that's redundant," but it doesn't work and fizzles out.

We plop Indian-style on the sparse grass and dirt and lean against the tires. I watch Rena start to take a bite of the pretzel, the inevitable avalanche of salt particles tumbling onto and into her loose, tie-dye-colored sleeveless top, and then the pretzel simply comes to rest in her mouth. The pretzel has docked. She sits there holding it to her lips, barely gnawing it, looking far away. Clouds part, and the light changes her hair, bringing out the hues hiding in what I usually interpret as simply "dark." I see two zits on her neck, but otherwise her skin glows, clear and clean.

Ollie tries to reassemble his sherbet stick, tube, and wrapper to make it look like he hasn't even opened it yet. He works with the intensity of a mad scientist. His orange lips are shiny and pursed.

Rena finally bites through the pretzel and chews it. She wipes her mouth with her wrist and seems to consider how to phrase a question. Rena doesn't fear properly deliberating things, which I admire. I remember how to think analytically, but my attention span rarely allows it anymore. I feel like I need to de-frag my brain. I need to reallocate some resources. I need to upgrade my firmware.

Rena and I watch Ollie bounce around in the moonwalk. We convince the seventeen-year-old attendant that Ollie is a fifteen-year-old with Down syndrome. Ollie stiffly claps his hands together as seven-year-olds laugh at him and he tumbles to the purple vinyl floor. The hit single "Fuck Yo Dead Mama" echoes distantly from one of the RVs in the parking lot. Ollie has had twenty-seven birthdays. He lets his tongue fall out of his mouth and his face scrunches further. He really milks the role.

I almost shit my pants as a small firecracker bursts behind me. Some little brown-skinned kid wearing a tank top with a weird octagon symbol flips me off and runs away. Rena flips him off, moving her hand to keep her middle finger directly in line with him as he weaves through the crowd before slipping between two obese women and out of sight.

"You want kids now, honey?" I joke.

Rena turns toward me, her full body.

"If you ever ask me that question again," she says, "I will cut off your asshole."

I break before she has a chance to play up a deadpan moment. I kiss her cheek and slap my hand onto her butt cheek, keeping it there for a moment when I feel a pleasant human warmth.

I see a cactus walking toward me, some big foamy green alien thing. I panic as I start to imagine how things could have come to this before recognizing it as a costume.

"Why's the asparagus monster at a fair?" I ask honestly.

"Scientists have been trying to answer that very question since the dawn of man," says Rena.

"Do you think I could be a trap—" I cough. "A trapeze artist?"

"No." She smiles sweetly. "I want you to stay on the ground with me."

I love her all over again.

◎

These are the sitcom ideas that I pitch to Rena and Ollie as we're walking back to Rena's car:

ROLLAIDS: Famous wheelchair-bound motivational speaker Harvey Rollins (as "himself") acquires an immunodeficiency and has to substitute teach on the wrong side of town in order to afford AZT, but comes to an unexpected understanding with a rag-tag gang of streetwise teens. Season finale: Rollins dies of AIDS. (If it gets picked up for a second season, then we do a prequel story. If it gets picked up for a third season, then it picks up chronologically after season one, and Rollins is now a ghost living with AIDS who has to teach streetwise ghost kids.)

BUTTER-SIDE U.P.: A hotel located in Michigan's Upper Peninsula sees a new "star guest" each week. The stumbling, self-effacing owner/operator of the hotel is always mistaken for a Hollywood lookalike named Bob Oldlung (but he sounds like he's from the U.P.). Not-Bob's wife is played by a stick of butter, and only Not-Bob believes that she's real. Season finale: Stick of butter is used to make a batch of poison pasties, leaving everyone at the hotel seemingly dead (cliffhanger and/or series finale).

TWINKEYS: Twin monkeys keep getting mistaken for one another by gullible zookeeper. Plenty of broad mischief.

EXTRA CELESTIAL: Heaven is overrun by aliens, who claim that they founded heaven eons ago and have simply been on vacation.

Uptight dead Christians can't understand the hard-partying aliens, and it amounts to some serious afterlife/space shenanigans. (Aliens CGI or puppets?)

JAILBAIT: Two fishermen are arrested for not throwing back an underweight walleye they caught on the Missouri River. Their lawyer (one of those actors with an unruly unibrow) plea-bargains to get them community service. Unfortunately, they soon find out that the community service has to be performed at the prison. Every episode, lawyer visits prison to sneak in some goods that they can barter with. One-season arc ends when walleye is big enough to be legally caught, and their sentence is commuted. Any consecutive seasons would play out with puppets replacing the live actors.

THE FIRST LEMMING: Guy Normal's name is mistakenly placed on the presidential ballot, and he's elected. At first a reluctant leader, he begins to remember all of the things that he disliked about politicians (flashbacks to Guy complaining to his parrot, and then his parrot squawks the lines out back in the present, jogging Guy's memory), and uses those ideas to guide his administration. Guy should be played by an unknown, but the cabinet is an array of recognizable character actors. Pages and interns are played by the newest Internet stars. Guy has the highest approval rating of any President ever, and people will pretty much do whatever he says. Season one ends when DC is leveled by terrorists.

We finally find Rena's little, green, foreign car.

Wind rapes my hair, terminal velocity forcing me toward the increasingly defined pavement, my clothes shaking like an earthquake, lips peeled back and teeth freezing from the excessive wind blasting at them, my mouth bone dry from air and screaming and fluids diverted to tear ducts and urinating myself. I fall toward the ground, shitting myself, wondering whether the words "undisclosed causes" will appear in my obituary, trying to remember—in order—all of the girls I've had sex with (the quantity is a single-digit positive integer).

This mimics my late friend Seth's suicide, or mocks it. Something tells me the term "homage" does not apply. Seth was a super-talented and closed-minded self-hater with prospects he ignored and a crazy mother who drove him to focus on his perceived failures. He died a virgin, more or less. The fact that he drove to a different state lent an air of mystery to the immediate circumstances, although the lead-up seemed passably rote under objective hindsight observation. Our friendship had fallen off in the year after high school, the year leading up to his death. I shunned him for failing to embrace and develop his talents, for turning down a full ride to a telecommunications college. We went our own ways, and he pursued a life of straight-laced business (in a pyramid scheme) and compressed frustration over non-instantaneous success onto his failure with girls. He internalized lost battles like no one I've known since, and let demons eat out his innards. I ran into him, meeting up with a mutual friend who had him in tow, about a week before he jumped off the tallest building in a neighboring state's biggest city. Seth said he had a cold. I sensed more than physical illness, and I ended up dropping him off alone at the apartment he had shared with his mother as long as I had known him. I said something weak in an effort to be comforting. "Call me if you ever want to talk." The subtext connected, I thought. A week later, some city workers had to clean residue from his impacted head from the pavement.

So I plummet, interpreting his death for my own reasons, feeling physical sensations, and disappointed by the lack of emotion. This is a flat performance. A director would ask for another take. Where is my character's motivation? True to form, I can't even muster the energy to kill myself, and the pavement dissolves to a mosaic of stars.

2 GRAFFITI

I realize it's the middle of the night, and cold sensations surge to my extremities. I sigh and feel light, floating slightly above barely damp sheets. In a parallel timeline, there might be a dog licking my cold bare feet, but in this reality, Curly became a ghost. Curly had been a hairless sheepdog, which I was told by the vet was an impossibly rare strain of the breed. I always thought he looked like a dog mummy. Curly died choking on Gary, the cat. Gary died not due to attempted consumption by a senile, alopecic canine, but a few weeks after that, due simply to being an old cat. Both of these deaths transpired in the same month a year ago, shortly after DC fell. Then Rena and I found ourselves in our tiny rental house that suddenly seemed disconcertingly big enough.

I don't feel or see Rena next to me. The hallway light sneaks in and illuminates rippled sheets that appear simultaneously oceanic and desert-like and frozen. I scoot forward to the edge of the bed and slide onto the waxy orange wooden floor. A nice breeze cools my ankles.

The dark living room is illuminated only by remainder light from the yellow bulb over the stove in the kitchen, which is really part of the living room, unless you count the shift from dirty beige carpet into off-yellow tiles as a cartographic delineation. Rena sits on the couch, hugging her knees.

"My dad died again," she says.

◎

Ollie leads us into the church where he says he was baptized. The

24

congregation has mostly dispersed following the late mass on Sunday. An uncomfortable warmth and the gamey smell of densely packed humans lingers, and I cannot stop glancing at the quarter-scale plaster Christs jutting from the side walls, each depicting Jesus in different uncomfortable positions, with labels like, "Stumbles on loose floor board."

Ollie leads us down the aisle toward the priest at the altar, a white-hair-and-glasses archetype with blotches of redness further texturing pockmarked cheeks, brow furrowed and eyes pulled tight in focus as he scribbles some notes in a black journal. Ollie walks with a determination I rarely see in him. The back of his tee shirt has a list of about fifteen dates from the tour of a band I don't think he's ever actually seen. The top of the shirt has a rather hairy-looking font spelling the word, Tu$h. Ollie's green corduroy pants and carpet-dampened footsteps make a decent establishing beat.

I notice that Rena has fallen behind. I turn to see that she stands several pews back, looking up at some stained glass, several colors of light and curling shadows creating a discotheque camouflage about her form. I can still taste her pussy. I have brushed my teeth and had coffee since I woke her up. I turn back and try to catch up with Ollie.

Ollie stomps up the three steps, hiccupping the syncopation, and stops with his hands on his hips. He looks like a superhero on an off day. The priest purposefully finishes whatever he scribbles, draws a red ribbon into the black book and pulls the corner of the front cover to close it. Only then does he clear his throat and turn to acknowledge Ollie.

"Hello," says the priest.

"Hey," says Ollie.

I stand in the aisle at the bottom of the three steps up to the altar, looking up toward Ollie. Ollie, the priest and I form points of a scalene triangle in a plane that would intersect the floor and the ceiling. I look over my shoulder and see a few more stragglers exiting the door at the back of the church, stark white from noon sun outside. I can see Rena, now just a silhouette backlit by the cold sunlight, and I hear her humming something. She drags her hands over her abdomen, spinning slowly to take in the art glass where the walls meet pitched ceiling. I turn back to Ollie and the priest.

"Did you enjoy the sermon?" says the priest.

"I didn't hear it," says Ollie. "I just got here." He breaks for a moment, and I wonder whether he forgot why he brought us here. He had seemed pretty purposeful in the ride over. I feel a drip of sweat down my lower back.

"I see," says the priest. He turns to acknowledge me. "Good afternoon."

"Hello," I say.

"Do you remember me?" says Ollie. The priest turns his head back to Ollie, and a politely confused smile crosses his face.

"Are you ... Molly and Dan Norfolk's son?"

"No," says Ollie. "Norfolk? No. My name is Oliver Pilgrim."

"Pilgrim," the priest says. He thinks, or pretends to think, and then remembers or pretends to remember. "I recall some Pilgrims in the church, although not for quite some time."

"Yeah," says Ollie. "I went to church here. My mom used to bring me when she was a kid. I mean, when I was a kid."

"Welcome back," says the priest.

"Thanks," says Ollie, not smiling. "You're Father Gorgon." Ollie says this so it might be a question, a slight tremor in his voice.

"Yes," says the priest. "I am Father Gorgon. Well remembered."

"Yeah," says Ollie, curling his fingers and tapping his left foot in no certain rhythm. "So, do you remember me?" Ollie's ears flush red. Ollie's arms look ghost white except for his elbows, gray and rough. I start to recognize whatever Rena is humming back there, though I can't quite place it. Father Gorgon looks back at me for a moment, his mouth drawn wider and more flat. He pulls his thin-rimmed glasses tighter to his face as he tilts his head to scrutinize Ollie.

"Oliver. Ollie?" my friend says to the old guy, using his own name as an interrogative.

"I'm sorry, I don't remember," says the priest. "When did you last attend?"

Ollie folds his arms across his chest. "You molested me. Do you remember that?"

Father Gorgon's brow now scrunches until it covers a fair portion of his nose. "Excuse me?"

"My name is Ollie Pilgrim, and you molested me." Rena stops humming, and now I'll never be able to figure out what the tune was. "Do you remember me?"

"I've never done ... I have never done that." The priest is breathing visibly, his black robe moving up and down. Ollie sighs and his head drops a little. He picks his head back up and tilts to the side a bit.

"Yeah, you did." Ollie's fingers dig into his palms. "You molested me, and I want to know why."

The priest is all red-faced now. This is just how I would have directed a scene like this. Just the right beats of silence and little bursts of dialogue with mid-range church reverb. Sonically, it really works. And the framing of these two men from my low angle seems to elevate the importance of everything. I am bummed I don't have my video camera, and that my phone is so old.

"You molested me, Father Gorgon. And I don't want money. I don't want to send you away. I just want ... to know why. Why did you do that?"

"But I ..." The priest is no longer so angry. Instead, he seems thrown. He grasps the edge of the pulpit. His head drops. His glasses slide off, clicking the wooden stand before tumbling to the carpeted floor. He starts heaving and drooling. His behavior doesn't quite suggest a heart attack, but I'm as worried as I am exhilarated. The priest starts whispering to himself. "How? How?"

Ollie turns to me and flashes a big smile. Then he turns back to the priest and, with as much gravitas as before, says, "Tell me why. Father Gorgon, just tell me why, and I'll leave you." Ollie is winning all kinds of acting awards. I'm starting to get an oddly timed boner. The priest's face lifts again, red outlines around his eyes where his spectacles had been. Sweat and tears ensure consistent lubrication, a really remarkable sheen. He looks like he got beat up in a nasty fight, like one with a prisoner or a sibling.

"I ..." Father Gorgon falters and looks away from Ollie. He turns back, locking eyes with my friend. "I didn't know ..." He sucks in or sobs. "... what else to do."

Ollie says, "OK. But don't do it anymore. OK? No more molesting. All right. Take care, now."

Ollie turns, a torrent of stained glass-filtered light catching him as he meets me at the bottom of the stairs. I turn, and we collect Rena on our way down the aisle. We stroll out into the white light of the October Sunday afternoon. Rena's face has distorted into a smirk of disbelief. She half-pushes me out of the way to get to Ollie. "Did that guy molest you?"

Ollie laughs and pulls his cigarettes out of his green corduroy pocket. He milks the moment, lighting up, his face smiling and mysterious. "What do you think?"

"I think," I say, giddy with mischief, "you just accused a random priest of molesting you, and he just happened to be a molester."

"Ding, ding, ding!" says Ollie. "I did a little research, but yeah, I never got molested … by a priest."

I laugh. Rena's face morphs into horror. "What?"

"That guy didn't molest me," says Ollie, dragging from his cigarette. "But he did molest someone. And now he won't do it anymore. I'm a hero."

"You're a liar," says Rena. "That's … I'm sorry, that's not right."

"But that priest fucking molested kids," I say. "At least one kid. You don't react that way when you've never molested a kid."

"You should know," jokes Ollie. He shakes his head, suddenly contemplative. "Wow. That was the fifth one I did and the first time I guessed right."

Across the street from the church is a billboard with a picture of Santa Claus with a black eye, holding a shot glass. The speech bubble sprouting from Santa reads, "Tell your mom I'm sorry."

Rena refuses to kiss me goodbye and hastily vacates through the front door of our house. I go online and look at porn and start to masturbate and I hear keys in the lock and I quickly navigate to a news site and the door opens again. She grabs her water bottle off the table by the door without even fully opening the door and slams it shut again and doesn't lock it. I zip up my fly and waddle over to lock the door and look out the window and make sure her car leaves the driveway.

I hate it when she gets mad at me for something Ollie did, like he's an appendage I can flex or not flex.

I waddle back to the computer, and now my boner is half gone, and I'm annoyed, seeing a cloud of interference over things like I do at work, and I try to navigate to a site that has computer-generated cartoons of people being maimed and tortured, but I mistype a letter and end up at a website that sells human muzzles. I complete the order form with bogus information and type in a random credit card number. I try to believe that everything happens for a reason. The blue fuzz seems to clear.

I log into everyoneyouthoughtyouknew.com and along with a picture I had downloaded from another site depicting a man kicking his own ass, I post this line:

Every mass murder starts with the first murder.

This may be as optimistic as I can get for the moment. I log off, and pull a shrink-wrapped gourmet lobster and Gorgonzola pastry from the freezer.

In my cubicle, I have two photos on the wall: One is a mirror in a bathroom where there were mirrors on the front and rear walls, so you can see decreasing iterations of myself tapering infinitesimally. The other is of Rena and I at the Grand Canyon. Rena came into the office once, and she had a line on the Grand Canyon photo: "You failed to push me in." The photo was taken by some guy in coveralls who had been pushing a broom around the pavement. If I remember correctly, he sort of looked like my dad.

Roy comes up, and he already has springs and wires shooting out of his collar, and I'm afraid his head is going to launch from his torso like coiled snakes from a can labeled as peanut brittle. He keeps referencing a spreadsheet containing certain red cells I should be concerned about. Three times within the four minutes he stands near my desk, Roy uses the phrase, "everyone on the distribution list." I look down, and he seems to be leaking motor oil all over the carpet in the corner of my cubicle where my chair normally rests. I catch glimpses of lights through the flesh on his short-sleeve-exposed forearms, some sparks or emergency lights going off in his cyborg skeleton. He smells like grinding gears covered by cologne.

Ultimately, Roy gets to the point of his visit, which is that some important person will be visiting next week, and that everything needs to be in order when he arrives. Roy makes this clear by buzzing emphatically, punctuated by alarm horn blasts. His googly eyes spill from his face and recoil awkwardly. His pocket protector contains every marker color produced.

I forgive Roy for spilling oil, and he looks at me strangely before proceeding to Berry's desk. Before I zone out for the remainder of the day, I hear Berry deliver this week's give-me-the-news catchphrase, "Dump it on me!"

For the third anniversary of our first date, I take Rena to her favorite omni-cultural kitsch-fest, Gregor Baloney's Authentic Cocktails and Chops Bistro Parlor. We split an appetizer of Genuine San Antonio Tex-Mex Whistler Rustlings, which taste vaguely oniony. I have one, and then use my second to repeatedly dip into the tangy orange sauce until Rena says something. I order and sip a Howell Derby Barrel-Aged Hopalong Wheat Draft, which is a beer. Rena finishes in about three big draws her tall glass of Randy McCormick Deep-Distilled Wilberry Rush Vodkesque Liqueur, which is a cocktail. The menu has more chapters than the novel I tried to write in college. Rena watches the 1/41-scale choo-choo train navigating the restaurant's interior on an elevated track. Popping out of the train's engine car is the restaurant's mascot, Gregor Baloney, a skinny anthropomorphic pig with big eyes wearing a blue top hat. Gregor Baloney bears something of a resemblance to Ollie, I realize as I try one of the complimentary Filo-sopher Fred Feta's Greek Flaky Flavor Bites, which sheds pastry bits like a scared bird de-feathering as I bite into it.

I start to ask Rena a question just as a herd of GBACaCBP employees shriek the opening strains of their non-copyright-royalty-inducing original birthday celebration song, which includes a lot of clapping. One of the employees in a wheelchair has their hands clapped together by another employee playing puppeteer. I feel hot and vindictive on behalf of the wheelchair bound employee for what I perceive as a slight at her dignity, until I see that she is smiling bigger than I have maybe ever smiled, and then I feel ashamed. Rena looks at me, and says sarcastically, "Hello?"

"Sorry," I say. "I got distracted."

When our food arrives, the plates are so big and numerous that the gayest waiter ever produced by science has to overlap them like cardboard box flaps in order to fit them all on the multi-color tile tabletop. "Hoo-boy!" says the waiter. "We've got ourselves a real puzzle here, haven't we? Well, good luck working through that, and if you have even the slightest sense that you need absolutely anything at all, please, under any circumstances, do not hesitate to ask. My name is Kenth, just like it says on my nametag." He curls a finger inward to touch the rectangle of plastic pinned to his Hawaiian shirt. "You two enjoy your delicious meals, now!"

Rena takes a bite of her Mickey Mussolini de Rigueur Farfalle en Potat Au Gratin mit Kartofelln Con Queso and Bowtie Noodles. "It's good," she says with her mouth full. "Not very hot, but it tastes good."

I spear my fork into a hunk of the Captain Shylock Gnochi-Sprinkled Porcine Abdomen Meat-Based Meal, causing unexpected juice to squirt onto my bib. I bring the fork to my mouth and taste salt and maybe some other flavors.

"Happy anniversary," I say, raising my stein. Rena lifts her empty-save-for-ice glass. "You too," she says. I can't see anything recognizable reflected in her eyes.

◎

The phone rings, and the display reads: UNAVAILABLE.

My cellphone seems to have gotten a virus, and I can't upgrade the firmware anymore, and now once in a while I get phone calls from someone who claims to be me from the future. Except I'm fairly sure that it's a pre-recorded digitized voice running from a program that can select from a branching array of audio files based upon whatever response it receives. My reasoning behind this is that most of the time the responses make sense, but once in a while it seems to mishear me, or to not have a programmed response for a given question, and it responds with either silence or something entirely non sequitur.

The phone keeps ringing, which means it keeps playing a really bad MIDI version of a popular song from the 1980s by someone who had been in a progressive rock band in the 1970s, which I realize describes about half of all 1980s music. Even though I like the tune and have other reasons not to answer, I press the button, holding the obsolete phone upright.

"Hello?" I say, sighing.

"Hello," Future Me says.

I wait, to see how it interprets my pause.

"Are you ready to listen to what I have to say?" Future Me asks.

"Sure," I say. "You have three minutes. I'm at work, so I can't talk long."

"Work doesn't matter," the voice says. The inflection is very much how I'd say it. "In fact, almost nothing matters. Do you understand me?"

"Not really," I say. "What are you selling?"

Future Me says, "This isn't about selling anything."

"Awesome," I say. "Glad to know what this isn't about."

"You can still have everything," it says.

31

"I think your program just shorted out a little," I say. "That didn't make any sense."

There's a pause. In the background I hear a coffee grinder, and I can't tell if it's from the phone or in the office kitchenette. I smell Cindy's awful toaster pastry from several cubicles away.

"Listen." The voice sounds pleading. The algorithms driving the speech patterns are really impressive. "You should stay away from the inauguration. And don't bring him."

"Who?" I ask.

"Nestor," says Future Me.

"Who's Nestor?" I say, picking something out of my teeth.

"You just met him."

I'm too numb to tell if I've shit my pants. Then, as my nerve endings burst back into practice, I get wise. My eyes squint and I sneer.

"Ollie?" I say. "Is that you?"

"No," says the voice. "You know who this is."

"Look, ass," I say. "I don't know how much money you've been given. Maybe you're doing research for a collector or something. I don't really care. But do not call me anymore. OK? Don't call. This is obnoxious. Your phone number is 'Unavailable,' and I'm going to ignore it from now on. OK? It's ridiculous."

Future Me "breathes" into the phone. After a pause, it says, "I don't know how to convince you. Uhh …" The digitized voice stumbles to add realism. "Look. What's something only you would know? Something you've never told anybody?"

"Why would I tell a stranger my innermost secrets? So you can help the IRS track me when I forget to receipt everything I claim? So you can digitally capture whatever I'm saying on whatever recording device you've got on the other end of that line and throw it on the fucking Internet for all the world?"

The robot or computer or whatever on the other end of the line just breathes more, and I feel a little victorious, like I outsmarted Deep Blue or something. There's a little bit of static or sniffling, and then Future Me says, "I'll call you the day after the election. Ruder is going to win the popular vote with a forty-one percent plurality. If I'm right, please take the call. Remember: 'Unavailable' the day after the election. Take the call."

"Alrighty, sounds good," I say. "Good hearing from you, Me."

"This isn't a—"

I hang up. My coffee's cold, and I feel peeved. I notice Berry looking at me, and he says, "Telemarketers, huh? They're worse than in-laws." Berry's tie has an airbrushed-looking image of an anthropomorphic chili pepper wearing sunglasses.

In the bathroom at Skizzers, the divider wall between the stall and the urinal displays some of the finest graffiti every scrawled by bipeds. I shake my penis, pull it in, and zip up, and, four beers in, I stand transfixed by some of the literary and artistic offerings.

- *Steffis cunt caused 7/11*

- *I faerted*

- *Gonzo is the muppet with the biggest cock AND THERE'S NOTHING YOU CAN DO ABOUT IT*

- *[a drawing of a small cock and big balls, and arrow pointing to it, and text near the origin of the arrow that says, "God fucked up."]*

- *[Ollie's haiku] My tasty trimmings / Filling grandma's Christmas pie / Eat up, everyone [I later told Ollie that technically, it should be "ev'ryone" to fit the syllabic structure, and he just looked at me]*

- *Pope Kong: The Biggest Pope*

- *My parents never taught me how to properly express myself.*

- *i got soft shell crabs*

- *I punched a hooker and all I got was this marker.*

- *Suck my dicks.*

- *One date with Britney Jones cost me $641. $41 for dinner and $600 for the abortion.*

- *[Written in small letters next to the previous text: "WHY, DADDY?!!!!"]*

- *If pot is outlawed, only potheads will have guns.*

- *Go back home, forners*

- *Let's gang-rape some fag.*

- *I smell poop.*

- *[A hangman head and body dangling from the crooked structure that looks like a giant number one.] D _ D*

- *Knock knock. Who's there. Fuck. Fuck who. Who do you think.*

- *I beat my girl so bad she needs braces for her teeth and her legs*

- *Eat whitey*

- *Jews could have come up with a cheaper way to operate Auschwitz.*

- *SHARKS SLEEP WIDE AWAKE*

- *[Pointillist rendering of a big-assed woman eating a donut or a bagel.]*

- *[Cartoon rabbit flipping off.]*

- *[Chinese characters that look like a rake, a satellite, Stonehenge, overlapping Band-Aids, and a cat's game of tic-tac-toe.]*

- *[Nine amorphous blobs outlined by pencil. Caption: "My jizz."]*

- *This stall needs spellcheck.*

- *yea riht*

- *Stop reading this! You should concentrate on pissing!*

- *I got away with murder.*

- *I got a way with murder.*

- *this is a cry for help*

- *[Some strange fusion of a yin-yang and a swastika.]*

- *the president is the real tearist*

- *fuck yalls ignorant*

- *Don't bother fucking a pumpkin. It's already filled with seed. —Socrates*

- *I'm pretty sure that was Plato.*

- *celebritydeathbettingpool.gov*

- *let me babysit yer kidz*

- *[An asterisk that's supposed to be an asshole. Arrow pointing to it. Caption "You."]*

- *my band sucks*

- *IF YOUR BAND GETS HURT, GIVE YOUR BAND AIDS*

- *It cost me four shiny buttons to bang a retard*

- *but I gots 4 buttons now*

- *BOY, THIS MESOTHELIOMA IS A REAL TREAT*

- *so this is it?*

Some other guy comes in the john and I snap out of it. I rinse my hands under cold water in the dirty sink and shake them as I walk back to Rena at the corner table.

◎

Waiting in line at the grocery store, I see in an adjacent line a young pregnant girl smacking gum and complaining to her friend about a television show they both watch. They both look about sixteen. They have a full-sized cart containing three bags of different kinds of potato chips. I hold a hand basket, which carries a full roasted chicken enclosed by a clear plastic shell and a can of corn. I realize that I forgot to grab milk, and I look around to see if there are any bottles of milk in the last-minute convenience coolers capping the checkout lanes. I see strawberry milk, and I try to imagine how it would taste on raisin bran before I give up on the idea. Three people have joined the line behind me, and I don't want to forfeit my place in line to go get regular milk. The pregnant sixteen-year-old says, "I know. She's such a slut."

I try to think about my life as a timeline. I see rows and rows of different colored packs of gum. I try to understand how my first thoughts as a toddler may have influenced how I perceive things now. A magazine with a blurry picture of a celebrity caught in a transition between two facial expressions has an italic, sans-serif headline: *"MISSING DAUGHTER: 'I SAW HER IN MY DREAM!'"* I find it difficult to focus. The cashier at the front of the line runs the same carton of orange juice over the scanner over and over again, sighing in rhythm. I feel myself aging. I overhear the shrill voice of the pregnant sixteen-year-old, who is now mostly obscured by candy bars and toenail clippers and single-pill packets of headache medicine and five-dollar sunglasses and processed, corn-based snacks. She says, "Yeah, I'm sure that card works. Run it again. Jesus." I can hear a song my dad used to play on guitar spiritlessly reinterpreted as elevator music, distorted by shoddy supermarket speakers. I feel like falling to the ground and dropping everything and crying until they take me away. I see a dim blue as daylight escapes beyond the high, wide windows at the fore of the store. The chicken in my basket used to walk around. I smell perfume that could potentially fuel a small vehicle. My legs feel hot and my ears are numb. At one point in my mid-twenties, I decided not to spend money on anything that I couldn't touch. Then I got a ticket for driving with lapsed car insurance.

On the way home, the windows rolled down, I feel cold air gripping my face. My foot on the pedal feels almost stuck. My vehicle careens through intersection after intersection, in sync with the timing of traffic signals, things working out in a relatively meaningless yet satisfying way. A heavy sentiment overcomes me as the last light disappears from the purplish sky.

At home, Rena has paper plates and metal forks set on the table. A rerun of mustache-era-Trebek Jeopardy plays on the television. A commercial for a toy that has resurged in popularity twenty years after its introduction starts off the break before Final Jeopardy. The category is, "History Repeats Itself."

Rena heats up the corn and talks about her Tuesday/Thursday job at the medical clinic, which is one-third done for the week. Today, she had to cover for Danielle, she says. "So I had to check in patients and juggle transcripts and work the phones."

"That sucks," I say.

"I hope she's planning on taking one of her vacation days, because I don't know how many more freebies she's expecting."

"Doesn't she have, like, severe diabetes?"

"I don't care if she has to have both feet lopped off," she says. "Unless she wants to give me part of her paycheck, I'm not doing double-duty anymore."

"Well, good for you," I say.

"Are you being sarcastic?"

"No," I say. "I just, you know, think it's good that you're sticking up for yourself."

"I'm not," says Rena. "I'm just ... pissed off."

"Oh."

Applause and the 1990s synth version of the Jeopardy theme music fills in for whatever should be said next. I missed the Final Jeopardy question. The chicken tastes all right.

"What's it about?" asks Ollie.

"I don't know, I haven't seen it," I say.

"What does it say on the back?"

I flip the case over and read aloud for Ollie and the nearby video store clerks. "'A small group of slackers kill time in the suburbs while life passes them by. Sex and drugs do nothing but make the hands on the clock spin around and around. Rated R for strong sexual content, pervasive language, violence, two abortions, and jokes about terrorism.'"

"I think I saw that one," says Ollie.

"There's a whole shelf of movies like this," I say.

"What's the one with that guy who in real life got run over by a train?"

"You're thinking of *Life Wasters Infinitum*."

"Yeah. That's the one where they're so bored that they decide to smoke that pipe with bleach in it, and when they get to Hell, the Devil makes them live their lives over again?"

"Yeah."

"Do they have that?"

I look for a minute and find the case. "It's checked out."

"Darn," says Ollie. "We should just download something."

"Wait," I say, looking at the case next to it on the shelf. "They have a Danish remake of it. *Forever Spilde Tiden*. It looks the same, but with all blonds."

"Does it have those words?"

I crease my forehead.

"Subtitles?"

I look at the case. "It says it's dubbed in … Scottish."

"That's like English, right?" Ollie looks like he needs a nap. His shirt has an iron-on image of Ronald Reagan riding a unicorn.

"What about this one?" I say, picking up another box. "'Farmhands hunt down a pest that has infested their soy fields: A ghastly hybrid of man and skunk known as the Smunk. When they capture him and put him to death, things get even worse, and the Smunk becomes Demon Smunk. Rated Adults-Only for excessive gore, surprising vernacular, outlandish pacing, and unsettling editing.'"

"I saw *Demon Smunk*, but I'd see it again," says Ollie.

A woman screams, and Ollie and I look to the corner of the video store, where a bald man in a green army jacket holds a knife to his own throat. I hear him hiss, "This is how it ends!" He pulls the knife across his throat, spraying the nearby woman with jetting red-black blood. The woman screams until she passes out. The man stumbles, his eyes rolled up, spins a bit, and drops out of sight behind some video shelves. A security guard runs over to where the guy has dropped.

"Wow," says Ollie. "Spoiler."

"That's the first one I've seen this month," I say.

When the Golden Gate Bridge collapsed on Valentine's Day, at first everybody assumed it was the same terrorists who hit DC. High definition surveillance footage recorded via satellite later revealed that no fewer than twenty American citizens of diverse backgrounds walked onto the bridge between 4:00 and 4:05 p.m. Pacific Time, spacing themselves out evenly, each near a pivotal structure point, and all twenty detonated the C4 explosives they wore strapped beneath light jackets or blouses or flannels within about ten seconds at 4:10 p.m. Twenty blasts broke apart all supports and the bridge, and all vehicles, drivers, passengers, cyclists, pedestrians, and security personnel exploded and fell into the bay. The wires waggled and grasped like mindless robotic tentacles before flailing and plummeting, following the massive chunks of torn iron to which they had been fastened for so many years into the wicked undertow.

I remember it well because an emergency news pop-up interrupted my online porn session. Just as an old clip of Lana what's-her-name that always got the job done was getting to the good part, a fucking red alert stomps in and cockblocks.

Rena was out of the house with Janet. On the clips I later watched over and over again, mostly uploaded cell phone videos, the sound was like a breaking of the sound barrier followed by the slow, orgasming death of a whale the size of the moon. Twenty folks from all over the country, men and women, young and old, a representative spectrum of skin tones and cultural affiliations, participated in what became the biggest mass-suicide bombing of all time. I had to click the pop-up closed about ten times before it stopped re-spawning and took the hint so I could finish jerking off.

"You mean a website about William Shakespeare?" I say.

"No," Ollie says. "It's Shakespeare's website. He has all his poems and plays on it."

"William Shakespeare died hundreds of years ago," I say, inhaling from the kangaroo dick. "He's like … way dead."

"Well, why would someone else put up all of Shakespeare's writing? That would break Shakespeare's copyright." Ollie looks at me, his mouth pulled tight between responses, frustrated that I'm not getting it. A car passes by outside, splashing in the fallen rain, its bass-heavy radio blaring the hit single, "Put It In Before I'm Sixteen." Through the open window, low-hanging orange leaves drip consistently as the rain intensifies above. I exhale blue smoke.

"Yeah," I say, scratching my neck as my tendons flare. "Shakespeare should definitely sue them for breaking his copyright. In fact, we should probably let him know. Do you want to email him?"

"Well, if it's not his website, Harland, how are we supposed to email him?"

"Touché," I say.

Ollie turns to the screen and opens a browser, typing the address. When he locates the site, his middle finger continuously works the scroll wheel on the mouse, blowing through a list of classics.

I begin to lose focus, thinking of my mom on her deathbed. It was the first time I had seen her without makeup in a long time. "I let things that didn't matter get in the way," she said to me, her voice unusually dry and unwavering. She gripped my wrist. "I have loved you. I want you to know that," she said. She became blurry like everything else in my sight. "I'm sorry I didn't give you more time." Feeling her strong bony fingers press onto my pulse, I was overcome with a simultaneous warmth and a chill. A cool gust through the window brings me back to my living room.

"There's one I wanted you to see," Ollie says. "It's a poem. And I think it's about how people should be afraid of the future."

"Aren't all poems about that?" I ask.

The old twenty-six-inch picture tube television is muted. On the screen, a cell-animated condom ("C-O-N-D-E-M") bends over, crying hysterically. The condom looks sad. A pink diaphragm wanders over and pats the condom on the back. The closed-captioning reads:

DIAPHRAGM: It's OK. The pill doesn't really work, either.

Ollie keeps scrolling through poems. Light from the kitchen part of the main room backlights him, and I feel like getting up to get my camera, but I feel sort of amazingly tethered to my chair. An orange lei I got at a New Year's party hangs from a bowling trophy I received when I was twelve years old. I touch the scar on my forehead and recall every frame of the raft flipping over and the slimy sharp rocks beneath the rapids on my seventeenth birthday. I feel pretty great about all the nothing happening. On television, the pill shows up and spoils the party. The rain intensifies, and somewhere a fire alarm goes off. Rena is across town doing craft night at Janet's apartment. Ollie's cowlick starts to look like horns. I smell muffins. It occurs to me that the first moon landing was real, but that the original footage was used to fake every subsequent "landing." I'm definitely feeling it now.

I feel a pang at the memory of having a mother. At some point, my actual mom turned to stone, and being her son, I half-turned to stone. I retained my ability to walk around and fuck things up. She drank from a stationary position and doled out soundbites of saccharine laced with sarcasm when I dared to visit her unassuming lair of an apartment. Her mantle had a row of little white figurines that I guess harkened to an innocence she felt she had lost by marrying my father. Their divorce left them equally broken, though with vastly different symptoms. My mother chose to portray a disingenuous complacence with her shambles. She sipped what I wasn't supposed to know was gin from a travel coffee mug. She knitted a variety of shawls to cover her useless little legs. She had the television remote velcroed to her wheelchair armrest. She looked at me without trying to really appraise me, seeing her son as some template or representation. Her deep, unspoken need for me to feel sorry for her made me resent her more and more. The kind and funny woman who had raised me became this self-hating, unfunny jester with a sinister self-interest that gained her nothing. I came to regard her in the broad strokes that she painted everything besides herself. She could not reflect. It was too painful for her to look inward, so she turned out and off. She lashed out with self-righteous criticism cloaked in unanswerable rhetorical questions. "So, your father must be proud of you?"

By the time Ollie has located and starts reading what he still protests is a poem by Shakespeare, I'm wiping tears from my cheeks and trying to swallow something hard and hot. I feel itchy and held-down. Ollie reads Sonnet 155:

> Timid footfalls breach this hostile quiet.
> Soiled oily bandage entrail cords pull
> Twisting from twin bonemen, poison pour'd full;
> Shrunken casks spell truth as they deny it.
> You approach this wicked den for solace,

Ne'er considering the tracks you follow.
Twice have warnings fallen harsh but hollow,
Sieved through ears not tuned to render malice.
Pain-drawn eyes seek wreckage, blink and tighten,
Dark pursuit fulfilled as devil's riddle.
You ingest sharp nectar, lips to middle
Flake, revealing skeleton to frighten.
    Round again, the same path worn from blind shoe,
    Rid yourself before the futures find you.

"That sounds trochaic," I say.

Ollie looks at me and says, "Are you crying?"

"Shakespeare didn't write that. And yeah," I say. "I'm crying a little. Sometimes I feel … and I'm not …" I look around. "… ready for it?"

Swatting away a fly, I accidentally get barbecue sauce on my ironic hipster T-shirt. It stains a very obvious place in the fabric, not anywhere near the ironed-on graphic, where at first glance someone might just mistake the blob for one of the undead animal puppets.

"Fuck," I say, mad at myself.

Rena turns from her debate with the bartender about the likelihood of electric vehicles exploding to look at me like I sneezed on her.

"I accidentally touched my shirt," I say.

"I'll call the paper," she says.

"Never mind."

I wipe my fingers on a disposable lemon-scented cloth and wad it up, leaving it on my massacred pile of orange chicken bones. The wet nap unfurls on the plate like it's coming back to life.

I'm almost to the bathroom when I'm halted by the sight of a familiar face in my periphery. I change directions and realize that I have pushed some woman out of the way, and I have to fake like I'm drunker than I am and apologize (barely). Black Me sees that I'm coming toward him, and his eyes open wide, and when his teeth show, it's somewhere between a polite smile and a grimace of embarrassment. I stabilize and come to a halt in front of him, consciously putting my hands down by my sides so I don't seem threatening.

"Hey!" I say, maybe a little too enthusiastically. "You made it out! Cool!"

"Yeah," he says, smiling, looking around maybe to see if he knows anyone. "This is … a cool joint."

"Yeah," I say, mesmerized by how much the guy really does bear a lot of my features, more than I remember from the Provisional Secretary of State's office. "It's wing night, so …"

"I don't know if I caught your name," he says.

"Oh," I say. "My name is Harland."

"Cool," he says. "I'm Nestor." He reaches out to shake my hand, and I realize that my right hand is only half-clean, wiped down by a lemon cloth but still sticky from wing sauce. I awkwardly offer my left hand, twisting it acrobatically to shake his right hand. He says, "O … K."

"Sorry," I say. "I was on my way to the bathroom to wash the sauce off my right hand."

"Looks like you got a little on your shirt, too," he says, looking and pointing at the stain.

"Yeah," I say. "That sucks, too, because I got this shirt at a garage sale and it's basically irreplaceable."

"Bummer," says Black Me. I try to start thinking of him as Nestor, but I'm finding I have a mental block about it.

"So, Nestor, let me just run to the john. I'll introduce you to my girlfriend and buy you a beer."

"Oh," says Nestor. "OK, cool." He looks around, and I wonder if he's planning to split while I'm in the bathroom. I realize I'm hovering near him, and he says, "Don't let me hold you up. I'll see you in a minute."

"OK, sweet," I say. I feel like I'm in junior high, or just learning to walk or something. "Be right back!"

Washing my hands in the rust-stained sink, I spy myself in the mirror. I notice wrinkles that I haven't noticed in other mirrors. I realize that Nestor is probably at least five years younger than me, closer to Ollie's age. I bring the paper towel with me as I exit the bathroom, so excited that I forget to throw it away while I'm still in there. I wad it up and throw it on someone's dirty plate at the corner of the bar, and it expands like it's resuscitating. More evidence of how hard it is to truly kill a napkin.

As luck would have it, Nestor has wandered over to the bar, and he's not far from Rena. He sees me, so I don't have to decide whether to tap him on the shoulder or shout, "Hey," over the music.

"So, what's good here?" he asks. He's so good at small talk. I'm a little jealous.

"The wings, man," I say. I get momentarily self-conscious about pitching chicken to a black person. I then consider whether irony outweighs fear of latent racism. Before I get too sucked into the vortex of my own neurosis, survival instincts force me to keep talking. "The BBQ are awesome, but if you like habañero, you'll love the hot ones."

"What'd you have, BBQ?"

"Yeah. They're pretty awesome, dude. Man." I keep shitting words. "So, Nestor, what are you drinking?"

"Just a beer, I guess. Whatever's good on tap."

I interrupt Rena and the bartender to order Nestor a beer and pull Rena over. "Rena, this is Nestor. We met at the Provisional Secretary of State like, what? A week ago?"

"Must have been," says Nestor. "Rena, is it?"

"Yeah," says Rena. "Nice to meet you." They shake hands, and Rena scrutinizes him a bit. I can tell she sees the resemblance.

"So, what brought you to the Secretary of State that day?" I ask.

"You want to talk about the Secretary of State's office?" says Nestor.

"Yeah, you're right," I say. "Let's not waste time. You look just like me."

"Yeah," says Nestor. "And you look like me, but a little older and white."

"That's nuts," says Rena. "Harland didn't mention you." She turns to me. "You met before?"

"Yeah," I say. "I was getting my renewal license."

"When's your birthday?" asks Nestor.

"October twenty-ninth," I say.

"Mine's October twenty-second," says Nestor.

"Not the same day," says Rena. "What are the odds?" She smirks through a sip of some red drink.

"Rena, come on," I say. "It's still within a week. That's pretty interesting. Happy birthday-ish, Nestor. So let's see," I say, turning back to Black Me. "What else do we have in common?"

"Well," he says, "What's your favorite band?"

"No fair. That's almost as bad as favorite movie."

"All right," he says. "One in the top five."

"All right ... Drunk Orphans."

"They're good. Not in my top five. I'd say Lump Loadz ..."

"Yes."

"... Crayonion ..."

"Yes! Holy crap!"

"... Tu$h ..."

"No, but they're OK."

"... and Blope."

"Not bad. Three out of five I like."

Rena looks at us like she's waiting for something she doesn't want.

"All right," says Nestor, gulping his unfiltered ale, "What's your family like? You got any brothers or sisters?"

"No," I say. "Only child, raised in a vacuum."

"I have a sister. She's younger. Half-sister, actually. Same mom."

"You still have both your parents?"

"My dad died a couple of years ago," says Nestor, his smile disappearing for the first time.

"So did mine," says Rena.

"Both parents are gone," I say.

"Well," says Nestor, "that's OK to drink to."

We bring our glasses together with a few sloppy clinks and swallow in turn.

"I've got a good one," I say. "What do you think about life?"

"Uh ... What do you mean?"

"Just," I say, "what do you think is going on with all this shit?"

"Like in general?"

"Yeah. Like why do you think we have to be here?"

"Because ... we can't think of anything else better?" Nestor smiles, but not fully.

"I think we should definitely hang out," I say.

Ollie meets us behind a billboard next to the interstate. Rena looks like she's fellating some 99 percent invisible marsupial. Nestor laughs so much that he starts choking and braces himself, grabbing his stomach. I make shadow puppets using light from my screwed up cell phone. I tell them about Future Me, and Black Me starts telling me he thinks he got a similar call. Ollie keeps grinning big and looking back and forth between Black Me and me. Ollie takes one third of a Red Delicious apple into his mouth in one bite. Rena warns him about swallowing seeds, and I say something about how Rena knows what she's talking about when it comes to swallowing seed and Nestor cracks up and almost rolls down the hill into traffic but catches himself. I make some joke about how he can't die or we'll be accomplices to a hate crime. A semi truck blares its horn, almost ramming a motorcycle in the right-hand northbound lane. The semi's trailer bears the logo of a company called Excess Meat Ruiners, LLC. Rena starts singing some R&B song her class sang together at sixth-grade graduation. She's singing it like a cartoon chippie in a way that reminds me of my mom at her most intentionally grating. Ollie offers us applesauce by opening his mouth while I'm trying to hold smoke in, and I cough wickedly, producing some uncomfortable inward burp, but it's so funny that the pain is almost a benefit. Nestor talks about what the new government should be: A nation where everyone is a monarch and has complete reign over their personal space, and if anyone encroaches on another, then it is an act of war punishable by being kicked in the genitals. I say that might be as close as we'd get to doing it right. Ollie one-ups by mentioning that Sweden is already testing this exact scenario in a biodome. Rena says that if she had the time and money to travel, she would poke holes in every bubble she could find. Dancing in the light-polluted blue-gray night sky is a cloud that looks a bit like my dad.

I pull a receipt from my wallet and a pen from my cargo pocket and scrawl a picture of people on the first escape pod from Earth. Ollie likes the old '50s car-style fins on the pod, and agrees that that's what it will look like. Nestor comments that it looks like all the people on the pod are white. Nestor then mentions that he's gay. It comes out so casually and out of context that I almost miss it, and I follow up by asking Nestor when he first realized he was gay. He says it was during a computer-animated movie about calculators who team up to solve the world's hardest math problem. I never saw that one, because it came out when I was a teenager. Nestor says that two of the same kind of calculator became best friends and that's when he realized that he didn't like girls like most of the boys did. He asks me when I realized I was straight. I tell him about the time I played private parts peek-a-boo with a girl who lived two doors down when I was four. The two of us sat Indian-style in the dirty doghouse behind her house and peeled back our underwear to show each other. Surrounded by the romantic aroma of stale dog feces, I put my finger to the slightly damp pink flesh and brought it to my nose. I can't remember the girl's name anymore. It was gross and wonderful at the same time, I tell Nestor, and that's what sealed the deal. Ollie says he hasn't really decided, but that girls are probably better because they smell better. He clarifies that he's not just talking about genitalia as sampled in a doghouse. Ollie says he has never been with a man, but the girls he has been with haven't fully convinced him. Rena didn't know this about Ollie, and she suddenly seems less annoyed by him than usual, tilting her head and straining to listen, strands of her dark hair falling across a cheek.

Nestor talks about growing up the black gay kid in a straight white neighborhood. Nestor says it wasn't fun, but that he has a great life now. Nestor pulls up his shirt and shows us a bruise he says he got when he was thirteen. It never faded. Nestor says he doesn't desire anal sex with anybody, just kissing and oral sex. I am surprised to hear that, I say, because hardly an hour goes by where I'm not bugging someone for anal sex. Ollie dies laughing, and the core of his apple goes tumbling down the grassy hill into the southbound freeway. Rena adds that Hitler had a poor sense of humor. The males nod, we hit a lull, and then we laugh at the lull.

The billboard on the hill on the opposite side of the freeway reads, "Don't just change your oil. Change your whole attitude about oil. Paid for by Friends of Oil." I'm not sure what the billboard we're sitting behind says, because I forgot to peek. The kind of breeze that only occurs in the middle of the night engulfs us. Rena curses the thinness of her jacket. I'm supposed to be at work in five hours. I'm exhausted and wanting the night to go on forever.

3 BLACKOUT

A company-wide sexual harassment seminar is underway in the cafeteria. Behind me, I hear Berry occasionally mumbling, "Done that" as transgressions are bullet-listed in a slideshow presentation. I can hear his smirk. Our company has a twenty percent female workforce, almost completely secretarial or non-managerial. There's one token female executive, a Human Resources rep who talks like a toddler and looks like an airbrushed mannequin. I was only a half hour late this morning, and no one said anything, and I saw a few sideways glances. The seminar, which began at 9:00 a.m., was apparently prompted by a recent incident that was supposedly resolved internally but came pretty close to arbitration. One male executive, Paul Jabber, hasn't been seen in the office since the alleged incident took place. No one but HR knows exactly which girl was involved, but three of my co-workers each have twenty dollars riding on the outcome. Last week I overheard Berry say something to the other two about "double the money if Jabber's fingers got sticky." According to the pixelated display on my crappy phone, it's 10:41 a.m. I have a headache in part from not having had any coffee yet.

"'No' isn't just a word," says the handsomely dressed business woman in the current video clip, "It's the most important word there is." A wave of low-pitched giggling emerges from around the room. Certain higher-ups scrunch their foreheads and cast stern looks.

I notice two women sitting in the front row of folding chairs tighten their jaws and hug their own arms and stare with greater intensity at the screen, ignoring to the utmost the disrespectful males surrounding them.

I'm with them, but too lazy or scared or unimaginative to do anything to help. At the same time, I sort of want to bang both of them. I find my morality as wavering as my attention span. My sense of right and wrong feels comically context-dependent. I find myself giggling at my own horribleness until I realize that if I'm caught giggling, I will be considered as bad as the chauvinists I detest. This sobers me, and I reign in my outward expressions, become stony, become a crash-test dummy, become a pillar of shit.

Cindy flips on the overhead fluorescents as the presentation concludes with what is supposed to be a memorable motto: "If you're unsure of your Self, keep it on your Shelf." This line precedes a registered-trademark symbol. Some people grab danishes and cookies from the tissue paper-covered table on their way out of the cafeteria. I approach the table and grab a Styrofoam cup for coffee. As I approach the big silver canister, I hear Laurel, one of the receptionist girls from the front row, say something to Dana. I can't hear what is said, but Laurel looks like she's on the verge of tears. I turn back, pull a black lever, and start to hate myself ferociously as I push a black button to release steaming coffee into my cup and wonder how much Laurel's eyes would tear up with my dick lodged in her throat. The difference between me and the assholes I work with, I tell myself silently, pulling my finger back before the coffee overflows, is that I sublimate my poison before it can escape me.

Back at my desk, I access a form on the intranet and nominate Laurel for Employee of the Month. This is the kind of guilt-driven psychology that elects black presidents and funds orphanages. I search the online dictionary for a word that means reflexively positive external expression of unbearable self-hatred. Somewhere down the hall, I hear Roy say the same exact sentence twice in a row without trying to modify the emphasis.

"We cannot underestimate the implications. We cannot underestimate the implications."

I actually say, "TGIF" to a co-worker with whom I've never had a real conversation and smile as I walk to my car, answering a phone call from Ollie, who recommends an apple orchard that has a very small staff and many bales of hay in the apple fields. He means to just sneak out into a field and eat apples and get high, but as he continues to talk, his scheme is so detailed that I wonder if he's not also planning to break into a safe or kidnap the farmer's daughters or something.

"Yeah, OK, sounds good," I say. I hear myself talking and I hear my father's voice, and I feel a chill. Upbeat, appeasing, amiable, calculating. Ollie keeps talking, telling me about a documentary he saw on cable about a country that clones itself, and then the two identical countries go to war and destroy each other. I ask Ollie if he's sure it was a documentary. He responds by saying it was on public television, and that everything on public television is true. I can't think of a good argument, so I ask him when and where we're meeting.

"Your house," Ollie says. "Seven o'clock. Wear warm clothes. Do you think Rena will come?"

"She likes cider," I say. "I don't know what she had planned tonight. I think tomorrow is the anniversary of her father's death." I say this as immediately as I recall it. Somewhere deep down, my brain still works. "So, I don't know what she'll be up for. She might want to be on the phone with her mom for three hours." The inside of my car smells like fast food. "Can I invite Black Me?"

"You mean Nestor?"

"Yeah. It's his birthday. Or was. What's today?"

"OK," Ollie says. "But probably no more than that because my car is not clean."

"O … K," I say. I think this is Ollie's passive-aggressive way of being jealous of Nestor. I think Ollie is unhappy not to be my newest friend anymore. On the other hand, I'm not sure Ollie would have ever taken a bullet for me. I hear him breathing, maybe thinking, for about five seconds.

"Are you guys coming to my play tomorrow night?"

"Yeah," I say. "Sorry I didn't reply to your email. I was looking at porn when it popped up and I forgot to write back."

"OK," he says. "I just didn't know whether to reserve seats."

"Are you expecting it to sell out?"

"It's free to get in," says Ollie. He pauses long enough that my question must be assumed to have been addressed. A half-mast flag ripples.

"OK, thanks," I say. "I'll see you at my house."

Nestor tells us about working at the morgue. He tells us about a journal he keeps. He writes descriptions of everyone who comes in to identify a body, how much or how little they weep, their relationships to the deceased, to whom or what they pray, clothing appearing pulled on hastily on the way out the door after receiving the worst phone calls of their lives. Nestor sits with his back against a large bale of hay. He looks like a giant snail. He tells about how he's pretty sure that once or twice as he pulled back the sheet—standing there with a doctor and a next of kin, watching the eyes of the relative or boyfriend or neighbor—he has seen a murderer. Nestor tells us about a few occasions where the eyes did not change as the sheet came up, or the eyes glimmered with secret smiles, or faces froze with no surprise or concern, as Nestor puts it, "like they were getting one last peek at their deeds."

He goes on to tell some really awful tale about twins; one twin dies and the other one lives. Nestor doesn't think this was a murder situation, but the surviving twin broke down and started bawling about how his mother had always loved his brother more. Hospital security eventually had to drag him back to the elevator because he wouldn't stop hugging his brother's corpse. Nestor recalls that as the elevator door closed, the surviving twin kept repeating the same line between sobs: "Now Mom won't love anyone! Now Mom won't love anyone!"

Ollie exhales a plume of smoke that twists into a noose before the October wind sucks it into its own lungs. Ollie's glazed, tired look morphs into a Cheshire grin, and he claps his palms together, rapping, "Now Mom won't love anyone. Now Mom won't love anyone."

Nestor starts beatboxing, and his nasal snare sounds make me giggle. Rena even starts doing a syncopated owl hoot. I volunteer a vocal impression of a slap bass to counterpoint Ollie's words. We become a working machine, ringing out at dusk in a remote quadrant of an apple orchard that we found without the help of wireless technology. The song ends abruptly, with Nestor doing a "Shave and a Haircut" riff. Ollie tells us that at a drugstore, he saw an apple-based aphrodisiac called Gettin' Cider. I can't tell if he's joking. I can't tell if we're actually here, or just playing a video game with characters modeled after us.

Rena admits that she told her boss to fuck off today, and that she might be out of a Monday/Wednesday/Friday job.

"So that's why you were home before me," I say. "Good for you. Bad for us."

She says, "I'll be happy to explain the situation if you'd let me."

"Good idea to wait 'til we're in the middle of an apple orchard and stoned."

"I'm not stoned," she says. "I'm the designated driver."

"Well, I guess responsibility comes and goes."

"Why'd you quit?" asks Nestor.

"I didn't quit," says Rena. "And I didn't literally tell my boss to fuck off. I just told her that I'm sick of covering for Diane when she's always late, or calling at the last minute because she has to pick up her kids." She pauses, grabbing the pipe from Ollie. "I'm not going to suffer because some other bitch couldn't keep her legs closed or figure out how to swallow a fucking pill."

"… or just swallow," pipes in Ollie.

"Thanks, Ollie, for helping," I say, straight-faced. "So you didn't actually say, 'Fuck off.' What did you say?"

"I said," says Rena, "I'm sick of being the one dying for everybody's sins."

"Whaaat?" says Nestor, kind of buckling, pulling his knees into his chest with what looks like involuntary force. His eyebrows lift from his face. "You compared yourself to Jesus for working at a Chinese restaurant?"

"That's awesome," says Ollie, taking a prime opportunity to say something nice about Rena. "What did she say?"

"Yeah, Rena," I add, unnecessarily.

"She said that I should be prepared to die for anything. And then she let me leave early."

"She let you leave early, or she sent you home?" I don't know why the distinction matters, but I have to ask.

"I think she was sort of mad at me and sort of felt bad for me." Rena's lipstick is dark, and her mouth appears to be an amorphous ring floating and squirming. "English is like her third language. She's menopausal. She eats eels. What do you want from me?"

"Just let me know if I need to get another job, I guess." I'm saying this just to be a dick, I quickly realize. It's poor form, especially in front of friends. Whatever buzz I was riding has evacuated my system. "I'm sorry. It's just not what I expected."

"Sorry to defy your expectations," she says. She exhales something cold and more opaque than condensed water, signaling that I have become the designated driver. We all turn when an owl hoots. There's a rustling that will never be explained. We have to take for granted that someone is always watching. A brief stream of radio static buzzes from the phone in someone's pocket. A cold drop of rain or dew fallen from a leaf chills my forehead. I take a moment to consider the years I've known.

I look at Rena and she sees that I'm sorry, and I don't have to say anything right now. Anything more in front of the others would be tacky, scab-picking. Rena sometimes drinks milk as a stand-alone meal. I like the way she looks. I am itching to get out of my skin, but it's not her fault.

"Do you think it's OK to eat the apples?" Ollie asks.

"Are you fearful of knowledge?" I say.

"I just want an apple," says Ollie, not smiling.

"I'll bet Adam and Eve were bored as shit," says Nestor, looking at the first stars visible through the deepening purple. "Nothing to talk about because nothing had happened yet. I bet that sex got boring real quick."

"Have you even read the Bible?" says Rena.

"I saw the movie," Nestor says, smirking, then cupping his mouth and guffawing through his fingers. "It was rated X."

"Yeah," says Ollie. "I heard the Bible is really violent."

"It makes video games seem damn near …" I search for a word, "… biblical."

"I read part of the Koran," says Nestor. "It's pretty didactic."

"Fuck," says Rena, "have you read the Bhagavad Gita? It's more chatty than a fucking Woody Allen movie."

"Personally, I've always respected the Talmud for being unabashedly boring." I gesture with an invisible martini glass and raise an eyebrow.

"One time, I dated a guy who didn't know the difference between the Shurangama Sutra and the Kama Sutra," says Nestor. "Instead of trying to fuck me, he tried to help me ward off meditative delusions."

"What's the difference?" says Rena.

"Did you ever see …" Ollie asks Nestor about a television show that's been off the air for years. Rena and I groan in unison.

"I couldn't follow it," says Nestor.

"Well, you have to watch all of it to get it. I read a lot of theories about what it means, but here's what I think it really means …"

"I'm sorry," I say to Rena, as I grab the kangaroo dick from her. "I can't stay sober for this."

Ollie's theory has almost nothing to do with the television show he's supposedly explicating, let alone any fiction I've ever heard of. I can't follow his every word, so my brain paraphrases for me as Ollie starts rolling a joint with the scraps from his baggie.

After a three-minute synopsis of back-story, Ollie takes an unnecessarily long drag from what looks like a firecracker pinched between his index finger and stubby thumb and says, "Then a plane crashes."

I wake up to light and constant rain on Saturday and feel an amazing breeze through the window screen. Rena is still asleep, snoring barely, like a puppy. I think of Curly the hairless sheepdog, who gave himself rashes trying to keep clean. I touch Rena's shoulder lightly enough not to wake her. I think back to Saturday mornings with rain, the feeling of not having to go to school, not feeling like I'm going to have to run around and get sweaty, a sense of freedom and possibility. I could stay in and draw or build something from clay or make a song on the computer. The feeling of waking to no expectations is, I recognize, one of the things I use to motivate myself to keep going. I have the time and space to make something, to do something good, to not jump through someone's hoops. As comfortable as the bed is, I rise in hope that today can be one of those days, where I can do something with what I have instead of being kept working for it.

I pour beans into the grinder and press the button, two of my fingertips turning white as the blood goes elsewhere under my skin, hoping the necessary racket doesn't rouse Rena quite yet. I realize that when Washington, DC went away, we all got another chance to do what we wanted. We had a national rainy Saturday. The slate was wiped, not completely, but enough for everyone to reassess what they wanted and consider the possibilities of actually doing those things instead of putting them off or saving up for them or feeling like they would offend someone. The gift the terrorists gave us was the opportunity to start over from closer to scratch than we ever thought we could. I let go, remove the cap, and pour the fine brown powder into a bleached white filter. A lot of reactionaries swore to vengeance, and some opportunists saw the moment to get their third party off the ground, but what really happened was that, with the sacrifice of a tiny minority of public figures, a lot of people got a moment to breathe. Some people got out their easels. Others got their laptops. Some went outside for the first time in a long time. Some got divorced, or proposed. Some committed suicide. Others called their grandparents.

I pour water from the carafe into the chamber. I press the START button and look through the kitchen window, through the drizzle at some trees and the side of my neighbor's house. For a few months, I felt like I could do anything. I wrote short stories, I made a comic book. I recorded four songs using computer software so advanced that they were basically composed on my behalf. I went and helped at a church homeless shelter (just one night). I planted a birch tree that's still living, in the strip of grass between the sidewalk and the street. Technically, it's city property, but that hasn't seemed to matter.

Then, after a while, things slipped back to an uncomfortable pattern. I slept late, didn't make time to do things, started watching a lot of TV again, put weight back on when I stopped walking. Society got on the mend, and I felt worse and worse.

Three years ago today, not long after we began dating, Rena got the call that her dad had dropped dead in the middle of a department store. He had been holding a box set of awful action movies. His wallet contained eight dollars. I like to think he was going to steal the movies, although his wallet also contained two credit cards. Jack had been a garbage man. When I met Rena, she said that her family had a rich history of garbage. At the banquet following his funeral, I remember Rena telling me that in the few years before he died, her dad lost about forty pounds without even trying. He claimed it was because after working with garbage for so many years, he had voluntarily willed away his sense of smell and he couldn't really taste food anymore. I remember going to Rena's parents house not long before her dad died, and Jack had made what ended up being pretty amazing burgers for having been prepared by someone who couldn't smell or taste anymore. It was an old recipe, he said, and he put the platter on the table, shouting, "Yippee-ki-yay, burger-eaters!"

Comedy is the difference between something happening to you and me observing it.

I scribble this on the wall in the men's room at Skizzers. I piss, glancing over at the still-drying marker letters. I shake my penis and tuck it away, zipping up. I take the marker back out, scribble out the word "observing," and write in "causing."

Old Fuck flips off a busboy and says like he's realizing it for the first time, "Your mother babysits cocks with her asshole." He spins slowly on his stool and yells over his shoulder to no one in particular, "Shitmouth took my pint before I was done with it." He turns back to where the busboy no longer stands. "That kind of betrayal could get you tossed in the snake pit, 'f you're in my brigade." He turns to face the lady bartender right in front of him. "Get me a free refill, tits."

I sit in a high-top chair near the wall, drunk and watching The Old Fuck Show, my arms stuck to the burgundy vinyl tablecloth. Rena was tired and took the car home after I convinced her I could walk home, even though it's dark and I'm drunk and the terror alert is red. I reminded Rena that the Terror Alert Color System is now controlled by Canker Cola. Rena responded by saying that's why she drinks cocktails instead, and then she left.

Old Fuck talks so loudly that I can hear him clearly through the Tuesday midnight crowd at Skizzers when he's fifteen feet away and all I can see is the scraggily gray back of his head.

Old Fuck tells the best way to eat a peach: "Avoid the fuzz, get juice on your whiskers, and watch out for the brown pit."

Old Fuck says why he drives American cars: "I'm not getting into anything Japanese unless she's under sixteen."

Old Fuck recounts his stint in prison: "I didn't drop the soap. I didn't have to."

Old Fuck spells the word "divorce": "R-I-C-H C-U-N-T."

Old Fuck explains the New Testament: "Bullshit."

Old Fuck thumb-wrestles some college guy, loses, and later kicks the guy's stool out from under him. The guy and his two big friends make like they're going to kick Old Fuck's ass, and Old Fuck pulls out a hand grenade from his coat. The college guys are freaked out and leave, and the bartender yells at Old Fuck, and Old Fuck complains that it's a dead grenade.

Old Fuck says why he hates children: "The meat is too stringy."

On a widescreen television in the corner of the bar, a non-widescreen video image is stretched to look widescreen. Soldiers in gray fatigues surround a house and shoot machine guns at it, breaking windows and porch railings. The white text on a red band across the bottom of the screen reads, "Nebraska."

Alone at my tacky table, I scribble a golf pencil on an upturned placemat. I shade in the cloak on a wizard who's shooting lightning from his big veiny cock. I take it up and show it to Old Fuck. Old Fuck nods approval and says, "I miss my dad, too."

Rena and I arrive at the Drama Memorial Theatre at 7:05 p.m., a small converted warehouse downtown. We're not the last ones to arrive.

We make eye contact with Ollie, and he smiles closed-mouthed and waves, but doesn't leave his front-row seat to greet us.

In the first scene, the entire cast is onstage. With a quick count, I determine that the performers slightly outnumber the audience members. As a black guy wearing a sash and a crown starts chanting about "sons of the Apocalypse," leading a band of hippie-ish stormtroopers in a figure eight around the stage, I scan the single-page leaflet of a program. Ollie is listed as a co-author of *The True Story of the First King of Earth After the Destruction*, along with his would-be girlfriend Sesha. I see Sesha in the front row with a tablet computer, using some sort of finger-painting application to make notes and graffiti that may or may not be in response to whatever is happening onstage. Ollie sits next to her in an identical metal folding chair, hugging his knees to his chest. I sense the energy between them, one direction, from him to her. He doesn't eye her, but I've heard him talk about her with tenderness and admiration. Ollie says that Sesha told him she's asexual, which Ollie thought was pretty hot until he found out what it meant.

A few scenes down the line, two actors in papier-mâché dragon costumes step on small-scale papier-mâché buildings and have some sort of cryptic dialogue about politics. I feel fairly sure that Ollie didn't write this scene (except for maybe the detail that they're dragons).

"Only ghosts believe in a free market," says the first dragon, kicking over a building.

"The living know that you can't rely on entrepreneurs," says the second, squishing a small painted paper car.

Accordion music cues lights leading into a five-on-five arm wrestling competition, which clunky dialogue reveals to be a metaphor for the UN. This is topical because lots of Americans hate the UN for stepping in when the federal government was wiped out. Although, to be fair, a lot of Americans simply hate.

When the lights come up, someone on an offstage microphone announces to the house that the intermission will be ten minutes long, which slays my hope that the thong-wearing fat man doing a solo consisting only of grunts and armpit farts was the last scene of the show and not a cheap cliffhanger.

Rena and I wander to the sparse slab-floor "lobby" and approach the fashioned-together and one-coated plywood booth that works well enough as a concession stand. We pay four dollars for a plastic cup of red wine to share. Floodlights in the high corners of the cinderblock walls illuminate the space oddly, with most of the middle of the large room cast in faint crossing shadows. It smells like dust and paint. I half-whisper to Rena, "I wish I had thought of this," and it echoes a bit.

We see Ollie standing next to Sesha, who stands with a scoliosis slant in glimmering fabrics that comprise the neon rainbow, sipping a drink from a coconut half. She must have brought her own, because I didn't see that offered at the bar. The pair is standing by a statue about as tall as them, as if a third in their party. The statue looks like an octopus on its back, tentacles flailing everywhere. On second glance, I see that each tentacle is a penis, and whatever this multi-phallused creature is, it belongs in a Japanese cartoon. I have to pull Rena with me as I advance toward them Steadicam-style, even though she half-heartedly resists, saying through her teeth into my ear, "I already know I don't like her."

"Heyyyyyyy!" says Ollie, extending the syllable into abstraction. He's wearing a powder blue tee shirt with a tuxedo screen-printed on it and brown corduroy pants that are baggy enough to fit two of him and long enough that I can't tell if he's wearing shoes.

"Hey," I say, "heck of a show so far."

"Thank you so much," says Sesha, her sleepy eyes fluttering for some reason. I guess Ecstasy. "The second half completely negates the first, which is why it's my favorite."

"I'm Rena."

"Sesha, this is Harland and Rena," says Ollie, gesturing with a flattened hand. "Harland and I dropped out of film school together."

"I didn't drop out. I just couldn't afford it anymore. The scholarships dried up pretty quickly after 7/11."

"Oliver has a decidedly filmic eye," says Sesha.

"Two," says Rena.

"Three," says Ollie, laughing. Ollie has never made a movie, but he has pitched hundreds of "what-if" scenarios. If conceptualization were sufficient to sell tickets, his lack of follow-through wouldn't seem so sad. I feel mean, guessing that Sesha is the only reason that whatever we are watching tonight has made it to the stage. Because she appears so sedated, this seems particularly tragic. I sneak a glance at Ollie to see if he can read my mind or if I have gotten away with my unfriendly thoughts.

"Well, it's very avant-garde," says Rena, checking off an obvious item on the list of positive things to be said. "Dreamlike," she says, stealing my addendum before I can utter it.

"Yes," says Sesha, "its surface has the quality of dreams. Yet every waking day contains more absurdity. Consider the parking meter."

"A limbless robot you feed metal chips so he won't get mad about your car being there." Ollie seems to have memorized this line.

"A parking meter," I say. "Yeah. Totally."

"Many have seen the igloo isolating us, but few have had the inspiration to bore through the ice floor. We thaw from the inside and find our way out."

Rena looks blankly at Sesha, and I see Ollie looking like he's waiting for a cue. Nothing happens, and Sesha keeps talking.

"Everywhere there is light. In stars, in hearts, in pain and torture and oblivion. These are the totems we carry near to our souls."

I can't tell if I'm throwing up in my mouth or chewing my tongue.

"In superior universes, the idols we feign to represent assume our true modes. The parallels are clear to me, but for some it takes years or decades to make the connection. I've had readings done, and I have done them myself. Have you ever had a reading?" Sesha doesn't seem to be addressing anyone in particular.

"A reading?" says Rena. "Like a palm reading?"

"A spirit reading," Sesha corrects. "If you check in on the status of your soul, you can manipulate the very essence of the constructs that bind you to this world."

"I see," says Rena. "Good to know."

"I can tell," says Sesha, "that you have yet to trace the path to the core. But there is the opportunity. Several left in this cycle, in fact."

"In *fact?*" Rena says, starting to breathe more quickly. Her cheeks flush, and I feel concurrently sorry for her having to deal with this and excited about the potential of her kicking this girl's ass. "What makes that a fact? What are you talking about?"

"We serve greater purposes, but the mechanizations interfere and distract from our organic processes." Sesha pointedly pronounces it "process-ease" like a Brit.

"Like when the phone rings and you're taking a dump?" I say, wanting to ruin this Sesha character. I've quickly acquiesced to Rena's instinctual assessment of this phony bitch. "Or when you go to have sex and there are already, like, three dildos in her pussy?"

"Harland," says Rena weakly, needing to admonish me for being gross but also happy that I'm giving her a hard time.

"No, Rena, I think that's what she's saying. Right, Sesha? Did I nail it? Did I just spoil the second act?"

"You'll have to wait and see," she says with a slightly stiff smirk, letting everything roll off. The intensifying itchiness I feel inspires me to contemplate a variety of methods in which she could be disemboweled.

"Garth's waving," says Ollie, his smile gone. He walks over to the wall and flicks a light switch off and on twice. "You should head back in. We need to start back up."

As we turn around, Rena grasps my elbow and leans into my cheek. "Can we leave?"

"Yeah," I say. "I'll tell Ollie we had to … get an abortion?"

"I don't care what you tell him. I don't want to see anything else that that witch produced."

We enter the performance area again and take seats in the back corner. I see Ollie sitting next to Sesha in the front row again, this time with one empty seat between them. When the house lights dim to near-black and some audio recording of splashing and droning monk voices gets piped in, Rena and I get back up and race to the exit door.

Safely in the car, Rena says, "What the hell is wrong with him? It's like he forgets who we are when he's around other people. Like he pretends not to know us or something."

"I think he's under the spell of someone named vagina," I say. "And he can't tell whether or not she's made of bullshit."

"He's not that stupid, Harland. How can he like her?"

"She tricked him into helping with her show, making him think he had a hand in it, and he likes the attention, even if it's sexless. Men are dumb enough to think that 'no' means 'maybe.'" My thoughts return to the sexual harassment seminar.

"Yuck," says Rena. "I want a shower."

"I can connect the shower idol to the core essence," I say airily.

"That's enough of that shit … like, forever."

Most of a week later, in the middle of the night I awake hot and itchy, kicking off the comforter. I pick up my phone and flip it open. The digital date display indicates that it is now my birthday. Some force compels me to punch in the digits of my own phone number. I listen to the ringing, encouraged when I don't hear a busy signal. After two rings, I hear someone answer; my own voice. Just as I'm freezing with disbelief that my hunch worked, I realize that the me on the other end of the line is speaking my outgoing voicemail message, verbatim. It's Past Me, of sorts. I leave a message . Future Me will get it, I deduce.

Still in my Casual Friday jeans and shirt, I burn my tongue on hot and sour soup at Orange Bamboo, waiting for Rena to get off. Rena's boss walks by and either pretends not to recognize me, or is still annoyed with Rena and taking it out transitively, or is just menopausal.

I see a heavy man walk up to Diane and ask something. When Diane says, "No, I'm sorry, there's no buffet," the man's face drops, and he walks back into the mall, defeated. I try to figure out how to craft this into a proper joke, but I get hung up on puns using the word "buffet" and eventually I drop it.

When Rena comes out from the kitchen, she's on her phone. I hear her tell someone it's "going to be OK." She thumbs an end to the call and swings into the other side of the booth.

"Janet," she sighs.

"What's the matter? Did her teeth shrink?"

"Harland," she scowls. "She's my friend."

"Right," I say. "So it's not the teeth?"

"Brad is working a lot of hours."

I do my best to interpret this. I feel individually exploded tastebuds rubbing the roof of my mouth.

"Her fiancée, Brad?"

"Yeah, Brad," I say. This guy does not exist.

"And Brad admitted to Janet that he's grown attracted to a woman at work that he's working on a project with."

"That's big of him," I say.

"It is, actually," Rena says, maybe annoyed that she agrees with my sarcasm. "And I told Janet that the fact that he told her means that he really wants to be with her—"

"Her who?"

"Janet!" Rena says, looking at me like I just appeared out of nowhere.

"Right," I say.

"She's still worried, but I told her that he's admitting it because he wants to nip it in the bud."

"Sounds like he wants to nip that woman in her bud," I say.

"Jesus, Harland," she says.

"Just Harland," I say.

"Look, I know it's not about you, but she's my friend, and I'm just trying to talk with you."

"OK," I say. "Let me know when I should submit my half of the conversation."

"How old are you now?" she asks, implying something.

"Seven for the fifth time," I say.

"Cute."

"Buffalo parfait," I say. "Buffet?"

She looks at me.

Sitting on my front porch in a granny rocker at dusk, a rippling awning keeps drizzle from hitting my thin hair. Ollie pulls up and emerges from his beater with a large whiskey bottle in one hand and a crumpled copy of what I quickly deduce is today's local paper containing the review of *The True Story of the First King of Earth After the Destruction* in the other hand. Ollie's eyes are red from crying and/or pot. And/or whiskey. I hug around his arms, since he can't really grab me with the stuff in his hands.

"'Fuck it, dude; let's go bowling,'" I quote.

"What?" he says.

"You didn't write it," I say, consolingly.

"No, but I read it," he says, looking at me earnestly. I realize he's referring to a review.

"I mean, you didn't write the play."

The pause seems loaded.

"I mean, did you?"

"I helped to create it, Harland."

"OK. I'm sorry. I'm sorry there was a bad review by some loser at the local paper who wouldn't know drama if it was slowly finger-fucking him."

"So, did you like the second half?" he asks, his ears and cheeks the color of ham.

"I'm sorry, we left. Rena was tired, and I was tired, and that girl weirded her out."

"Sesha's an artist. And she listens to me, and she likes my ideas."

"Good, Ollie. I'm glad she does. So do I. I just don't have enough clout or energy to get anything produced. But by all means, if that makes you happy, keep doing it."

"Are you gonna walk out on the next one?"

"I don't know. Hopefully not. I like you. I don't have to like her. And that play was fucked. Maybe it was good-bad. I don't know."

He looks hurt. I try to feel bad. "But she and I—" He stops. "I like her, Harland."

"I know," I say. "I'm sorry."

"What do you mean?"

"I'm sorry that she's the only female who's given you attention lately."

The light rain has made his gray tee shirt almost black. A cop drives by, and Ollie sort of hides the bottle behind his belly. Somewhere an open window lets out the opening strains of the new hit single, "Dead Ol' Daddy."

"You want a frozen pizza?" I ask.

We wander inside. Ollie takes a seat at the kitchen table.

"I got fired from the charity."

"How the hell do you get fired from a charity?" I ask.

"I didn't work for free," says Ollie. "I got paid. But I went in late too many times."

"Oh shit," I say, and don't continue. I've managed not to get fired for that very offense for years. I think about the balance between time and money. I think about getting a blowjob twenty years in the future by some person who's not even born yet.

"And I sold pot to my manager, and another manager found out that I had sold the pot cheaper to that manager than I had to him, and that manager fired me."

"Oh," I say, feeling better. "How many managers does a charity have?"

"Four," says Ollie. He doesn't qualify it any further.

"So, like," I say, taking a moment to take a bigger bite of steaming hot thin-crust pizza, burning the top of my tongue, painfully blowing on it, the air hurting and helping my double-scalded taste buds all at once. "Fuck. Ow. Um, so like …"

"Are you OK?" Ollie says, biting into his own piece of pizza and burning his own mouth. "Ah! Ouch, ouch!"

"You OK?" I slur, my tongue pretty much melting out of my mouth. "Shit is hot."

"Happy birthday!" Ollie slurs.

"Thankth!" I slur.

The bedroom door opens and Rena shuffles out wearing sweatpants and a tank top, rubbing her eyes. "You guys aren't going to let me nap, are you?"

"Well, since you're awake, you wanna go out? It's almost eight already." I whine, refusing to be a grownup.

"OK. I need to wash my face and put on makeup," she says. "I'm not going out looking this tired."

Ollie wrinkles his nose and blinks a few times.

"I LOVE YOU RENA," I say in a goofy monotone to fill the lull.

"Happy birthday, retard," she says.

The combination of poisons I have ingested has turned me rabid. People I vaguely know sway in and out of my field of vision fisheye-style, their eyes and noses getting obscene and unnecessary, and some of them chant out birthday greetings that scare the shit out of me. My hands look like talons. It feels like someone shit my pants. I smell nachos and throw-up, but I might just be clairvoyant. Something Ollie-esque utters every other word of the punch line to a joke I like:

" …blood … out … clown …"

Nestor, tiny and far down the bar, is showing a few women his unhealed bruises, and I wonder what Nestor has to say to women. Maybe he's telling them what men are really like. I feel myself cringe dramatically.

I sense Rena, but she's not in my field of vision, and when I try to turn,

I feel medicine balls compressing the fluid between my stomach and my throat, and I have to stop or I will launch a cauldron's worth of bile onto a cast of extras.

I see a cartoon cutout of Old Fuck making the slit-throat finger gesture, a yellow hangnail trailing across an angular Adam's apple suspended in gray stubble and raw pink wrinkles. I fear living long enough to become that thing.

The hockey game in the corner is a biodome, I realize, with a dozen blue and red men bound on preordained paths, back-and-forth, spinning around, unable to tread other parts of their sterile prison. They chase an elusive black disc as a timer counts down and two gods look on and yell curses at one another, and I am reminded of Ollie's explanation of some television show whose title I've now forgotten.

My mouth tastes like breading.

Echoing noise sounds like an old rock and roll song about breaking up. Then, listening more closely to the lyrics I can hear, it seems like the song is really about the end of the Cold War, the bittersweet conclusion of an era when Americans thought they knew exactly who the enemy was. If I thought I could lift myself from the stool and stagger to the jukebox without otherwise injuring myself, I would be happy to break bones in my hand punching it for reminding me of simple truths I've spent so much of my life trying to complicate or ignore.

I get mad about remembering that I have cutely found wisdom in graffiti.

I get mad about not understanding the messages from Future Me.

I get mad about adhering to the comedic rule of three.

HDTVs used to screen stretched-wide Standard Definition signals concern me more than the somehow-ongoing abortion debate.

My mother used to call me Harold when she thought I was being silly. "Well, that makes perfect sense, Harold," she would say, her hands on her hips. I would laugh despite myself and protest that it wasn't my name, and then my silliness paled to hers, and she won by playing my game instead of halting it. I realize now, on the verge of tears—sorry for the times I didn't call her when I thought of it and could easily have called—that time is a useful organizational method even though everything happens at once (sometimes).

When my mom was being sarcastic or vindictive, she would call me Hal, which I hated. "You do whatever you please, Hal. It can't possibly affect anyone else."

The thought occurs to me: Who the fuck is still broadcasting SD?

My dad wasn't silly like my mom was, but he had a way of asking ridiculous questions that had no answer. When I was young, I would earnestly struggle to answer them, and not uncommonly, I would end up with a red face covered in tears.

"Why isn't silence louder?"
"How come we can't experience tomorrow as happens?"
"Who are you supposed to be?"

Rena asks me what's wrong, even though she seems a long way down the bar, even though she might be right next to me, even though she must know that what's wrong is the same thing that's been wrong, which is that no one can handle living in their own skin, or that no one can be honest about why it's not easy, or that articulating feelings is akin to rounding off to too few decimal places. Once this wave comes, everyone becomes part of the freak show, and I am scared not just for my life, but for the fact of life. We are crawling all over this planet, and even at our most dull, there is a horrifying amount of unpredictability. Something spills on me, and I'm annoyed, looking to see who's holding the empty mug hovering over my denim knee, and I recognize the hand holding it, and I follow it up the arm to my shoulder. I think about how a puppet must feel when there's no hand inside.

Something changes the mood of the whole place, but I'm not quite sure what it is, except that I'm definitely involved, but people seem happier, or at least not pissed off at me, and I get into the celebratory vibe. Something seems to lift me from my stool and allow me to levitate, which is nice. Later, after seeing some guy who looked like my dad shoving some other guy who looked like a slightly older version of my dad, people start coming up to me and congratulating me. I say thanks as well as I can. They push shots my way. Rena hugs me, and pulls me to kiss her, even though I don't like the smell of her breath in the moment, even knowing that mine could be three times worse. Someone pushes a shot to her, and she drinks it and drops the shot glass to the floor, and somehow it doesn't break, and a few people cheer. Someone makes an armpit fart. Nestor is saying, "That's so cool, you guys." Ollie is sort of smiling, maybe forcing it.

The jukebox literally catches on fire. The next thing I register is that I have been pushed into the alley. I see smoke and a fire truck, and somebody yells that everything is OK, and then I'm in the backseat of a car trying not to throw up.

My hand feels coated in tree sap when I wake up on the rug near the bathroom in Ollie's apartment. Above me, a marionette of a mime dangles, orange puffs of yarn atop its blue wooden feet. The memory of wilted nachos and a red digital alarm clock blinking 4:20 in a dark space lit by only open refrigerator light pulls like a mesh over the sight before me, and I keep hoping the clown puppet doesn't slowly tilt its head down to look at me. I stare up at the thing, and it keeps staring straight ahead, daring me.

A skittering sound followed by the sensation of talons on my abdomen convinces me that I have just been haunted by the ghost of Madonna the mole. But before any terrible beast can devour my belly, the skittering sound echoes into silence. I recognize that I have been spared. Perhaps food will taste better now.

I've ruined another one of my nice tee shirts with a witty declaration, I realize, looking down the length of my sprawled, aching body. Convulsions seem to have kept my muscles busy while I was in the black. I hear cartoons. The nastiness-covered cloth on my torso once read, "Fuck you in half." Now it is a mess of dried oral discharge and maybe the vague impressions of varmint prints.

My face is close enough to smell the carpet, which is full of four years of Ollie not wanting to spend money on a vacuum cleaner. The preeminent scent is the must of the pets of whoever lived here before he moved in, but traces of artificially flavored breakfast cereal and toe jam and instant noodle flavor packets sneak in while I try to ignore them.

Something bothers the back of my neck, and when I reach back to pull it from under me, I reveal to myself some kind of scrap of cardboard covered in plastic which has a repeating pattern on it, and as the pattern pulls into focus it becomes repeating words. As I regain the ability to read, I isolate one of the iterations: "Jerk Pop." It's now that I realize that some of the stickiness that has ruined my shirt is caramel-covered popcorn. And of course much of it is whatever becomes of human bile when exposed to air over several hours. I'm ready to open my prize when the bathroom door opens.

"Hello, my sweetest," says Rena, standing above me. She smells and looks showered. It's a porn angle, a perfect up-skirt, but for her pants and the fact of real life never living up to scripted notions.

"Hi Rena," I say, feeling miserable and self-conscious. She keeps smiling down at me. "Why are we at Ollie's?"

"Ollie drove. Neither of us was in a condition to drive after that celebration."

"Everybody bought us drinks," I say, not quite forming a question. "My birthday."

"Yes, your birthday, my thirty-five-year-old, and another little thing that happened last night." Her eyes sparkle. "Now get in here and take a shower with your new fiancée!"

Hot water opens the pores on my face as Rena scrubs my back. She moves a rough washcloth between my shoulder blades and recounts how much I caught her off-guard when I got down on one knee in front of everyone and asked her to marry me. I seem to remember having fallen off of my stool at one point, which must have been it. She tells me how, even though I didn't produce a ring, it was still very romantic, and she said yes right away. She playfully slaps my butt with the washcloth before draping her arms around from behind and talking more quietly into my ear about how surprised she was about everything I said last night, and how I really opened up and put myself on the line. That I took a day that was supposed to be about *me* and made it about *us*.

I turn around, making sure to hide my paralysis, and I say, quoting something I heard in a movie once, "I love you."

She looks into my eyes, through me, into whatever she's planning, and the water keeps rushing down on our heads, and this, I guess, is how we have become engaged.

4 BOX

At work, people I barely know come up to me and say, "Congrats," and I wonder which website is posting things about my personal life. Someone has left a bowling ball bolted to a rusty chain on my work chair, which I heft onto the ground, pinching something in my back, and the chain makes a clanking sound, and I'm sweating and itchy, and I know my ears have flushed red, and I can feel multiple pairs of eyes on me, and I hear giggling that I know belongs to Berry. When I don't react, I hear whispered conversations shift to Laurel having been let go, and I try to remember which one was Laurel.

With earbuds inserted and the soundtrack from some horror movie blaring into my head, I can focus on starting up my laptop and appearing to work. I see the toddler-talking HR woman bustling down a hallway, and I feel shameful warmth flow into my crotch.

The bowling ball rolls away from its seemingly stationary spot next to my desk, dragging the chain with it, revealing after how many years that this floor has never been level. I don't even pretend to go for it. It's someone else's problem now. I almost sneeze but can't, and I feel a little flattered by the fact that someone went to the trouble of assembling the thing to poke fun at me.

Nestor has called an emergency meeting, including myself, Ollie, Rena, and Nestor's friend Dave. Dave, like Nestor, is a light-skinned black guy, though he doesn't look much like me. I realize that the appropriate adjective to describe Dave is "generic." He's not an extra, but he probably doesn't have many lines. He definitely doesn't have a last name. I can't tell whether Dave and Nestor are romantically linked, and then I wonder about whether anyone would assume Rena and I are romantically linked if they had just met us. At some coffee bar on the side of town that caters to optimists, in some warm-hued corner near a real fireplace with a real log on fire, Ollie munches a brown pastry out of a napkin, crumbs spilling almost continually into his lap. Rena waits for her tea to over-steep. I have a double espresso into which I'm dumping thimbles of half-and-half, mostly to observe the colors shift. Dave has both hands delicately folded around a hot cocoa, looking prim and sweater-vesty. Nestor sips something foamy with nutmeg sprinkled on top and then gestures in a more overtly gay manner than I'm used to seeing, and I chalk it up to the presence of Dave.

"You guys," says Nestor. "We had a terrorist in the morgue today."

"Oh my god!" Dave whispers, gasping for emphasis.

"Really?" says Ollie.

"I think so, yeah," Nestor says, licking the tip of the whipped cream mound. "OK, so: I'm cleaning this woman. She blew her brains out, so she's barely got a head. There's a policeman in the office talking with my boss—"

"A policeman!" I laugh. "Was he with the fireman and the spaceman?"

"You know what I mean," says Nestor, blushing in a way that only black men can. "So Doctor Thule is in there with the police guy, and the door is mostly closed, but not like, shut tight, and I hear the police guy asking if anything was found in her stomach. So I'm like, well, that's weird, because obviously she blew her brains out. Did she poison herself, too? But then I hear the policeman—"

"Oh my god!" I whine. "Can't you just say, 'cop'?"

Nestor looks at me like I just deleted a cancer cure. "Anyway ..." he sighs, "then he starts talking about the Golden Gate Bridge, and how when they were searching her apartment they found an unused one-way ticket to San Francisco, dated February twelfth."

"Abraham Lincoln's birthday," says Rena. The males look at her for a second.

"That's two days before Valentine's Day," says Nestor. "This woman was supposed to have been there when they blew up the bridge."

"Just because she had a plane ticket?" says Ollie, crumbs on his chin.

"Well, a plane ticket, and the fact that she blew her own head off. And not with a gun, either. The cop said she had a small explosive. It's not exactly uninteresting." Nestor takes a sip, gets foam all over his upper lip, and wipes it off with his non-drinking hand, which he then wipes on his corduroy pants. "Doctor Thule asked why the cop asked about her stomach, and the cop asked if he found anything, and Dr. Thule said no, and then the policeman said that when they recovered parts of a couple of the bodies from the Golden Gate bay or whatever, they found objects in two different people's stomachs. And then they found a few more of these objects at the bottom of the sea floor or whatever, which they think must have come out of the stomachs of some of the other people when they blew up. And these objects were all the same, or something."

"What were the objects?" says Dave, his mouth wide open as the question hangs.

"The police guy didn't say. I don't know if he didn't know, or wasn't allowed to say, or what. But Dr. Thule hadn't actually checked the stomach. He was pawning her off on me so he could go play golf when the policeman showed up."

"Undertakers play golf, too, huh?" I say. I take a sip of my lukewarm espresso-flavored half-and-half. "This tastes like my mom."

Rena glances sidelong.

"So he didn't look for whatever might have been in her stomach?" Eight of Dave's fingertips are on his lips, at the ready for fingernail nibbling.

"No, he went to play golf," says Nestor, now sitting back and taking a long gulp of his cinnamon mocha disaster.

There's a beat where the only sound is spoons clinking coffee cups and some salsa music being piped in.

"But today I became a surgeon." Nestor's face stretches into a grin that makes me uncomfortable.

"Nestor," Rena stage whispers. "Did you … cut that woman open?"

"In my defense," says Nestor, "there was a bigger hole in her when she showed up."

"Oh crud," says Ollie. "That's gross."

As my respect for Black Me exponentiates, he continues.

"I made a lateral incision into the abdominal tissue, and I pulled this out of her." Nestor reaches into the gray backpack at his heel and retrieves a gallon-sized Ziploc bag. Through the blood-black, condensation-fogged interior of the bag, I can make out an object that at first strikes me as a

71

clamshell case that might bear a ring.

"You're making us accessories to a crime!" Dave whispers giddily. Rena squints at the bag, mouthing something to herself. Ollie looks scared.

"This," says Nestor, milking it, "is a black box."

About to heckle him, I catch myself. "You mean like on an airplane?"

"I think so," says Nestor. He brings the bag in closer to the center of the group, hovering over a crumb-covered saucer, and I start worrying that the thing is going to start leaking post-mortem syrup. Nestor rolls the object within the bag so that a new edge is visible through the plastic, and a tiny green LED flashes in a seemingly random pattern. I start looking around the coffeeshop, trying to see if anybody is watching our fairly conspicuous show-and-tell session. The level of disinterested self-involvement all around us is, for once, reassuring.

"How do you know it's not a bomb?" says Ollie, who has crumbs in the corner of his mouth, making it look abnormally wide and cartoonish.

Nestor rolls the object another ninety degrees and presses it tight against the interior of the plastic bag. Dark biological fluids squeeze away from the object's surface, flat droplets pulling back to reveal tiny white text on the black metal, a brand and a serial number. "I researched it," Nestor says. "It's a black box. A personal one. It's produced by a company called TBL."

"So it … records …?" says Rena.

"Yeah," says Nestor. He scratches his nose, and it makes my nose itch.

Rena's furrowed brow smoothes slightly. "What does it record?"

"The website says it … interprets and outputs audio."

"Interprets what?" says Ollie. One crumb from the corner of his mouth falls near my drink, and I move my drink.

"It interprets what it records," says Nestor.

"Yeah, but like how?" I say, sipping. "Like it gives an assessment? Like it offers an opinion?"

"I don't know," says Nestor. "The website didn't say."

Dave wrings his hands, releases them, and scoots back from the table, raising his palms to the beige tiled ceiling. "This is weird. And that," he says, pointing at the plastic baggie, "is a biohazard."

"This," says Nestor, "could be worth a billion dollars."

He's exaggerating, but I'm intrigued. My penis is halfway-erect. I'm thirty-five years old, I recognize. I could be halfway to death. The warmth of the coffeehouse and the scents surrounding me feel suddenly romantic. I start to fall in love with the possibility of the inexplicable. I expect my cell phone to start ringing. I speak smoothly and quietly, taking focus.

"We need to find out how to get the recordings out of that thing."

"There's a device," says Nestor. "It connects wirelessly to the black box. They sell it online. We could buy one."

"How does it cost?" says Ollie. I wonder if anyone else has noticed that he somehow forgot to include the word "much."

"The list price on the website is eight thousand."

"Holy shit," says Rena. "Is it made of diamonds and babies?"

"It's got some special encryption, and it's not, like, a mass-market product." Nestor pulls the Ziploc back down into his backpack. "The corner store doesn't have them, OK? It's, like, sci-fi technology. Probably no one buys them but governments and insane people."

"That's redundant," says Dave, lifting an eyebrow.

Ollie's other crumb falls out.

"Well," says Rena, "It sounds like twenty insane people acquired them and blew up a bridge in San Francisco."

"Actually," Nestor says, "the black boxes are cheap by comparison, only four hundred. It's the media conversion device that's really expensive."

"Anyone can keep a diary, but it will cost you if you want to read it," I say, wishing I had a cigarette for some reason.

"How did she swallow that?" says Ollie, looking down at the backpack in which the black box is now hidden. "That thing looked too big to swallow."

"It's probably at the upper range of what one could swallow," says Dave, and I guffaw. Dave smirks at me and tilts his head, probably learning not to expect better from me.

Rena finally pulls the teabag from her mug, dangling it in the same space where the nasty baggie had dangled. Ollie's eye follows the saturated bag.

Ollie says, "Why don't we just rent one?"

Drunk driving feels like a video game. I keep an eye out for the cops and try to stay in between the lines. The graphics are somewhat lifelike but also kind of fake. Expectedly, the replay value has diminished, but there's something to be said for knowing the course, in this case, the optimum route between Skizzers and my house to minimize the likelihood of mission failure.

I have to take a common detour because I need Taco Bag. Rena argues, drunk from the passenger seat, that I don't *need* Taco Bag. She's wrong, and I quell an impulse to spit in her direction. She smells like a lot of perfume and sweat and smoke and ginger, the last of which is due to the fact that Chinese restaurant odors never completely wash off. I decide to try to convince her to blow me using ten words or fewer.

"I love you," I say, spending a powerful three.

She looks sternly at the road, folding her arms, hugging herself around her seatbelt, huffing a bit.

"You smell good," I say. Another powerful three. Four left.

I reach out to caress her far shoulder, straining and grunting a bit, not feeling young anymore. My fingers dance on her sleeveless shirt strap, going in between that and the bra strap. I kiss her neck, craning my head to keep one eye on the blackness and strobing yellow through the windshield. I breathe lightly into her cheek.

"Remember Florida?" I'm referencing some vacation where a similar set of tactics worked two years ago. She turns, pulling her face slightly taut and skeptical. She's resisting playfully, though, and a smile starts to break through her stoic pretense. I wait, let the moment float there, let time do its thing. I pull back to my side of the car a little, showing that I'm willing to abandon the pursuit if she's really not interested. I want to tell her that I liked watching her dance to music I hate earlier, but I only have two words left to use. I wait, and I peek out of the corner of my eye to see her body language warming. I take the beat, inhale, and play my trump card.

"Fiancée," I say, smiling straight ahead at the streaking colors on the dark background. I turn back to her slightly to see her pulling the shoulder strap around her head and bending toward me.

Outside, wind moves high-reaching, skeletal trees, and stars blast by like bullets, a barrage all miraculously missing the car. In the distance, a yellow speck grows into yellow bell with its clanger perpetually askance. It's not Taco Bag, but it will do. A unique and wonderful music plays from my lap. I still have a word to spare.

I had mocked Ollie for suggesting that rental was an option, but he was headed in the right direction. Scouring the Internet for anything besides a specific pornography is generally fruitless, or at least an empty satisfaction, but now as I find a few leads, I start to feel like a proper detective. I have to disable the company's proxy server to avoid the web filter, but that's only about four clicks. My cell phone can access the Internet, but only some handicapped, tiny version of it that's too annoying to use, so I find a way to justify in my own mind risking my job by using company equipment to hunt for spy equipment at ten in the morning on a Wednesday. Roy comes by, and I have to minimize the browser and open a spreadsheet and pretend to be updating it until he catches fire, blows up, and leaves. As he walks away, I try to remember the task he's just asked me to perform.

When I find a website that sells information about other websites— which sites have arisen with surprising swiftness in the wake of the government-*in-absentia*—I know I've struck gold. Backstabbers can get things cheap. I submit a request for a list of every sale from the black box site to anyone within a two hundred-mile radius of my ZIP code. The report, which the confirmation claims will be emailed within a week, costs me seventeen dollars, which I pay for using an account which uses my spam email address set up in the name of my elementary school enemy, Brock Davis. A few years after setting up the account, I once got an email from the real Brock Davis's bail bondsmen, which made me very happy. My unsigned reply to Brock Davis's bail bondsmen read:

Not if you want to see your daughter again.

Having accomplished my day's goal by 10:30 a.m., I go wandering around the office, smelling the fake ferns and peeking over cubicles, pretending to be social. I wash my hands in the sink by the coffee station, hoping that someone will come by so I can make small talk. Instead of wasting a paper towel, I shake my hands into carpet the color of damp sand and continue on my aimless rounds.

I get to the Accounting department, and I take a secondary seat next to a desk in the cubicle of Julius Zorro, according to the placard, and the name rings a bell. He's on the phone, talking numbers, doing a heck of a job. He has a laminated calendar hanging in front of him with several November dates circled in red. I notice that one of them is Election Day. Julius Zorro is tan, which makes his big teeth look even whiter, and stylishly shaggy dark hair hangs down to his eyebrows. He has sculpted cheekbones and a narrow chin with no sag beneath it, which convinces me that he's still in his twenties. His blue shirt is fully buttoned, and a shiny purple tie hangs over his thin chest. He looks healthy and efficient. When he finally hangs up, he turns to me and says, "Mr.—?"

"Just Harland," I say, leaning over his desk to shake the hand he quickly extends. I see him wince because my hand is still slightly damp.

"Julius Zorro," he says in the congested tone of the smug.

"Yeah," I say. "Cool."

"How can I help you, Harland?"

"Well, Julius Zorro, I work down at the other end of the building. You been there?"

"Yes," he sort of laughs and his brow creases. "Actually, if you check your email—"

"It doesn't matter, Zorro," I say, realizing I'm sort of doing an impression of my dad, feigning the confidence of the self-employed. "But I'll tell you what. Nothing in this building is gonna kill me."

"Right," he says, sinking a bit, perhaps realizing that his role in this conversation is that of the straight man.

"Let me ask you something, Zorro," I say.

"It's Julius," he says.

"Sure, sure," I say. I realize I'm doing an impression of every salesman I've ever met. "Let me ask you something, Julian. Do you intend to die in that chair?"

Julius Zorro smirks at me, blinks as he inhales, and says, "No."

"Exactly!" I say, pointing at his tie. "No one does. It's not a bad chair— looks more swivelly than mine, and probably has great lumbar support— but it's not the kind of place where you'd want to permanently lose consciousness."

In between my bursts of propaganda, I hear multiple clocks ticking slightly out of sync.

"I got engaged last week. I didn't mean to, but I did. I might have a family to support sometime before long. Are you married, Jules?"

"No, I'm not, Harland," he says. His smirk has frozen in an ugly way. "What can I do for you today?"

"Thanks for asking," I say.

"You're welcome," he says.

"I know how valuable I am to this company," I say.

"This is probably something you want to take up with HR," he says.

"No, no," I say. "What my issue is, is really a money issue."

"Yes," says Julius. "I don't set pay rates. We have different employee classifications, and Human Resources maintains ..."

"So they do payroll?"

"No," says Julius, his smirk gone, his jaw still set, "Accounting does payroll. We do."

"Then you 'sign the checks,' as it were?" I say this, making a little hand gesture. "You can direct where funds come from, and where they go. I can direct where information goes. I can't really influence where it comes from—that's a little ontological—but I can influence where it ends up."

"Are you—?" He backpedals. "What are you suggesting?"

"I want what should be coming anyway, but what people are too obtuse to bother to recognize."

"Look, I need you to put this is concrete terms. I don't know if you're proposing something, or trying to force something, or if you're threatening something ..."

"Why would you say the word 'threat'? Don't you think that's inherently threatening?"

I can see Julius Zorro's teeth again, and I feel satisfied. I stand up.

"I'm going to remember this, OK?" I say. I walk out of his cubicle. I want to punch something out of fear and exhilaration. I'm down the hall. I pass the second drinking fountain and it begins squirting water in a sad little arc, the response of some proximity sensor or ghost. The buzz ignites in my pants pocket. I answer the phone, and a familiar voice speaks.

"So you have a ball and chain now."

"Yes," I tell Future Me. "So you know when you're reaching me?"

"Approximately," says the voice. "So you're ready to make big life decisions."

"That sounds," I say, "exactly like some vague line a psychic would dangle to imply something without really saying anything."

There's a beat, and I hear a sneeze on the other end of the line.

"Bless you," I say.

"Thanks," says Future Me.

"Why are you calling me?" I say. "The election isn't for another week or something."

"Two," says Future Me.

"And who was it you said was going to win? Rudy?"

"Ruder," says the voice. "A plurality. Forty-one percent."

"Right," I say. "So what, do I help rig the voting machines? Is that how I know this?"

The voice takes a moment, maybe to calculate from its array of potential responses.

"Oh, sorry," I say. "Did I confuse you by referring to you as me, even though obviously you're just a fabrication of some programmer's fantasy?"

"You're a programmer," says the voice.

"So maybe I *made* you?" I try to make it extra sarcastic.

"Maybe I made you," says the voice, and I hear static interrupt the line for a moment.

"Good one," I say. "You're obviously real mature."

"No," says the voice. "But neither are you, and obviously there's not much I can do about that at this point."

"Then why are you calling me?" I look around for something to spit into.

"You miss your mother," says the voice.

I look across rows of cubicles, one or two heads of taller workers peeping above the parallel panels. Far beyond, there are some windows, and beyond the window are clouds in the sky.

"And you don't?" I say.

"I do," the voice says.

"Glad not much changes," I say. "Glad I'll still be a boring, ineffectual fuck when I get to be you."

More static, then: "Is that how you see yourself?"

"Looking forward to catching up to you," I say. "Except not."

I hang up. I wince at a pain in my hand. Somehow, I have a splinter in the tip of my ring finger, and it reminds me that I still need to make it official with Rena. Even though it seems that I have yet to make the decision.

At the mall that white people don't go to anymore, I walk around looking at flimsy banners for clearance sales which may or may not have passed, and darkened, gated stores vacant since well before DC fell. The once bustling and elaborately decorated central intersection of hallways where Santa's throne stood—where for a string of years my parents would bring me to sit on said stranger's knee and request lavish material goods they had no apparent means and/or intention of procuring—now evokes a shadowy temple, a dark vast space with stray plastic plants towering and somehow overgrown, a single column of light tilting to the floor, revealing dust spinning from dirty tile up to the angular breach in the structure's apex that I struggle to think of as a skylight. Where I stand now is where I stood in line almost thirty years ago, a cranky child waiting endless moments to posit a petty proposition to a false incarnation of a fictional character. Which, I find, sounds like the central motif of any given religion.

I walk past the closed Hunan Bowl, its cartoon panda picking with chopsticks at a bowl with cartoon squiggles of steam emerging almost menacingly, forcing me to reinterpret the panda's seemingly docile expression. I imagine Rena in the mall five miles north at the Orange Bamboo, and I wonder how long it will take to scare the white people out of that mall. There is, after all, another mall five miles further north. I pass a closed novelty store, and through its mostly soaped window I notice a stray, motionless Dancing Condom figure with google eyes and, almost certainly, Chinese batteries corroding in its plastic belly. I marvel at how efficiently the relocation of a few major industries and the resulting urban sprawl has resurrected racial segregation in the metropolitan area.

I pass a clothing store that might be open—two of the five florescent beams inside are flickering—and beyond a dozen racks of neon and pastel garments, in the dim rear of the store, I see a black woman or girl on a large cordless phone. Sleeves of a thick gray sweater cover arms folded around her large torso, and I estimate that her age falls within the range of 12 to 40. She paces behind the counter, and as I pass, I hear her say, "How I'm supposed to do that myself?"

I pass a row of coin-operated rider horses, yellow, green, gray, and blue. Each horse bears a frozen expression of comic glee, large oval eyeballs with Pac-Man-shaped pupils, each tied to a post with three open coin slots and one blocked slot. Seventy-five cents a go to tilt back and forth for a minute must have seemed like a bargain when rich white wives brought their gaggles here years ago. I catch a glimpse of a spider hanging in the cobweb between the two middle horses, and it looks like it's shitting silk out of boredom.

I get down to the slightly populated region of the mall, near the bargain multiplex. The dollar theater's interior marquee displays a list of movies, some of which I can't believe are still in theaters, the rest of which I can't believe anyone put up money to release.

CASH BLIMP, starring Ronnie Murphy, Jr. and the computer-generated likeness of the late Ronnie Murphy.

LOVE DATE, featuring whoever was on a sitcom three years ago.

AIN'T NUTHIN BUTTA PLAYA PARTAY, for which someone amazingly spent time writing a script.

SPACIST, a sci-fi comi-tragedy about a racist starship captain who learns to love all creatures only after he finds himself confined to a space wheelchair.

THE DARKNESS OF HAUNTED SCARY, an old-fashioned non-3D cartoon.

I DON'T GIVE A SHIT ABOUT YOUR LAWN, a revenge comedy.

JESUS CHRIST: BOUNTY HUNTER, the final film by an insane maniac before he burned down his compound.

YOU, ME, THEM, US, WE, I, WHO, a feature-length version of the like-named website.

MCMART, a somewhat fictionalized account of when they merged.

YOUVIE, the experimental mirror booth where you go for 90 minutes and pretend that you're in a film.

I also see a poster advertising buy-one-get-one movie tickets if you donate plasma.

When I reach the jewelry store, I see a man at the counter paying for a thick, gold-colored necklace. The man is wearing a puffy green jacket with a horned head on the back, and airbrushed lettering beneath the image reads, THA DEVIL.

The clerk, a thin woman wearing glasses with a clear plastic frame—the only white person besides me in this mall, by my observation—asks, "Credit or debit?"

The man says, as far as I can tell, "Crebit."

The woman swipes the card and something beeps, and she swipes it again, and the beep happens again. She exhales, and she says to the man, "Do you have another card … you could use?"

"Try it again," says Green Coat Man, who turns both ways, looking over his shoulders, catching me in his periphery and pointedly ignoring me.

After five minutes of increasingly hostile exchanges, including the man gesturing at me at one point and saying, "Y'all gonna just give *him* shit," he agrees to not take the necklace and put ten dollars toward layaway. Before the receipt can fully print, he barks, "I'm gonna need a receipt!" When he grumbles his way out into the sporadically lit hallway, I advance toward the counter and the flushed, pale woman looks at me, and says, "Thank you for waiting. How can I help you?" She looks like she has not smiled in weeks.

"Hey," I say. "Hi. Thanks, um, my name is Harland."

"I'm Dina," she points to a nametag pinned to her sweater that I can barely read.

"I am looking for a ring," I say.

"For you, or …" she lets it hang.

"For my fiancée," I say.

"A wedding ring?"

"No, an engagement ring. I forgot to get a ring when I proposed. Honestly, I was pretty fucked up. The next day I was covered in Jerk Pop … Anyway, I just need a simple ring. No blood diamonds or whatever. Do they still do blood diamonds?"

"Yes," says Dina, cheerily enough.

"Yeah, she wouldn't like that. So I guess like a sapphire or plastic or something?"

"What sort of price range are you looking in?"

"Uh," I say, really not knowing. "What's the going rate?"

"Normally they say it's two months' salary, though lately the trend is to get whatever's least expensive, since some analysts have predicted that goods may not retain value after the election."

"Right, right," I say, peeking slightly over the counter to look at Dina's body, which is predominantly covered by her long beige sweater. "So, what kind of ring would you like?"

"Me personally?" she says. "Well, I like … topaz."

"I don't know what that is," I say.

"Well, it's a precious stone," she says, biting her lip, or I imagine her biting her lip. Maybe she starts running her fingertips up one hip, feeling a contour that is hidden from me. "Most of them are blue. And like many stones, the ..." She points to something inside the case, though my eyes don't follow. "... *cut* is what makes it valuable." Her mouth hangs slightly, lower teeth visible and glistening.

"You must need something pretty hard," I say, "to cut through a topaz."

"Most gemstones are cut using diamonds or silicon carbide, which is made by man," she says. "It's called lapidary." Her head is tilting, and she's short enough that she has to look up at average-height me. I listen to her inhale and exhale following her statement.

"I'd like to know more," I say, looking dead into her eyes. "I want to be educated before I make a purchase."

"Well," she says, breaking her eye contact with me to lean far over the case toward me. Her breath fogs a small portion of the glass and she brings a fingertip to rest in the middle of the fog. "You see how this stone has a simple geometry?" She's talking into the glass, so her words bounce off of it. "Compared to this one?" She drags a line clean through the evaporating fog to point at something else within the case.

My eyes follow her finger, but nothing beyond it. I lean in so I can smell whatever soap she uses. She does not wear perfume, which I appreciate. A few strands of hair curl behind the ear closest to me, which is pierced but contains no earring. I can smell cherry lip balm and fabric softener. I can almost hear her heartbeat, and I see tiny capillaries in her cheeks filling, warming, her face heating visibly.

"That's more complex," I say, still not looking anywhere but at her face as she looks down. I record every second of this in my memory. I bring my clammy hands to the internally lit surface of the glass, within inches of hers. I exhale, and I inhale more deeply.

Ollie says, "He started out as the obvious bad guy," breaking to gobble more caramel corn, then continuing, "but then in the middle seasons, you weren't sure whether he was a good guy or a bad guy. I mean, he obviously wasn't a good guy—he killed people and stuff—but you didn't know if he was fully bad, you know? Like, he was killing people for a reason, to protect other people or to pave the way for something greater than himself. But then—"

More brown sugar-coated popcorn crunches as he sniffs enough air into his nostrils to continue with his mouth full. " ...by the end, it's like you didn't really know whether he knew whether the things he did really meant anything. Like, did he know that there was a purpose, or did he at least believe there was, or was he always just looking out for himself?"

I assume that Ollie is talking about the character on the television show he's making me watch, but then I wonder if he might be talking about Hitler or God or somebody else.

Pulling an incredibly dense smoke into my lungs and holding it long enough to recite the alphabet backwards and forwards in German in my mind, I delicately balance the pink glass pipe on the now-very-long glass coffee table, release the smoke through pursed lips, whistling a monotonic pattern that probably has a mathematical significance. I rely on my subconscious to record it for later analysis. I say, with a husky cadence that might come across as skepticism, despite my intent, "So that's ... like ... the bad guy?"

"Well, I just said, it's hard to tell. But he always has the best lines. He's real deadpan."

"Deadpan," I parrot.

"Yeah, deadpan," says Ollie. "He should have died in a pan."

"How does he die?" I ask.

"Him? Don't you want to watch and find out *if* he dies?"

"Just tell me, Ollie."

"Well, I don't know, really. The end of the show is weird because you kind of know what happens, but there's a lot left to the imagination."

"That's stupid," I say. "Deadpan. Deadpan stupid. That shit is deadpan stupid." It becomes a rhythm, and we start to repeat it until we giggle.

"I'm telling you, Harland, if you watch until the end of this season, you're going to be hooked."

"Right," I say, "like a fish; like a john."

"John who?"

"That's right." I try to focus on the action of the program, but people talking to each other suddenly seems very stupid in the abstract. What could they possibly have to say to one another? I point at the television. "Those two? They're really the same. Right? They're the same person?"

"No," says Ollie. "Well, I mean, what are you thinking of? Did you hear something about season five?"

"No!" I whine, swatting an invisible insect. "I don't care about the show. I'm just observing. Those two—they're arguing, and they're playing tug-o-war, but come on. They're really the same, right? The same thing?"

"I don't know what you mean," says Ollie, not having fun now. His face is serious, threatening to show annoyance. His brow is dry. His mouth is flat.

"You want me to like this thing that you like," I say. "That's cool. We're friends. You want me to like what you like, and I am happy to see the show. OK? I am just telling you, with words, that I have observed something that I find meaningful, and if it does not fit into the bigger picture—" I feel only dryness in my mouth as I try to enunciate, "—then I apologize for muddling the perspective."

"OK," he says, picking up the kangaroo dick. "Let's watch the show."

I face the screen. I tell Ollie, "I face the screen."

He doesn't respond.

I say, "Harland looks at the television to understand the characters and the plot."

Ollie looks straight into the television, flicking his lighter, holding its flame to the open bowl. He pointedly ignores me, and I want to stop and be the bigger man, but I overrule my better instincts and choose not to.

"Harland watches television," I say. "Harland sees moving pictures on flat rectangle."

"Shut up, Harland," Ollie finally breaks. "We don't have to watch it if you don't want to. I thought you might enjoy it, but I'm not forcing you."

I don't turn to look at him, and he eventually gives up on me returning eye contact.

Some things that I don't understand occur on the screen, and it feels too much like watching my own life go by unattended. I get up to go to the bathroom, and Ollie doesn't bother to pause it.

In between setting up blog accounts under aliases to post my poetry, I do some search engine searches and find all sorts of hints that someone out there is well aware of my existence and is interested in contacting me. I see targeted advertisements in response to my search terms, some even using one of my alias names that must be captured in a cookie (I picture a small nebula of nothing but text and chocolate chips). I see offers to get me started on a program that will lead me to what must be my ultimate goal, based upon the microseconds of psychotherapy the server has just performed, using my input and its search optimization indexes. My keystrokes get interpreted, harvested, rendered, dissected, julienned, filleted, snapped wide like they're split up the sternum. Some faceless mathematician plugs my immediate desires into a function that yields precise yet limitless ways in which I should spend money.

I receive a notification that the seventeen dollars I spent on the black box distribution report is being refunded because the snooping website has gone belly-up. I swear and purposefully spill my coffee.

◎

The Flying Saucer is decorated as expected. Dark walls, strings of blinking LEDs, inset video screens simulating stars passing by beyond, recessed backlights illuminating neon foam board planets—most of them with Saturn-esque ellipses encircling—all of this surrounding a circular floor with a couple dozen circular tables with bucket chairs circling them. The four of us sit centrally, in the nexus or the nucleus of whatever's going on here. We are served crayon-colored drinks in Erlenmeyer flasks with tiny floating ice bulbs.

"Brownstack," says Nestor.

"Is that your nickname?" says Ollie. Rena sort of laughs.

"Wow, racist. Anyway, it's a pawnshop about an hour north." Nestor stirs the ice in his flask, the light orange liquid swirling. "I talked to the proprietor on the phone, and she thinks they have one."

"The thing?" I say, trying to think of synonyms for *thing*. "The, like, object ... device?"

"Yes," says Rena. "Do they have the 'object device'?" She tilts her head and scrunches her face and goes cross-eyed as she turns to look at me.

"You know what I mean," I say to the table.

"Yesh," Nestor says, slurring and looking surprised. "Yes." Beat. "What the hell is in these?"

"Alien juice," says Ollie. "That's what the menu said."

Nestor takes out a folded square of notebook paper and begins unfolding it. He reads aloud, "QBBR231, the Quiet Black Box Receiver."

◎

At work, in between checking the UPS tracking status of the Revelations trading cards I ordered, for fun I write suicide letters on behalf of all of my coworkers. I have a fancy-looking spreadsheet open too, in case I need to appear as though I'm working. The title reads EBIT.

Berry's letter reads:

> *This cloud of blackness is inescapable. Each day the same, the Nothingness will not let me rest. I can't forgive myself for all that Iv* [sic] *done. I have wronged so many, most of all my children. And to Lisa, I am sorry to say that the man you married never existed. Oh, and I cheated on you with with* [sic] *the receptionist who got fired, Laurel. She was the only real woman I ever had. I cannot bare* [sic] *the guilt anymore. I'm sorry. Please hug our dog. Berry.*

Chad's letter reads:

> *I can't stand this bullshit. My teams arent'* [sic] *winning, my gal's a bitch, and I can't even get it up anymore because porn ruined my expectations about sex. Thanks a lot, life. Thanks for nothing. —The Chad*

Roy's letter reads:

> *Dear Jesus, I'm finally coming to see you. After a life of stoic withholding and countless evenings of penitent self-flagellation, I am finally ready to embrace the hedonistic free-for-all that is Heaven. No longer will I sit silent in my well-kept, three-bedroom home, silently pushing down my innermost desires out of love and respect for You; indeed I will vacate the shackles of my Earthly prison and strip myself completely nude, every shred of cloth shed shamelessly from my quivering body, so that I may mount each angel in glorious ecstasy and defile each in turn, reveling in base, carnal deeds, which will now be blessed by Your hand. I will put my manhood unto each one I desire, and they will scream with fulfillment. And then, finally, Lord, I will take Your p—* [sic] *into my mouth and imbibe the truth of Communion. Then, when you are done Communioning in my mouth, maybe we can go out for some sodas. Love, Roy*

I receive a text message from Rena that reads, "Plz take tomorrow off." That's all the excuse I need. I don't bother asking permission, counting on the fact of my relative invisibility in the scheme of things.

Nestor's hybrid is tiny and I keep bugging everybody by complaining about it in less-and-less subtle ways.

"It sure runs quiet," I say. I scratch my nose, wincing at a billboard for Fissure Fixer suppositories. I take a bite of my meatball sub and say with my mouth full, "Must be due to that zero horsepower."

"Since when do you care about cars?" asks Rena, riding shotgun, kitty corner from me sitting behind Nestor, her mouth full of a bite of tuna sub.

"How much longer?" I ask, at first meaning the pawnshop. I suck through a straw the remaining dregs of some unnecessary variation on one of the major non-cola soft drinks from between ice chunks in the thinnest plastic cup possible. Then I add, "I mean, 'til you have to return this thing to the toy store?"

"At least I'm not driving a gas guzzler." Nestor didn't get a sub; he got soup and ate soup while driving, which I gave him shit about earlier, until he finished it without spilling or crashing, to my chagrin.

"Yeah," I say. "What's this, technically … a cum guzzler?"

"What?" says Ollie, who has a booger on his wrist from wiping his nose. He opens his mouth and burps in order to make room for another huge bite of his Italian sub.

"That was real stupid," says Rena, squinting through dark-rimmed glasses she doesn't really need.

"It's pretty cool that they make disposable, one-time-use cars now," I say. It annoys me that Nestor isn't getting more irritated. I want a reaction. I realize that I WANT A REACTION should be tattooed on my forehead. I bite into a meatball and something hard clicks between my teeth. I maneuver the bone speck to the forefront of my palate and inconspicuously spit it at the childproof door handle. I see it stick in the middle of a tiny reflection of a severely warped version of my head. Then I conspicuously fart, which sounds like a missile dropping from T-minus four.

"Oh come on!" is the general cry as windows roll down (necessarily).

The car comes to a stop with nothing but a slight gravelly noise in the dusty parking lot. We exit the "car" and I feel a sharp November breeze ripple my windbreaker. Beyond the rusted brown-on-beige BROWNSTACK PAWN sign, a diffused orange sun sinks in deepening purple. I turn to face my friends, and there's already deep night sky beyond them, too cloudy for stars. Thursday evening, and not going to work tomorrow—things could be worse.

Bells suspended from a leather strap jingle as Rena pulls the door open. We step into a comforting warmth and disquieting must. Something stinks of gingerbread and wicker. Maybe a menthol-infused humidifier from a back room. We squeeze between shelves of radio-controlled cars, bunches of fake flowers, leg braces, snorkels, framed certificates, and discontinued board games. We pass between piles of stacks and heaps of mounds, all under intermittent fluorescent tubes and the occasional bare spiral bulb. My hand brushes against a pussy-willow branch jutting from what I guess is a five-gallon gray vase covered in a luster or patina or shimmer that I associate with filmic portrayals of portals to another dimension. I pass a three-quarter scale mummy that sort of looks like my dad. Next to the mummy is a corresponding sarcophagus painted in what looks like flat acrylic, with an Egyptian-looking face, yellow and purple headdress, and huge tan breasts with brown nipples. A sign hangs just below the breasts, reading, "King Tit." I nudge Rena's sweatshirt-covered back, and she turns around, and I gesture suggestively at the sarcophagus and its big breasts. She looks at it, then back at me, and doesn't bother to say, "What?"

We pass puppets and shields and traffic cones and neon signs that read "ATM," and an actual ATM that's been converted into a Ms. Pac-Man machine, which is already making this worth the trip for me. We shuffle past sepia-toned grandfather clocks with pendula resigned to rest position, a box for a late-1960s home film projector with early-1980s action figures peeking out the top, a bathroom scale with hieroglyphics, a pop-up bible opened to the Garden of Eden, with the serpent bent up into a number seven shape. A Polaroid picture from mid-2000s Guantanamo Bay hangs from yarn in a popsicle stick frame adorned with yellow puffy paint and tiny plastic jewels. The magic marker caption reads: MOMMY.

As we approach a counter at the now-visible rear of the shop, we pass a mannequin that looks like Max Headroom's pituitary-disorder-inflicted cousin wearing a space suit. Taped to his left cheek is a rounded piece of cardboard that sticks out as if his head has a solitary wing. I realize that the cardboard is meant to be Big Headroom's speech bubble, which reads, in what looks like an old ribbon printer output of a large serif font, "Shop Lifters Dont Think About It" without any punctuation, which I silently reread to myself with different word emphases until it's utterly meaningless.

Behind the counter is what I at first glance interpret as a scarecrow and then realize is an actual woman. The patchy brown fabric covering her hunched, lumpy frame may as well have straw bursting from the seams. Her nest of gray-on-gray hair tangles in all directions. I follow behind my friends, and as we approach the counter, I see that she has a clear eyepatch over her right eye. Through the clear plastic that covers her socket, I see what looks like a speculum shot from a particularly coarse porno, something indeterminate but reddish, puffy, moist, and invasive-looking. I can't help but think of her eye socket as prolapsed. I burp and taste meatball sub, which does not bring me pleasure.

The closer we get to the counter—behind which the clear-eye-patch scarecrow stands, waiting for us to get on with it and stop being so cinematic—the more I smell wasabi. We keep dragging out our approach, which must be cut in slow motion to allow the degree of scenic description required for an immersive entertainment experience. I'm somehow in a pitch meeting in my head. I see yellowed posters with early color process prints of movie stars who died over seventy years ago, eroded edges flaked away and cracked like a desert floor. I hear a faint howl that I assume is a wolf and which I hope is far away and outside. My allergies start to bug me, which means dust and/or pollen and/or cats.

"Hey, that bookcase," I say, gesturing to a far wall, bypassing formalities. "The books on that bookcase look fake." The woman's good eye seems to look at me. Her non-eye seems to flare up or flex or spasm. Behind its clear container, it struggles to emerge. "If you pull on one of the books, does it, like, spin around into a secret room?"

"Yaw," she says. Her voice sounds like a harmonica.

"Can we see it?" I ask, feeling on a roll.

"Naw," she says.

"Oh," I say. Now I obsessively struggle with whether this revelation is just a red herring, or whether it might be meaningful closer to the climax.

"Hi," says Rena, breaking whatever tension may have built there. "I left you a voicemail yesterday."

My focus gets pulled away by a water stain in a sagging ceiling tile. An orange jelly has accumulated at one of the seams. I get pissed off trying to discern whether this is meaningful or just atmospheric. I begin, probably irrationally, to resent the trappings of narrative. Thankfully, while my mind wanders, the others have cut through to the core of the matter.

"Black box," says the scarecrow woman, although Rena is now calling her Courtney. This is by far the most haggard and witch-like Courtney I've ever met. "I think I know 'cha mean. Hold on, or hang on; your choice."

She disappears through a doorway, leaving an earthy bead curtain jangling. It seems sort of cliché; like the rest of this place, it's just screaming, *Hey, look at this weird setting.* I look over to the far end of the counter, expecting to see incense even though I can't smell any amidst the hodgepodge funk. And there's a stick ready to go, dangling at its ten-degree angle over a floral tray that looks like half a kayak. I lean way over and light it. The edge of the counter against my pudgy belly reminds me of the jewelry store where I bought a four-hundred-dollar ring for Rena that I have yet to give her. I try to remember the clerk girl's name.

Courtney the scarecrow/witch/pawnshop owner basically drops the gray box on the counter, and I can't believe the glass countertop doesn't shatter. I feel chills at what doesn't even happen. The thing looks like the old quarter-inch tape decks I learned to edit on in high school.

"This what ya want, this here?" the scarecrow woman asks. Her voice sounds processed, not quite like a voice box, but like a chorus effect. It sounds … unlikely. On the side of the box are white-stenciled letters which read, "QBBR231."

"Think yer gonna tell yer fortune?" Her forceful wheeze morphs into a raspy chuckle. And I sort of want to punch her in her probably grossly soft face and say, "What's so funny, devil lady?" I feel my stomach lurch as I envision peeling her whiskers off my knuckles. I begin to notice the incense, which smells like tartar sauce.

"That's the one," says Rena, showing off by knowing simple facts. "How much?" Sometimes I remember that I'm with her for a reason. She doesn't fuck around.

Rena drops four bills on the counter. They are hundreds.

As we're exiting the store—all this build-up for a simple transaction—I hear Courtney call, "Yer just like yer father." This could apply to any of us.

Getting more high than I have ever been in my entire life, my legs walk away and found their own colony. The rest of me remains slumped against a wall in my surprisingly well-lit garage. That I even have a garage seems amazing, and I am superlatively grateful. Deconstructing the lineage of the concept of a garage brings me to tears, and this is when I realize I have shit my pants, which normally would stop me. Instead, I power on, figuring that one minute is longer than can be dealt with. I can't wait for someone to join me in here so I can detail my plan to get a tattoo, which reads: "[Delete from first draft:] even one page a day doesn't write itself." Some version of Ollie comes in, and I tell him some version of a version of an iteration of a repeating, if diminishing, sequence just came in, Ollie-like. He sort of guffaws abortedly. His tee shirt, powder blue like the hood of Virgin Mary, hosts a screen-printed likeness of me with a mustache. I recognize that he got high separate from me, which makes me jealous, until registration of his zoned face makes me sympathetic/in-love/not hostile. There are crumbs of fried batter on my shirt and a pasty texture on the anterior of my tongue.

"This is day one," I say, meaning it.

"But tomorrow's day two," he says, taunting me, even though I know it.

"We're not arguing," I argue.

"False," he admits.

Once the arm-wrestling starts, I realize that I'm by myself, even though Ollie wandered in at some point. I sort of weep. I sort of weep extremely. Tears shoot out of my face and hit a dartboard that I recall buying at a garage sale, even though I would deny owning a dartboard on principle. Land ownership seems a bit classist, I tell what I hope is Ollie. Whatever that is slurps soggy cereal, evoking unjust assonance of the consonant type.

Do you want to know what it says, he says in quotes to me as dialogue. I'm afraid, I say, also in quotes. This is a conversation we're having with words in a well-structured paragraph series. Thankfully there is no record of the actual exchange.

The next morning, the Friday I've actually not sought approval to take off work, I awaken with a cigarette butt all the way in my mouth and a paper pirate's hat. I allow a vague cinema show projected on my frontal lobe, showing a cramped electric vehicle pulling into a retro-themed fried-fish drive-thru at 2:15 a.m. We ended up at my garage, I see. My pants are miraculously shitless.

Around 1:00 p.m., everyone has gotten as bathed as they will for the day, and Nestor takes us through the donut shop drive-thru at Ollie's pleading and my seconding, despite Rena's veto. Rena won't even submit to a coffee, clinging to some principle. When we get to Nestor's apartment, Dave is just coming home from his early shift at the bank. We say hi, but Dave skirts us as much as possible, griping something about "supervisor" as he closes his bedroom door behind him. Nestor leads us into his bedroom, explaining about how Dave is between places, and I smart-aleck about how we're all technically between places.

Nestor retrieves the black box receiver from the mossy paper bag that has cradled it for the past most-of-a-day. He immediately flips it upside-down, and some sort of white crayon marking on its dull black underbelly reads a scrawled date, which happens to be my birthday. Nestor pulls what looks like a pocket protector from his desktop. He pulls a thin Allen wrench from it.

"That the one-thirteenth?" I say in a mock-New-England-manual-laborer voice. "I'd, ah, suggest that there three forty-firsts. That'll do ya pretty."

Rena snaps out of her funk to chime in, "I'd try that, ah, four-bit manual doohickey."

Ollie says, "Yeah, I'd use a wrench." Ollie then giggles like a girl on purpose and curls all of his fingers up into his open mouth.

Nestor makes a stupid retard face that's so absurd that I blurt out a laugh that sounds like a disastrous tick disorder. He removes a screw, squeezes it between precisely clamping pointer finger and thumb tip, and rotates it over to the dresser top like a crane arm. He slides off a small panel, also placing it on the dresser, and in its opening, where I expected to see batteries, are what look like googly eyes.

"These receptors are supposed to hook up to a DC source." Nestor brings his retard face back for an encore. "Faaahck!"

I sort of urinate a few drops abruptly, and it itches my tip over the next two minutes.

"I'm gonna have to rig this."

"Are you frigging MacGrover?" asks Rena, and I wonder if she's making a joke or just mispronouncing.

"You have the stuff you need?" I ask, willing to remove limbs. "I'll give you cash if you need it."

"Thanks," says Nestor. He faces away again, flinches a fist at the machine. "I might need a few more bucks."

"Can we help?" asks Rena, picking a rear tooth with her thumbnail. "Or should we leave you to it?"

"Yeah," says Nestor. "I'll give this a crack, and I'll call you guys later. I'll probably get frustrated with you guys watching."

"That's incredibly honest, negro," I say. Nestor doesn't so much laugh as smirk an expression of sympathy with some guttural throat noise.

We leave a bit disappointed that we don't get to play with the new toy right away, but I'm secretly glad, because I haven't gotten to play my massively multiplayer online game during normal business hours in several weeks, and I have to verify my guess at how many experience points have been beaten out of my proxy *in absentia*.

The non-news from Nestor fails to interrupt my game, which turns into a whole-weekend thing. Translation: I get bed sores. And carpal tunnel. And not laid.

At work on Monday, I read Nestor's email, which is a bulletpoint listing of grievances about the non-functionality of the Black Box Receiver, his tinkerings with it all weekend long, that he thinks he somehow has contracted HPV, that he has worked at the same job for six years, only two of which has he received "annual" cost-of-living wage increases, that he feels self-conscious about complaining via email to relatively new friends but that the Backspace key on his phone does not work anymore, that we should ignore his overuse of punctuation, that he feels he cannot fully convey himself without italics, that he's gotten off-topic, that there's no way to ensure that anything is truly random. His email signature reads, "— Nestor[two line breaks]Please consider paper cuts before printing this E-mail."

This day feels like filler, some padding to postpone the inevitable, a meandering path that will get back to the main road but which may or may not offer up sightseeing worthy of the delay. Having failed to stop for coffee from The Coffee Shop®, I am four dollars richer and regretting it, sipping and tasting (so to speak) whatever it is that I dumped from the silver-medal tier spherical pot into my sheepdog mug. From the flavor (so to speak), I gauge that hot water was poured over dirty rocks held by a porous shoe insert.

The thought occurs to me, prematurely, that it might bode well to start wiping down every handle, knob, button, receiver, and latch that I've necessarily fondled in this place. My fingerprints are everywhere. As I imagine what we'll find when we finally connect a black box to a functional receiver, multiple permutations of succeeding events end with me having to erase any evidence of my former life. Granted, most imaginary scenarios I play out further than ten or so moves end up with me having to erase any evidence of my former life. In these mental worlds, I live at the top of a teetering Jenga pile, but a bitter cold requires that I continually burn the uppermost blocks.

Around 10:30, I realize I've been at work almost two hours, so I close the webmail and open up my work email for the first time today. Three emails have little red exclamation points, which is my cue to delete them unread. I find it's best not to lend any credence to that which others hold in elevated regard. I *eenie-meenie* between the two remaining, and it's from Roy, blank subject. The email reads, "See me when you get in." My stomach drops a bit, and I start really regretting not having wiped my prints clear.

Roy's office, beige with beige highlights, is framed by two sepia lithographs on opposite walls of ostriches with their heads conspicuously not underground. The door is ajar. I call in, trying first for levity, "The jar is a door."

Roy, on the phone, glances up with a one-minute finger and no facial expression change, leaving him with the right eyebrow high, upper-left lip curled up like he's painfully squeezing out a side fart, or on day two of stroke recovery. I feel naked when I realize I didn't bring a pad of paper or laptop or any reasonable business instrument. I take out my phone and pretend to peruse its paltry memory for business notes. As I open the notes application, I see a limerick I remember typing in the stall in the men's room at Skizzers, drafting it for possible etching in the stall wall:

> Harland dismounted the stool
> Hence dropping the kids in the pool
> "I'll miss you," he cooed
> "For you used to be food"
> Then he flushed them away like a fool

"I can trust you, right?" says Roy, not asking.

"Absolutely," I say, my voice as deep as it gets. The con is on, even though I don't yet know whose or how.

"You're aware of the situation with Paul?" He asks, acknowledging my perceptiveness as he never has so obviously. Granted, the Paul Jabber-on-leave-due-to-sexual-harassment-allegations situation is more or less legendary, but I'm happy to take an implicit compliment. Roy looks at one of the ostriches, seeking words or his reflection superimposed over a long bird neck. Roy sighs. "Yeah," also comes out as a sigh. "Well, it's not good. It's gone beyond arbitration, and it could go public and hurt this company in a very bad way."

"Really?" I ask, honestly intrigued by this tabloid.

"Did you know that Zorro guy?" asks Roy.

"Zorro? That swashbuckler?" I ask. I make a little sword-waving gesture. "Accounting," I add, suddenly caring about not looking stupid.

"Yeah, well, he's gone. Gave two days' notice last Wednesday, no real explanation. Herbert was understandably upset. Then, this morning, this arrived."

Roy spins a piece of paper on his desk so I can read it. The fax shows large, highly granulated hand-scrawled words reading at an angle, "Nothing happened." Inches below, smaller letters read, "Ask Harland."

I think of the go-cart that my dad made for me when I was seven years old, a four-by-eight piece of plywood with rubber wheelbarrow wheels and a tacked-down semi-frustum of plastic sheeting that formed a hull, and how I yanked back on the wooden hand break, speeding off the path in the woods, burning rubber from the right front tire, skewing the path just enough that velocity created a spin that shuffled me, scrapes and cuts, into a pricker bush, one calf suffering multiple splinters as the plywood vehicle continued spinning out from under me, continuing down the increasingly steep slope, spraying wood chips until it disappeared out of sight, leaving me to crawl to peer over the cliff to see its fractured frame in the rocky ravine dozens of feet below.

"Weird," I say, furrowing my brow in what I hope looks like concern over the situation and not just my ass. "Strange, that." I gesture with a flat hand as if I'm a penguin hosting a home shopping program. I feel awkward in my body; I'm reaching a secondary puberty.

I picture a large, grainy, projection television screen with my disgraced faced, apologizing to constituents. It seems fairly disingenuous; not the apology so much as the scenario. I realize I'll never be important enough to face true humiliation. If I could think faster, I might interpret this and use it to my advantage.

"Paul Jabber," I say, improvising, "he connected to Zorro?"

"I don't know," says Roy, his face alone shrugging, the frown remaining after his brow resolves smooth. "I don't think so. Zorro was meek, right? Quiet, studious. I don't think Jabber would have given him much notice."

"Yeah," I exhale, joining Roy in looking down at his desk, vaguely at the fax that might as well be glowing and covered in blood. I'm mirroring him, being on the same side. We're two partner detectives, solving this mystery together. I try to edge my way around to his side of the desk. We're architects reviewing some blueprints. I see him glance out of one squinted eye, and I take a hint and edge my way back to a subordinate position.

Roy scans me from head to feet, having to x-ray through his desk for the latter, and I feel a red laser capturing my essence in three dimensions. I have never regarded Roy as fully real, but indeed I have underestimated his cyborgish nature. I fear that if I am driven to mush in his face with desperate fingertips, I will hit metal. I sincerely hope it won't come to that, because the only thing worse than fear is confirmation of its validity. As I begin wondering about how one might go about disassembling Roy, he resumes talking.

"Zorro," he says, "how well did you know this guy? Were you friends?"

"Naw," I say, absentmindedly mimicking scarecrow/Courtney. "Naw. We warn't friends."

"What am I supposed to make of this note?" I try to read Roy's smirk as annoyed that he has to deal with this kind of thing, as opposed to annoyed with me, or finding evil in my presence.

"That's a strange fax, Roy," I say, finding my own voice again. "That's pretty baffling to me. I mean, I talked to Zorro once. Just once, really, I think was our only communication."

"What," says Roy, not sinister even though I'm totally receiving it that way, "did you talk about?"

I find the list of alternates to my sort-of-joking attempt to extort the company via my vague threat to Julius Zorro. "Payroll," I say, a half-truth that I can get behind. "Direct deposit," I add. I wonder whether I should stop now, and then I forcibly add, "Because the split between checking and savings—I needed to change how much was going in savings." This is too much fabrication. I'm not leaving myself wiggle room. I can smell Cindy's distant toaster pastry and I want to kick something.

"Huh," says Roy. He squints at the ceiling. As he gives me this momentary reprieve from the third degree, I try to reconstruct the details of my previous, spontaneous threat. Had I actually implied violence against Zorro, or suggested that I would get him fired? Who had I thought I was? What was that all about? The only detail that fully surfaces is that the exchange ended with the phoned-in interruption by Future Me, that prick.

"Well, the thing that's got me concerned," says Roy, closing his eyes for this first part of a spiel that must be so trite that the cue cards are faded, "is that this company can't afford to be handling multiple harassment lawsuits right now. Can you assure me that this is nothing?"

I force myself to remember something that has not happened. I have to see it and believe it before I can say, "Oh, Roy, you know what it is? I remember Julius mentioning something about his dad." This is good; it's vague.

"His dad?" says Roy.

"Yeah," I say. "He was going to see his dad, or help him or something." If Julius Zorro's dad is dead, this will reflect poorly upon me. "'Nothing happened' must mean he's all right—the father."

"So, 'Ask Harland,' means that he would expect you to mention this?"

"I don't know, Roy," I say, chuckling. "He was kind of a weird, meek guy. Who knows what was going on there?"

Somewhere, I sense a parade forming. I hear marching band music. I smell fried dough. I feel a cool breeze. I'm at the Thanksgiving Day parade prematurely, only in my mind, taking note of what I'm actually thankful for.

"OK, thanks, Harland," says Roy. "How's the workload?"

"Manageable," I say. "Never enough time, but enough to get the important stuff." This sounds great; I want it on a sash.

"You want to get lunch?"

"I brought mine," I lie. This lie feels totally acceptable.

Nestor's mass-text reads, "My job is interrupting. Start n stop on this sucks. It should be done by now. Rrrrrg!!! :P"

Rena and I shrug in unison. "You want shells and cheese?" she asks.

"Let's go out," I plead.

"We have to stop doing that on Mondays," Rena says. "We can't afford to go out more than twice a week."

"We can if we keep paying the minimum balance on our credit cards," I say. "Besides, even if we default, do you really think the provisional government is going to come after its constituents over the same kinds of evil corporate bureaucracy that was supposed to have been wiped clean on 7/11?"

"Jesus Leftist Christ," says Rena. "I didn't realize you were stumping. Do go on."

I smirk, exhaling, "Mac and cheese is always good. You want to smoke?"

"Not right now," she says. "I have to finish my blog. And I don't want it to turn into one of your blogs."

"Speaking of partisan claptrap," I say. I run two blogs under aliases. One is an extreme leftist named Spanx Johnnie, a biracial, transgender atheist who claims that a return to big government-subsidized abortions is the only path to something or other. His foil is a gun-nut Baptist named Granch Depravo who vows to only participate in the new government if all people with skin shades darker than Premium Interior Creamy Beige are sent on a wooden ship to the great, mysterious continent of Africa. Their rivalry is as popular on the Internet as championship-level chess. I thought of them one day when I saw an old *Mad* magazine opened to a "Spy vs. Spy" comic when I went to the dentist for a cleaning, just to take advantage of a legitimate day off of work five years ago.

We eat macaroni and cheese sitting at the dinner table. I always get nervous eating without the television on, but Rena has things to tell me.

"[Something about her blog]"

"[Affirming response]"

"[Query referencing a specific detail from my response]"

"[Repeating the question, with slightly different wording]"

"[What appears to be genuine contemplation followed by self-convincing]"

"[Disbelief just to see where it will lead]"

"[Confusion trying not to be injury]"

"[Mangled explication of prior comments]"

"[Resignation betrayed by a need to pick scabs]"

"[Quote from a long-dead philosopher]"

"[Antithesis via quote from a living philosopher]"

"[Admission to never having heard of said living philosopher]"

"[Accusation that I invented long-dead philosopher]"

"[Denial of several core tenets of philosophy in abstract]"

"[Skepticism regarding the severity of my cynicism]"

"[Sarcasm]"

"[Fake laughter and real tears]"

"[Desperately trying to undo]"

"[Posing hypothetical scenario where no one interacts with anyone else]"

"[Comment on non-sequitur]"

"[Defensive aloofness]"

"[Exhaustion shrouded in apology]"

"[Cute anecdote as peace offering]"

"[Cliché]"

"[Eye-rolling verbalized]"

To cap things off, I grope under her breast and she actually slaps my arm. Later, in bed, damp sheets stick to cold legs, and I hand her a joint and ask if she remembers what we fought about.

5 USA

After a week of not hearing anything more about Julius Zorro and his maybe-shrouded attempt to rat me out following a mysterious exit from the job he only held for seven months (and to be fair, a complete ball-dropping on my part regarding any independent follow-up or investigation), I've gone through my various denial-driven moods: anxiety, anger, depression, hunger, sloth, extreme sexual arousal, loathing. I have said nothing about this to Rena or my friends, because I fear it's disconnected, and I underestimate them generally, which is directly attributable to my defensive fear of being judged as a poor person. Indeed, everything wrong with my life stems from fear. But I'm afraid to resolve all of that.

I consider using a *deus ex machina* I have scrawled on a sticky note taped flat against the underside of my desk, reachable only if the keyboard stand is fully extracted. But there are too many co-workers around, too much business, too much potential sabotage, so I am forced to delay that avenue. I've only used it twice in the three years since it was bequeathed to me, and I've incubated it like an insurance policy.

Temporarily foiled, I just sit around, drive to work, sit in my chair at work, get up, go to the bathroom, wash my hands, go to the vending machine in the lunchroom, walk out to my car as if I forgot something important out there, sit in it, maybe turn the key halfway to get accessories so I can listen to blank-wing pundits expound on things that have no consequence (and take mental notes for my blogs), return to emails I can't bear to read, wait out the day, return home, don't exercise, miss the footsteps of my dead dog, argue with Rena about what we're not going to eat, finally get convinced of what we should eat, eat it joylessly and too quickly, wonder about dessert, get distracted by television, hope for the best, fear the worst, fail to make meaningful contact with Rena, joke with her in a way that annoys her instead of entertains her, step out onto the porch and register the month of November in a really helpless sort of way, purposefully wait until my hands are almost frozen because even no sensation is a difference, go back in and get forced to appreciate what I have in a fairly primitive way.

Rena wears pajama bottoms, white with mint green vertical stripes, and a pink tee shirt which reads, MILK MILK. I wear gray sweatpants and a dark blue hoodie and thick red socks that I got from my grandma for Christmas the year I hit puberty. On the not-oversized television, a talk show host explains the best way to lie to your spouse about an affair. I ask Rena if she wants to smoke and she says no. The talk show host says, "I'm way too busy at work to even think about that sort of thing." I feel like I've caught this out of context, but I try to find meaning in it. My cellphone vibrates. It's Thursday night and I'm not at Skizzers, which must mean we're poor. Ollie's text reads, "Tomoro Nesters got it!!! [sic]" I have to think this is good news.

In bed, I roll and sigh and struggle to force myself into a hibernation. Rena snores softly, and I see a wall illuminated, a gradient from amber to smoky gray. Somewhere out of my eye line a nightlight keeps the meter spinning. I hold my breath and picture a single sheep. I can't bear to make more than one, blushing in the dark at this childish tactic. Can I count the same sheep repeatedly? What if I clone it?

Chilled with only the sheet, sweaty with the comforter, this seems like any given moment. Once it turns 2:30 a.m., I realize that since I won't get enough sleep anyway, I might as well make use of my time, so I crawl out of bed, pull my sweatpants back onto goosebumped legs, and wander to the bathroom mirror. I flip on the light, seeing a bloated, beleaguered version of the youthful mental picture I tend to retain of myself. Thirty-five. Engaged. Going nowhere, and taking the scenic route. The phrase crosses my mind and I feel the need to brush my teeth.

I locate a cinematography textbook in the spare bedroom, a thick, glossy hardcover filled with theory and screen captures labeled as "Fig. A" and "Fig. B" with italic elaboration to the core text. The book's title is *Monolith: Symbolism and Discourse in Modern Cinema*. This bedroom, I register, is filled with all of the required reading that I never quite had the attention span to engage. As I walk to the living room, I sense a trail left behind. I don't fancy to glance behind me, but I imagine a snake of frames, each one a choice, something that's led me here. So many of those frames seem to be empty. I try not to dwell on the prospect of legacy, but solitude at close to three in the morning the night before a workday holding an unread textbook in a dim house for lack of sleep figures as well as any context to prompt speculation about the nature of one's impact upon the world. The two words well up again and push themselves through. I pull the chain on the lamp.

Future Me.

The slowest Friday in recorded history begins with Rena snapping in my face, saying, "Not gonna tell you again. I gotta go, and you're gonna be very late if you don't get up now."

I grumble resentment, clench fingernails into palms, register a kink in my back from an odd angle on the couch, and see a ray of sunlight through the blinds, which means I do not have enough time to properly prepare for the day. A streak of brown across the words "Dolly shots evoke an air of control and elegance" implies a paper cut that I failed to notice as my body gave up on my mind. I recall Nestor's email signature and grin slightly at whatever he has to show us tonight.

A rather grim sector of my brain suggests a wake-and-bake, something I've actually not done before work, but I remind myself that this is an especially bad idea in light of the unspoken probation I'm facing due to the oddly departed Julius Zorro and his vague fax. I tell myself, aching as I reach my full, unimpressive height, that I will have wasted this day if I don't spend as much time as I can scouring the Internet for information on this guy.

Rena says she loves me from across the room, and I croak that I do too. She's gone when the door slams, and it takes everything in me not to lie back down on the couch. I turn on the television, knowing that my hatred for morning programming will motivate me to leave. Immediately, some blond dipshit woman is cackling about something called "Powder Puppies," and I want to discharge a firearm into her hair-shaped helmet. The jaw guy, made of tan, replies, "My two daughters are going to want that. One each, if I know them!" Unrelated text skates across the bottom of the screen:

"Ruder in critical condition." I don't really make anything of it. I slap myself in the face, for real, and I say, "Go. Get coffee, and just make it through. Tonight is going to be awesome, and you'll appreciate it more if you go to your stupid fucking job first." Blond dipshit can't seem to stop cackling.

◎

I slink into work with a thirty-two-ounce coffee from the gas station nearest the office, and I get a glance from one of my supposed peers that makes me feel guilty, resentful, apathetic, and stoic all within five seconds. My jaw is set as I take my seat as quietly as I can. I'm only about forty minutes late.

My computer is still booting up when hefty Cindy and her mass of orange clown hair approaches my desk, bringing the horrid cloud of uncut air freshener that apparently gets hosed on her each morning.

"Harland, did you sign up for the flu shot?"

"What?" I ask, trying my hardest not to sound like I'm intentionally being a dick.

"I came around earlier to see who was going to get the shots, but you weren't at your desk."

"Flu shot," I say, trying to imagine why I'd want that. "I already got one."

"You dee-id?" she scrunches her nose as she asks me with unnecessary syllables. "You should have waited, silly, you could have gotten one for free. All the employees get them for free. It's part of the benefits package."

"Awesome," I say. "But I …" [invent something] "I make my own."

"You do-oo?" she asks, her eyes glazing as she tries to calculate how this can be. "Wow. You never told us you were also a doctor."

"I never told you I'm also an astronaut," I say. "Or that I can see the future."

"Harland, you're a funny fella." She's already wandering away, looking at her notes. "I'll let Judy know that we can reallocate your dose to one of the contractors."

"No, not a contractor!" I fake-yell. "They don't deserve health care!"

Cindy's clown head disappears behind beige drywall, and I remove the thin plastic lid from the paper-covered Styrofoam cup. The scent of coffee gradually heals my wounded nostrils.

At some point I recall the headline that passed the bottom of the television screen before I left my house this morning. I go onto the news headlines site, and there it is: RUDER IN CRITICAL CONDITION. Future Me said something about this dude. The first link I follow has this story:

SEVEN CORNERS, PROVISIONAL CAPITOL, 14 NOVEMBER

Provisional Government Senator John Ruder (I-MI), is recovering at the recently opened Washington Memorial Hospital from an injury sustained during a recent campaign stop at an area paintball arena. On Thursday evening at approximately 8:30 p.m., Prov. Sen. Ruder was posing for a photograph in a full-body paintball protective outfit at one of the "lookout points" within Paint Shotz Sport World when he was unexpectedly struck in the chest by a paintball. An eyewitness to the shooting, fifteen-year-old Darryl Maddingly, said, "I could tell Senator Ruder was shot by a paintball and not a gun because he was all green, not red."

Unfortunately, the commotion did not stop then, because Ruder was apparently knocked backward by the force or simply by surprise, and stumbled backward over a ledge, dropping 10 feet to a padded floor. When arena manager Maria Montegue, 43, tried to revive Ruder, she claimed, "I could not stop crying or shaking him, and he would just not wake up. It was awful. I'm definitely going to vote for him."

Spinal Specialist Darius McAllistair, MD, stated, "Provisional Senator Ruder appears to have acute brain stem trauma that seems to have been caused by his impact with the floor of the sporting facility. He has been given a one for all three, Eyes, Verbal, and Motor on the Glasgow Coma Scale. Not many people outside of the medical community are familiar with the scale, so I've been asked to note that one is bad."

A presidential hopeful who announced his candidacy in July from the epicenter of the former site of Washington, DC—exactly one year after the former Capitol was vaporized by terrorists—Ruder, a middle-of-the-road Independent whose campaign platform focuses on taking advantage of the "Opportunity for a fresh start" the nation may be facing, has two major competitors. New Mexico Democrat Phil Brandley has roused up equal enthusiasm and skepticism for his "America pays for everything"-themed campaign. And Florida Republican Morton Shemp's "Not in my country" campaign has its expected following. As of Monday's "America Today" poll, the three shared an uncanny 30/30/30 tie.

Authorities continue to review details of the incident, including security camera video feed, to assess whether the incident was a freak accident or a possible assassination attempt. The shooter has yet to be identified, and receipts from the Paint Shotz Sports World ticket office are being reviewed to identify possible suspects or witnesses beyond those already interviewed. Seven Corners Sheriff Trenton Byutch was quoted as saying, "We're gonna figure this one out, don't doubt that."

Up-to-the-minute updates on Prov. Sen. Ruder's status can be found on any of the 475 major news media outlets.

Over the next couple of hours, I spend too much energy avoiding my boss, who I'm now convinced considers me translucent. I need to get it to transparent. I don't want him to see my guts and my feeble and mostly meaningless lies. I consider how much drama draws from people not clearly stating what they mean. Then I consider how frequently I don't even know what I mean. Maybe that's ripe for drama.

My blood sugar feels all over the place, and I'm shaking from some combination of exhaustion, malnourishment, alcohol withdrawal, and possibly atheism. I've got DTs that feel spiritually sourced. I count the number of buttons in all of the toolbars in the spreadsheet application, and it feels like cloning sheep. I toggle off the seconds on the computer clock display because I cannot bear the sluggish way they shuffle onward. The coffee tastes like a worn boot.

When 11:45 finally arrives, lunchtime may arguably begin without too many glaring eyeballs burning retinal lasers into my posterior or whatever. I receive a glance identical to the earlier one as I walk past the same judging coworker on my way down the hall. I pass doorway after doorway, executive offices with frosted glass windows which reveal enough of my blurry pastel silhouette to reveal that it's indeed me if they happen to look over in the middle of jacking or whatever it is they do in there. Roy's office, I note, appears dark, and I start considering the likelihood of getting caught if I fail to return from lunch. It wouldn't be the first time I've gotten away with it.

I pull into the drive-through lane at Bearger. "Large Double Cheese

Bearger combo with Canker," I say. I get less change from my ten than I was hoping for, pull forward, and get a white bag that becomes translucent (like me) toward the bottom.

The car continues running as I sit parked in the Bearger parking lot listening to the tail end of a talk show where a hideously raspy man jabbers about the "election shakeup" in between fart sounds and clips from '80s movies. The fries give me heartburn, but I'm unable to stop eating them.

The next show, "Penetration Audio," is basically nothing but a music-free stream of the sound of people fucking. It starts out sensual and seems to get violent very quickly. It ends with a gunshot, and I realize that I have to make a decision about whether I'm going back to work. I weigh the pros of going back, the primary which is that no one could rightfully claim that I didn't go back. The main con is that I'd have to go back to work, meaning I'd have to consider once again what it is that I'm supposed to do while not doing it, an endless loop that ages me. Another argument for not skipping out is that I would have to kill that many more hours before meeting Nestor and Rena, although Ollie does not technically work and might be free. Nestor helps to evacuate the innards from newly former people, and Rena slings Chinese food that looks like how I imagine the innards.

Back in my cubicle with an extra-large cafe mocha to sip on—sweets being a trump-card self-negotiation tactic, meaning I've essentially bribed myself to suffer the afternoon at my desk by the consolation of further empty calories—I check the news links for further information on Ruder, find little new, then remember that I should check on the Zorro thing.

After taking a short walk down the executive hallway to see primarily darkened offices, I spin on my heel and decide it's safe enough to use the *deus ex machina* left to me by a disreputable former employee named Todd Crabs. Todd Crabs was the only coworker with whom I ever even remotely connected. He had a weirdo hippie mustache and short curly hair, and he wore short-sleeve yellow business shirts ironically. He spoke with a nasally twang, saying things like, "That thing got fucked, man," and "How'm I supposed to know, Tubs?" and "Everybody else workin' for the man, man. I'm rentin' out his wife." He kept snus in his lip, and he worked super early hours. "In at six, out at two, baby. Flex time, bitch." Todd Crabs had a tattoo of himself on his right bicep. Beneath the police-sketch-looking image (he had Unibomber sunglasses on), were gothic letters that read, CRABS. He claimed to have once delivered a baby at a mall. His desk had a bobblehead of Santa Claus, which had masking tape pulled across its base, on which black marker letters spelled out, "Dad?" The one time I spent time with a co-worker outside of work, Todd took me to a monster truck pull and gave me some pills in the parking lot. The truck race seemed colorful, with a wall of sound, and I ended up finding it deeply personal. When he dropped me off that night, he handed me a rubber band bundle of singles, barking, "Ya gotta hide this for me!" Then he snatched them away, sneering and laughing out the word, "Psych!"

Todd Crabs had put in his two-week notice not long after that. He told me, "Brother-in-law got me the hookup, Chooch." He called people "Chooch" sometimes. At first I thought this meant his brother-in-law got him a new job, but then he clarified at lunchtime. "Died, Brub." He called people "Brub" sometimes. "My sister's pretty sad, but this dude had a fifteen-mil policy, and I'm gettin' three of it." I suddenly hated him, and I felt bad about it, so my first response was, "Sorry." He hadn't heard my internal struggle, so he's like, "Shit, Chooch, you hear me? Three mil." I remember commenting that it was big of him to finish out his two weeks. "Good K , Brub. Karma. Before I leave, I wanna figure out what it is I'm supposed to been doin'."

Todd's parting gift to me was the fruit of all of the secret research he'd been doing during the year he'd worked there. It was a skeleton-key administrative account and password.

"Log up on in, do what you want. Just don't send no email. That'd be real dumb, Brub."

I find the file on Julius Zorro, copy it to a plain-text file, copy it to my C: drive, log out of the administrative account, log back in as myself, take a big swig of the lukewarm mocha, and open the file. I feel glad that I convinced myself to return to work.

> *ZORRO, JULIUS CAESAR*
> *ACCOUNTING, REPORTING TO H. KROHN*
> *HIRE/VACATION ACCRUAL ANNIVERSARY: 4/1*
> *[OTHER STATISTICS THAT MEAN NOTHING TO ME]*
> *11/13: Announcement of intent to resign position 11/15, verbal notification to Herbert this morning. Unresponsive to inquiry regarding immediacy of departure. No reasons officially sited. No known conflicts. No record of prior such departures. No hearsay or inference or noted grumblings. Informal peer assessment yielded nothing of note.*
> *UPDATE 11/18: Cindy Gaines claims Julius once "cut in front" of her on the*

way out of the office to the parking lot in mid-June. Technically, this might be considered precedent of hasty departure.

I open my phone, create a new contact record, enter his forwarding email address, phone number, Social Security number, allergies, emergency contact info, and the fact that he's left-handed.

I delete the file, empty the computer's trash, copy some random text to clear my paste buffer, make sure that my "Recent Files" has no trace. I itch for intoxication, but I have to settle for a pre-diabetic sugar rush. The blue fuzz seeps in. I try to think of creative ways to kill three more hours.

Nestor agrees to bring the thing to our place. I struggle to not light up a bowl as soon as I get home, but Rena helps convince me that we may want to remain sober in the name of science. I can barely eat the macaroni and cheese that Rena has sliced hot dogs into like we're five years old. I ask her for a juice box and ask her when naptime is. She looks at me, probably remembering we're engaged to be married.

Ollie shows up in his clunker, wearing some garish necklace that looks like it hatched from a plastic bubble for a quarter.

"It's a charm necklace," says Ollie. "Sesha gave it to me."

"She's still alive?" I say, trying to picture her so I can then picture her naked.

"It's supposed to be good luck."

"Too bad you got it from the girl who thinks that American history is best represented by fat Asians in diapers splashing soup onto the stage with a pelican's beak."

Ollie chooses to pause, forcing me to remember to feel guilty.

"Sorry," I say. "How … 's she doin'?"

Ollie chooses to pause again, then says, "Fine."

"Where'd she get the necklace?" I ask, actually curious.

"She made it," says Ollie. "From a kit."

I sharply bleat laughter. "Awesome."

"Yeah, it is awesome." Ollie smirks and his brow crinkles in this skeptical expression I never see from him. It breaks my heart. "Don't ask if you don't care."

"Ollie, I …" I hesitate, stumbling, struggling not to lash out defensively.

I don't like being the real bad guy. I am forced to recall my mom sniping sarcastically, her useless little legs cloaked by a quilt, which always struck me as a shield, an accessory that simultaneously allowed her to portray the victim archetype while concurrently attacking without motion. *"Your dad approve of that, Hal?"*

Rena walks in from the bedroom, inadvertently diffusing things before I can make them right.

"Oliver," she says, "You look well. I like your necklace. Your lady friend give you that?"

"Yep," says Ollie, forcing a smile and avoiding eye contact with anyone but her.

"It's cute," she says, smiling widely—offering no acknowledgement of her distaste for the absent gift-giver—proving herself socially superior.

I suddenly wish that there were no such thing as subtext and that we could all express ourselves without consequence.

We all have beers—even Rena—and we're on round two when Nestor's fake car pulls up outside. I note not to comment on it or do anything further to jeopardize our evening. Nestor comes in empty-handed, which freaks me out until I see that he's wearing a backpack the same green shade as his shirt.

"Nice backpack," I say, because I can't seem to shut up even when I have nothing clever to say. Rena looks at me, more confused than annoyed.

Nestor gently sets his backpack on the coffee table and says, "You guys are probably gonna wanna be high for this."

I exclaim something positive.

As Ollie cleans out the resin from the kangaroo dick, Nestor gives us technical details beyond our comprehension.

"When I soldered the replacement solenoids, I finally got the energy flowing to the power converters."

"From the Toshi Station?" I ask.

Nestor and Ollie prove with blank expressions that being a certain amount younger than me renders Star Wars references meaningless, and it breaks my heart again.

"So I think, from a schematic point of view, we've got the connections we'll need. But I took it no further. We're in this together."

I smirk and then warm. I say, "Thanks, Nestor. I know you put in a lot of effort. We appreciate you sharing this."

"Yes, we do," says Rena, perhaps with less certainty.

Ollie, whose left index finger delicately compresses the marijuana into its vehicle, declares, "We're ready for launch sequence."

I volunteer to hit it first, which somehow does not seem as martyr-like to the others as it did in my head. I take one enormous hit into my lungs and pass it. The others make small talk and take human-sized hits, Ollie, then Rena, as I try to remember my favorite plot twists from video games. By the time it gets to Nestor, I burst out a plume of smoke and say, "*Deus Ex.*"

"That's a superpower?" asks Ollie, the earnest little kitten.

"Superpower?" I scrunch my face into a cartoon of near-parallel lines, which represents, I think, everything I have to say in response.

"Seeing the future, absolutely," says Rena. "I want to know exactly when and how I will die."

"I want to fly," says Ollie. He giggles, then adds, "For the frequent flier miles."

"I'd want to be able to heal anyone." Nestor looks both serious and serene. Nestor knows his limits. I can tell he took a small hit. I try not to resent him for it, or resent myself.

"What if," says Rena, obviously feeling it, getting squinty and pensive, "you healed someone who turned out to be a serial killer?"

"Oh no!" says Ollie, slapping his hands to his temple. "That would be … wait, how could there be a serial killer if you could heal everyone?"

"He can't always be there to heal people in time, can he?" Rena asks.

"That's true," says Nestor. "Even if you have a superpower, time is always the enemy."

"Unless you're the master of time," says Ollie.

"No one's the master of time," I say. "Look it up."

"Harland, we're speculating here," says Rena, gawking at me. "You know what, if you don't want to play, you don't have to. Nestor's brought the thing here, and we're gonna do science. This is supposed to be fun, and you just … can't, sometimes. So just shush, and just sulk like the big-headed baby you are."

I worry a little bit before adding, "My superpower is not caring." As soon as I say it, it feels hollow, like a shot gut.

Out in the garage, Nestor's got the black box thing on the particleboard platform that stands in for a proper workbench along one wall. The fluorescent tubes overhead sway slightly from a draft, making the light shift rhythmically like we're out at sea. I get paranoid that it will make me sick.

Nestor's shadow moves back and forth across the black box receiver. His brown hands move methodically across the gizmo's anterior panel, precise fingers checking connections, verifying functionality, assessing vulnerabilities. I can only assume that this is where the delicate tendencies of homosexuality really pay off.

With the thing plugged into a chain of three different Comp Shack power-manipulating modules—Nestor refers to them by sci-fi names like "currency rectifier," "amplitude maximizer," and "proton deflector"—little green lights on its front panel begin pulsing in a way that is, admittedly, instantly hypnotic. I feel drawn into a trance on an embarrassingly short timeline. If I had any chance of interpreting Morse code, I'm sure I would be pulling in all sorts of meaningful subtext. Alas, I just sort of look at it, my jaw hanging involuntarily. A mesh of tones becomes audible. The just-discernible audio flowing from the daisy chain of equipment whose discrete functions I'll never fully comprehend is in fact a chord; each piece, I imagine, emanates its own mid-range note. As far as I can tell, and not that I would, none are of a piercing dog-whistle frequency. They blend together to form a chord that I suppose is mostly major, with a bit of dissonance thrown in for flavor. For lack of a better musical frame of reference, I assume that it is all the notes from the "Close Encounters" melody playing simultaneously instead of in sequence. The retained music theory from seven weeks of guitar lessons more than twenty years ago is not sufficient to deconstruct whatever may be playing out here. I lament, in a typically profound and high manner, that my attention span has never been worth a damn.

In my state of hypnosis, watching the tiny light show on the human interface portion of the QBBR231, and feeling drawn into the unchanging and yet dynamic stasis of the electro-choral soundtrack, I begin to hope that outer space life forms are involved in this plot, because even a cliché payoff is a payoff. I surmise that before this is through, I'll meet Alien Me and possibly Parallel Universe Me, if not Zombie Me. I feel a rash of annoyance as I begin to draw lines between my blind speculation and Ollie's enthusiasm for the mysteries in his mystery show that he keeps trying to get me to watch, which has already been off the air for five years. I console myself with the notion that exercises in futility tend to be harmless. Yet I still feel dirty, callow, unprepared. If I am sucked off this planet by a beam of light, I realize, trying to force a tear, I will be no more out of place in another world. Which I think is the shared mission statement of my favorite bands.

"Radio … it … make the light … afraid," I manage to say to my three friends, who look at me like I'm some kind of infant who doesn't yet possess the motor skills to ask for a specific thing. I recognize that I should be thankful that pot continues to affect me as completely as it does. My tolerance has not recognizably increased since my regular usage began, which I like to think is the universe's way of passing the savings on to me. I remember that I should probably pay Terry a visit, because the supply in Rena's "sewing kit" has run low. I recall Ollie mentioning that he doesn't deal with Terry anymore, but I can't remember why, and I'm apparently in no state to be asking questions.

As Nestor continues to fiddle with the machine, adjusting and calibrating and fine-tuning, Rena squints through her glasses, her dark eyes looking smaller than they are. Her face depicts a focus and patience that makes me at once jealous and warm-hearted. She appears to study without judging, taking in what she can without any of the solicitude that plagues me. She strikes me as—not complacent—but trusting in the worth of this while.

Ollie, meanwhile, chews on some beef jerky that he must have brought with him, a disconcerting aroma of teriyaki and preservatives wafting in my direction. His mouth smacks, speckled lips glistening with a cartoon sheen.

Nestor withdraws the gallon-sized baggie from his backpack. Within the wagging plastic walls, the familiar black-red soup oozes, the black box tumbling on end as Nestor slings the bag to rest atop the particleboard surface of the workbench. I can't stop clenching my butt cheeks, certain that the bag is going to snag on a splinter and dump a stomach's worth of biohazard all over the space I had taken ten minutes to clear.

"So, you didn't have the opportunity to clean that thing off?" says Rena, and I mentally jump to other contexts in which I've heard these words.

"Actually," says Nestor, sounding not nearly as defensive as I would in his position, "by all accounts I could find online, you get best results if you don't tamper with it. The fluids actually work as sort of an incubator for the device. It, like, maintains the integrity of the data. And it's not like it's rotting in there. I kept it frozen until I left my place. Although it's just about thawed out again."

Now Nestor removes a small cardboard box from his backpack, which reads NITRILE. Nestor breaks a perforation with a penguin-flipper hand and says, "I have a latex allergy."

"Bummer, sort of," I say, thinking condoms, trying to remember the last time I used a condom, trying to conjure a definitive image of the girl before Rena—Sandy, that emotional wreck that I commandeered and abandoned and salvaged and discarded and begged back even though it was too late. And maybe I was the emotional wreck. Despite the utter, drunken chaos and otherwise rampant irresponsibility and penny-stock volatility that were the hallmarks of our two rollercoaster years on and off, there were always condoms. My mother had been actively dying, and I had been spending the last years of my twenties burning every bridge I could. I took every risk that didn't matter and trampled other people's feelings. The image I conjure is of Sandy, on her knees, facing away from me, unclad, trying to lure me back into another three months of torturing each other, to which I tacitly obliged, burying my face in her ass. The definitive snapshot of that woman in my mental phonebook is faceless and NSFW.

"OK, guys, you ready?" Nestor says, plucking the sleeves of one of his non-latex gloves, the snap sounding a slap reverb off the walls within my mostly dark garage. "Let's see what Kimberly Relto was all about."

"That's her name—the terrorist woman?" asks Ollie, seeming a little sad and serious. And I force myself to admit that this is all a little sad and serious, even though my mind keeps wandering back to the narcotic memory of Sandy's naked ass. I struggle to pull myself away from a memory that I'm embarrassed continues to hold such sway over my psychic life. Focusing on the methodical movements of Nestor's hands—gently pulling apart the matching sides of the baggie, green back to blue and yellow, holding the bag upright with the left, reaching in with the right, like it's some unnecessarily gory game of Operation—I find myself drawn back to the moment. Nestor draws the slime-covered black box out of the bag and rests it on top of the QBBR231. A small puddle of liquid accumulates where the two devices meet, and I have to restrain myself from launching a comic jet of vomit all over everyone. It looks like Ollie might be struggling with the same. Rena grimaces, a strand of dark hair falling to the corner of her glasses in a lovely way. Nestor releases the black box, his open, gloved hand hovering over the pair of connected objects.

"So, you just put it on there, all drippy and everything? It doesn't, like, plug in or something?" I try not to sound like a dick, for once.

"Yeah," says Nestor. "From what I read, that's how it works. No plugs or wires or connectors. You just want them touching, with the black box in as close to a state that it was inside the subject as possible."

"That," I say, with every bit of earnestness I can muster, "sounds completely fucking wacko."

"Well, let's see," says Nestor, and he flips a switch on the receiver.

The chord I had been hearing becomes much more pronounced, evidently amplified by the internal speakers of the QBBR231. The tones waver a bit, and I hear a bit of feedback and static.

"Can you guys turn off your phones? Rena, can you turn mine off, too? It's in my back pocket."

"Sure," she says, and we all comply. I watch Rena hold down the power button on my stupid, obsolete flip phone until the screen goes dark, leaving a temporary ghost of the home screen.

The notes playing from the QBBR231 become more precise and beautiful. I can't tell if I hear a melody weaving through the notes, or whether it is simply an electrical pulse that gives the illusion of song. For a moment, the linked tones from the device are the only sound, and I feel lulled into a wonderful place. I feel an undue warmth and sense that we will find peace. A lifeless robot voice interrupts.

This is the final capture of subject Kimberly Ann Relto.

Ollie says what I'm thinking: "Oh no."

The robot voice—a male voice, I think, due to its pitch, even though it's speaking a woman's mind—something like the text-to-voice functionality of early personal computers, continues speaking its cold, dissociated words over the beautiful tones:

I have given everything I have to my husband Daryl. He is the love of my life and I have given up so many things for him. I never pursued publishing my poetry I stopped painting and I ruined my body to give birth to Hailey. Daryl begged me to leave Tom after we broke up the first time when I had just started college. I never should have agreed but I broke Tom's heart and went back with my first love. But our mutual love did not last even though he married me and forced me to quit college when I became pregnant. He slept with my sister Jess and she had an abortion to keep me from knowing about their affair. Even so I found out later and Daryl denied it every time until the time I got him drunk enough to admit it. When Hailey was hit by that car everything I had wagered on the future vanished. I knew Daryl would never let me leave even after what he put me through. I had nothing. No options. This was the only way. When I read about the Utilitarian Suicide Alliance I thought that I might as well make something of my death even if I couldn't make something of my life. I'm sorry to die in this way and I hope God understands but I needed something to have meaning. I hope that this cause actually solves what it says it will and makes things better for people. I'm so sorry Hailey. Please forgive me.

The robot voice pauses, and then repeats:

Please forgive me.

When I realize that Rena is weeping, I immediately go and hug around her arms from behind, but she seems cold and stiff. Ollie, though not crying, seems considerably broken up. Nestor's face is devoid of the excitement it had held throughout the setup; he looks at his shoes. Rena seems to relax slightly, and she allows her body to more fully fall into mine. I feel significantly sobered. The chord from the device continues ringing, and I feel a genuine fear that if the voice returns I won't be able to handle it.

Rena's cracked voice, measured and soft, asks, "Do we have to take this to the police?"

"I guess someone had to ask," I say. "I don't know."

"What would the police do with it?" asks Ollie. "I mean …" he seems to search for a way to say something. "She did it herself, right?"

"It would seem so," says Nestor. "I just … I could get in real trouble if we turn it in at this point."

"Yeah," I say. "That's no joke. I think we need to think about this. This might be the most serious thing I've ever heard."

"It's real sad," says Ollie, and he starts blubbering in a sweet, childlike way. His lower lip pouts cartoonishly, and huge tears stream from his eyes as his ears turn beet red.

Because I can't remember ever seeing Ollie cry before, it makes me start to cry, and I start sobbing wildly. I can't remember the last time I cried, so I suppose I'm making up for all the times I should have cried, and emotions are just pouring through me, sieve-style. Nestor joins in easily enough, and soon we're an eight-armed hug, head to head, comforting each other in between gasps and wailing, salty trails streaking every cheek. Huddled together under the swaying fluorescent lights in the garage, we are a giant weeping mess, and as I momentarily distance myself from the scene to picture it objectively, I can't help but find the display absurd. Thankfully, Rena catches on and she starts giggling, and soon we're all giggling and then laughing out loud, holding each other so we don't fall over.

"What the fuck are we doing?" I ask.

Later, the cherry pie Ollie swears he obtained legally from a grocery store is cooling on top of the stove, and the coffee pot fills drip by drip. I have a really hard time picturing Ollie having the forethought to purchase a pie for us, and I prod him to get him to admit that he stole it, which he won't.

"Drop it, Harland," Rena suggests.

"I would have stolen a pie, too," I say. "It's the perfect thing to steal, because no one would suspect that you would have the audacity to actually do it."

Rena's silence mirrors Ollie's, and Nestor is looking at me like I'm completely out of my mind, so I drop it. The microwave clock reads 12:00. Outside, clouds obscure all stars.

I turn the TV on and compromise by muting it.

"People are doing this," says Rena. It's an improvement on our prior lack of words. "They … think there's no alternative." She pauses, as if to draw from an absent cigarette. "They find no way to reconcile what's happened to them. I mean, suicides happen. But then there's this organization, or cult, or whatever it is, that offers them a way to use their suicide for a purpose. Is that what's going on?"

"Golden Gate," I say. "Those people, they blew themselves up. It was organized. The question is: Who's actually organizing this thing? Who's in charge? What's the motivation? How did this start? Is it nefarious, or is it somehow actually noble and we just don't have enough information to understand the martyr-hood aspect?"

"Martyrdom," says Rena. "And that's way more than one question."

On TV, a clown wearing a crown cannot seem to decide between two identically gross-looking burgers. Then a man in a sombrero shoots them both with dual six-shooters, and it turns out to be a Taco Bag commercial.

"But, I mean," says Ollie, closing his eyes to get the wording correct, which endears him to me, "how can it be a good thing? I mean, this thing, the suicide group—"

"Utilitarian Suicide Alliance," says Nestor, looking down into the same central area of the carpet as the rest of us. The percolator gurgles beyond Ollie.

"The Suicide Alliance," says Ollie. "Isn't it taking advantage of people, saying that they should kill themselves because it's going to help something? That seems wrong."

"Yeah, maybe it's cut and dry," I say. "But I don't think there's anything inherently wrong with suicide." It feels a little macho and disingenuous, but I continue to advocate for the devil. "People should be able to opt for that. I know it hurts other people's feelings in many instances, but we only have so much control over how our lives end up, and if you don't have the gall to stick it out beyond a certain point, why should you be forced to do so?"

"So you think the Alliance offers counseling services to talk people out of it?" Rena's tone is curt and all-offense. "You suppose they only recruit the ones who fail a series of tests or something? What the fuck?"

"I don't know, Rena," I say. "I'm not defending them. And either way, I agree that it is most unusual. But we simply don't know all the details, and we're all on the same side speculating here. I'm sure Kimberly was a nice woman."

Tears well up in Rena's eyes. After a long moment, she says, "I miss Curly."

This gut-punches me, and now I'm tearing up again. My throat gets all lumpy and I glottally croak, "I do too," as I get up, wiping my eyes with a flannel-covered elbow. "Who wants coffee and pie?" I blurt, choking back a sob.

We eat pie and coffee, each silently staring at the television as the fake-looking news woman recounts the latest lack of information about the supposed political race.

"Provisional Senator Ruder still lies in critical condition at Washington Memorial Hospital. Over forty-eight hours have passed since his tragic fall following an unexpected discharge at a nearby paintball arena, and doctors say that his condition has not changed, and has been extremely consistent during that time. He is still considered in critical condition, but doctors have said that his condition has neither improved nor worsened, meaning his condition has remained very much the same condition, which is consistently extremely critical."

I shut off the television and the others look at me.

"Did I tell you guys about Future Me?" I ask.

They turn slowly to look at me.

6 VOTE

In a windy, gray field, with dead leaves and the occasional bare tree, the landscape generator churning on its "autumn" setting, I stand among a small group of people who should be familiar to me, but they're all covered in scarves, hats, hoods, glasses, or outright masks to keep me from identifying them. One of them, looking around, trying to find an angle to legitimately get out of this situation, is a rotund man who's making it fairly obvious that he's my dad, even though no one is copping to anything. Nearby is an open grave hole into which my mother's casket is being lowered by a crane, which seems like overkill, pun intended? Dad's grumbling about how he's going to be cremated, and that this ordeal (he means the lavishness and elaborate, procedural nature of this event) was all my maternal grandmother's idea; meanwhile, she somehow blames my dad for my mother's death, as if my dad invented cancer. Just to punctuate the fact that this is a dream, a giant raven flies by, cawing and swooping down to pick up a scrap of barbecue chicken from an open container sitting atop a heap overflowing from a trashcan. Cannibalism? How close are the raven and the chicken? These thoughts apparently escape my mouth, or at least register with dad, because he says, "Birds are birds." Someone shushes him, and then he gestures harshly, just short of flipping them off. "We dropped the ball, Harland," he says, his voice creaking and warbling. "We … didn't end up where I always thought we would."

The crane backs away from the site, its job completed. "A crane is a bird, too," I say.

"It's a homonym," says Dad.

It occurs to me that this will be our last meeting, so I try to make it last, make it better than it really ended up. "So, you're going to DC?" I ask.

He just looks into the open rectangle with the dirt edges. I hear a familiar sound, some harmonic intervals seeping into the atmosphere. I see a light blue static cast over the scene. It occurs to me that I'm a character in a non-branching narrative, and I have to plod forward into the inevitable. I also realize that this is a consolidation of events for convenience. The actual last time I saw my dad was about a year and a half after my mom's death. But I understand the point of the heavy-handed graveyard symbolism. I go ahead and wake up, because there's nothing else I'm going to glean from the pantomime.

Just pre-dawn, I pull myself out of bed, pull on jeans, pull on socks and boots, pull on a windbreaker. I listen for the sound of my sheepdog, which does not come, because he's dead. Nor do I hear the skitter of my late cat. I wander out of the bedroom, through the kitchen where a third of the pie remains uneaten atop the stove, into the living room portion of the big open space. I walk up to my front door, twist the deadbolt out of its seat, turn the knob and pull the door open. I step into the doorjamb, pushing the screen door easily without touching the handle because it never latches properly, stepping out onto the porch, pulling the door closed behind me, and letting the screen door jerk itself closed, its upper pneumatic cylinder gobbling the rod an inch at a time.

I sit in one of the wicker chairs that Rena brought with her when she moved in. It's not comfortable and not attractive. I'm still trying to figure out the appeal. I look down the street to my left and see sunlight begin to break through the branches overhanging the street at the horizon. Soon a funnel of light expands into a shapeless haze that continues creeping down the street toward me. The forty-something Fahrenheit air chews through my pant legs.

The way my dad actually left was that he came by uninvited asking to borrow money. A title card announces the flashback: *16 months earlier.* After work on a Tuesday, Dad showed up at my door, and Rena had to call the pizza place back to up the order.

Over pizza and salad, Dad explained, "This is the one that will hit. This'll be it, or I'm out."

"What's that mean?" I asked with my mouth full.

"You can only kickstart things so many times, and then you have to say they're gone."

Rena looked at him with a lovely combination of compassion and skepticism. I clenched my jaw and waited to hear a dollar value. And after ten minutes of convoluted explanation (promotion?), it came:

"I've got five thousand. It's everything to my name. I need another three."

"Three thousand?" I said, maybe choking for effect. "For investment in a cult?"

"It's not a cult," he said. I'm sure he said that. "It's a for-profit reform movement. But I have to buy my way in."

"Frank," said Rena. "I know you believe in this ... organization. And we want to help in any way we can, but the money ..."

"I'm not giving you another goddamn cent," I said.

Dad set his jaw. His head dropped toward folded forearms.

"What happened to the turbo-laundromat?" I asked. "What about the group insurance? Or the fucking timeshares, or the super-vitamins, or the *Seinfeld* theme park? I'm probably into you for fifteen grand since I turned eighteen. There was no college fund, no trust, no safety net. I work a fucking dead-end job I can't stomach just to latch onto some semblance of the stability you never allowed us to have."

"Harland," Rena warned.

"No," I said. "No, this—Dad, I can't be part of these schemes anymore. I know—well, I hope your heart is in the right place. But I can't do it. Your promises are short-term and meaningless. I ask you about the last one, and you dissuade from it. You distract me, and try to get me to bite on the next. It's frigging maddening. I'm your son. It's not supposed to go this way. Who am I supposed to turn to if things fall out from under me?"

His head didn't rise. But he said, softly, precisely, "This was for you. You and your mother. I never had the muster for the nine-to-five, and I'm sorry. I tried it, and I just about put a gun in my mouth. These were me— they were ways of me trying to be creative, and if just one of them hit—just one—we'd be covered for life. I hope you'll notice I never stopped trying."

I was shaking, angry and embarrassed and deeply sad. I said through teeth: "Maybe it's time you stopped."

He stood up, not looking at anyone. I focused on the floor, and Rena drilled her vision through my profile. He stepped over, put his hand on my shoulder, squeezed firmly, and said, "I love you. Please know that this was all for you, in the only way I knew how."

He turned and walked out of my house.

Even though he was short three grand, I knew he was going to the convention anyway. Someone would fall for his pitch, I thought. Maybe even someone on the bus ride there. He'd show them the fabricated statistics about how The Bottom Line movement was going to help everyone, to eliminate debt, and truly revolutionize the national outlook. "We'll all get a fresh start," he'd say to them, like he had to me.

I have no doubt that my father made it to DC by the time the convention started that Friday. That Friday was July 11, the day that Washington, DC was leveled by terrorists.

Saturday night, Ollie and I drink beers at the bar in the one arcade remaining in the area, Planet Pi. It's been a night and a day since we heard that woman spill her final testament. Ollie plays a touchscreen video game like a savant, smearing it with his pizza-stained fingers but well on his way to the high score.

I scold Ollie to ignore his game and listen to me as I read the list of possible themes for when we finally make our movie:

- *Time theft*

- *Getting food poisoning on purpose*

- *Replacing HDTVs with regular TVs*

- *Putting up "missing" signs of yourself*

- *Stop going to work and no one notices*

- *Jacking off to your horoscope*

- *Everything falls apart and it doesn't change anything*

- *A maze that can't be solved*

- *The purpose of Esperanto is to reveal the end of the world to a select few*

• *Ghosts only brag about how much better death is*

• *Love only worked before people were educated*

• *Education is a distraction from self-discovery*

• *Self-discovery is a generally fruitless endeavor*

• *What happens after the water towers are poisoned*

• *Being the opposite of a martyr*

• *Selling guns out of an ice cream truck*

• *Monarchies are better because there's only one bad guy and everybody knows who he is*

Ollie has continued playing his game throughout, and I give up on him. "Fine, you don't get to hear the good ones," I say. Just when I'm about to catch the female bartender's eye, a scream comes from across the dark, strobing room. A man with a gun to his head yells, "I'm sorry, Tammy, but this is how it's gotta be. This is how it ends." When he pulls the trigger, his head explodes all over a change machine, and the bullet must have gone through, because the change machine bursts open, spilling thousands of quarters all over the colorful, zig-zag-patterned carpet.

Two swarms of young adults converge and momentarily sort themselves out: those fleeing from the gory scene of the suicide, and those scrambling to get fistfuls of quarters. The latter group clambers into the jackpot, most of them trying not to touch the blood and brains, but a subset of them simply grabbing indiscriminately, getting equal parts quarters and skull fragments and flecks of the dead guy's frontal lobe.

"Another one," says Ollie. "Do you think he was—you know, part of the Alliance?"

"I don't know, Ollie," I say, taking a swig from my heavy mug of amber beer as I watch a hilariously underprepared security guard arrive on the scene. "By the way, how come we had to go through a metal detector on the way in here if crazies are getting guns through so easily?"

"Good point," says Ollie. "It's no fair if only some people have guns."

"That wasn't quite my point," I say, grimacing.

"What if there's more than one?" Nestor says this, rubbing it in that he's the brainy one.

"Alliance?" asks Rena, proving she's the second-smartest.

"And what if they have different methods?" I say, trying not to be the dumbest.

"Yeah," says Ollie. "There would be two. Or more." Ollie then spills lemonade all over his overalls. "Aw, man." he says. I hold out a napkin and snicker, feeling assured.

"And I only say it because the one you described seeing at the arcade—that doesn't sound like ours. The gun—that's what's different. Kimberly Relto didn't use a gun. She used some kind of localized explosive. It took her whole head off. The people at the Golden Gate Bridge used explosives, too, although admittedly they were much more powerful. Those cut through steel supports."

Skizzers is busy for a Sunday night. I see Old Fuck leaning forward, almost tipping his stool, grabbing some jock by the collar of his polo shirt. I hear a snarling voice speaking a slew of words that I can't completely comprehend. At some point I hear the phrase, "shit bigger than your cock."

Ollie, wielding a lemonade-soaked napkin, firms his brow and says with an undue dignity, "So you think one group blows themselves up—that must be the Alliance—and another one shoots themselves with guns. And maybe there's another one who cuts themselves with knives, like that guy at the video store last month. And another one who poisons, and they all have their own—wait! What if they all record their messages in different ways?"

"Their messages," says Nestor. I assume he understands, but his face is almost completely expressionless.

"Like the Alliance have the black box. But maybe the gun people write emails or leave behind word puzzles?"

"The news probably would have reported something about a string of word puzzles left behind after a string of serial suicides," I say, pretty sure of myself and looking it.

"Maybe," says Rena, not giving me eye contact, so I can't give her a dirty look.

Nestor's face continues its streak of non-breaking. "I think the idea of separate suicide organizations is actually likely. You don't see anything in this country without three other people trying to make a shitty copy of it."

Old Fuck explains how to tell if someone is lying: "They're talking out loud."

Old Fuck explains foreplay: "Hankie with ether."

Old Fuck explains religion: "God left."

I wander back to join Rena, Nestor, and Ollie. The jukebox blares the beginning of the new hit song, "Break That Thang Off Up In," and Ollie starts dancing without getting out of his chair. I see Rena's friend Janet at the far end of the bar, turning around just in time to catch my eye, and her face becomes exaggerated with happy surprise. Apparently she's blocked out everything I've ever said to her.

Rena greets her by standing up and hugging her, which is slightly hot when their boobs touch through four layers of cloth.

"Hot," I say.

"Nice," says Rena, meaning the opposite.

"How are you guys?" says Janet. "I was just about to leave. I met Kaylie, but she had to get home to Jaden."

"Fascinating," I say. "Great backstory. How do you see your character arc playing out? Tidal wave? Goose attack?"

Janet chuckles, and her brow furrows. She's so dumb and nice that I want to punch her in the head. Rena literally pinches my arm under the table, and I verbalize a reaction to the pain.

"How are you, Rena?" Janet is pointedly not looking at me, which makes me warm with desire to pulverize her.

"I'm good. Very intrigued about this election. We haven't seen a good three-way race in a long time."

"Yeah," says Janet, glazing over, not knowing what the fuck. "Who are you voting for?"

"It's impolite to talk politics," I say, folding my arms. Rena's glare melts the right side of my face, but I continue grinning coldly at the blond.

"Janet, have you met Nestor?" asks Rena, deflecting expertly.

"Hi," says Nestor, actually standing and offering his hand. I like to think this is the first black person Janet has touched and that she's got some really fucked-up preconceptions. They shake weakly, and Janet says, "Hi, I'm

Janet."

"Janet's also engaged," Rena says to the table, for lack of anything new or noteworthy.

"How's your fiancée?" I ask, my arms still folded, defensive. My tone is rote. I play up the small-talk angle, and I make it obvious that I could give a shit about the response. I picture Janet naked, and I get instantly livid with myself.

"Brad's good," she says, dragging out the syllable of "good" far too long, making it obvious that the situation is anything but. "We're looking forward to the holiday. Brad's coming to my parents' house for Thanksgiving."

"Oh, Jesus Christ," I say. Ollie and Nestor look across the table at me with what looks like morbid curiosity.

"That sounds nice," says Rena. "How are your parents doing?"

"Good, I think." Janet seems almost in a daze, maybe seeking some substance in her life. "Mom's very busy with the soup kitchen, and dad is retiring next year, so he's getting ready for that. It's still tough, it's going to be our second Thanksgiving since Jason passed. But having Brad there will be good. Even though it can't be my brother, it'll be good for my parents to have a boy back in the house."

"That's nice," I say. "My parents are dead."

"Look," says Janet, her face screwing up, eyes right at me. "Do you have a problem with me? Or what?"

"No problem," I say. "Just making conversation."

"Right," she says. "I'm friends with Rena, OK? And you don't have to talk to me if you don't want to. Whatever."

She turns around and starts walking away, and Rena gets up to go after her, not even bothering to glance at me to scold me.

"What's that all about?" asks Nestor. "Did you two used to date or something?"

"No," I say, grimacing crazily, overcompensating. "Are you kidding? Gross. I just—that girl is so superficial."

"She seems nice," says Ollie, dissenting, betraying me.

"What the hell?" I say. "Are you serious? She's a robot. I'm fairly convinced that she's not even a person."

"Weird," says Nestor. "I think she seems nice, too. A little airhead-ish, maybe. But nice."

"She's the devil," I say. "And I never overstate my case."

"The devil's pretty cute," says Ollie. "She's got big teeth, but … Do you think Brad is really the one, or do I have a chance?"

"Ollie," I say. "If you ever had sex with her, I would kick you both in the taint, mid-coitus."

"You need a cold shower, Harland." Nestor raises an eyebrow and sips from a thin, pink straw.

"What do you know, gay?" I say, trying to burn bridges and realizing that I have indeed got a mean drunk going. "Sorry."

Nestor's face turns into a poster of skepticism. I'm losing whatever credibility I've held with these two, I realize, and I begrudgingly begin to backpedal. "I'm a drunk a-hole." I wait a beat. "I'm not in my right mind. I'm—" I try to think of what I am. "I'm jealous."

"Of who?" says Ollie.

"Of people who don't see everything through a fucking ironic lens." I hope this is close enough to the truth to suffice.

"Well, that's ironic," says Nestor. After a second, Ollie starts to giggle and raises his mug to his mouth.

A couple minutes later, Rena re-enters the bar with thunderous footsteps and fire shooting from her eye sockets. By the time she strikes me with lightning I'm already forcing myself to black out.

Three days before Thanksgiving and the day before the sham that is Election Day, I arrive at my cubicle at work at only eleven minutes past the required arrival time, so I'm off to a good start. Less than fifteen minutes late is early for me.

I get some slop from the silver-tier coffee pot, dump a pile of non-dairy creamer on top and watch it slowly sink into the abyss. I take a moment to be mesmerized. I grab a thin plastic stir and head back to my desk. The very shaggy sheepdog on the mug winks at me. He looks nothing like Curly, the late, bald beast. Curly was Dog Me, and he's gone now. I wink back anyway. We're up to something, I realize. In cahoots.

I dismantle the proxy server and get into a web window with no history tracking. I check out comments on my blogs. Spanx Johnnie's heavily slanderous disavowal of Republican presidential candidate Morton Shemp (entitled, "Shemp: The next bin Laden") has received a new record number of comments. The most recent is a terse tone poem from a user called

KILL_N_WORDS: "YER GUNNA DIE FAGGIT WHEN I SHOOT YOU IN YER FAGGIT MOUTH. [sic]" It really wouldn't work without the caps. Granch Depravo's blog entitled, "Why Phil Brandley is Mexican and should be Deported" has fewer comments, but some equally resounding. The most recent comment, from B. Davenport, reads, "You don't know what your talking about, you ignorat racist. I hope you go back to 1930's Germany where you belong. If your address ever becomes public your in big trouble. [sic]" And that's America to me.

I check my webmail, and Nestor has sent a novella that I can only skim because I've yet to have a sip of my coffee, which I'm reminded to stir. The crux of his email is: "I ordered 4 black boxes." Black Me is also up to something.

Next I scour the Internet for personal information on Julius Zorro: his allergies, sexual proclivities, deepest fears. Sadly, all of this comes from one site that aggregates data posted on a handful of social networks. Julius Zorro wants the world to know who he is. Anyone dumb enough to use his real name on the Internet deserves to be harassed by me, I decide. (Later, I will post this sentiment from the persona of Spanx Johnnie.)

I log in using my alias "Brance Michelton." Brance is a self-important armchair philosopher who has a comment for any discussion of no cosmic consequence. In that way, he is the soul of the Internet. Brance sends a message to Julius Zorro: "Hey, I think we went to elementary school together. You went to Faulkner, graduated from 6th grade in 1998, right? Remember Mr. Chalmers? What a spaz that guy was." So far, this is all just regurgitation of his extensive lists of affiliations and achievements, personality mirroring by cut-and-paste. This is the basis for modern scams. I have the passing desire to attempt extortion, but I'm afraid it will botch my somewhat-covert data mining effort. I don't want to lose focus. "So, what's been going on? You still hang out at [name of childhood hangout]? Still seeing [listed significant other]? Did she go to our school too? I remember how funny it was when [funny anecdote extracted from profile]."

The aim is to gain his attention, not his confidence. I don't care if he's suspicious. I just want a reply.

By the time I finally sip my coffee, it's cold.

When I return home Monday evening, having stopped to pick up a bucket of fried chicken, Rena is already home and lying down in the bedroom. I lean into the darkened room and whisper.

"I got chicken."

A moment passes. Then, from under the covers, a croaking voice says, "I'm laying down."

I interpret this the only way I can, backing out, gently closing the door, taking the bucket of chicken to my recliner, scooping the remote from the side table, turning on the television, scaling the volume so low I that I might as well turn on the captions, and sighing. I watch cartoon robots fight the forces of evil while I eat chicken and think about what I've done. This is being grounded all over again. Rena's become my mom, and I'm just a misbehaving boy. I eat greasy leg after greasy thigh, feel myself fattening, and feel like a piece of shit. I keep eating for about ten minutes beyond when I've had my fill. I wonder about whether things might have been different if I had eaten my words and scrounged up three thousand dollars for my dad. Presumably, he still would have gone to DC. But maybe the universe would have been different enough … I lick my fingers in lieu of dessert. I feel a bit sick.

Cartoons transition into nightly news, and this time the computer-animated robots are a pair of news reporters with perfect skin and disarming smiles and amazing tits and presumably a big cock who talk about a nation on the verge of a new order, which I have a hard time believing, but they say it with such conviction that I feel consoled by the idea that at least someone believes in something.

The news people talk about the trials that America has endured, that even in its darkest hours heroes have emerged, and our greatest strengths are sometimes only evident in the throes of struggle. I feel unclean listening to this sober, but I remain tethered to my seat in a post-ingestion stupor, too lazy to go get my drugs. I'm riddled by uplifting sentiments about the human spirit and the beauty of mankind's ongoing explorations, both internal and into the frontiers of the unknown. This shit is relentless, I think, trying to escape the moment, but the production values suck me back in, and I'm inundated by a resounding chorus of angels evoking the underlying hopes of each person, that points earned in this realm may be redeemable in a future one. It all makes some kind of sick sense.

Then the female robot strips off her top, and she's wearing a pristine white bra with a complex paisley pattern, this incredible garment holding two enormous, perfect breasts, just magnificent specimens of the benefits of evolution (this is the thought process even though she's obviously an android). The camera is straight on her now, and she unclasps the latch in the middle—one of those amazing front-fastening bras no one bothered to tell me about before high school and which I discovered in probably one of the most elating moments of my life—and she peels back the cups to reveal big, perfect breasts. And that's when I become convinced that, despite my prior viewpoint that there is absolutely no reason to do so, I probably will go vote tomorrow.

At work the next morning, my cell phone buzzes against my thigh, and I can almost feel a tumor blooming beneath it. Rena is actually calling, not texting, which makes my stomach feel awfully low and heavy. I spin my chair into a far corner of my cubicle and duck down.

"You OK?" I pant.

"Danielle," Rena speaks with a whispered urgency that doesn't ease my anxiety, "is saying that I'm not allowed to leave to vote, which I'm pretty sure is … unconstitutional."

"Does the Constitution even apply anymore?" I ask, actually wondering.

"I never heard anything about that being off the table. The point is, I know we're supposed to be let out to vote. I read an article about measures you can take if you receive resistance from your employer. But I really want to keep this from becoming anything close to litigious. That would be very f-ing annoying. I just don't understand why she has to be such a selfish …"

"What about your lunch hour?" I ask.

"Everybody and their mother is voting at lunchtime. I wouldn't get back for three hours, and then what? I'm gonna get docked, or fired, or worse, I'm just going to get a month worth of guilt and bullshit from this fucking woman."

"You really shouldn't be put in this position," I say, which sounds diplomatic and unhelpful. "You know what you should do? Tell her that you're a write-in candidate, and that it's going to hurt your chances if you don't show up to the polls."

"That's weird," she says, maybe sniffling, maybe static coming over the line.

"Tell her your dad and you used to go vote together, always at two in the afternoon, and that it would be a betrayal of his memory not to vote then."

"Do you hear yourself?" she asks, somehow sweetly. I hear a smile break.

"Tell Danielle that you'll vote for her while you're there. Get her order like you're going to get lunch."

"You're a silly man," she says.

"Tell that lazy bitch that you'll grab her insulin on the way back. Tell her you'll cover for her the next time she has to go get liposuction. Tell her there's a warm cherry pie in it for her. You know Ollie will steal one."

I hear giggling.

"Just assert your rights, Rena. You're allowed to go vote. You think you can't get another Tuesday/Thursday job if it hits the fan? Employers everywhere are scrambling to find lovely vixens to helm desks on Tuesday and Thursday across this great land. What do you think this election is all about? It's about a woman's right to choose where she works the two days a week when she's not bringing people Moo Goo Gai Pan and Egg Drop Oops-I-Just-Jizzed-In-This-Bowl Soup. You are woman, hear you roar. You're my lovely queen, and your voice will be heard."

The giggling continues. I spin from the corner of my desk and see that Cindy has been waiting for me, and she looks like I just took a dump in her lap. I guffaw and spin back around.

"You go vote, Rena. It's your right." I feel energized, like I'm making a difference. Then I realize something, and ask, "Who are you voting for?"

"I know it's a little strange to vote for someone in a coma, but I'm voting for Ruder," she says without hesitation. "I did a bit of research, and it sounds like things could be very different in a positive way with him in charge."

"Paintball guy?" I say. "Huh. Cool. I don't know who any of these jackals are. I'm gonna look it up before I go after work."

"It's going to be so busy, Harland. You should try to get out during the day."

"Yeah, I might," I say. Remembering Cindy's there, I add loudly, "It's pretty busy. I've got a big workload, so I'm going to have to tear through that before I go exercise my unalienable rights. Because this company comes first, and my personal agenda always comes second."

"You're full of lovable shit," she says. "Thanks for making me feel better."

"I love you," I say. "I'm sorry about the Janet thing."

"We'll talk about that later," she says, deflating me.

"OK. Good luck. Love you."

"Love you, Harland."

I collapse my cell phone and spin around slowly, presenting a Cheshire grin to Cindy. "Hello, Cindy. How may I help you?"

Cindy's face is still sour. "Everything OK?"

"Fine," I say. "Voting day dilemmas. How may I … help … you?" I can't make it any more clear that she should walk away right now.

"This came for you." She holds out a single piece of paper. I snatch it from her hands, not caring if I give her a paper cut.

"What's this?" I ask before even attempting to read it. Then my eyes focus on a matrix of printed splotches, which I soon recognize as a familiar-looking facsimile. The printed pattern implies a wrinkled source, and the dark streaks imply something written in black marker. The message says:

> Harland G:
> Dad's fine. Thanks for your concern. But no thanks.
> —Julius Z.

I try not to throw up all over Cindy as I scramble to determine how it's possible that my cover story about Julius's Zorro's dad got back to him. I feel a long shadow cast over everything. I would not be surprised if Cindy turned to stone and crumbled. But she keeps standing there, her nest of cartoon-colored hair bursting everywhere. Her foot is literally tapping, forcing me to ask, rather curtly, "What?"

"I don't know if you saw the memo last month, but it's very important that the fax machines be reserved for business-related faxes only."

"What?" I ask, squinting at her, my mouth askew.

"We have to ask that you please not use the fax machines for personal faxes."

"Yeah," I say, getting that somehow she doesn't realize I'm being haunted here. "I didn't request this. I barely know this guy. I've never used the fax machine since I've worked here. I can't believe there's even still a fax machine. Why aren't people using email?"

"Well, Harland, this appears to be addressed to you. So would you please ask the sender to not use our central fax number for personal messages?"

"I don't know this person. As far as I'm concerned, this is spam."

"So you're not going to comply with the policy?" she asks.

Ready to find a sledgehammer and knock her head clean off, I say, glaring crazily and with my teeth gritted together like a monster, "Do you not hear what I'm saying? I did not send this fax. I did not request this fax. I don't want it. I don't know what it's about, and I really don't know who sent it."

"This fax," she says, matching my methodical pace and tone, "was sent by a former employee who left under questionable circumstances, and with whom you obviously still have contact."

"Look, I know you're pissed he cut in front of you leaving the building, whatever that means, but don't take this out on me."

"Who told you that?" says Cindy. "That was confidential."

I freeze. I flail without moving. "He said something about it before he left. He was a real piece of work." I have to make Cindy believe we're on the same side.

She pauses, dumbfounded. Her face cycles through a few expressions and finally lands on blank and cold. She speaks clearly: "You're on a short list."

"What the hell does that mean?" The same-side plan is failing extremely rapidly.

"Watch your language."

"'Hell'?" I exclaim. "Are you fucking shitting me?"

She spins on her fat heel and briskly waddles away.

"Fine," I yell down the hall, "I'm going to vote!"

In line at the precinct at the elementary school in my neighborhood, I use the crippled, tiny Internet browser on my obsolete phone to see if I can find out where Julius Zorro may be living or working or hiding out. I don't find any of that, but I do find a lot of two-for-one deals at participating local merchants. Then I perform some last-minute research by checking the wiki pages for the presidential contenders to see if anything has emerged to actually distinguish one from another.

The voting booth smells like ginger ale. With the curtain drawn behind me—which itself seems a lovely artifact of this antiquated process—I see some words scribbled on the right-hand wall: "Like this is gonna change anything."

I slide the tall, single-sheet ballot onto the platform and pick up the ballpoint pen chained to the wall in front. A small, official-looking notecard is adhered just beneath the short fluorescent tube that illuminates the booth, reading: "Please leave booth when done voting."

The presidential candidates are at the top, and I review the list for kicks:

MORTON SHEMP – Republican [line drawing of the heads of Reagan and Lincoln]

PHILLIP BRANDLEY – Democrat [line drawing of the heads of JFK and FDR]

JOHN RUDER – Independent [line drawing of the Comedy and Tragedy masks]

LARK LUCIANO – Independent [line drawing of an Ace of Spades and a dollar symbol]

HUGH JORGAN – Independent [line drawing of a two-headed monster]

DAVE "TOKEMAN" CRUTHERS – Green [line drawing of a Pez dispenser and a cannabis leaf]

CASEY BEAKMAN – Reality [line drawing of a remote control and a television]

Despite a momentary itch to vote for Tokeman, I remember the awful music he used for his infomercials, so I fill in the box to the left of Ruder's name with my number-two pencil, participating in the manifest destiny of Future Me and, incidentally, agreeing with Rena and avoiding those arguments. As I assume most people vote, I am going with whatever I guess will cause me the least short-term grief.

I skim the rest of the ballot, but the only other thing I bother to vote for is Proposition 6, which proposes that all fences be raised two inches because dogs are getting taller. I surprise myself by farting, and the dampened acoustics in the booth give it the sonic intimacy of an audiobook. It also sort of stinks in an unfamiliar way, so I exit, hand my ballot to the oldest woman alive, and start humming the hit song, "Sell That Kid By The Pound."

When I return to work, there are no new emails, no notes on my desk, no major indications that this place is still in business. It's nice. I put my head down on my desk and nap through lunchtime.

I slip into REM sleep during my nap and find myself falling through air, the poor choices I've made pulling me down instead of gravity. This is my friend Seth again, but I'm his first-person proxy, because I'm supposed to derive meaning from this. Looking down, I see my mom wheeling away and my dad looking at his watch. I close in, unable to yell.

When I pull my head from the desk, a temporarily stuck dime falls from my forehead, spins, and lands on tails.

Ollie arrives at our place around seven p.m. I'm playing my videogame on the console while Rena's actually taking the time to make a lasagna, which I think has happened all of once previously in the term of our relationship.

"Oliver, you like zucchini?"

"Sure," he says, falling onto the couch. "Thanks."

I capture a little purple alien in my jar, holding down the square button while tapping R1 to remove all the air from the jar, and his head explodes all over the interior.

"Sick," says Ollie.

"Yeah," I say. "It's based on the Sylvia Plath book."

"Who's that?"

"She founded the Alliance," I say.

"You boys want to play cards while it's baking?" asks Rena.

"You guys want to get baked while it's baking?" asks Ollie, a cherubic smile.

"Those don't sound mutually exclusive," I say, saving my game.

Rena deals as Ollie packs the kangaroo dick.

"Where's Nestor?" asks Ollie.

"He's working late, I think," I say. "He said that someone quit, so he's doing two doubles this week."

"Did he get to vote?" asks Rena.

"I don't know. His text said, 'Stuck with stiff til ten,' or something like that. Hopefully he got out earlier."

Ollie winks unintentionally and says, "Did Nestor see that guy who killed himself in the arcade?"

"No," says Rena. "I asked him, but he said the guy must have been taken to another morgue."

"Morgue Wars," I say. "That would be a good videogame."

The light hanging over the kitchen table illuminates us in the otherwise darkened house. Amazing aromas seeping from the oven fill our nostrils as Ollie lights the pipe. Rena produces a hand with all four fives, and with the jack of clubs up, she's got maybe the best cribbage hand there is. The tableaux recalls game nights with my parents in my prepubescent years. Sometimes they'd invite friends over, sometimes it would just be the three of us. I felt included, grown up. I'd still get frustrated when I wouldn't win—my parents never believed in letting me win for the sake of phony esteem-building. They allowed whatever self-esteem I was going to garner to be organically obtained. Prior to their divorce, they were anything but manipulative. And at that preteen age, I never thought about us being poor or lower-class or limited in any substantial way. They were my parents, I was their kid, and they asked me about school, sometimes helped me with art or science projects, encouraged my interest in music (and didn't seem too disappointed when I couldn't muster the attention span to really pursue it), and sometimes just played cards with me at night, not only because it was a virtually free thing that we could afford. I was part of their functional plan. And then, when the plan fell apart, I became a token of the fallout.

When they divorced, the memories of happy times became anachronistic artifacts. Recalling a family dinner only raised a lot of speculation about what wasn't being discussed. Recalling Mom sneaking a kiss from Dad only drew attention to the compromises they endured. Seeing the one studio portrait photo we ever had done, the three of us in matching mustard turtlenecks, all I could see was an airbrushed façade.

I'm smoking absently, not really inhaling, laying down a shitty hand that's got six points total, passing the glass tube left to my fiancée. Somewhere about half my life ago my family ceases to exist, and then it was no longer dad the inventive provider and mom the loving supporter. Now, per Mom, Dad is the conniving huckster. And per Dad, Mom is the undermining saboteur. Each one says the other brought us to this, and I'm somewhere in a nether realm, grasping at a crumpled tapestry depicting our former life as it's sucked up into the eye of a tornado. Whatever happened, what becomes clear is that is the new order. The old ways are rendered moot, old assumptions crumbling under scrutiny, old hopes cast as foolish fantasy through the lens of newfound cynicism.

Rena easily wins, and I'm happy for her, and before I can fully commit to shutting out this unwelcome rush of epiphany, a parallel I'm almost embarrassed to recognize emerges, which is that America is now surviving post-divorce. We have broken into the unknown, unhappy mirror world; we've crossed through the looking-glass, where each fanciful glance back yields a distorted view of everything we should have seen coming, all the ignorance and best wishes.

I sit at my kitchen table as Rena uses a spatula to transfer steaming, gooey lasagna onto colorful ceramic plates, and I see myself with Rena and with Ollie, a funhouse proxy for an evening with my parents in the time before any of us knew better. Practically, it's no different, but perception ruins everything.

Rena's humming a song from the one musical she likes—the one about mummified Martians who are rejuvenated by Earth's nitrogen-rich air and then take over Hollywood. I ask permission for us to eat in the living room in front of the television, and Rena, in her motherly, nurturing mode, is on board with monitoring the election results.

"That cartoon is attractive," says Ollie, pointing at television. I'm not convinced that the girl onscreen is actually animated, but I concur.

"She looks like a platypus," says Rena.

"At least it's a mammal," I add.

Over three hours of virtually nonstop advertisements for cars, boats, land, legal services, the lottery, private schools, private prisons, weapon registration, cosmetic surgery (especially gender reassignment), milk, beef, a video game which pits milk against beef, and too-late campaign ads meeting their on-air quota, the outcome is whittled down, with only a few non-imperative western states like Oregon not fully reported.

"With ninety-eight percent of precincts reporting," says the female android onscreen, her nipples virtually popping through a pink sweater, "the first President-Elect of the new government—one among many firsts tonight—is John Ruder, the Independent Provisional Senator from Michigan, with a forty-one percent plurality of the popular vote. As the Electoral College process was voted down in May's preliminary election, it is the popular vote that holds sway, and it is, again, Provisional Senator John Ruder who is our new President-Elect. Morton Shemp, the

Republican Governor from Florida, is the closest runner-up, with thirty-nine percent of the popular vote. Democratic Senator Phil Brandley fared much worse than early polls had indicated, bringing in only twelve percent. Experts attribute this drop to a response to what is being called a 'slip' in one of his rally speeches over the weekend, when he referred to Texans as 'fat-alecks.' Three percent of the popular vote went to a candidate who many are claiming is simply a practical joke. It is still unknown whether 'Hugh Jorgan' actually exists or could have taken office if elected. The remaining percent of votes was split between the remaining candidates and various write-ins."

I keep watching, waiting for my phone to ring, cold sweat down my neck and back.

"John Ruder is the first candidate in United States history to be elected to the Presidency while in a coma. We take you now to the Ruder victory party in Lansing, Michigan."

Onscreen, an exterior of what looks like an expensive home is swarmed by awkwardly dancing, well-dressed people. Confetti hangs in the air, and the strobe effect of ceaseless camera flashes make it look like a bad disco. A stocky, balding man in a gray suit approaches a podium sprouting a dozen microphones. A red band across the bottom the screen appears, and white letters across the band tell us that this is VICE PRESIDENT-ELECT THOM GARNDER.

"Fellow citizens, this is a night for healing. Our great nation has seen many trials and has won many victories. We have been, at times, torn apart, but now is as important a time as any for us to come together." He wipes a glistening eye. "Our President-Elect, John Ruder, is not able to celebrate with us right now, but I have every confidence in his ability to fully recuperate, and to lead this new government and our great country, to stress the importance of community, helping one another, and giving back where we have been helped. As his running mate, many have raised questions about whether [the screen cuts to a slowly zooming-in image of the pasty President-Elect lying motionless in a hospital bed as Garnder continues to speak] I will follow John Ruder's lead. Of course I will. Because John Ruder ... will ... lead. Just as this country was set back by the destruction of the District of Columbia on 7/11 and still marches onward, John Ruder has been set back by his tragic paintball accident while fraternizing with his constituents. Set back, not defeated. Not taken out. And certainly not dead. I look forward to President Ruder's tenure, and I know that a resounding plurality of Americans feel the same way." The screen returns to Garnder. "Thank you, America, for believing that we can all have an Opportunity For a Fresh Start, and that includes John Ruder. When he wakes up, I think America too will awaken to a new morning. Once again, I'd like to offer my gratitude and support to the Ruder family, especially Rose, who has been a rock throughout this tough past week. And of course, to my wife, Tabitha, and our daughters Tammy and Tabby. We finally did it, girls! Daddy's the VP! Hoo!"

I mute the television. I turn to Rena and to Ollie. Neither speaks, and I try to process about ten different things to say. After most of a minute, as smiles begin to break on their faces, Ollie finally breaks the silence:

"So we just elected the potatohead?"

7 CRABS

Rena drives, the two of us heading to her mom's house just across the state line, about two hours from our place. Rena's mom's place is the de facto location for Thanksgiving, since she's the last parent still hanging around the land of the living. The compromise, or maybe ultimatum, is that Rena has to drive there and back, and she can't get mad if I nod off on either trip, while the contribution from my end is attendance and endurance of Rena's mom for seven hours. Thankfully, we're a couple years beyond the "How can you love me if you don't love my mother?" debates.

The first flurries of the season fall through cold, dry air as the lime green junker speeds down a four-lane freeway. Some husky-voiced, breathy female moans about a relationship gone sour atop over-compressed piano pounding, some new clone from the emotionally damaged female singer factory. I can't complain aloud about the diegetic soundtrack, because the driver controls the radio, and some rules are to be taken seriously. Still, it beats the country-fried Christmas carols I had to endure on the way to Sandy's family's double-wide four and five years ago.

We cross into our neighbor state to the south. I rub my eyes, having dozed at some point.

"Future Me hasn't called," I say.

"Right," says Rena. "The Ghost of Christmas Yet To Come."

"Maybe it was a telemarketer," I say. "But he knew things." *Like I know things that I shouldn't know about Julius Zorro.*

"So this guy predicted the election?"

"Yeah," I say, convincing myself. "He said forty-one. He nailed the percentage."

"So maybe it's rigged, like every other election."

"Maybe."

"Please don't bring this up in front of Mom."

"Oh, come on," I say. "She needs more twigs for her Harland bonfire."

"Who started that fire?" She glances over at me, smirking. I notice that she's wearing green mittens, one of those details keeping her youthful.

"I'll take the blame for the metaphor, but not for her dousing me in gasoline, so to speak."

After a few more minutes of aimless banter, Rena turns into the frosted cul-de-sac, a loop of indistinguishable houses built around the time her mother was born. A white haze swirls over everything.

We pull into the driveway behind a station wagon or stunted SUV. Towering next to it is a pickup truck the size of Africa.

"Whose is that?" I ask through a yawn, stretching.

"It looks familiar, but ..."

After a series of admittance rituals soaked in saccharine, Rena and I are finally allowed to sit in separate living-room chairs. The mystery guest is announced by a flushing toilet. Rena finally asks:

"Who's that?"

"Terry," says Rena's mom.

"Who's Terry?" asks Rena.

"My boyfriend," says her mom.

Rena's eyebrows reach her hairline in a way that I will not forget.

The sound of a door creaking open precedes a shadow cast along a far wall. The shadow grows until a man emerges. He's got to be six inches taller than me, and has the swooping features of a vulture, from his apparent spina bifida to his hook nose. Then it occurs to me that he is my pot dealer.

Terry gawks back at me, and even though it takes his scrutinizing face longer to resolve and register this connection, I'm completely mute, so he speaks first.

"Small world," Terry says, a glazed glint in his eye accompanied by a guttural chuckle. This was not exactly the greeting I had been hoping for in the last three seconds, because he did not say, *"Hi, I'm Terry, I don't believe we've met."*

"Hey ... Terry," I say.

I stand to extend my hand, and he grabs it and we shake tentatively.

"You two know each other?" Rena and her mother ask, more or less in unison.

"Yeah," I say, scrolling through all the possible things I could say to Rena's mom to not look suspicious or lowbrow. For a moment I feel like I might be completely splattered in shit. "He's a friend of Ollie's."

"Hmm," says Rena's mom. "I assumed he sold you pot, too."

Now Rena's face becomes wrecked in disbelief. My stomach growls.

Once all the steaming dishes are scattered around the dining table and side tables, Terry agrees to lead us in a prayer.

"Dear ... Lord? Thanks for this great-smelling dinner, and thanks, Lorraine, for inviting me. It's been a few years since I had a real Thanksgiving dinner, so this is just great. And I'm glad to be able to see Harland again, and to meet Rena." His prayer has efficiently morphed into a sloppy toast. "Let's get into some turkey, huh?"

Forks and spoons scrape an interesting cacophony against china as we fill our plates, and I'm studying Rena to see whether she's going to burst at the seams.

"So, when did you start smoking pot, Mom?"

"Oh shit," I fail to whisper.

"When I was about twenty."

"Oh, really?" says Rena, in a humorously hostile way.

"Yes. Your dad smoked marijuana, too. You know that we met at a Neil Diamond concert, so obviously we weren't completely straight."

"What about the times you grounded me in high school when you caught me smoking pot?" I'm glad to see Rena exorcising these demons. The gravy tastes pretty good.

"We were being good parents, obviously. And you got caught. If you hadn't gotten caught, you wouldn't have gotten grounded."

"Good point, Lor," says Terry with a mouth full of mashed potatoes. "You gotta work under that radar if you don't want the grief."

"You should know," says Rena.

"I do," says Terry, not defensively. "I only break the laws that I know I can get away with breaking."

"I can't believe the Provisional Government even kept it illegal. Seriously, when I heard that, I thought, 'Great, nothing's changing after all.'" I'm now diving into this conversation, thankful we are all on the same agenda.

"No shit, dude," says Terry.

"So, you just, what? Smoked behind my back while I was growing up?"

"No," says Rena's mom. "I quit when you were a baby."

"You mean you smoked while I was a baby?"

"I said I quit when you were a baby."

"So you smoked pot while you were pregnant with me?"

"Yes," says Rena's mom, and I snicker way too loudly.

"You were a pot baby!" I say, putting my arm around her, which she sharply shrugs off. "It's no big deal. I'm probably an FAS baby."

"So when did you start up again? When I moved out? As soon as it wouldn't make you a huge hypocrite?"

"I started smoking marijuana again a while after your dad died. I was afraid that I was starting to drink too much, so I decided to smoke the funny stuff instead." Lorraine takes a dainty bite of turkey covered in cranberry sauce into her pursed mouth.

"I can't believe what I'm hearing," says Rena. "This is just … too bizarre."

"Not really," I say. "My mom started drinking a lot after my parents' divorce. So did I. I didn't really start smoking pot regularly until after 7/11, though."

"Harland!" Rena says, as if protecting me from something.

"I think it's fair to say there are no bones at this point," I say, pragmatic as ever. "By the way, Lorraine, you're correct; Terry is my dealer. He's my friend Ollie's friend, too. That wasn't bullshit."

"You should have invited Ollie," says Rena's mom.

"Yeah, we should have," I say. Rena looks at the ceiling, searching for something.

"You know, some very famous and successful people have smoked marijuana." Rena's mom says this so matter-of-factly that I want her to record a podcast full of similarly dubious proclamations. I can picture her rabid fanbase huddled around their hi-fi stereos in dens and family rooms, listening to sixty-something Lorraine from the Midwest claiming, *"Heroin is what they call a gateway drug,"* and *"There's no such thing as an unimportant acid trip."*

Later, Rena lights Terry's jade bowl while her mom holds it. I find it endearing, and I note that this is probably the closest I will ever get to being in a situation like those porn-folklore letters about mother/daughter action.

Terry says if I come by on Tuesday, he can get me some sweet Durban Poison. I can't stop giggling as I watch Rena's mom exhale a puff of blue-gray.

Over the weekend, for a cross-section of reasons I can't clearly identify, I feel the need to just get super, super drunk. I drink bourbon, gin, liqueurs, maybe a little distilled isopropanol, a bunch of lite beers, about twice as many full-calorie beers, some cough syrup, a few tin cups of moonshine. I also manage to wrangle from Old Fuck the number of a guy who has ether, so I huff a little of that, and at some point I open one of those little packets of silica beads and eat those, too.

I'm clearly acting out—at least in part—because my parents are not around anymore, and I'm not ready to be a man. Maybe part of this is a dream, but it's kind of hard to tell because I really am pretty fucked up. At some point, my mom appears and explains to me why she was so reluctant to issue positive reinforcement, which has something to do with the fact that her parents were cold and stoic and uninvolved and religious and looking forward to the promise of something uncertain instead of focusing on what they could control. I understand all of this, not that it makes me feel much better.

I also work up the nerve to open my phone, scroll through contacts to the Js, and click the SEND button with Julius Zorro's cell phone number selected. I get an outgoing message in which he seems to be doing an impression of some rapper, and I hear myself whining like the spoiled kid who once got a different toy than he expected for his birthday and proved all sorts of theories about commercialism:

"Look, Julius, I don't know what your, like, angle is. I'm kind of put off by those faxes. It's drawing all sorts of weird attention to me at a time when I really don't need that. Call me back at this number. [beat] And who faxes anymore? This is Harland, obviously."

I'm still fairly drunk as I close my phone, and the clock says 3:41, and it's dark out, and I feel pretty sorry for myself as I fall asleep on the couch.

Monday morning, feeling like I've been ravaged by demons, my hands somehow operate the computer keyboard atop the desk before me. How I even made it into work seems ambiguous, perhaps miraculous. Nestor explains by email that the additional black boxes he ordered should be arriving before Christmas, which somehow doesn't sound particularly festive. I write back, worrying about which government agency is going to intercept it and arrest everyone, remembering to ask how he came up with thirty grand to order the things, and if instead of pursuing whatever it is that we're pursuing, maybe we could use that money to go on a vacation. I have a last-minute urge to crumple up my message and toss it in the wastebasket, but that would require printing the thing, so I go ahead and click the SEND button.

Cindy walks by, purposefully ignoring me, maybe even uttering an audible, "Hmmph." I try to think of something equally cliché to do in retaliation, but nothing comes to mind, so I just flip off her back. It feels pretty good, because I don't get caught. I make a note in my phone that I want to make tee shirts that say, "It feels good because I don't get caught."

A few weeks go by, and I barely take note. Rena catches a cold and sounds like a jazz singer for a few days. Ollie gets another "job" handing out flyers for the band Tu$h, which he claims is getting signed by one of the corporations and is primed to "blow up real huge." I ask him to think about what he wants to say before speaking out loud. At one point, camped out by the billboards on the freeway again, which is a stupid idea because it's very cold out now, Nestor explains the sudden appearance of black box funds by noting that his company has a "discretionary R&D fund," and that he convinced his boss that the black boxes may represent the future of autopsy. I argue that it may be interesting to capture the last moments of life, but that the real focus should be on trying to capture the first moments of death. After debating the semantics of this, I realize that I'm onto something major that I will never have the energy to pursue.

Meanwhile, President Ruder's vitals remain uncannily static. His heart beats, his blood flows, and that's about it.

A few days before Christmas, I'm at work making copies of my hand for this last-minute Christmas card idea I have when a fax rolls into the output tray. The familiar digitized marker scrawl is present, Julius Zorro's latest dispatch, "HG—Got your vm. Sorry for delayed resp. Reception is bad here. Hope you make it to April Fools'.—JZ" I immediately crumple it up, uncrumple it, fold it in half, fold it in half again, and put it in my front left pants pocket.

Then I hear this ominous whistling, some horrible song from the '80's that's way too familiar in whistle form. I peek over my cubicle wall and see the big, red, sweating, salt-and-pepper head of Paul Jabber wandering down the hallway. He doesn't see me looking, and maybe it's on purpose. His greasy, puckered lips disappear behind a beige wall, and my faith in humanity sags a bit lower.

I knock on Roy's office door, peeking through an unfrosted strip in the otherwise frosted glass. I see a hand beckoning me in. I suddenly feel guilty for having willed this guy to explode so many times. He's on the phone, rolling his eyes up to the ceiling, pointing at the phone with the hand that's not holding it, and lifting his chest and lowering it procedurally, silently sighing. Some percentage of this is meant to amuse me, so I twist my face into a sympathetic smirk. This is good; we're starting out on the same page.

After a moment, he sets the receiver of his desk phone back in its cradle and stares at it, sighing again.

"Business or personal?" I ask.

"I don't know," says Roy, dry as the desert.

"I saw Paul Jabber," I say, leaving it an outline for Roy to color in.

"Yes, Mr. Jabber is back in the office." This is about as non-committal as what I said.

"He was whistling," I say.

"He's probably in a good mood," says Roy. He's making me color it in myself.

"So he's back-back?"

"Yes. She—" Roy's stop and start is somehow both abrupt and fluid. "There was a settlement. And not nearly what executive management thought it was going to be. And, they see … strategic advantages in retaining his services."

I struggle to get the sentence past my lips, but I do: "Does the company see … a strategic advantage in hiring back Laurel?"

Roy seems to register what I'm saying, and replies with maybe a hint of disappointment: "No."

"I see," I say. "Can I ask how much this cost the company?"

"That's confidential," says Roy. "Nor do I know. I have an idea, but I cannot confirm anything."

"How are we supposed to take this? The employees who didn't leverage our positions to touch people who didn't want to be touched?"

"Harland, I would advise you to let this go. It doesn't involve you, and there's nothing to be gained from it."

"What about the people who worked hard and won't get a bonus, because that money went to paying for bad behavior?" I'm obviously not referring to myself, but I feel like debating, even if it means sticking up for the common people.

"I take your point," says Roy, still diplomatic and not defensive. "It is not ideal. I have not heard that bonuses will be impacted."

"What, was there an insurance policy to cover executive molestation?"

"Harland, it is inappropriate to insinuate things that you cannot back up. No charges have been filed. This situation is resolved."

"What, are you getting money from this, too?"

"I understand that you are upset about this, Harland. I know that some people are going to be upset by this circumstance." Roy seems like a robot again. I see him forming calculations and following a digital decision tree.

A cloud formation appears to accumulate and then makes its way from the room. I ask, "Any more word from Julius Zorro?"

"Not that I'm aware of. Well, Cindy mentioned another fax, but I never saw it. What was that one about?"

"Beats me," I say, which feels quite honest. A series of miscommunications is both keeping me employed and threatening to unseat me. I feel like I'm wearing a sash that says, "Fuck with me."

Roy says, "Thanks for your professionalism regarding this." I assume he's back to placating me on the Paul Jabber situation.

"Thanks," I say back, spinning on my heel.

At the food court at the mall that white people still go to, Nestor delivers a lecture. I spoon nasty French onion soup into my mouth while Ollie licks a multi-hued ice cream cone. This mall is a few minutes away from the hospital where Nestor works, so he has time to meet here for lunch. Ollie has incorporated this into his "work" schedule, as he plans to litter every unguarded wall in the mall with duct-taped Tu$h flyers. A few hundred yards away, under the same meandering roof, Rena, understandably unable to take her lunch break during the lunch rush, brings fried noodles and mysterious curries to fat faces.

"We are going to test the black boxes ourselves," says Nestor, almost maniacally.

This sinks in, and I raise a pointer finger. "Nestor, quick question: Are you going to kill us?"

"No, Harland. I'm not going to kill you. And you don't have to kill yourself … not quite."

"What do you mean?" says Ollie, a ring of orange around his mouth.

"Ollie's got clown mouth," I say.

"I'm convinced, from what I've read, that the black boxes won't actually record anything unless the subject is in a life-threatening peril." Nestor seems to be repeating something he's memorized word-for-word. "There's a theory that the human body emits a special hormone when it believes it is dying. Some scientists call this hormone 'Thanatopside,' but it's not widely recognized yet. Anyway, the black boxes are supposedly activated by this."

"I have a strong feeling that this is the kind of thing that will provoke the government to murder us," I say with a mouthful of melty cheese.

"Couldn't we just buy some?" asks Ollie.

We halt and look at him.

"Buy what?" Nestor's face is in its blank-slate mode, which I realize he uses both when he's bored and when he's skeptical.

"Some *Thanastopide*, or however you say it."

"Well, Ollie, like I was saying, scientists are still in disagreement about whether this stuff even exists, so the likelihood that there's a warehouse of it somewhere is very low. But good thinking."

I kind of snicker at Nestor being a dick. It's a rare treat.

The fattest and most androgynous person I've ever seen waddles by, carrying paper bags with twine handles in each hand. I admire that this person is not using a fat-person scooter. Ornate logos on the bags read, MAX and MIN. There are either stores with those names or there's some symbolism I'm missing.

"Good luck convincing Rena to almost die in the name of science if it's not going to help orphans or something," I say. "Why don't we outsource this one?"

"We can't risk involving anybody else in this," says Nestor. "I haven't even told Dave."

"How's Dave?" I ask.

"I don't know. I'm getting pretty sick of cleaning up his dishes."

"When are you getting the things?"

"The tracking info indicates they're here on Friday."

"You're going first, Black Me," I say. "It'll be like a movie. Black guy dies first."

"Nice," says Nestor, smirking.

Ollie says, "I'm gonna go smoke."

In his car in the parking deck, Ollie's in the driver's seat, hunched over, rolling a joint on a Tu$h flyer on his lap. I nervously glance around to make sure no mall cops are snooping around. I see a sign indicating that this is section B EAST. I make small talk about what I might get Rena for Christmas. I know that there are three things for which she dropped fairly obvious hints, but I failed to write any of them down.

Driving back to work seems pretty fake. My right foot functions independently while my hands make the wheel thing turn as necessary. I'm pretty sure that I even use my turn signal appropriately. It's fun, or at least not nearly as stressful as sober driving.

By the time I arrive back at work (my flipped-open phone tells me it's about 1:35), it's really starting to get good. Standing outside my car, thinking seriously about crawling back inside and taking a nap, I hear jingly Christmas music. I can't tell the origin, and where I work is located in an industrial area that is not known for random bursts of festive audio, but I appreciate it all the same and carefully step my way up to the side entrance door I normally use to sneak in. When I swipe my pass card and pull on the handle, the door doesn't open. My first, panicked thought is that I've become extremely weak. I try again, and the door stays locked shut. I swipe again, hear the expected beep. I try again, pulling with both arms, my feet sliding toward the door so my profile becomes what must be some kind of scalene polygon.

After another long moment of deliberation, as the chill of December starts to permeate my coat, my shirt, my skin and fat, I resign myself to trudging around to the main entrance.

When I get there, I peer through the layers of glass doors to see if there's anyone in the lobby. I see only the receptionist, Rachel. I see her tufts of short, curly hair, and her bony, pale face bent over, working on things, or pretending to be working. I decide that it's now or never, so I pull open the main door, step into the decompression chamber, then pull open the secondary door. In the dim, dark wood and sparsely lit lobby, it occurs to me how few times I've actually entered Hell through the main gate.

Rachel's ghostly face, cast in blue from her computer screen, jerks up to identify me with round bug eyes. For a sick moment, I expect her to launch into my horoscope and explain the nature of my failings in a grizzled demon voice. She then morphs her poltergeist visage into the most wan smile that I've seen, which is almost worse.

"Hey, Harland," she says.

"Hey," I say, processing, processing, "Rachel."

I walk down the hall, fretting about how I almost asked her out five years ago. The carpet moves beneath me like a futuristic conveyor, nuances in the brown-on-brown pattern spelling out hints and foreshadowing. I make out the word "future" and the number 41. I become convinced that my third eye has glaucoma.

I pass by Berry's desk and he's half-whispering into a strange device that is either a telephone or an oboe. I hear the words, "never shoulda sold your hot rod, buddy," which seems like code for his intent to capture me. I make a rough crucifix with my pointer fingers, but he only sees me if those eyes protruding from the aft of his buzz-cut head are real. I have to remember to tell Ollie that that joint was laced with something. Or else it was just weed and I'm kick-starting myself into an adrenaline-driven hallucinogenic state. "Fugue" does not seem like the right term, though as soon as I think it, the soundtrack of my life becomes a complexly interwoven pattern of complementary themes. I fart a heroic crescendo, which may or may not be capped by the crash of cymbals.

As I round a cubicle wall to reach my desk, I see a large troll rummaging through my belongings, which soon resolves into a no-less-disturbing image of blood-haired Cindy shuffling papers.

"Can I, uh, help you?" I say, trying so hard to sound like a human being.

"I left you a voicemail and sent an email," says Cindy. "And I didn't have time to wait for you to get back from wherever you were."

"I was in the bathroom," I say. "I'm" —*try not to let this be the truth*— "sick."

"I'm trying to find that fax you received from that Zorro person. We've been getting a lot of unwanted faxes, and I'm submitting a list to our telephone provider to block certain numbers."

"Good," I say. "We don't need them wasting our precious resources. Right on."

"Where is that fax from the Zorro? I need the number."

"I think I filed it," I say, smiling at the idea that I would organize things. "I'll try to find it."

"OK," says Cindy. Her tone is short and harsh and violent. I almost cower. "I need it by four o'clock."

"Well, I will try to find it, so …" I shrug and yawn in her face.

She stares at me, trying to destroy my brain with her mind the way I do to Roy. So I stare back, willing her to unravel into a pile of snakes. It doesn't work, but I feel empowered. I stand with feet welded to the floor, forcing her to waddle around me in way that I hope makes her feel itchy.

"You know," I say, dead-eyed and monotone, "Adults are just the babies who survived childhood."

She freezes, turning to me and hissing, venom spilling from her maw, "Don't you dare talk about children!"

When the witch has wandered back into the wilderness, I extract my thick wallet and pull out the thick rectangle of folded paper. I unfold it until all three faxes are arranged in front of me.

Nothing happened.

Dad's fine. Thanks for your concern. But no thanks.

Got your vm. Sorry for delayed resp. Reception is bad here. Hope you make it to April Fools'.

As my cognitive potential begins to regenerate, a horrifying vibration throttles my right thigh. I pull the cell phone from my pocket and peel it apart. The listed number is "Unavailable."

"Hello?" I say quietly, curling into a ball in my office chair.

"Ruder won, just like I said," says Future Me. "Do you believe me now?"

"Yes," I say, shivering.

"OK, now listen. This is simple."

"OK," I say, mirroring Future Me. High and scared, I am exerting amazing amounts of energy trying to identify the voice, which still sounds digitized and filtered. Maybe this is the sound of a voice as it travels through time, I think. My voice?

"You have to go to the *inebriation*."

"What's that?" I say, not recognizing the final word in my state.

"The swearing-in ceremony of the new President." Future Me says this patiently, and waits a long moment for me to respond.

"I'll see if I can take it off," I say.

"It's very important that you attend." The voice sounds pleading, less android-like than I remember.

"How far out are you? Months? Years? Why don't you just go back to when I was a kid and make things different then?"

After a pause, the voice says, "Believe me, I would if I could." I hear static that might be a sniffle.

"Yeah, me too," I say. I register that I'm agreeing with myself, which seems pretty arrogant.

"I'll see you then," says the voice. Now my skin erupts into a mesh of bumps, and I hear my teeth chatter. I cycle through any number of scenarios to find one that does not pose a paradox of time and space. Before I can break my stunned silence, I hear the familiar click of an ended call. I feel borderline weepy at the fact that my buzz has been so abruptly stifled. I use both hands to fold the phone shut. I log back into the computer at my desk and look up the date of the planned inauguration. I know it was pushed out from January because of some clause in the Provisional Government contract, but I can't remember when it's supposed to be. Amidst a list of search results from forums and bulletin boards full of people complaining about conspiracies and Illuminati and extraterrestrial influence, I see the date:

April 1.

I stare at the date, my brain spinning within my head. I force myself to look away from the computer screen, all of this information that doesn't add up weighing on me and making me feel alone. I notice a list containing only the number 41 on the side of my left leg, and I realize that it is a mostly-clear sticker with excessive iterations of the inseam measurement of these too-big pants. I peel it off, fold it in on itself and throw it in the trashcan. I find this troubling, because I'm fairly sure I've owned these pants for over a year.

At a disconcertingly dark 5:30 p.m. on Christmas Eve, my car fishtails over the coating of slush. The potholes actually help to stabilize the direction of my car, as the tires slip into them as if the road is a slot car track. I pull into the large, largely vacant parking lot outside the mall white people don't go to anymore and manage to find a space right next to a handicap space. I remember Rena mentioning that "handicapped" people should be rebranded "unlucky."

I step out of my car under a glaring wash of light spilling down from a high pole and see my breath as a yellowish mist, my shadow cast over my reflection in a shallow puddle. It's dark upon dark, murky and distorted.

Inside, the dollar show has most of the same movie posters that I saw on my prior visit, although I notice that there's now a film called *Pro Janitor*. As the blurb on the colorful poster states: "His dad's a janitor. His mom's a janitor. The only way to escape the shadow of his heritage is to turn pro."

The nexus of the mall is vacant, a crisscross of shadows, and again I see dust swirling in the beams of light coming down from the high center. This time it's a few sparse columns of artificial light, as the skies beyond the skylights are black triangles. There's an ominous quiet. I sense the echoes of distant elevator music more than I actually hear them. My shuffled, reverberating footsteps create a semi-regular rhythm that seems small and lonely.

Passing into one of the grim, main corridors, six out of eight store entrances dark and gated, I feel a rush of hot blood, beads of sweat breaking through pores. Beneath my coat and my shirt and my undershirt, my fatty skin becomes sticky. The tickle of my fingertips on my palms heightens the tenseness in my jaw. I suppress a sudden need to urinate. I feel the flesh behind my knees begin to itch.

I slow my pace to a halt and peer through a glass wall into the jewelry store and see the clerk behind the counter, askew in a way that suggests she's leaning into it. The store is dim, but a halo of tiny spotlights give her form a soft glow, and her short, kempt, brown hair seems to blend into the atmosphere surrounding it. I see no customers, and she doesn't see me, and I start moving again, walking through the open space into the store. I move directly to the counter, and she turns with a dreamy delay to meet my eyes.

"Hello," I say first.

"Hello," she says, her voice velvety in tone.

"Do you remember me?" I ask. Whatever I am impersonating is confident and certain of what it wants. I do not break eye contact.

She takes a moment, her eyelids pulling tight, and speaks with a quiet deliberation: "I don't know."

This is good, I think. I am anonymous.

"I remember you." I enunciate with a volume befitting our proximity.

Her eyes become large and sad and hopeful. A front tooth pulls on her thick lower lip. I see her rub her fingers against her palms. Her chest, covered in a thin brown sweater, rises and falls. I hear her breathe.

The bottom drops out, in a sense, and my fears fall away. The context beyond this moment evaporates, and I can't conjure my name. I feel my nostrils flare, and I see a strand of her hair flutter over one cheek. In the high-contrast portrait of her face, I see her cheeks flush.

Something extends my arm, and soon my fingertips feel the side of her face, under the strand of hair. The hotness of her skin warms my cold fingers. She does not pull away from them. Our temperatures begin to compromise. I stroke behind her ear with four fingers, my thumb grazing her temple, pulling gently over straight, fine hair. She does not look away. She breathes quickly.

She grabs my other arm with both of her hands and pulls me sideways. We move sideways, the metal and glass counter passing between us. I feel fingers clinging to me with a magical urgency. She pulls me at an angle across the barely padded carpet to a door in a far corner, letting go of my arm with one hand to reach behind her and grab the doorknob.

We fall into the back-room office and the door closes by pneumatics or predestination. A faint light of uncertain origin transforms her silhouette into a tapestry of blues and grays. Her breaths come in little bursts of sibilant sound and sweet humidity. My knuckles contact hers and soon our fingers are entwined and grasping. My palm feels the pulse through her wrist. I take her other hand with my other hand. With this, her body presses to mine. I feel her breasts push against the top of my full abdomen. The heat permeates several layers of cloth. She directs her breathing to my neck, hot puffs that drive an incomparable sensation to my heels and toes. Now her fragrance is close and dense, some wild blend of flowers and cinnamon, and she becomes the air I breathe.

Her head moves back slightly, and through the dim light, I see tiny reflections of a human form in her eyes. Her mouth closes, and then she whispers: "Please."

Our mouths come together. She emits tiny sounds as she presses more firmly against me. Her hands unclasp from mine and begin to cling to the back of my coat. She then retracts them, sliding them inside my coat, over the back of my shirt. Her tongue comes into my mouth, and the sweetness of her breath brings another shiver that targets my knees. I realize that I'm moaning, breathing heavily through my nostrils as I lick her tongue and kiss her mouth. My hands go to her waist, and I'm exhilarated to find flesh so easily between her sweater and her skirt. The skin is soft and warm, despite the texture of tiny bumps I feel as I run my hands further across her back. My hands slide up her back to the bottom of her shoulder blades, and her soft vocalizations of pleasure intensify. I find the clasp of her bra and unhook it with one hand on my first attempt.

My hands gradually slide around to her abdomen and continue upward from her navel across warm skin to the lower border of her bra. I simultaneously slip both hands beneath the cups and feel hot, full breasts sticky with the slightest coating of perspiration. I squeeze her breasts gently, and she moans, her hips grinding against my pelvis. She kisses me harder now, pressing her face full force into mine. My fingers slip to her nipples and tug delicately. She responds with her entire body.

My hands drift down, sliding back around and into the back of her skirt. I press my fingers close to her skin to slide beneath her silky underwear. One of her hands slides down to my khakis, and rubs firmly over the two layers covering my insanely hard penis. As I hunch to slip my hands all the way into her skirt and grab her warm butt cheeks, I grunt, bending sharply, feeling her hot mouth move to my left earlobe and envelop it in warm wetness. I move my right hand down and around. As the rapidity of her breathing increases, my hands approach the hotness between her legs. Then I stiffen, croaking out a foreign noise, my body surging and then relaxing. I feel a stickiness like magma within my boxer briefs and realize that I have unceremoniously ejaculated.

"Um," I say.

She brings her head around to face me, still panting hungrily. Her expectant face, mostly in shadow, soon mirrors the disappointment that must be plastered across my own.

"Did you …?" She stops, knowing.

I sigh heavily, feeling my face blush in the dark.

She slowly withdraws, pulling her arms from under mine. She reaches around to refasten her bra. I bend over, thumbing the waistband of my boxer briefs away from my gut and feeling a rush of cold air permeating the dampness within. I let go of the waistband, and it snaps obnoxiously against my hairy belly.

She opens the door and exits the office into the glowing realm beyond. The door closes behind her. I stay in the dark, looking into a void.

In the parking lot, I imagine that there is a large crane with a camera looking down onto my car, recording the pathetic, husky man inside bawling like a baby. Once I have cried myself to exhaustion, I turn the key and hear an advertisement for "Her Pleasure" condoms. There's a generic rock riff and a sultry-sounding woman with a lisp. Soggy tissues litter the floor in front of the passenger seat. My headlights shine into a foggy, glistening expanse of vacant pavement. I turn the key and shift into Drive. I remember that I have to do my Christmas shopping.

I arrive home before midnight. As I pull into the driveway, I notice that the kitchen light appears to be the only one lit. I turn the key and shut off the headlights. The dome light remains momentarily and then fades away. I consider the text message that I sent to Rena earlier, which literally began with, "Ho ho ho." An overwhelming trepidation rattles me, and I fear that I will not be able to bring myself to leave the car. Then my hands unbuckle my seatbelt. Then I open the car door and get out.

I bring in the bag of groceries first, unlocking the door and expecting to hear Curly, then remembering. I put the eggs and sausage and bread in the refrigerator. I throw the plastic bag in the bigger plastic trash bag. It occurs to me that I forgot to grab coffee cream. I say "Fuck" to the microwave, and it looks back sympathetically.

I peek into the dark bedroom, and the faint light coming in from the kitchen reveals a pile of blankets that is Rena. I whisper, "Hey." No reply.

I strip my clothes and step into the shower. I step in while it's still cold and refuse to budge, even though it takes a full minute to warm up. I'm trying to prove something to myself, I think, pushing away the thought that I'm punishing myself.

Dried off, I pull on pajama bottoms and a tee shirt. Then I put on boots.

Back outside, I open the trunk of my car and grab the handles of two large McMart bags, clenching the bulk of one of them between my elbow and my knee in order to close the trunk without putting anything down. The trunk almost closes, pops back up, and I turn into a black and white slapstick reel as I repeatedly try to bat it closed while hampered with two heavy bags. I finally get the thing shut and am a little disappointed that I don't hear applause.

Back inside, I wrap the presents over the course of an hour while watching the muted television. The closed-captioning on a talk show is amusing for its phonetic spelling of the shit being shouted by members of the audience. "Yal dono nussinbow hata raza baby," says one. "Yo daddy gone, he don wanyo assnomo," says another one. Later, a heavyset white woman wearing a fuchsia blazer holds a penis-shaped microphone and says, "There's always a point where the innocuous turns malignant."

Somehow, even with probably three or four fewer hours of sleep than Rena, I awaken first of my own accord, yanked from a nightmare about mirrors that stop working. I start the coffee. I scour the cabinets and manage to find some non-dairy creamer, which is on the minor end of compromises that Rena is going to have to deal with if we are to stay together.

Slumping into a hard kitchen chair, I see a vision of a Christmas when I was eight years old. I came downstairs to my giggling parents. I remember thinking at the time that they were laughing at me, at my disheveled straight-out-of-bed and cowlicked appearance. Now I believe they were probably laughing at something unrelated. Maybe it was evidence of their connection. Or maybe they were just passing the time with a joke. The point, I guess, is that it didn't have to be about me. Which still hurts.

I remember opening a book of riddles, not from both of them, nor from the recently discredited notion of Santa Claus, but specifically from my dad. It was *Ridiculous Rick's Big Book of Tricks*, or some such mouthful of a title. Anyhow, I soon found that the thing was mostly full of puns, shoddy wordplay but not what I would call logic puzzles.

Q. What do you call a lemming who doesn't follow the leader?

A. A lemon.

Further in the book, arranged according to supposedly increasing difficulty, some of the "trickier" riddles were actually riddles. One in particular stuck with me:

Q. A man was on trial for robbing a bank. The man claimed that when he went into the bank vault it was empty. The prosecuting attorney responded that he could prove that the alleged thief was lying. What did the attorney say?

A. "If the man was in the vault, it could not have been empty."

I remember feeling outraged at that stupid logic. I remember thinking, *But what if the man was also empty?*

◎

Rena calls my name with a broken morning voice that startles me.

"Merry Christmas," I say, catching my breath and strolling into the bedroom.

"Come lay with me," she says.

"OK," I say.

I crawl under the covers and she slides next to me. Then she reaches down and touches my crotch. I hold my breath.

We have quiet sex, and neither of us can reach orgasm, and after a while we stop.

◎

I push a spatula into a frying pan full of runny eggs. We eat breakfast and drink coffee and Rena talks about something. When a withered piece of sausage bursts between my teeth, I feel sick.

Later, Rena tears the wrapping paper from a few movies. Her reaction is polite, and I wonder if maybe I confused which redheaded actress it is that she likes so much. She unwraps a box containing a fruit juicer. She looks at me quizzically, asking, "What's really in here?" She smiles knowingly.

I say, "A juicer."

"No it's not," she asks, still smirking, seeming to be in on a joke I haven't told.

"Well, I hope it is," I say. "But I still have the receipt if it's not."

Her face falls. "Oh." I hear wind blowing outside. "Thanks. Thank you."

I smile stoically, fake like my mother. "You're welcome. Merry Christmas."

She's sitting next to me. She seems awfully far away.

I open boxes with pants and shirts that I'm going to have to wear. Then

I open what is thankfully a videogame that I've actually been wanting, the new Lee Harvey Oswald FPS.

"'Death Depository,'" I say. "Thanks, honey." I flip the box over to read the blurb on the back aloud:

> *Are you a disgruntled ex-Marine with a political axe to grind? Or are you being set up in a high-level conspiracy involving Wolf Nixon and Cuban Vampires? You decide! Fight your way to the truth and emerge at the moment of your destiny. Beware sinister Jack Rubies, befriend decoys on the grassy knoll, and discover the Magic Bullet to achieve unique Kennedy Kill Kombos™.*

I tear off the plastic and turn on the television. My self-hatred eases as I enter the alternate reality.

Nestor texts that the things have arrived and that he has to find an angle to smuggle them out of the morgue. For some reason he is fixated on doing the experiment on New Year's Eve.

Because I had burned my vacation days earlier in the year when Rena and I went up north to her uncle's cabin to sit around and wonder what it would be like to afford a proper vacation, I have to go into work for the days after Christmas, for which all of the reasonable people have saved their vacation days. So I'm basically in the office alone, save for the scattered others with poor planning skills and one bummed-out manager whose name I have yet to learn who's low enough on the totem pole to be stuck as our babysitter.

I walk around and see the office, some of it dim and completely vacant, and I resist multiple urges to curl up under a cubicle and nap. I also resist some (not all) urges to open people's desk drawers. I find a snack in one of the three I do open, which seems like good odds. I chew on a name-brand premium granola bar as I continue my exploration. I find a door open to the warehouse, go back into the long aisles lit only by sparse exit signs and try to jog my memory as to what it is that this company I work for actually does.

Lapping back to my desk, I check my email to find the status quo. I count the contacts in my cell phone. There are twenty. Six of the names are people who I can't really picture anymore. I look at the pictures I have stored for Ollie and Rena (the only contacts whose photos I have bothered to store). Ollie is grinning big and looking above the camera. Rena is chewing on her thick glasses, feigning to appear pensive or studious. I still have my dad's phone number, and a part of me wants to press SEND. I bow out at the thought of a ghost answering.

I find the Human Resources office door locked. Accounting office is also locked. President's office: locked. I see somebody in reception, but it's not Rachel or the albino girl. I wander up. She's got a black bob haircut and rosy cheeks. She looks like that black-and-white cartoon chippy that my mom used to talk like when she wanted to be both funny and condescending. I hold my breath as I approach the desk.

"Hey," I start.

"Hi," she says. She seems pretty normal, which sort of bugs me.

"I heard Jabber mention yesterday they're letting us out at two today if we don't have work to finish up."

"Oh, really?" I can't tell if she's calling my bluff with sarcasm.

"Yeah," I say. "I'm Harland." I hold out my hand, which will feel warm to her because it's been buried in my pocket. She shakes it weakly, and her hands feel like they would work pretty well in a sex situation.

"Roxanne," she says, her voice a little rattly now, which suggests that she smokes. "I actually just started two weeks ago."

"Nine years," I say. I sigh for her benefit. "Big doin's."

"Wow," she says, according to some script for scenarios like this.

"Have you met Jabber yet?"

"No," she says. "He's a … VP, right?"

"I don't know what his title is now," I say. "Just watch out for him. He'll try to rape you."

"What?" she says. "That's not funny to joke about."

"I know," I say. "I'm not. He was supposed to have been fired for sexual harassment, but he cut a deal. He was on unpaid leave for like six or seven weeks. But I think he had some dirt on one of the other execs, so they caved."

"We … shouldn't be talking about this." She seems to shiver, and she looks over her shoulders to see who might be witnessing this.

"This isn't a practical joke. I just wanted to give you the heads-up."

"Thanks," she says, looking disgusted. She looks down at the desk, then back up at me. "You shouldn't joke about rape."

"I wasn't," I say, whining like a kid again. I inhale and exhale. "Sorry … Roxanne. I didn't mean offense. Just don't want you being another statistic."

She seems bored now, which makes me feel like I should apologize much more emphatically. I count backwards from five, seeing sheep jumping a fence. I force myself to walk away. I feel her looking through me from behind, like I'm some kind of creep.

By some stroke of luck (probably careless cleaning staff), Roy's dark office is unlocked. I wander in and push the door closed. I stroll over behind his desk and sit in his chair. The room is dark, and the dimly lit hallway appears warped through the frosted glass wall in front of me. I glance to each side and see the twin ostriches, their heads bowed, but significantly not in the ground. I feel no sense of power in Roy's chair. It's not very soft or comfortable. I feel a bit sorry for him, and I struggle to assure myself that the notion is not strictly a defensive one. The framed picture on Roy's desk shows a woman in her forties and two girls probably in their late teens or early twenties. *If they're not legal,* I think, *I'll sacrifice my hands.* Nevertheless, they look very chaste and reverent, which doesn't exactly hurt the fantasy. Roy is probably with his family right now, and they're probably wearing similar sweaters and not thinking anything of it.

I take a moment to contemplate what it is that I want out of life. I only get as far as determining that it is not in this building. I try to open Roy's desk drawers, but they're locked. At this point, I notice a crocheted cloth hanging on the wall to the left. It bears the words, "You can't win them all."

On the thirtieth (New Year's Eve Eve) I go to this bar a few cities over where Julius Zorro supposedly hung out, according to all of his long-cached Internet bragging. I wear a baseball cap and smoke a cigarette, which I try to convince myself is sufficiently *incognito*. I meet this woman who looks like she has been in a war, and she explains the best way to show a man a good time: "Bite the pilla'." I call her Old Fuckette and she doesn't seem to hear me.

I order a double whiskey and Canker and drink it too fast. A neon sign at the far end of the bar reminds everyone that this place is called "Slaggers." A poster beneath the sign depicts four mop-topped young men in black suits, all wearing Groucho glasses. This place is empty except for some bar flies and touristy people. It does not look like a place where young professionals would want to hang out, so I assume there must be some ironic appeal. Then I remember that I am not particularly young or professional, so maybe I don't know anything.

I feel out of place without anyone I know to crack wise at. My security blanket is missing; my yes-man was uninvited. I doodle on a napkin and wait for something to happen. The doodle is a heavy-browed madman whose jagged-toothed mouth opens into a sharp, dangerous-looking speech bubble, proclaiming, THERE'S NO ESCAPING ME!!!

The muted television shows some kind of ball-kicking game that's popular overseas but whose name I can't recall for some reason. I order another double. I begin wondering if I could will myself to grow some ultimately benign tumors just to get a paid medical leave from my job. I wonder how funny my mom would think that idea is.

I picture Washington, DC, a scab picked from a map tattooed on a big, battered arm. It has scabbed over again, I realize, and soon new flesh might thrive there. To evoke real change, someone must be thinking somewhere, you're going to have to remove the whole arm.

The bartender, who looks like a gorilla wearing an apron, refills my glass from a bottle and the soda nozzle. He doesn't offer new ice, but I don't really care. I assume that he must know some basic sign language to communicate with his trainer. I find myself beginning to pour my heart out to him without either prompting or resistance.

"… and I like to wonder whether my Dad's scheming ever meant anything. You know? Like, you—you probably have your own stories about growing up. You grew up a certain way, and like, I don't know, that's just what you knew. I had this situation, but I didn't know that it was or wasn't supposed to be that way. It was just my life. And now I'm cursed with this ability to think about things, to analyze them and shit, just tear them apart and break them down. Like, deconstruct, you know what I mean?"

The gorilla wipes the inside of a glass with a rag and keeps paying attention to me with tired eyes. Only two of his huge fingers fit inside the thing. I can't tell if the musty smell is from him or just the age of this place. The nostrils on his snout flare. I feel certain that he could kill me with a simple extension of his arm into my chest. Then I'm continuing, just babbling to him like he's my therapist in a way that strikes me as stereotypical and comforting.

"… because that's how you're meant to be. You can't really choose who you are. Not really. I mean, you hear about the 'self-made man,' but Jesus, who has the audacity for that? The only people willing to strike out and try to be themselves are fucking assholes. Meanwhile, the people with real potential are too busy worrying about how they're gonna approach it. When's the right time? When do I pounce? All I know is that, you try, you try to work outside the system, and people are gonna resent you for it. That's what my dad did, and my mom ended up hating him, or at least claiming that she did. Then my mom tries—pretends—to be this holier-than-thou victim and gives herself cancer, and I resent her for not just nipping things in the bud. I could have just as easily been an abortion. And now, tomorrow night I gotta pretend to kill myself just to see if this magic device works on the living … that probably sounds crazy, but that's just too simple an answer … I want things to work, but I feel like a sellout when I'm happy. I can only get hard on conflict, you know?"

"Fuckin'-A, Brub," says a familiar voice.

I turn around on my stool to see the bony, mustached face of Todd Crabs.

"I'll tell you how things is going, Harland. Shitty. Things are real fucked up and stupid, too. Did you know that divorce costs a million goddamn dollars? A fuckin' million, Chooch."

"Bummer, man," I say, sipping my third drink, now in a booth across from my curly-haired ex-coworker.

"First Uncle Sam takes a third. OK, three million down to two. Fuck it. That's how it is, even now. This was before DC, but shit ain't changed. You get three mill' today, they're taking a third of it. Fuck it. They can suck my cock 'til eleven o'clock. Bite the fucker off, might as well. Bite a third of it. Ass-pumpers. And then I cain't buy shit without sales tax. What the fuck, Brub? Ain't that a double-stick 'em up? They gonna tax my tax now. 'Oh, I see you paid a million dollars in taxes. Well, there's tax on payin' taxes now.' Fuckin' animals. I see Uncle Sam tomorrow, I'm 'a kick 'im in the tip."

"Exactly," I say, pointing at him for emphasis. He could be saying anything and I'd be agreeing.

"So then this donkey-show-level tramp I used to call my wedded wife waits 'til that shit's in the bank. She's checkin' the Internet website every day, lookin' at the bank balance. I mean, we both are, 'cause I want it too.

The day—the very day—that shit registers, she prints these divorce papers and hands 'em to me. And I'm up shit's creek, because I ain't got no pre-nup. Not that it would prolly matter anyway, 'cause we got this as a thing while we're married. And she didn't say shit why—I mean I gotta guess it was in part because I cheated with her ex-best friend. But fuck, I never woulda touched that tattooed skank if I knew it cost a fuckin' million dollars. Million-dollar pussy. That's expensive pussy. That's like two-hundred-grand-for-a-handjob expensive. Fuck that shit. I hate it. Stupid fuckin' bullcrap. I mean, yeah, I still got a million dollars. But shit, I had three million like two weeks before, Brub. That's a bad gambling trip. That's a shoppin' spree where you gotta walk home 'cause your car broke down. Fucked up. Plus, I got a STD."

"What?"

"Yeah, Chooch. My shit is burnin' up. I got so depressed after Traci left that I didn't do nuthin' but bang hoes for like three months straight. And now I got like the clap or simplex two or some shit. My dick's a fuckin' flamethrower, Chooch. Now I gotta rubber-up and I got the drips. Not a good thing, Harland. Double-bag that shit. Keep your pecker in a sleeping bag. Them skanks got it all, and they're ready to share."

"Damn," I say, beckoning someone I hope is a waitress.

The conversation with Todd Crabs quickly unravels into a drinking contest, and I have a handicap of three. We start/I continue with Bloody Marys because, according to Todd, "You don't wanna end with 'em, Plumps." "Plumps" is my new nickname, because I'm about twice Todd's weight. I call him "Pegleg," but it doesn't feel quite right, so I just go back to calling him Todd Crabs.

"I can't really pull off nicknames," I explain to no one in particular. "I sound like an old man trying to fit in." I burp and taste celery.

"Aren't we the same age?" says Todd Crabs, not really asking.

We make a horrible mistake by following with eggnog-based shots the homely waitress with glasses that are too big for her face calls, "Reindeer Cum."

Todd claims to have once been dishonorably discharged from Basic Training, although I don't know enough about military protocol to judge this one way or the other. He says he got his bachelor's degree at a community college in six months. He pulls up the bottom of his black ASK ME ABOUT MY STUMP t-shirt to show me a tattoo below his navel that reads, SUCK MY. I also notice what I guess is an appendix removal scar.

"Nah, Plumps," he groans. "Kidney. That bitch Traci got half my kidneys too, even before the divorce."

"Wow," I say. "Was she on dialysis?"

"I don't know, man," he says, his head sinking and shaking. "She was just a needy-ass bitch, I guess."

"Yeah," I say. The waitress brings two tumblers full of what she says is primarily pickle juice.

"Picklebacks," she says.

We down the shots, and I vomit a little in my mouth and swallow it back down. I pull off my red baseball cap and rub the saturated lining with my thumb.

"I ain't spent shit, man," says Todd. "I mean I got a new TV and a car and that's it. For a while, I couldn't even look at my bank statement. Made me sick. It was big, but so much less than it was supposed to be, you know? But after a while, I started to realize that maybe it was good I was so pissed off when I got the money, 'cause I didn't feel like spending it. Still just sittin' on my ass, drinking cheap-ass beers, thinkin' about how to go back in time and divorce her ass three months earlier. So I didn't go crazy like some stupid fuckin' rap monkey who spends every last penny on bling before he finds out his second album didn't sell shit. And that ain't racist. Buncha one-hit-wonder white monkeys did that shit, too."

"White monkeys," I say, focusing on words to avoid vomiting.

"I got resources, Brub, and I still don't know how to change the world."

"Resources," I say.

"Cash, bitch." He squints. "You drunk? You punk-ass motherfucker, you're drunk. What the hell, Chooch?"

"I had three 'fore you got here," I try to say.

"What?" He looks at me like I just farted, which I may well have. "You're a mess, Harland. You still at that stupid fuckin' place?"

"Yeah," I say, my own head drooping.

"Damn," he says, puckering his mouth to one side, forehead wrinkling. "That's fucked up."

"Yeah," I say.

"You ever use that password I gave you?"

"Yeah," I say. "Not long 'go."

"Oh yeah? You fuckin' shit up?"

"Trying to find this quit jerk," I say. "A real … fuckin' d-bag. Started way after you left, like eight months ago. Then he quit. Now he keeps faxing me."

"Faxing?" Todd looks offended.

"I know. That's almost the worst part. I don't know, I think he's trying to get me fired or something because he left after I sort of started to maybe threaten him so he'd rig me a pay raise that I don't even really need, I guess. I was just bored. Then when my boss asked me about it, I told him that he was just a weird dude and he quit because he had to go take care of his sick dad. But then somehow Zorro finds out about it and faxed me about it and it just freaked me out."

"Zorro?" Todd Crabs slams back a beer, gaining on me.

"That's his last name. Anyway, now I'm supposed to go to the inauguration on April Fools' Day and—Future Me told me to meet him there."

"You're not makin' much sense, Plumps."

"I don't know," I slur. "I get these calls from myself in the future, and I'm real condescending."

"So this punk who quit is faxing you, and yourself from the future keeps calling you on the phone?"

"Yeah. I know."

"And they both want you to go to the inauguration for the vegetable?"

I try to think about what I've said. "Fuck, what's wrong with me?"

"We should go and kick both their asses, Plumps."

I think about this. I don't have any better ideas.

"Yeah," I say. "If I don't die swallowing that death box tomorrow, we should totally go."

Todd Crabs looks at me. "Right on, Plumps."

166

8 GHOSTS

My garage is the de facto location for New Year's Eve, because it's the only place with adequate space where no one will care if we vomit on the ground. A space heater is doing little to combat the dry freezing weather seeping in through the two poorly caulked windows. My body feels recently reconstructed from spare parts. I try to remember the name of the bar from the previous evening, and it hurts my head. The reconstructed image of Todd Crabs seems artificial and contrived. I search for a "reset" button.

"Isn't that what astronauts use?" Ollie grins.

"What?" asks Nestor, focusing on delicate placement of a large purple duffel bag on the particleboard workbench.

"A space heater."

Nestor tilts his head forward and glares at Ollie. Rena looks like someone kicked her in the stomach and says, "No more jokes from you. You're banned."

"Knock knock," says Ollie.

"Who's there?" I ask.

"*Deathto.*"

"Death to whom?" I ask.

"The infidels!" Ollie cackles weirdly. I smirk, surprised he actually knows that word.

"So, what's the exact purpose of this ill-advised pursuit?" Rena asks.

"We're going to verify the functionality of the black boxes," says Nestor.

"Didn't we, like, do that a month ago?" I taste tartar sauce and smack my mouth, grimacing.

"We heard the output supposedly captured from a woman who died," says Nestor. "I want to see if we can get them to work without actually dying."

"Well, I like the not-dying idea," I say.

Nestor unzips the duffle bag, peeling back a large flap to reveal four semi-shiny black objects. I notice from the unfurled flap that the interior of the purple bag is red, like its guts have been cut open.

"Those look bigger than I remembered," says Rena.

Nestor shrugs. "I think they're the same model as what we saw before."

"You guys are completely out of your goddamned minds if you're really going to try to swallow those."

"Hey," I snap, "*We're* swallowing them. All of us. We're in this together."

Rena turns and looks at me without anything in her face.

"Come on!" I whine. "You can't just ditch us at the last minute."

"I don't want to die, Harland. I'm sorry. It just sort of occurred to me."

"You're not going to die," I say, "necessarily. Right, Black Gay Me?"

"I am certified in CPR, and I've administered the Heimlich maneuver multiple times," says Nestor. "I've dated my share of chokers."

While I try to parse what Nestor is saying, Ollie simply looks mortified.

"And I said I would go first," he says. "Or you did, Harland. Black guy dies first. I know the rules. Rena, you know CPR, right?"

"I have to because of my job," she says. "But I really didn't learn it for use in situations where it's planned that we might need it."

I work to comprehend what Rena means, but from Nestor's continued activity situating materials, I take it that she has implicitly accepted the plan. Once Nestor has placed all four devices on this felt cloth he has laid on the table, he pulls out a canister of shortening.

"Oh shit," I say. "Are we gonna have to get buttfucked, too?"

"This will help get it in and out," says Nestor.

"What did I say?" I ask, mugging.

After miscellaneous preparations for which I have zero patience, Nestor is finally seated in the folding chair as Rena, Ollie, and I stand around him expectantly. He holds the greased black plastic thing in his flattened palm as if he's serving it. Or as if he has just received the weirdest tip of all time. Its rounded corners are white and shiny with shortening. Nestor chews his lip nervously, and I'm transported to a jewelry store for a moment, returning with hot cheeks, a cold neck, and a burning sensation in my stomach. For the first time I'm realizing what this thing might reveal when it's pulled from my stomach.

Nestor leans his head back and pushes the thing into his mouth with two fingers, coaxing it down his throat. While I acknowledge that my concern should be with my friend as he risks his ability to breathe in the name of some kind of informal science, I can't help trying to quickly piece together which of the things I feel guilty about have actually happened and which were depressing wet dreams.

Nestor squints like he's been sprayed by something, both hands wiggling extended fingers in front of him like he's a monster trying to get us, giving the effect of some sort of temporary palsy. Then he visibly swallows the thing. Now it's in him. He opens his eyes wide and gasps. When he catches his breath, he says, "It's in."

"Was that enough?" I ask.

"Enough what?" he asks, starting to grasp his abdomen with both hands.

"Enough of a death effect?" I don't know how to phrase it. "Is that enough—like, were you even choking? Do you think the death effect happened?"

"The death hormones," says Ollie, helpfully. "The *Thantostoppies*."

"Thanatopside," says Nestor. "I don't know." He looks uncertain for the first time. "I guess I thought—the—the process of swallowing would trigger it. But I didn't really choke. It was not easy to swallow, but that was only about twenty seconds. And I never really felt scared like you would when you're choking."

"What the fuck are we doing?" Rena bends her palms into her eye sockets.

The pause that follows seems long. The garage seems to get colder.

"We could try to drown you," says Ollie.

I watch Nestor's reaction as it morphs from horrified to admiring.

While I rinse the plastic tub, Nestor recounts the guidelines for a third time. We're back in the kitchen. Nestor still has that thing in his stomach.

"You'll hold my head under until you feel me start to struggle. Then you hold it for fifteen more seconds. No more. Rena will keep track on her phone. This should make me freak out enough that I go into the death throes. And if it doesn't, we might be stuck, because I'm not willing to see the netherworld for this. Anyway. The water—it should be cold but not freezing. That will add to the effect, and in my panic I might think I'm drowning in a river. Warm water would be too welcoming. Like being born."

◎

Back in the garage, Ollie and I use a combined four hands to hold Nestor's head down, pressing his face against the bottom of the plastic tub. A few bubbles pop up on either side of the island created by Nestor's head in the water. Ollie and I look at each other, reciprocating with rare, genuine eye contact. I glance at Rena, whose expression suggests that she feels helpless to stop the apparent murder being committed before her. I kind of chuckle as I realize that this has all of the aesthetics of a hate crime with none of the intent.

After what must be close to a minute the cords in Nestor's neck suddenly tense, and I feel his head jerk. I yell at Rena: "Start counting!"

"Fifteen," she says, tears in her eyes. "Fourteen."

Nestor flails and grasps at Ollie's hands and my hands. He grips one of my wrists, and his fingernails dig into my skin.

"Ow!" I yell. "What the fuck?"

"Nine," sobs Rena.

"We're really drowning him!" Ollie looks scared and small.

"He said fifteen seconds once he started struggling. He must know his limits, right?" I'm pleading with my mouth and fighting the desire to let go.

"Sih-ix." A saliva bubble has formed on Rena's distraught mouth.

Ollie starts bawling, inhaling with horrid gasps, and now I'm doing the bulk of the drowning.

"Come on, Ollie!" I yell, tears falling down my cheeks. "I'm not going to be the only one who drowns him."

"Three."

I start to panic as the resistance begins to wane. His hands fall away from mine and Ollie's wrists.

"Two one! Let him up!" Rena screams, her hands covering her face as she involuntarily lifts herself on tiptoes.

Ollie and I let go, and Nestor doesn't rise.

"Oh fuck!" My stomach feels poisoned.

Ollie and I pull Nestor up by his collar, water splashing us and dripping from his limp head. His eyes are one-third open, and for a split second I expect to see translucent secondary eyelids like a drowsy cat.

"Oh fuck!" I yell. "Oh fuck."

We lay Nestor on his back on the cement floor of the garage. Rena takes off her coat and starts to put it under Nestor's neck.

"Call 911," Rena snaps at me, bending to her knees.

My whole body goes numb, but I manage to pull my phone from my pocket and pry it open.

As Rena leans over Nestor's face to begin CPR, Nestor gasps desperately and sits up, impacting Rena's nose audibly.

"Ahhh!" yells Rena, leaning back on her knees, falling backward onto the ground and cupping her nose with both hands. "Oww!"

"Oh no," says Ollie, his sobs slowing.

"Holy shit," I say. "Nestor, are you OK?"

Nestor, looking like he's mid-stomach crunch, blinks a few times and looks up at me. A guttural voice says, "That had to be more than fifteen seconds."

Ollie and I pull an unopened, white garbage bag flat on the garage floor, and I grab a roll of duct tape and tape down the two corners nearest me. I hand Ollie the roll and he tapes down the other corners.

"OK, Captain Vomit," I say, feeling twice my age. "Do your worst."

Nestor hunches over, palms on his knees, and starts heaving violently. He lunges repeatedly, producing more and more drool but no black box. The sound and/or sight of it is too much for Rena, who visibly gags and covers her mouth with a fist. She turns around and yells over her shoulder, "I'll be in the kitchen."

Nestor keeps heaving. "Push," I say, giggling. "You're at thirteen centimeters."

Nestor ends his bow, looking at me like I tried to kill him. "You're so funny."

"Come on, bro," I say, "you made it. And that thing's probably covered in Thanatopside."

Without a reply, Nestor bends over and heaves. I see a degree of blood intermingled with the drool now, and I see that Ollie sees it too. Once again, we're making that meaningful eye contact, and I suddenly have a very sad thought that one day we might be making that same eye contact through the bulletproof glass of a prison visitation booth. Despite the vividness of this vision, I can't tell who's inside and who's visiting.

Finally, with a crackling sound, the slime-covered black box falls from Nestor's mouth. The thing lands with a thump onto the white garbage bag, runny redness splashing outward in an objectively pretty pattern. He begins to bend back to his full height, and the garage is unnervingly quiet. Then he suddenly leans down again and launches a wave of reddish-yellow vomit all over the thing.

"Damn, Nestor," I say. "You didn't have to get all bukkake on it."

"Looks like macaroni and cheese with ketchup," says Ollie, grimacing. This causes my stomach to lurch and I almost join in the puke party. I catch myself, exhaling in disgust.

Nestor stands up for real this time. He wipes his sloppy lips with the back of his hand and slurs, "Let's see what it says."

Having spent three whole minutes convincing Rena to come and join us back out in the garage, Nestor is now using sterilized salad tongs to place the vomit-, shortening-, and hopefully Thanatopside-covered black box directly on top of the pristine QBBR231.

"You sure you shouldn't clean that off?" says Rena, grimacing.

Nestor's lack of response implies that her question was rhetorical. I note to remember that tactic. He's intermittently having spasms, his gut still in heave mode. He tips back a water bottle and squirts it into his mouth like a boxer between rounds. He swishes and spits into a small, plastic trashcan. I watch Rena's sour expression.

Soon, the familiar combination of tones begins to resonate, meaning that Nestor has switched on the receiver. The garage is very still and quiet now, a single weak bulb illuminating us, the aroma of regurgitation minimized by the cold. I get chills. My arms swell with tiny bumps. I feel all sorts of things that I can't handle processing. The pulsing chord from the QBBR231 and its daisy-chained array of auxiliary devices is very warm. I embrace the trance. When the detached, sterile voice begins speaking, I'm not nearly as scared as I would be without the tones.

This is the final capture of subject Nestor Desmond Little.

I can tell that we all get chills at the words "final capture." The cold, dissociated voice continues its abhorrently rigid speech pattern.

Oh my God they are killing me. They are killing me. These horrible motherfuckers. These homophobic crackers. I thought they were my friends. Harland you fat asshole let go of me. Get your stupid pothead friend off of me. You fucking losers. I will kill you. There is no way it has not been fifteen seconds already. I have so much left that I want to do. I want to write that novel about the detective who finds clues about his own murder in a time loop. I want to see Paris. I want to run a marathon. Let go of me you horrible fucks. I am worth so much more than you. I actually contribute to the world. I do not want to end up in the morgue. No one should end up there. This is not fair. This is not how it was meant to be. If somehow I do not die I am going to be a millionaire. But if I die then there is no point. They will not know what to do. I want good in this world. I want good and I am failing. Oh no. This is dying.

The voice stops, and the beautiful harmony continues, somehow swelling in the vacuum left by the now-absent voice. Nestor looks at his feet. His shoulders rise and fall slowly. I can tell he's mortified. I step forward and his head rises, large wet eyes. I grab around his sunken shoulders and pull him into me, hugging him as completely as I can.

"Hey," I say. "Hey man. You're … fine. I totally understand. We understand. Right?"

Ollie and Rena nod, and then Ollie says, "Yeah."

"You thought we were killing you," I say, as softly and precisely as I can. "It was desperation. You didn't mean it. You can't help what you think. And we're not taking it the wrong way, right?" I glance at Rena and Ollie, nonverbally begging for support.

"Yeah," Ollie says again, nodding more obviously.

Nestor's head sinks into my chest, and soon he's bawling in what must be complete catharsis.

"It's OK," I say. I feel Rena's arms around my sides, so now I'm the middle of a hug sandwich. Ollie joins, and we're one big group hug, each of us crying in varying degrees.

Once the hug disbands, I clear my throat and say, "Who wants to watch the ghost of the Top Forty guy?"

"Just to be clear," says Rena, curled on the couch, pulling the blanket up to her neck, "No one else is swallowing one of those. No one. We're done with that. Agreed?"

"Agreed," says Ollie, without hesitation. He sits in the blue easy chair, his arms crossed and his hands rubbing opposite elbows.

Nestor follows, "Yes, agreed. No one else needs to go through that. We verified that it works. We found out what we needed to find out."

Rena looks at me, waiting. I let her wait. Finally, she says, "Harland."

"Yeah, I heard you."

"Do you agree?" She's becoming my mother again, stern without anything to back it up.

"Yeah, sure, whatever."

"Harland," she says, "I don't want you dying for no reason."

"Dying for a cause is overrated," I say. "I'd rather die for nothing."

On television, some plastic-skinned woman with bright red lips and bleach-blond hair is saying something very emphatically into a penis-shaped microphone. Behind her halogen-illuminated mask is a crowd of people in hats and scarves and coats and mittens, some holding champagne glasses, many making high-pitched vowel sounds. The scene takes place at night, but the degree of artificial light is severe, so it almost looks like a stage play. Rolling waves of people in the crowd create an indiscernible static whose echo keeps folding in on itself. It's relentless. I find the amount of enthusiasm on display for this simple passage of time to be deeply troubling. I pass the kangaroo dick to Nestor, and the televised image switches to the top of some skyscraper (or a green-screen studio with the image of the skyscraper top digitally inserted) where some ugly puppet slurs incoherently into a microphone that obscures most of his jowls. Ollie claims the person on TV is still alive, but I argue that he died three years ago, and that Hollywood animators have resurrected his likeness in the name of tradition.

"Why would they make him look like that?" asks Ollie, biting into a chocolate bar.

"Because they want to fool people like you into believing he's still alive," I say. "Give me a bite of that."

Ollie hands me the remaining half of his candy bar. I dislodge it from the wrapper and shove all of it into my mouth.

"Hey," he says.

"*Whuh*," I say with my mouth full.

"*Frr blafed mlopnu*," says the puppet on TV.

"See?" I say, swallowing chocolate, which tastes unbelievably good. My brain begins clicking back to functionality as the THC hits my core.

"Nestor, dude. You said—in the black box, I mean—you said that if it worked, that you were gonna be rich. You'd be a millionaire. What was that?"

Nestor pretends to be focused on lighting the pipe.

"Hey," I say. "Pot hog. You hear me?"

Nestor takes a big toke, leaning over the corner between the sofa and the loveseat to pass the glass pipe over to Rena. When he exhales, it looks like a mushroom cloud. I know he's ignoring me, and I follow his gaze back to the television. On the screen, an apparently homosexual wizard in a shiny blue suit makes wild predictions about the economy, the weather, which divorced celebrities will get back together. It cuts back to the blond cyborg, who says, "Thanks, Chance," with an affected lisp, which seems like it would have been difficult to program. "This New Year's Eve telecast is sponsored by Gravity. *Gravity: You're Not Going Anywhere.*"

"Hey," I say, beginning to get pissed. "Black Me."

Nestor finally turns. I can't tell if he's scowling on purpose, or if he's exhausted or wasted. "What?" His mouth seems a little out of sync with the audio.

"What's that about? The millionaire thing? What's going to happen? What got proved?"

"*Proven*," says Nestor. "The thing works on the living."

"Yeah," I say. I wonder if I look as beat to shit as he does right now.

"It works on the living," he repeats. "You don't have to be dead. Near-dead is sufficient. Or maybe in a deathlike state."

"Yeah?" I say. "And?"

"Like a coma," says Nestor.

I try to process what he's getting at. I realize that the candy bar wrapper is still crumpled in my hand, and I look at it as if it's an oracle.

"Ruder," says Rena. "You think if they put one in … in him? That they …"

"He might be able to communicate." Nestor says this with dead-eyed clarity.

"Well, thanks for telling us now," I say. "You could have died."

Nestor turns back to the television. "Ball's dropping."

January and February happen, and I barely notice. A certain kind of suicidal depression sets in, which isn't helped by utter gray and the cessation of particle motion as the temperature approaches zero Kelvin.

I almost get intoxicated enough to start admitting dark secrets to Rena, but a lingering uncertainty of what I've really done becomes even less clear when held up to the meticulously crafted universe of my incessant fantasy.

I masturbate constantly, watching depraved pornography hidden in the crusty recesses of Eastern European websites. As a result, my libido practically evaporates. I cannot perform as a man in situations involving more than myself, and Rena is left disappointed and sad and self-conscious like it's her fault.

I look in the mirror and begin to see Future Me, thinning hair, additional faults in my face, fatty skin hanging below my chin. On multiple occasions I pick up the phone to ask Nestor to bring me a black box so I can capture a tone poem as I blow out my brains. I never manage to press SEND. Cowardice or reason wins out.

There's no communication from Zorro, and I guess that maybe the weather has gotten to him, too.

Mid-February, a network television special commemorates the first anniversary of the Golden Gate Bridge collapse. About once a week, Todd Crabs and I get drunk in a series of sixties-rock-band-themed bars, during which I am treated to more stories about his ex-wife. I learn how blinded by love Todd had been.

Ollie says he has been promoted within Tu$h from flyer distributor to actual band member, even though I can't remember him ever demonstrating a shred of musical ability. He's expectedly vague when asked about it.

I become convinced that I have scurvy because I eat too many cookies and zero fruit and I feel like trash.

Nestor claims to have formalized his pitch to the Ruder administration. Meanwhile, the three unused black boxes sit in a locked case in the morgue where Nestor works. He says his supervisor has never even asked about them, meaning that Nestor deals with the same kind of apathetic management that I've grown to take for granted.

On the first weekday in March, the sun actually shines through the massive clouds and I talk myself down from slitting my wrists with a box cutter and get in the shower. I make it to work by 8:35. I feel proud. I look at the picture of Rena stored in my phone. She holds her glasses and looks quite attractive. I try to think about where I've gone wrong.

Walking down the executive hallway on my way to an early lunch, I hear a plaintive female voice say loud enough to be heard through frosted glass windows, "Mr. Jabber, please. It's not appropriate." I keep walking.

I get a voicemail from Todd Crabs, and I curse my obsolete phone because it never even rang. Todd's disembodied voice says, "Listen up, Brub. Let's meet up for a beer real soon. I got some shit I gotta tell somebody, and I fired my therapist, know what I mean?"

I take the long way home from work, driving through slush on the ruined roads leading to the mall where white people don't go anymore. I pull into the parking lot, the sunlight falling through gray clouds in a horizon littered with abandoned buildings. I bounce in my seat as the worn tires of my ten-year-old mid-sized consumer vehicle dip in and out of wet potholes. The shock absorbers, more or less absent, force me to take the brunt.

When my parents brought me to this mall, I would get excited for hot pretzels and orange cream coolers. I would want to go to the toy store and find the best toy that ten dollars could buy. (Ten dollars was the upper limit of what I could reasonably convince them to spend on a toy without a special occasion prompting the purchase.) Generally, the optimum pick in the price range was a mid-food-chain dinosaur that would turn into a robot, something well down the hierarchy of the robots-who-change-into-other-shit pantheon. It still had the logo, though. It wasn't like it was some off-brand trash. It was genuine, but never one of the main guys. The main guys cost too much. I knew I had to settle. I covertly learned that lesson.

Then I would take the toy home and meticulously remove it from its packaging, often preserving the box, which would always depict the character in a much more exciting action pose than one was likely to achieve with the actual hunk of plastic. Then I would change the thing back and forth, sometimes as quickly as I could, to simulate the effect seen in the cartoon. Frequently, this rapid transformation would lead to dismemberment or decapitation. But even when it didn't, it was just back and forth: reptile to robot, robot to reptile. Not a drop of warm blood in the whole scenario.

Closing my car door behind me, I walk toward the dim entrance, a rusted framework enclosing foggy glass. The heat in my stomach tries to surge into my esophagus, but I will it back down. My fingernails cut into my palms. A chill hits my face, no harbinger of spring.

I grasp the filthy handle and pull the heavy, dirty door open. I walk down the dark, vacant hallway, soon arriving at the discount cinema. The same slew of garish movie posters hang, some peeling from the wall. The only one I don't recognize features a blue-hued man with frost covering his bearded face. The movie's title is, *Self Preservation*, and the poster's blurb reads, "He wasn't meant for this time, so he decided to risk the cold."

Further along, the main crossroads at the center of the mall hangs in darkness, none of the electric lights lit. I taste the dust that must be swirling about, unseen, and the high skylights reveal only an opaque gray beyond. I realize that the outline of the triangular windows in the ceiling create a sort of tangram shape that looks like a large arrow pointing back where I came from. I continue on in the wrong direction, contradicting the arrow's guidance.

In this hallway, the furthest from where I entered the building, I find seven stores completely dark, leaving only one store lit with signs of life. This store is on the wrong side. Its red and white illuminated sign reads, "Traitors."

Where the jewelry store had been stands a retractable metal gate and a generic sign that reads, DOLLAR MOVIES: STILL OPEN, STILL ONLY A DOLLAR! SOUTH ENTRANCE. Through the gaps in the cage, I can see the vacant, lightless store, its merchandise removed. In the shadows, I can see the form of the long metal counter with its glass top. I squint to see a rectangle hiding in a far corner, what might be a closet door. I try to remember her name, and I realize that my heart is beating uncomfortably. Sweat bursts from the pores on the back of my neck, and I actually whimper, feeling weak with panic.

The sound of up-tempo footsteps echoes through the hallway, and more than ever, it occurs to me that I am traversing a ghost town. My luck diminishes with each step, and I begin to hear the rattling of chains and the gnashing of teeth and the echoes of a scream. It might be a dollar movie's soundtrack seeping through the walls. However, the fingers I feel creeping along my spine cannot be part of a movie.

When I push the filthy, heavy door open and the sharp wind stings my face, I know that I have escaped.

◎

Rena and I eat the macaroni and cheese that she's made. We eat with the television on, some game show where people trade their hopes and dreams for temporary employment. We don't talk much.

Later, once Rena has fallen asleep after another mutually failed attempt at sex, I get up. I go out to the living room and load a website on the laptop called "Stupid Czech Runaways" and I finish in about eighty seconds. Then, out of a profound boredom and inability to sleep, I scour the long-untouched archives on the computer's hard drive. I find old poetry, a couple demo songs I recorded in college on a four-track, emails from high school, scanned photographs whose physical counterparts have been lost, static-image pornography retrieved during the graphical Internet's infancy. Each rediscovery seems to bring up equal parts nostalgia and embarrassment. In the file path "C:/HUG/Stuff/Old Shit/Older Shit/nonsense/from old pc/dads" I find some of my dad's old files that he had asked me to transfer before I left home from the IBM clone he bought new when I was ten. I find many plain-text files, recipes, a list of addresses of contacts that he had from one of his consulting businesses. I find several game files, and I make a mental note to seek out an emulator, because I decide that it would be a crime to die before seeing whether "Terminal Hospital" holds up as the masterpiece of the rolling-hospital-bed-in-a-maze genre that I recall.

When I see the file called "will.txt," I assume the worst. I decide to smoke before opening it, thinking I might need something to cushion the blow. I concurrently realize the ridiculousness of preparing for what might be an emotional moment by trying to defuse my nervous system. My superego gets voted down, and I light the pipe, sucking in a big hit and holding it for a while. I exhale, take another hit, then another. I almost get so bored that I close the laptop, and then I remember the purpose.

I double-click "will.txt" and see this:

Maryann, Harland,

This is my last will/testament. And I'm sorry that it's not more official, but we can't afford an attorney right now.

Maryann, to you I leave both the equity we've earned on the house and my vehicles, including the Dodge in the garage (if I am unable to finish fixing it up and sell it), and 50% of the money in my bank account. If they try to freeze the account again, call Stan. He'll know what to do.

Harland, I leave you all of my books and Popular Mechanics, and the other half of my bank account money, which your mother should keep for you until you're 18. I also want you to have ownership of my pending patents, in case one of those ends up being worth something.

I'm sorry that things did not work out. I always tried hard, always did what I could do with the skills I had developed. I know it wasn't easy on either of you, and my biggest regret is that I couldn't provide for you the way I wanted.

I don't want you to think of this as a suicide note. Just think of it as my last chance of telling you how much I love you, and how I really did want the best for both of you. Sadly, I know that the best doesn't include me. With my death, there won't be the mess of divorce. It will just be cleaner.

Love you more than anything.

—Frank

Staring at the laptop, I start to piece together when this must have been written. I look at the "date created" in the file properties and find that it was the fall of my junior year in high school. About three years before I realized that a divorce was even a possibility.

More significantly, Dad didn't go through with it. He could have died for something but could not stomach it. He left this horrible, informal note, but never followed through with the suicide. I try to remember what he was doing around this time. I think it was somewhere between the "glow golf" venture with his ex-partner Stan and the direct-mail campaign promoting magnetic visors.

Staring at this evidence of the death that did not happen, I begin to wonder whether it would have been worse. By the time I see Rena standing in the doorway from the bedroom, I am already hiccupping and crying like a baby.

"What's wrong?" she asks, tenderly.

"My dad didn't kill himself."

9 FIGHTS

Todd and I meet at a bar out near his house called Sticky Fingers. He tells me that he's being sued by his ex-wife for withholding assets during the divorce.

"So, guess whose fuckin' boyfriend is my ex-best friend?" Todd Crabs turns to the wall next to the booth. A speck of something flies from between his teeth. "Mine." He squints and shakes his head once. "I mean, my fuckin' ex-wife's."

"What?"

"Traci," he sneers. "She's fuckin' Toby, my fuckin' ex-best friend. Fuckin' Toby, like he's not already stabbin' me in the heart bangin' my girl, tells Traci that he lost four grand to me playin' Texas Hold 'Em back when we was married. So Traci's suing me for two grand. She already got a fuckin' million. Now she wants two grand plus another five for 'emotional damages' because I didn't tell her about it. And I'm gonna just have to pay it, because even though it's small claims shit, it'd cost me more to fight it. Seven grand more. Fuck that, and fuck money, and fuck divorce. That shit is retarded. And now my beer glass is empty. Brown sugar!"

The waitress rolls her eyes and comes over, forcing herself to smile.

"What's more important than money?" Todd asks the waitress.

"Oh, great, a quiz," she says.

"I'm serious," says Todd, glancing at me for support. "What's more important to you?"

"I don't know," she says. "My health?"

"Good guess," says Todd. "But you're wrong. Love. Love, baby. That's the end-all."

The waitress makes as if to respond, but Todd keeps talking.

"So why's it that love is so fucked-up and temporary? If that's the most important thing, why's it so shitty?"

"Can I get you guys another round?" she asks, trying to make her gritted teeth appear like a smile.

"Yes, please," I say. The waitress takes her opportunity to leave, and I feel like I've done my good deed for the day.

"That girl you got," says Todd. "You better be good to her and keep her on a short leash."

"Those seem contradictory," I say, gulping the last of my beer.

"If you're good to her, she won't care if you keep tabs. Otherwise, you're a dick, and she won't want you pokin' around. Then she's gonna step out, or try to get your shit."

"That's pretty simplistic, Todd Crabs."

"Well, Harland, it ain't a fuckin' complex situation. You keep her happy and keep her close, or things are gonna get fucked up."

"Yeah," I say, processing whether Todd's template for relationship quality has any relevance for me. "Maybe I'm the problem."

"What'd you do, ass?"

My head drops. "I don't know," I mumble.

"Yeah, you do." Todd doesn't sound like he's making light anymore. "You step out on 'er?"

"It seems like I did," I say, staring down at the glossy wooden table, some dark reflection looking back at me. "Doesn't religion say that if you do something in your mind, then you're guilty just like you actually did it?"

"What religion?" Todd asks.

"I don't know," I say. "The main one."

"That's pretty screwed, Brub. I don't think I heard that one before."

"Yeah," I say, lifting my head again.

"So, what, you fantasied that you did something? Or you did something?"

"Yeah," I say. "I can't remember."

"Were you drunk?"

"No."

"Shit," says Todd. "Then I don't know. You doin' out-of-body shit?"

"I don't have what it takes to just walk up to a woman and make her want to have sex with me."

"What, you don't got a dick?"

"Not that," I say. "I just—my body, my personality. I'm not suave. I'm an awkward asshole. I don't really relate to people. The whole idea of it—I just don't buy it."

"You don't buy that you talked some chick into fuckin' you?"

"We didn't fuck," I say. "It ... ended short of that."

"Aw, fuck, Chooch." Todd scrunches his face.

"Yeah," I say.

"So why don't you think it was real?"

"I don't remember leaving. I ejaculated, and then I was back in my car, crying."

"Crying?" Todd looks disgusted. "What's goin' on with you?"

"I know," I say.

The waitress sets two beers on the table, and no one does much to acknowledge it.

"So you do this a lot?"

"What?" I ask.

"Do shit and you don't know whether it's real or not?"

"I don't know." I close my eyes, trying to think. "I blow up my boss sometimes."

"Uh-huh," says Todd, offering more empathy than I would have suspected.

"But I'm usually pretty clear that that doesn't actually happen."

"I blew up like five of my bosses, Harland. In fact, I prolly blew up some o' the same motherfuckers at the same time back at old what's-it-called. It's just something folks do. Don't sweat that."

"And I proposed to Rena and don't remember it. I guess that's the opposite, though. Because that actually happened, and I just, I guess, blacked out."

"Damn." Todd looks stumped. "You got mental problems, right?"

"I guess," I say. "Maybe. I mean, I think I need to talk to somebody, but the company doesn't offer mental health coverage. And I can't afford to pay that out of pocket."

"Fuckin' deductibles are bullshit." Todd looks up at the ceiling while taking a gulp of his beer.

I see someone in the far corner of the bar who looks just like my dad, and I start to panic.

"Whoa, what's the matter, Plumps? You look like you seen a ghost."

"Nothing," I say, chugging the majority of my new beer. I stare at the figure in the corner until it becomes blurry enough to be unidentifiable.

When I arrive in the parking lot of the apartment building, I see Terry's white pickup truck with the hood up. As I pull in next to it, I notice that Terry is leaning into the exposed engine, tinkering with something.

"Harland," he says, looking up as I exit my car. He thumbs at his truck and says, "Fucker only runs downhill. Come on in."

I follow Terry into his apartment, which is cleaner than I would have suspected.

"Lorraine's in there laying down," he says, walking past a hallway and into his kitchen.

"Oh," I say. "OK. I didn't know she was in town."

"We're going to the flea market tomorrow. How's Rena?"

"Good," I say. "She's been painting."

"You posin' nude, dude?"

"I wish," I say. "Trying not to eat so many cookies."

"Well, this ain't gonna help," says Terry. He pulls out a Ziploc bag full of reddish buds. "Satan's Polyps."

"Nice," I say.

"Normally forty premium for this, but since you're basically family now, we'll do your normal quarter rate."

"Thanks, Terry," I say. "That shit looks nasty."

"Oh, it's nasty," he says. "Seven outta ten dentists can't fix teeth after one puff."

"Good one," I say. "I like statistics."

Terry then opens a drawer and withdraws a CD case. He hands it to me. "Check it out," he says. "It's our new one. Some real hot tracks on this one. Our manager tried to talk us out of pressing, but I can't stand that digital distribution bullcrap. I need a disc. I want a booklet. I was ready to press vinyl, but we couldn't afford it."

I look at the cover, which shows a zombie about to bite into a large chocolate chip cookie shaped like the contiguous United States. An ugly green font reads, CULTURE VULTURZ. A smaller red font, what I deduce is the album's title, reads, FREEDOM FRENZY.

"This for me?" I ask.

"Yeah, man. Check it out. And let your friends know. We're playing the Ground Lounge in two weeks."

"Wow, weed discounts and free CDs," I say, pulling a series of twenties from my wallet. "Thanks, Terry. Maybe I'll see ya up there."

"Check out the back cover," says Terry, getting excited on my behalf. "It's like the 'after' picture of the cover."

I flip over the disc and see that the zombie is vomiting, while the ground around him is littered with cookie crumbs.

"Isn't that nasty?" He says. "My brother Jeff airbrushed both of those. He's sick, man. Sick genius."

"Pretty awesome, man," I say, now scanning the text on the back of the disc. I seize up when I see a name I recognize and have to re-read it.

> *Culture Vulturz are:*
> *Terry Johnson, lead vocals*
> *Gunner Mankin, lead guitar*
> *Herbie White, lead bass*
> *Julius Zorro, lead drums*

"Your drummer," I say. "He a skinny guy with dark hair, long bangs, tallish? Like over six foot?"

"Julius," says Terry, "yeah, he was. I mean, he was our drummer. But he quit, man. We're actually playing with a guy named Rod now, who Gunner—"

"What happened to Zorro?" I ask.

"Julius?" Terry halts and scrutinizes me. "You know him?"

"I used to work with him. But he quit, like three months ago."

"Yeah," says Terry. "That must have been right after we finished mixing the album."

"Why'd he quit?" I ask, trying not to sound too desperate or crazy. "Where'd he go?"

Terry looks off to the side, then back at me. "This is gonna sound crazy, dude."

Smoke pours through the translucent green glass dragon's nostrils as Terry removes his lips from the tail. He passes me the dragon, which takes both hands to hold. Just then Rena's mom emerges from the hallway.

"Harland," she says. "How are you, dear?"

"Fine," I say, momentarily unsure. "How are you, Mrs. Pealey?"

"Please," she says. "Call me Lorraine. Where's Rena?"

"At home, Mrs. Pealey. Lorraine."

"Tell her to call me," she says. "I don't want to interrupt you two. Go ahead; I'm going to fix a salad."

Terry lights the dragon's mouth and talks to me as I inhale.

"You heard about the Golden Gate Bridge cult, right?"

"Yeah," I say, coughing out a cloud. "The suicide cult."

"Right," says Terry. "Well, Julius Zorro's girlfriend was one of them. She blew herself up at Golden Gate. She was one of the twenty. If you watched the anniversary special on Valentine's Day, they talked about her."

"Holy shit," I say. "Are you serious?"

"Yeah, man. It really messed him up. They'd been together for a few years, you know? And then she decides to be part of this thing and killed herself, and killed a bunch of people, actually. Julius almost quit the band then, but I convinced him to stay on. I told him it would help him deal with his anger and depression."

"Did it?" I gesture for Terry to re-light the thing.

"I don't know, man. It's hard to read drummers."

"He's an accountant, too," I say. "A drummer accountant. That's messed up."

"Yeah," says Terry. "But they both take precision, though."

"I guess so," I say, exhaling a fog.

"Anyway, so when we're in the studio in the fall—we did it piecemeal, you know—four- or six-hour blocks as we could afford it—Julius starts hinting that he's probably not gonna be able to gig and help us promote the album. Frankly, I got pissed. I told him he shouldn't have played on the album if he wasn't gonna be in for the long haul. I told him drummers are a dime a dozen, but appearances count in this business, and I said some shit I'm not proud of. I hurt his feelings pretty bad, I think. Then, in late October, he says that he has to move, and he's out. And I said, 'Dude, we've got a killer album on our hands. How can you walk away?' He says something about 'an important mission for the USA,' and then I never see the skinny twerp again."

"The 'USA'?" I ask. "Did he say 'United States'?"

"No," says Terry, bending low, showing more of his fading hairline. "He kept saying, 'USA.' 'I'm going to join the USA.' And I'm like, 'Dude, we're in the USA.' And he says—I couldn't believe this, 'You don't know the first thing about the USA.'"

"Terry," I say, "he meant the Utilitarian Suicide Alliance."

"But that's not the same group that did the Golden Gate, right? Wasn't that just an anarchist group?"

"What do you think the USA is?" I'm sweating, my eyes watering. "It might be the same group, or a different group who does the same kind of thing." Something seems to click. I speak absentmindedly: "April Fools'."

"What, you're joking?" Terry shrugs.

"No, man," I say, looking down at my bloodless knuckles. "Julius Zorro said he'd see me on April Fools' Day."

"He did?" Terry seems concerned and confused. Rena's mom comes out from the kitchen, looking worried.

"Inauguration Day," I say frantically. "That's the day Ruder's getting sworn in. Oh shit." I feel like I'm breaking the fourth wall. "The USA is going to kill the new President!"

"We have to warn them," says Rena, removing a formerly frozen pizza from our oven. "They'll think we're heroes."

"They'll think we're in on it, or that we planned it. And we only have conjecture." I crunch a potato chip. "They might think we founded the Alliance."

"But we didn't," says Ollie. "Can't we just take lie-detector tests?"

"I suppose you'll want us swallowing black boxes next," I say.

"We need to keep this to ourselves," says Nestor. "At least until I've worked out a deal with the administration. I'm serious. If we go to them, there's no way they're going offer us anything for the black boxes."

"Why don't they just go to the manufacturer directly?" Rena asks, removing the plastic wrapping from a tray of fresh vegetables.

"Because they don't know who makes them. They don't even know what they are. I pitched it as a product that could potentially interpret Ruder's thoughts during his coma. They don't know that they're the black boxes. And I don't think they would be very receptive if they realized that they are the same black boxes used by a terrorist organization."

"Why not?" I ask. "This country has a rich history of selling technology to terrorists. Why not buy some back?"

"Nevertheless," says Nestor, "if there's a dime to be made—and I think we're going to need a pretty big dime bag—we have to secure an arrangement quickly, before they find out that I'm just a middleman."

"Dime bag," Ollie laughs.

I dip a piece of cauliflower, leaving it covered in way too much Ranch dressing, and shove it into my mouth.

"Hey Nestor," I say, showing chewed cauliflower, "we should all go. We're your company. They'll think you're legitimate if it's more than just you. My dad was always way more successful before he burned the bridge with his partner, Stan. If you have people on your team, people won't think you're a rogue or a kook."

Nestor's face reveals that he is struggling to find a way to politely decline or find a brilliant alternative. His tightened mouth finally opens and says, "Yeah, OK. We'll be a company."

"So what is our company called?" asks Ollie, eating a ranch-covered baby carrot.

Rena bites a stalk of celery and says, "How about Voice ..." she pauses, looking up, "... Tummy?"

"'Voice Tummy,'" I say.

"I don't know," she says. "I'm just brainstorming. Or Tummy Voice."

"No, it's a good idea," I say, picking up more cauliflower. "We should brainstorm."

Ollie says, "How about Grave Tones?"

"Interesting," I say, crunching. "How about Death but not Dumb?"

Nestor completely ignores me and says, "Lifewave."

"I think that's a brand of granola," says Rena. "But I like playing up the life aspect instead of death."

"Life Term." I shrug.

"Lifesavers," says Ollie. "That's candy, though."

"Medium," says Nestor.

"That was that shitty show," I say. "And it's like in the middle, not good or bad. Medium. Boring."

"We're brainstorming, Harland," says Black Me. "Right?"

"Lightvox," says Rena.

"Lightvox," says Nestor. "That's ... pretty good."

"Well, that's a resounding endorsement from Nestor," I say. "Lightvox: *The light at the end of your coma tunnel.*"

Rena looks at me like I made a bad smell. "We'll worry about a slogan later."

◎

The following Tuesday, Rena and I have called in sick to our jobs. We're joining Ollie at Nestor and Dave's apartment. Dave answers the door when we arrive.

"Hey," says Dave, looking annoyed. "They're in Nestor's room."

Rena and I try not to give each other a "what the fuck is his problem" look, and I'm not sure that we succeed in resisting. Dave goes to the couch and resumes watching a game show on television. I recognize it from the music as "What Is Your Child's Education Worth?"

I tap lightly on Nestor's bedroom door, and it opens, and I'm a bit disappointed that a cloud of smoke does not pour out.

"Come on in," says Nestor.

I see Ollie sitting cross-legged on the carpeted floor, rolling a thick joint.

"Jesus, Chong," I say. "Feeling pretty confident that a celebration is in order, huh?"

"This is that Satan's Prolapse stuff from Terry," Ollie says.

"Polyps," I say. "I think. Maybe Prolapse is better. By the way, I keep forgetting to ask you—what the fuck was in that shit we smoked when we met at the mall before Christmas? I thought I was going to get fired or be eaten by demons."

Ollie's face goes blank, and I guess that he's thinking.

"Do you remember that? We kept getting paranoid about mall cops?"

"Oh yeah," Ollie says. "I think that was the *boat.*"

"Aw crap," I say. "That shit was soaked in embalming fluid?"

"I forgot I had it with me."

"Hey, Lightvox," says Nestor. "Let's focus. We're about to place a call to a future cabinet member. If this works out, you can smoke whatever you want."

"Why do we have to do this here, again?" My stomach rumbles.

"Because," says Nestor, "I'm the only person under thirty who has a land line, and I can't risk a drop due to shitty cell towers."

"Good thinking," says Rena.

"All right." Nestor picks up the receiver of his red desk phone. "Let's not fuck this up." He pushes buttons deliberately, and I can tell from the cords visible on the back of his other hand how tightly he's gripping the receiver.

I hear the faint sound of a voice on the line. Nestor replies, "Sleeping Beauty." He turns slightly and covers the lower half of the phone, whispering, "It's the password."

We watch Nestor wait as the call is transferred. His forehead becomes shiny. His heart rate becomes visible in his neck. When a voice comes through the line again, Nestor becomes rigid.

"Hello, Mr. Vice President-Elect, my name is Nestor Little." Nestor turns to us and mouths, "HOLY SHIT."

"Yes, sir, that's correct. We believe that the technology we have tested—"

A rambling sound interrupts, and Nestor pulls the phone from his face. Nestor seems to stutter, trying to find an opportunity to continue speaking. He nods repeatedly, listening impatiently to whatever the rambling conveys.

"Absolutely, sir. It may be of great benefit to the Ruder administration. We at Lightvox—That's correct, sir. We—"

Rambling.

"Yes. If you can avail your Medical team to meet with us, we can demonstrate—"

Further rambling.

"Exactly, sir. I believe that this will allow The President-Elect to communicate openly prior to his revival. In fact—"

We watch as Nestor listens to the response. A smile spreads across his face, and his eyes grow large.

"Absolutely, sir. The thirtieth. I will watch for the email. My three colleagues will join me, the Lightvox team who have—"

The rambling responds. Nestor says, "Thank you, Mr. Vice President-Elect. We look forward to working with your administration."

Nestor looks blankly at the receiver before replacing it in its cradle. He then picks it up and hangs it up again. Then he says, "They're giving us an hour. And they're flying us in. Commercial airline, but business class. We fly in March thirtieth, and meet with them the next day."

"The day before the inauguration?" Rena asks. "They're cutting it a little close."

"Garnder said they're booked until then. Plus, I think, if it works, they may want it to be a surprise for the inauguration. Maybe Ruder can be properly sworn in."

"If that black box is the new voice of the President," I say, "that's gonna be creepy as shit."

Waiting for menus at a fancy restaurant that we both assume only assholes would normally patronize, we are dressed fancily, celebrating our rash decision to quit our jobs and just bet everything on Nestor securing a contract and sharing the proceeds with the other members of Lightvox.

"If this doesn't work—and I totally recognize that there's a fair chance this all could fall through—then we'll apply for Registered Homeless status, and hopefully we'll be placed in a nice camp." I smile, and I raise a glass of red wine. "Cheers."

"Cheers," says Rena. We clink glasses and enjoy a swallow. "Harland, there are other jobs. And even if we end up with less pay, at least the change will do us good." She pauses, continuing to look at me. Her expression dims. "Do you really think we'll be OK?"

"Of course," I say. "We're getting married. We'll be there for each other no matter how little we have."

"We could be making a horrible mistake," she says.

"Maybe this right choice will only serve to illuminate the long trail of horrible choices we've been settling for already."

"Yeah," she says slowly, "maybe."

I realize what Rena thinks I've suggested. Her face seems to be crumbling.

"Not you, Rena," I say. "I didn't mean that."

"I know," she says, not meaning it.

"Rena, I'm serious." My throat thickens. My voice becomes quieter. "I'm serious. I love you, and even though I can't really remember proposing to you, I'm really glad we're going to be married."

Time freezes. A record scratches. That whole thing. All is quiet and still. The couples at the other tables are mummies, wax statues, and mannequins. Steam from a bowl of soup seems solid, like a twisted tapestry. Several forks are held near mouths, full of food that does not glisten or drip. Because PAUSE has been pressed, not even crickets chirp. But Rena blinks, and I see her huffing.

"What do you mean, you *can't really remember* proposing to me?"

"I …"

"Why would you say that to me?"

"Rena," I say. "Rena—"

"Harland? Do you have, like, a drinking problem or something?"

"Well, probably," I say. "Don't you?"

"I guess so," she says. "But we're not talking about that. Are you serious, though, Harland? You really don't remember?"

I'm thankful for the fact that time has begun to thaw. Particle motion becomes mildly apparent. I see some guy slowly poke himself with his fork and begin to wince at it.

"It's true. I can't remember." Speaking a guilty truth feels wholly foreign, and a part of me feels excited despite the remainder of me feeling terrified. "But I must have meant it, because I did it, right? When you're drunk you do what you really feel."

"Really?" Rena says. "So you don't do what you feel unless you're drunk."

"Not necessarily," I say. Now people are chewing at a moderate pace, and conversations are morphing from slow, low tones to a moving mid-range. The second hand on a nearby clock takes about three seconds to notch. "I just … sometimes I'm scared to do the things I feel when I'm sober. Or say things."

"I'm well aware of 'liquid courage,' Harland." She chooses her words carefully. "What else are you afraid to do … or say?"

Time seems to slow down again, but maybe my perception is problematic since I'm being put on the spot and am sweating like a boxer. "Nothing." This is the worst thing I could have said, because it is the only response that has no chance of being true.

"Yeah," she says, the tip of her tongue sliding between flattened lips as she looks up and away.

"Well, not nothing," I say. "Obviously."

A tear falls from one of her eyes as she turns back to smirk at me. "Obviously."

"I mean, I want to do crazy shit all the time. But I have, you know, a moderating psychological force. I can stop myself."

"What would you want to do that you can't bring yourself to do?" She's asking for a novel, but she thinks she's asking for a pamphlet. "*Specifically?*"

"I don't know—"

"Yes, you do."

My intestines seem to be spilling from a gash in my abdomen.

"What is it, Harland?" The menus arrive, and the fancily dressed man may or may not say something before he leaves. I can't tell, because Rena needs to complete her question. "You want to fuck someone else?"

"Rena," I say, "what do you—?"

"That didn't sound like 'no.'"

"I don't want anyone but you," I say. "I mean, I've had fantasies, but those are just passing. They don't mean anything. And they're not always with someone real."

"I have fantasies, too, Harland." Rena's speaking at a level that makes me uncomfortable. The people around us, now back to full-speed, can surely hear all of it. "But I never let them interfere with my love for you. Fantasy is always on top of what's real, never in place of it."

"Come on," I say. "Are you serious?"

"Yes," she says. "I don't want a replacement for you, or for our life. There are things I want different, but I know that we don't always have the energy to pursue them, or to fix them. But anything more I would want, I would still want with you. Not in *place* of you."

"Yeah, of course," I say.

"Of *course*? Are you sure you mean that? Because, since I'm pretty sure you can't go back in time, the time has to be now if you have something you need to say to me."

I take a moment to parse what she has said, and then I realize what I have to do. "OK, this is embarrassing and humiliating, and I feel ashamed even though I don't know whether that's appropriate."

Rena's face is stony until her eyebrows rise and her face tilts forward, meaning: "Quit stalling."

"OK, so, here's this. I went to Blackshire Mall to get your engagement ring. There was a girl there—a woman, you know. She helped me to determine what to get. And—OK, this is stupid—but I thought she was cute."

"You motherfucker," says Rena.

"Hold on," I say. "You have to let me do this." Too much oxygen keeps finding its way into my lungs. "I thought she was cute, and as she was placing the order, I started to get turned on."

Rena looks anywhere but at me.

"And I didn't do anything. I bought your ring and left. And you like the ring, right?"

"I like the ring, Harland. Go on."

"So then, a few weeks later, I go to the mall again. And then—oh my God, why are we talking about this here?"

"If you don't finish telling your story, I'm going to murder you. Fuck these other people. They're adults. They can handle it."

"I—" I lower my voice. "I had this idea that I would go in and seduce her, and it was completely creepy and awful, and then I maybe jerked off in my car in the mall parking lot."

Rena wagers looking at me again and looks like she smelled something bad. "Are you fucking serious?"

"It was a very vivid fantasy. It was right after Ollie and I smoked that boat—I think I was getting a second wave of the embalming fluid high—and it seemed real."

"So you not only fuck this fucking whore in a fantasy, but you're jacking off to it at the mall, where you went to stalk this woman or something."

"I wasn't stalking her," I say. "I didn't go in. It just … seemed like I did. And I didn't fuck her—we didn't even get to third base."

"Third."

"We were just fooling around in the fantasy. And then I came."

"You came in the fantasy or in reality?"

"Both," I say. "I prematurely ejaculated in the fantasy, but I just regular ejaculated in the car. And then I sat there for about twenty minutes crying. Completely hysterical."

Rena—suddenly looking curious instead of disgusted—asks, "You were crying?"

"Yeah," I say, "I was bawling like a baby."

"Why?"

"Because I felt awful, and I felt gross and creepy and guilty and bad that I would do that to you."

"Why wouldn't you trust me enough to tell me?" She seems almost compassionate.

"Why do you think?" At this point I realize that everyone in the four tables surrounding us is staring in disbelief at us.

"When was this?" she asks.

I look down at the table, unable to read anything on the menu. I finally inhale deeply, exhale, and say, "Christmas Eve."

Rena's head leans against the passenger-side window as lights streak across her hair and her shoulders and her dress. No response comes when I ask if she wants any fast food. My stomach growls, and she turns to look at me as if I'm a disease. Then she turns back and resumes looking at the road or the stars, or anything that isn't me. I feel icky in the dark gray suit I've squeezed into. I'm not suitable for nice clothing. This is maybe the third time I've worn this suit since I bought it for my mother's funeral. For a fleeting moment, I wonder whether I might be buried in it, but then I convince myself that anyone who knows me would assume I want cremation. Unlike my father, I have yet to write an informal (premature?) will. Our bill at the fancy restaurant was only $41, for the two glasses of wine. As we walked out, leaving two twenties and a five on the tablecloth, there was a tacit understanding that we would not soon return to Le Façade.

"Why are you mean to Janet?" This voice seems to come from nowhere.

"What? Janet? You mean your friend Janet?"

"Is there another Janet?"

Silence.

"Why am I mean to Janet? Am I mean to Janet?"

Silence.

"I mean, you know, I guess I'm not totally friendly. It's just … she … I can't … What are you looking for, here?"

"Harland, if you don't stop bullshitting me, I'm going to do something bad."

"Don't be so vague and melodramatic," I say.

"So I'm the melodramatic one? Interesting."

"I've never been melodramatic in my whole entire life," I say. "I can't believe you would think that of me. What a personal attack!"

Silence.

"She gets on my nerves, OK? I can't stomach that happy-go-lucky bullshit."

"You can't stand other people being happy?"

"It's not that sweeping, OK? It's just, I can't take it when someone is so saccharine sweet. She's a phony. She's a cardboard cutout. She barely exists."

"Why do you think that?"

"Because she and her big teeth will just smile about everything and look to the future. And her brother died in 7/11—just like my *father*, if you'll recall—and she won't even let that bring her down. Where does she find the energy, and how does she have the gall? I don't understand it. She doesn't have anything intelligent to say when you have a problem; she just says some cliché and tells you to have a nice day."

"You don't know what we talk about," she says. I wonder if this is supposed to lure me. It does.

"Well, what do you talk about?"

"We talk about life, art, friends, possibilities. I like that she looks forward. Everybody has bad things happen to them. She doesn't let hers stop her from getting the most out of her life."

"Well, good for her and fucking Brad," I say. "That's his name, right?"

"I'm surprised you remember." I feel Rena looking at my profile.

"Does he even exist? Or is perfect Brad just a figment of our collective unconscious?"

"You've met him," Rena say, following with a quick burst of a sigh. "You block out everything you can't stand. You think that's healthy?"

"So I should start being healthy now? Rena, we're fucked. We're fucked big-time. Even if we get money from Nestor's scheme, we're going down. Nothing is going to save us from ourselves. We're drowning in our own tears and too scared to stop crying. There, is that melodramatic enough?"

"You ever masturbate to Janet?"

"Sure," I say. "Those beaver teeth get me really hot."

"Harland."

"Who cares?" I say. "We're burning in Hell as we speak. The President's a cactus. Our friends are more focused on what the dead have to say than the living. I'm not quite clear on how I earn money. I'm uncomfortable without marijuana and apocalyptic sarcasm, and I think I'm being haunted by my father. And I've already ruined things with you, so who cares what turns me on in the ten seconds a day when I'm not completely fixated on hating myself?"

Outside, the wind sounds dangerous. I taste red wine or blood. The strobe effects beyond the windshield seem half-assed. I smell my own sweat and want to vomit.

"Is that what it's really like for you?" Rena's voice begins to break. "Are you really that sad?"

"Harland isn't really a person." I find myself speaking the same off-putting third-person shit I wouldn't tolerate from someone else. "Harland is a loose collection of ideas that has no center."

I hear her break down, but I cannot do anything but look straight ahead and drive onward into the ugly blur.

◎

"Roy," I half-whisper, "should I come back?"

"Come on in." Roy is holding the office phone to his ear, but I foster a suspicion that he's faking the call to seem important. Roy now talks into the receiver to maintain the illusion. "OK. Sounds good. Monday afternoon. Uh-huh. Very well. Thank you, I'll see you then, Carl." He hangs up, grinning.

"Carl?"

"Yes," says Roy. "McKenna. From Supply Industries. They're interested in our—"

"Roy," I interrupt, "I need to put in my notice. I'll type it up if you need me to."

"Really?" Roy almost indiscernibly slumps in his chair. "OK. I'm surprised."

"Yeah?" I ask, feeling anger. "Why's that?"

"Well, I didn't know you wanted to leave." Roy says this in a typically open-ended way.

"Uh-huh," I say.

"Have you spoken with HR yet?"

"No," I say. "Should I?"

"Well, I can, but it would be better if you did as well. I expect that they'll want to arrange an exit interview."

"Why?"

Roy looks stumped for a moment and then improvises. "I think they like to keep track of the comings and goings and reasoning behind why headcount may fluctuate."

"Headcount," I say. "Statistics. Right. So I'm a statistic."

"Hardly," says Roy. "You're a solid employee. You're a skilled worker with a professional outlook."

I look at Roy like he has lost his mind.

"So, what have you got lined up?"

"Let's see," I say, pulling back the fingers on my left hand one by one with my right hand. "My side company is poised to sell a device that will translate the new President's thoughts as an interim measure until he vacates his coma. After that, I'm going to try to find Julius Zorro and kick his ass, if he hasn't already exploded according to the mandate of his cult. And then, assuming that my fiancée doesn't leave me for having a waking wet dream and generally being awful, I guess I might try to get my friend Todd to finance a movie about why Pangaea split up."

"OK," chuckles Roy. "You don't have to tell me. Just curious. Well, we'll surely all miss your hard work around here, Harland."

I allow this to sink in for a moment. "Do you have any idea who I am?"

"I should hope so," says Roy. "You've been here, what, five, six years?"

"Nine," I say.

"That many?" Roy squints. "You sure you don't want to hang on one more year? You'll earn your ten-year plaque."

"As great as that sounds," I say, not bothering to finish the thought.

"So, you'll finish out the two weeks?" he asks.

"Sure."

"Well, I'll see you Monday, then."

"Yeah." I stand up tentatively. This has not gone like I imagined it. No screaming, no blood. "Have a good weekend?"

"You, too, bud. Enjoy it. And have a safe St. Patty's Day. Don't have too many of those green beers, huh?"

As much as I'd like to see Roy explode, I can't muster it.

My mother awakens me, leaning over from her wheelchair.

"Guess you've made up your mind," she says.

I respond wordlessly, and she understands.

"Well, you better, Hal. Or should I say Harold?"

Neither of these are my name.

"I'm not worried about me."

There's not much I could say to that.

"But you're going to have to figure out whether you can forgive your dad."

I'm not sure that she did.

"That doesn't matter. You have to keep living for a bit."

Prove it.

"You remember your friend. The squirrelly little guy."

The one who fell to his death.

"Threw himself to his death."

Sure.

"He had some pretty unrealistic expectations, I'd say."

Is that what this is about?

My cell phone buzzes. A text message from Rena reads, "Home late."

I notice a reminder that I have a glut of voicemails wasting server space. I listen to the first seconds of each and delete them one by one, halting at the last and earliest-recorded of the bunch, left by someone calling from my own phone number back in October, in the earliest hours of my birthday. A tired voice speaks at an agonizingly slow pace.

"Hey, you ... me." Harland from months ago fades in and out, crackling. Past Me.

"... gotta move forward and stop being afraid, right?" The drowsy speech pattern mirrors my groggy state. "By the time you get this, you could well be engaged, maybe married. You might be dead in a ditch, though. If you hear this, take note. They dropped you off, but they didn't mean for you to stick around and wait for them. Maybe if you stepped out of the shadow and all that. Also, consider how blame ever helped anyone. All right, goodnight. Don't bother calling back."

My finger hovers over the key that would delete the message. A few things cause me to hesitate, the primary of those being that this seems indicative that time travel does exist. I also recognize that this seems to constitute some forethought to the proposal, and that maybe Rena would be receptive to entertaining the idea that I don't consider it a mistake (even if a serendipitous one). For some reason, I press the button with the red X on it.

Burning bridges feels pretty comfortable, natural. I shake off any nervousness about informing Rena that I actually rendered my notice today. I let any fear that Rena hasn't followed suit sift through me into the aether. I rub my eyes and pull my fat ass from the couch.

She walks in with a brown paper grocery bag.

"Hey," she says, flat-faced.

"Hey," I say, stretching and yawning like whalesong. "I thought you were going to be home late."

"Don't believe everything you read," she says. "Are you still going to Ollie's thing?"

"Yeah," I say. "Are you?"

"Probably not." She sets the bag down on the stove. "I'm making pasta primavera."

"Sounds good. Rena—"

"Harland, I'm not ready to talk about that." She faces away from me, removing vegetables from the bag.

"OK," I say. "OK." I mutely curse myself for deleting the voicemail.

Still facing away, she says, "But you should still go. Have a good time. Maybe meet some new friends."

"Rena," I say. "Come on."

"Go get drunk. Get high. Do what you want to do. If you make it home, we'll talk tomorrow." I recognize that she's not saying, "Go fuck other girls," which means that she is not actively burning bridges and will likely enter into negotiations. I mutely count my blessing.

"Can I help with dinner?" I ask.

Skizzers looks nothing like Skizzers, and the jocks are pissed off.

"Where's the fuckin' game?"

"The fuck is this faggot shit?"

Tu$h and their two crewmates—girlfriends, I'm guessing—finish setting up equipment in the corner of the bar where the pool table normally is. Ollie plugs a device into a laptop computer. I notice a pale young woman in a garish bohemian outfit sitting at a round table near the band. I stare at the profile for a moment and then realize that it's Ollie's maybe-girlfriend Sesha.

I order another green beer at the bar between two meaty-necked testosterone glands who complain alternately about the TVs being off and about this band obviously not attracting a female audience, which decimates the odds of scoring. I squeeze out from between them, tilting my wrist to avoid spilling foam from the boomba. I push between sets of people as the house lights are dimmed. "Hey," I yell, awkwardly holding out my left hand while balancing my still-full beer with the right, "I'm Harland, Ollie's friend."

"Oh, hello," she says, vacantly, but loud enough amidst the crowd.

"I saw your … play? Last fall, at the DMT."

"The stage performance," she says, barely smiling.

After a split second of almost telling her to go choke herself with a rope, I ask, "Mind if I sit with you?"

"The seat is not taken," she says.

Her phrasing annoys me, but instead of hitting her, I sit down.

"Hi!" yells Ollie, when he sees me, not moving from his station behind a black cloth-covered folding table.

After a few annoying minutes where I can't decide whether to press my luck by trying to engage Sesha in conversation, the lights fall away except for those illuminating the makeshift stage area. The drummer plays a typical pop-rock beat and a bassist does a syncopation against it. I'm kind of annoyed that I don't hate it. I don't want these poseurs to have any credibility and I want Ollie to fail just so I can reprimand him. I realize that I've already drunk my beer, and I try to peek through the crowd to see if waitresses are nearby. The guitarist comes in with a catchy, fluid overlay. And then odd electric rhythms get superimposed over the mix. I realize that Ollie is triggering these layers with the laptop (which isn't his own). Ollie grins dumbly and nods to the music. He gets approving glances from the other band members in turn. My mouth gets dry.

"All right," yells the guitarist into his microphone. "We gonna get fucked up tonight?"

Some of the crowd reacts to this approvingly. I'm among the indifferent others. In a far corner, Old Fuck looks livid. He recognizes, as do I, that this repurposing of our bar constitutes a sort of rape. I assume he's only sticking around to beat up some punks later, or to try to finger one of the waitresses again. I recall what he told me about the word *no*: "It's Latin for 'stick it to me harder.'"

"This is a new one. 's called 'Tongue Me Into Bed.' Check it out." The band morphs its groove and some start "wooing" like animals. I turn to Sesha, stare into the side of her face and say, "I'm going to have sex with you. Tonight. And it's going to ruin everything." She sort of turns toward me, head bobbing to the music. She smiles with tight lips. Then I realize she's looking beyond me. I turn away and see a brunette woman with large breasts squeezed into a tight light-colored sweater. The brunette smiles beyond me at Sesha, showing tooth-whitener-white teeth. She scoots her way through a few less-attractive women, making some nasally sound loud enough to be heard through the noise pollution.

"Sesha," she whines. Then she says some more inane greetings, the brunette leaning over me, blocking my view of the band with her bust, and they do some kind of barely touching wrist-hug.

"Siddown," Sesha says, like it's one word.

The brunette sits to my left, and now I'm squeezed between these women, not that either seems to notice.

"Hi," I say, turning to my left.

"Where's Rob?" Sesha yells behind my shoulders.

"He's at the bar," whines the brunette. "I hope he hurries his ass up. Fuckin' retard. I can't believe I let him talk me into blowing him on the way here. I need a wisp."

"Me?" I ask. "I'm doing great. How's a lovely lady like you doing tonight?"

"You wild woman," says Sesha in a yelled monotone.

"Both of you?" I ask. "Absolutely I'll bang both of you. Maybe we should grab a cab."

"Do you know this band?" asks the brunette, spitting a mist on my neck as she yells. I cringe to think of what is probably in that mist.

"I'll probably have you both get on your knees, and then I'll just go back and forth between you. Sound good?" I look back and forth between them, my eyebrows raised. "Little three-way and then we'll all kill ourselves? Sound good?"

"The keyboardist," says Sesha.

"He's not playing a keyboard," I finally yell loud enough to be heard. "It's a computer."

"What?" asks Sesha, looking annoyed.

"Ollie," I say. "He just pushing buttons on a laptop. He's not a musician."

"Who are you?" the brunette whines at me.

"Who the fuck are you?" I yell.

"Fuck you!" she yells.

"You wish!" I yell.

"My boyfriend is right over there!" she yells.

"Well, get your boyfriend! I'm sure his balls are small right now!"

"You're spitting, you fat asshole!"

"You should try it sometime, slut!"

"That's a friend of Oliver's!" Sesha yells. "He's just a drunk! Ignore him!"

"I'm not his friend!" I yell. "He's an untalented piece of shit!"

Then a large fist is scrunching my collar, pulling a few of my sparse chest hairs. Then I'm yelling at the large, angry testosterone gland. Then more large, beer-stinking hands are grabbing me, pulling me backwards through the crowd, out the door, into the alley. Then fists punch my face and ribs. A hard shoe impacts my crotch. I immediately fall onto my kneecaps and vomit on one of the hulks. The frequency of punches decreases as the nausea fades and I actually try taking a few swings. Nothing lands.

"You watch your fuckin' mouth, you piece of shit." This is grunt-whispered by one of them.

The taste of blood and vomit almost brings more of the latter.

The silhouettes seem to evaporate. I can't even get a good count, let alone identify faces, due mostly to the tears welling out from my eyes. I see what at first glance I think is a good chunk of my tongue lying on the damp asphalt. Then I realize that it's a worm, or a gummy worm.

I lean my head against the dumpster. This is the first time I have ever been in a physical fight. I struggle to find meaning in it.

My thigh begins to buzz, and it hurts my hand to extract the phone from my pocket. The display reads: RENA.

I start to whimper, panicking. I finally decide, flipping open the phone with a blood-stained thumb.

"Hello?" I croak, trying not to sob audibly.

"Hey," says Rena. She pauses. "Are you OK?"

"Yeah," I say. "I just … fell down."

"You fell? Are you OK?"

"I think so," I say, shrugging for no one.

"When can you come home?"

"I—" My vision separates and then comes back together. "The band just started."

"OK," says Rena. "You should know that I'm pregnant."

10 DROPOUTS

I feel extremely cold as I see Sesha's forehead bobbing at my crotch. I completely recognize that this part of the scene is nothing more than an incredibly sad, fleeting fantasy as I lay sprawled, my head bent oddly against the cold metal of the dumpster. She jerks her head hungrily, wanting me. There are no consequences, and Ollie and Rena will never know. This has no meaning. I indulge it because there are no reasons against it. "You can't hurt feelings because they're locked up," I say out loud. "They're put away."

Nodding off, my hand goes into a small, cold puddle. I awaken fully, my body aching. An intrusive light glares down, giving everything in the alley abysmal shadows. It occurs to me that Ollie has not come looking for me. I tell myself to stop regretting the ridiculous things I have said. "You're not going to find anything of consequence looking where you're looking." I say this to the wind blowing through the alley. My arms feel cold, not exactly numb. The winter has subsided just enough to have kept my body alive during my incapacitation. "Blessings are tricks."

There are no street sounds. No booming bass from inside the bar. I pull my phone open to find that it's four in the morning, meaning hours of blackout.

I sneeze and see a splatter of red on my palms. I moan as I attempt to stand. Eventually, I stand, feeling twenty years older. *Future Me*, I think. It seems that Rena had something important to tell me.

I wake up in our bed and I notice little bits of glass in my rust-colored palm. Rena sits cross-legged on top of the bed, hovering over me.

"What the hell is going on with you?"

"What do you mean?"

"What happened last night?"

"Some guys beat me up."

"Why? What did you say?"

"I didn't say anything. They were just horrible people, and they captured me. It was a total sneak attack. Don't blame the victim."

"I'm not blaming you. Are you OK?"

"I don't know," I say. "How do I look?"

"You look near-death."

"What's new?"

She does not react. She pointedly inhales, maybe forcing herself to be patient. She exhales. "So, we have a situation."

"Oh no," I say. "Are you serious? I thought that was just something I dreamed before I passed out."

"Sorry to disrupt your fantasy world," she says. "I'm not sure how I feel about it either, if that brings you any comfort."

I try to remember the last time I felt comfortable. My brain produces an "out of memory" error.

"What do you think? Are we going to abort this thing, or pretend to be adults?"

"Rena," I say. "I love you. But I'm barely functional. I don't want to ruin any more lives."

She starts crying, and I try to interpret it.

"Rena, if I hadn't convinced what's-her-name back in high school, I'd have a seventeen-year-old running around, paying for a whole new slew of abortions."

She stops crying long enough to look baffled.

"I just mean, this whole cycle of shitty life has got to stop somewhere, right? My parents bailed before they could really witness the destruction."

"Why do you hate everything so much?" Her breathing settles down, and now she's trying to be pragmatic. "Why can't you just be normal?"

"Do you really think there's such a thing?"

"Yes."

"Well, that's one difference between us. And do you think little Harland Junior or Rena Junior would have a chance in a million of winding up normal? Happy? Satisfied? Free from the weight of a legacy of horrible decisions and the plague of selfishness?"

"Yes."

"Really? And who's going to raise this little bundle of whoops? If you and I are in the picture, I can't see that happening. We can barely keep ourselves together. And children are not meant to be pawns. I think I should know that."

"Harland, your parents split up when you were like twenty! You are not a 'child of divorce.' You just refuse to take any blame for the way you are. How can you have the balls to say such insane shit and not have the balls to own up to what you—you—have made of your life?"

I try to imagine how my parents would react if posed with this line of questioning. My mother would smile, shut down, and pretend that she was asked about her knitting. My father would point to the competitive market place and lament the woeful position of the self-starter. "How much are they running these days? A grand? More?"

Rena's curled mouth shows teeth. Her lower lip shakes.

"By the way," I say, starting to pick glass from my hand, "I went ahead and quit my job."

Sitting in the chair at my desk at the office, I dial nine and then dial the digits of Nestor's cell phone number. I have more minutes than I would ever use on my cell phone plan, and even though my phone is an obsolete piece of shit, it still gets decent reception. Nevertheless, as I'm now officially into my final two weeks of "work," I have a side-goal of wasting as many company resources as possible.

Earlier, I started a batch of coffee with the carafe sitting next to the machine. When Cindy discovered the coffee spilling all over the counter and onto the carpet, her shriek was frightening and then hilarious. I also lit a roll of toilet paper on fire and threw it into one of the toilets in the men's room. Then I flushed the toilet and it overflowed onto the floor.

I hear the tones indicating that Nestor's phone is ringing, and I almost get so bored that I hang up. Then, the fourth ring is cut short with a click, and Nestor's asking me to call back in ten minutes, and I tell him that I'm more important than whomever he's talking to, and he says that he would normally agree, but that he has to let me go. Then there's a click, and I say, "Shit" and Berry leans out from behind his cubicle wall.

"Stubbed my toe, Chooch," I say, wondering absently if Berry would remember Todd Crabs.

"Oooh," Berry says with mock empathy. "Can't stop the inevitable." This is his new catchphrase. He disappears behind a cubicle wall, and somehow I realize that I will never see him again.

Ten minutes later, I once more wait as the phone rings, and again, I almost get bored enough to hang up. This time he picks up after the second ring. When Nestor speaks, he sounds completely distracted.

"Hey," he says. "Hey ... Harland."

"Hello, Black Me."

"What's up?"

"Just, you know, running out the clock," I say. "I got the shit kicked out of me, and Ollie won't return my text messages, and I'm trying to convince Rena not to have a baby. The *uge*. How's the morgue?"

"More suicides," says Nestor. "Maybe Alliance. Maybe something else."

"Wow," I say. "How many?"

"Three," says Nestor.

"That's not insignificant."

"Right," he says, maybe condescendingly.

"You think this is a sign of, you know, the end of the world?"

"Hold on," says Nestor. I hear him saying something to someone else, the phone held into his shirt or something so I can't really hear what's going on. Then he says, abruptly, "I gotta go."

"Fine," I say, slamming the receiver into its cradle.

Ten minutes later, my cell phone buzzes with a text message from Nestor which reads: "Boss snooping, looking at receipts, collecting for tax return, asking uncomfortable questions."

I text back: "Welcome to my world."

As if on cue, Roy appears in my periphery. I realize that I have not even turned my PC on yet, so I ruffle some papers, feigning productivity out of habit.

"Harland, got a minute?"

In Roy's office, the ostriches continue grazing, heads above ground. I want to grab their long, frilly necks and shove their faces into the dirt. The coffee I drank has made its way almost to the tip of my penis—that's how much I have to pee. But I'm in no position to beg off this impromptu meeting. Biological requirements would only be read as a stalling tactic against whatever inquisition I'm facing.

"You get in a fight?" asks Roy, smirking.

"Plastic surgery," I say. "I'll look just like you when it heals."

Roy's smirk darkens, his eyebrows lowering.

"I got beat up," I concede, for some reason. "At a bar on Friday night. I think they thought I was someone else."

"Really?"

"Yeah. Completely savage. Just a sad commentary on the state of society."

"Wow," says Roy, his expression serious now. He thumbs a corner of his mouth, for lack of a more meaningful gesture. "Did you have a co-pay at the hospital?"

"Well, Roy, I'm on the low-deductible plan, but I didn't go to the hospital. I just kind of passed out bleeding and then wandered home when I came to."

"Did you file a police report?"

I look at Roy like he's a new species. "No," I say. "I sort of just want to forget about it."

"Good lord," says Roy. "That's terrible." His brow rises, and then he sighs, sitting. I sit across from him, his big desk between us. On my right, the gold-framed photo of the women in his life is turned toward him so I can't see it. In the photo I imagine in lieu of remembering, the daughters are sluttier-looking. It brings a smile to my face, and I feel my dry lower lip re-split open.

"Ow," I say.

"Oh dear," says Roy, seeing my wound, and reaching for a tissue, handing it to me.

"Thanksh," I slur, dabbing the blood.

"So," Roy says, pausing, possibly with a purpose. "The Accounting department was trying to reconcile some of their records between the old database and the new database, and, long story short, Human Resources determined that it was acceptable to open the archive of Julius Zorro's emails to try to track down some of the incongruous data. They found this, and wanted me to ask you about it …"

Roy spins a single sheet of copy paper on his desk, and the blur of letters resolves to a short email:

FROM: Zorro, Julius C.
SENT: Friday, October 8, 20[coffee smudge], 8:07 A.M.
TO: Grant, Harland U.
SUBJECT: USA

Harland, we need to discuss the future of the USA. Please see me for details. I didn't want to email for non-business-related affairs, but I've tried coming to your desk a few times, and you're never there. Also, apparently you don't check your voicemail before deleting it. Anyway, I think you'll be interested, especially in light of what's become of your family. I've had some personal tragedy in my life, and I believe we have some things in common.

Ball's in your court. If you don't come by in the next few business days, I'll assume you're not interested. I'm in Accounting. Just mention the "USA" and I'll know that you got this.

Regards,
Julius Zorro

I look up at Roy with what may be zero blood left in my cheeks. Roy's intense stare feels more ominous than he probably intends. I feel an off-brand toaster waffle try to inch its way back into my esophagus. It takes the strength of muscles I rarely acknowledge not to urinate all over myself.

"I don't think I ever got this," I say.

"There was an electronic receipt," says Roy. "It was opened."

"Yeah," I say. "Maybe I deleted it by mistake."

Roy just waits.

"Even if I did—and I don't remember—I don't know what it means." I hide my hands below the surface of the desk, out of Roy's line of sight, because they are tensing up involuntarily. "Why does Zorro want to talk to me about the United States?"

"Harland, I need you to be one hundred percent straight with me. This is very serious. HR tells me that the USA is a terrorist organization. One of those new, domestic 'kill yourself for a cause' fads. The Universal Suicide Agreement or something."

"Utilitarian Suicide Alliance," I say, giving in, or seeming to. "Yeah, I've heard of it, but I'm not part of it."

"Well, Julius Zorro's fiancée was part of it, and she was one of the people who destroyed the Golden Gate Bridge last year."

"Oh my God," I say, doing award-winning acting. "No."

"Harland," he says. "I know you know about this. IT has records of your web searches, on the company-owned computer, on company time. Now, we both know you're not the only one guilty of doing a little web-surfing. But the fact is, you know about this situation, and now you need to tell me what you know. We can't afford another legal fiasco, and I'm certainly not losing my job over it. So what is it? What's going on with you and Zorro and this suicide cult?"

"All right, Roy," I say, sitting up straight, and rubbing my hands together. "Here's what I know. OK? Here: Zorro worked here, and I was joking with him about trying to get a raise, and I think I pissed him off, and then since he left, he's been harassing me with these confusing faxes. At first I thought he left because of me, but then I figured out that he probably left because of something related to the situation with his girlfriend in the USA who blew herself up, and he wants me to meet him at the inauguration for Ruder, where, incidentally, I'm supposed to meet myself in the future— I got a bunch of phone calls from him, or me, or whatever. And I know it sounds crazy, but I swear, at most I'm just a pawn in this thing. I don't know what the fuck is going on, and I'm quitting my job with no backup, and my girlfriend—fiancée—is pregnant, and I can't think straight, and I don't feel right when I'm sober, and sometimes I feel like the only way I could ever actually tell the whole truth to somebody is to off myself with a black box in my belly and let them dig it out of me. OK?"

Roy looks horrified. When I feel wetness on my balled hands I realize that I'm crying. Roy's office phone rings, and he looks at the display and without picking up the receiver presses a button that silences the ringing. He looks back at me.

"How old are you?" he asks.

"Th- thirty-five," I blubber.

"Ah-ha," he says. "Well, I wish I could tell you it gets easier."

My sobbing slows. I catch my breath.

"You've obviously got a lot on your plate. And since you're moving on anyway, I think it might be best for all parties if we just wrap this up. Go ahead and clean out your desk. Grab your personal items, and turn in your swiper to IT. I'll make sure payroll pays you through the end of next week."

"Wasn't there supposed to be an exit interview?" I ask.

Roy sighs. "I guess this was it."

A clock ticks. I stand up. "I didn't mean to burn any bridges," I say, looking just below Roy's face. I feel Roy scrutinizing me. I turn to leave, expecting him to take the final line, but he allows my disingenuous words to hang.

I arrive at Skizzers and find that it looks different in the daytime. A blue-gray glow pours in through the street-facing windows, a dull, naturalistic feel, converse to the artificial fluorescent-and-neon glare found at night. I see that the pool table has been pulled back into place. I tremble, recalling the shitty band that stood in its place Friday night.

A couple of guys wearing ties sit at one of the round high-tops near the front windows. I overhear one of them say, "She could use some analysis … up her butthole."

The bartender is a young guy I've never seen before, with long, dark bangs, and I realize that he sort of looks like Julius Zorro, which pisses me off. I order a draft beer with as few syllables as possible, being rude. "Draft," I say.

"Tall or short?"

"Tall," I say, letting my facial expression do the work instead of adding, "obviously."

After a few beers I send a text message to Rena: "Roy let me leave. At Skizzers. Nobody's here. You put in your notice yet?" I press the SEND button and wait in horrible anticipation for several minutes before I submit that she must be too busy to respond.

I drink nine beers in three hours and notice that it's almost four o'clock. "Pretty awesome Tuesday," I say at the bartender.

"You talking now?" he says, being a dick.

"You don't know me," I say. "I might be your next boss. Better be nice to me just in case."

"Right," he says. "Need another?"

I push the empty boomba at him. He walks down to the end of the bar. Then I see some fat asshole staring at me, and I get ready to yell at him, and then I realize that the fat asshole is my reflection in the mirror behind the bar. It takes some restraint not to yell anyway.

"Number ten," says the bartender, pushing the glass back at me, a glop of foam spilling over one side. "Shoulda brought your punchcard."

"Dude," I say. "You're a bartender. You don't wanna work here, why don't you just—I don't know—work on a boat or something? You think this is the best place I could be?"

"Well," says the young punk, "let me think about that."

"Whatever," I say, waving him off. "Your shift ends at what? Seven? Six? I don't have to deal with you much longer."

"Wow," he says. "You're gonna be here 'til six? That's really sad, old man."

"I'm not old," I say. "Just sad."

"Oh, boo-hoo," the dark-haired kid says.

"That's right," I say. "Life doesn't make sense, and I'm just another sad motherfucker, OK? Why should I feel bad about that? I'm typical. I'm just a normal slob. This is what happens when there's no clear path, OK? And make no mistake: You're not making fun of me. We're both making fun of me. I don't have feelings. None that matter, anyway. You're absolutely right: boo-hoo."

He makes a whistling sound and motions a pointed finger in a circle next to his ear.

"That's what I'm talking about," I say, but not like a rapper would say it. "My autobiography has serious narrative gaps. Don't you find that disconcerting?"

"You've shaken me to the core," he says. His sarcasm skills are impressive.

"Well, OK, tell me this, dude. Do you have a clear idea of where you've come from and where you're going?"

"No offense, *dude*, but I'm not telling you anything about my life. This is just a job."

"Let me guess: Perfect family, perfect parents, trust fund, you only work to seem like a normal person."

"I don't give a shit about my parents," he says.

"Living or dead?" I ask.

"I'm not telling you," he says.

"Come on, man," I whine. "Just tell me: Are they living or dead?"

"None of your beeswax."

"Dude, I don't care, I just want to know to prove my point."

"They're alive, and happy, and I … don't … give … a … shit." The bartender's eyes bug out at this. "All right?"

"All right," I say, backing down. "I guess we're exact opposites, then."

"I hope so," he says.

I continue drinking at the established rate until the front windows darken to black and the artificial lights pop on throughout the bar. The young bartender slips out at some point without fanfare, and I curse a missed opportunity to bug him again. The new bartender is a female who I've seen many times and whose name I still haven't memorized. Her hair is short and brown, cropped just below her pale ears. Her face is plump but clean looking and I debate with myself about whether I should flirt with her.

Instinctively, I flip my phone open to see if I've missed any calls or texts from Rena, but I see nothing. The phone indicates it's 7:41. I check my wallet and realize that I don't have enough cash to cover what I've drunk, meaning more credit card debt.

Old Fuck enters from the hallway to the rear entrance. He uses his cane every few steps, then leans it against the bar, taking his corner seat. The female bartender brings him a tumbler of whiskey as rote, and she says, "Hey."

Old Fuck says, "There's only one way to tell someone's future: Shoot 'em in the fuckin' head."

With this, Old Fuck pulls a gun from the pocket of his camouflage jacket, sticks it in his mouth, and blows his brains out. Flecks of brain and skull splatter the fiberglass drop-ceiling tiles above the corner of the bar, and Old Fuck's headless body falls backward onto the floor.

My car crashes into a plastic garbage can in my driveway. I kill the lights and turn the key. Still shaking with chattering teeth, I notice there are no lights on in the house, and Rena's little car is nowhere in sight. It seems that I'm once again alone in the universe.

Still drunk, I stumble in through the backdoor, lament the non-sound of scampering feet. I don't bother to flip on any lights. I find my way to the uncomfortable couch and slump into it. I start to worry about Rena, and then I get distracted by this creepy black blob in the middle of my old-style television. In the faint light, it seems to be oozing out, and as I lean in, it seems to grow. And then, of course, it's my stupid reflection again.

This somehow doesn't ease my panic, and I flip open my phone and locate Rena's name in the recent calls list and press the button to call her. It rings four times, and my blood starts to curdle as I expect her outgoing voicemail message to begin, but I hear a tiny click and then her real voice is saying, "Yes?"

"Where are you?" I try not to sound like I'm demanding something, but I don't have much control over nuance at the moment.

"At Janet's."

I wait for her to explain herself.

"What's up? We're in the middle of a conversation."

"Old Fuck's dead."

"Oh," she says. "That's too bad."

"Yeah," I say. "I was there. He shot himself."

"Oh my God," she says. "Where was this?"

"Where do you think? Anyway, I got the hell out of there before the police showed up."

"Harland, Jesus. You were, like, a witness. You should have stayed."

"Yeah," I say. "Probably."

"Where are you?"

"At home. In the dark."

"So you've been drinking?"

"Hello?" I say. "I was at Skizzers, so …"

"I'll be home by ten … maybe eleven."

"Are you still going to your jobs?"

The static is probably a long exhalation.

"OK, we'll talk when you get home. Tell Janet I said … whatever you want to say."

"Don't wait up for me," she says.

The call ends, and I resent that I don't hear a dial tone.

Two days before we're supposed to leave for DC, Todd Crabs has brought Rena and me out on his boat. Rena has gotten someone to cover the shift at Orange Bamboo, the job to which she has yet to tender notice per our supposed agreement.

"Slick shit, Chooch," he says. "Top of the line. Finally got around to spending some of that money."

"This is pretty nice, Todd Crabs," I say. "I don't normally like being under constant threat of drowning, but I guess this is the way to do it."

"Shit, Plumps, you afraid of water?"

"Just drowning," I say.

"This is nice," says Rena, focusing on the pleasant weather on the small lake, which must be a nice diversion from the near-constant active dismissal of me that she's been perfecting over the past couple of weeks. She looks pretty wearing sunglasses and a loose blouse over her yellow, one-piece swimsuit, her dark hair in a ponytail. I feel a horrible weight of regret. This regret fails to take the form of any words or actions on my part, so it just sits there.

Todd pulls down on a lever and we're jolted into motion. I dig my fingers into white padding on the seat before finding a chrome handle to grab onto. Wind pushes the fat of my face off to the sides, and I'm worried that it's going to start flapping like a flag. I entertain a passing thought that I should probably go for a walk and try to burn some calories at some point.

"Arright, Harland," yells Todd over his shoulder as he slows the boat near the middle of the lake. I'm startled by the fact that he has used my real name. "You're gonna learn to drive. First thing you gonna need, though, is a beer. Grab us some cans out the cooler. Rena, if you want somethin' girlier, I got some hard cranberry lemonades in there."

"Thanks, Todd," Rena yells. Todd kills the motor and the boat slows to a drifting speed. Then Rena adds, "I'll just grab a soda."

"Come on, Rena," I sneer, doing the peer-pressure bit, then remember. "Oh, right."

Rena hands me—without any eye contact—two cold cans, and I hand one of them to Todd. She cracks open her own off-brand can of lemon-lime soda but doesn't drink any. I slam my beer quickly and then, instead of having to ask a favor of Rena, get up from my seat, crouching to keep my center of balance low, and waddle past her to open the cooler and get another. "Todd, you want number two?"

"Like shit?"

I try to decipher this terse riddle while grabbing another can out of the ice.

While sipping my second beer, Todd shows me the basic controls, and I begin driving the boat around the lake, steering far clear of the shores. Once I've proven that I'm not retarded, Todd straps on a big slalom ski and jumps off the back of the boat. He pulls the rubber handle out into the lake, its twisting yellow nylon rope following.

"Arright, Plumps, when I say 'Go,' gun it and keep it at thirty-five 'til I wipe out."

I give a thumbs-up.

"He should be wearing a safety vest," says Rena, somewhat to herself.

"Go!"

I push forward on the chrome throttle and watch in the wide-angle rearview mirror as Todd's skinny, pale frame pops out of the water, white water spraying his already-frizzy mop of hair, his jean shorts dark and saturated. I ease down when I realize I've hit forty mph, glancing back to make sure I haven't jerked his arms off. As I round a curve near one end of the lake, the mirror shows a tiny Todd weaving back and forth, jumping the foamy wake with the single ski, showing its dark red underside. I find myself wanting to jump into the tiny mirror and be part of the little warped-perspective world.

After about three minutes, I see Tiny Todd let go of the rope and coast for a short distance before sinking into the lake. I ease off the throttle and curve the boat around to pick him up.

"You look like you've done that before," I yell as we pull up alongside Todd.

Todd, treading water, spits a stream from his pursed mouth, then yells, "Yeah, Brub. But don't it feel good off the back o' my own boat?"

Climbing up the few rungs onto a small platform off the back of the boat, Todd stands and poses like a muscle man, water dripping from his skinny arms. I think I notice some snot in his barely visible mustache, but I don't say anything.

"That was great, Todd Crabs," I say. "Looks fun."

"You goin' next?" he asks.

"Absolutely not," I say. "Thanks, though."

"I'll go," says Rena, surprising me. She places her seemingly full soda can into a cup holder. She removes and folds her blouse, tucking it under a cushion, and crawls over a row of seats into the back of the boat. Todd helps her to locate a pair of wide "newby skis" and jumps into the water with her.

"I'll be drivin', arright? Not that maniac." He splashes water up into the boat, and it barely reaches me. "Just teasin', Chooch." He turns back to her. "So you're gonna keep your knees tight up to yer chest, like yer doin' a stomach crunch."

"OK," Rena says, practicing bringing her knees almost to her chin, a blue life vest keeping her bobbing in the subtle waves. She tumbles a bit side to side, and I giggle, but not so loudly that she hears me over the breeze.

"That's good. So when the rope goes tight, you gotta pull back as hard as you can, and push up with your knees. It's gonna be tough on your legs and you'll feel it in your stomach, but just push and resist the water and you'll stay up. And remember to keep your legs a little bit bent. You wanna keep flexible."

"Got it," says Rena. "Don't go too fast, OK?"

"We'll go 'bout twenty, enough to keep you floatin'."

Todd crawls back into the boat, dripping, and flicks both hands at me, getting water on my face.

"Dick," I say.

"Yar whatcha eat," says Todd. "Psych."

Todd gets in the driver's seat and I sit to his left. I think to reach back and grab two more beers out of the cooler.

"Read my mind, Plumps," says Todd. "I was gettin' dehydrated."

We crack our new beers and I slam mine back. Todd calls over his shoulder to Rena, and I look back to see her head framed by her knees and an arm extending a thumb.

"Let's do it!" she yells.

Todd tips his beer back with his left hand and pushes on the throttle with his right. I turn back to watch the clumped rope straighten out and, to my amazement, Rena begins steadily lifting out of the water.

"She's up!" I yell.

"Damn straight!" yells Todd. "Natural!"

I squint to make out Rena's disbelieving face, wide eyes, pale knuckles gripping the rubber handle. Her blue life vest contrasts the bright yellow swimsuit beneath it. The wind streaks past my ears and blows around what's left of my hair. Then, with seemingly no provocation, her face distorts into a pained expression, and her knees come together. I tense up as I anticipate her wiping out, but she stays up, still looking agonized. When her knees come apart again, I see, through the mist of water, that her thighs appear to be covered in blood. She lets go.

Jumping into the lake feels heroic, and I try not to think about how lame it probably looks. Then it strikes me how freezing cold the water feels, and I remember that it's barely spring. I dogpaddle toward Rena, feeling like a fool, and I see her bobbing, everything but her shoulders and head beneath the surface, looking down at herself. When I get to her, I hear a clicking pattern that I realize is her teeth.

"Are you OK?" I ask. "Rena?"

"Let's get to the boat."

I pull us back to the boat using the tow rope with Rena behind me clinging to my soggy shirt. I step on one of the metal rungs on the stubby ladder to hoist myself up onto the shallow wooden platform off the rear of the boat. Crouching, I spin around, and I reach down into the water to help Rena up. I feel Todd's bony fingers on my shoulders, presumably to keep me from being pulled back into the water. With my hands gripping her forearms, she slowly climbs up to join me on the platform. Her face is covered in water, but the redness of her eyes implies tears in the mix.

She lies on her back on the smooth wooden platform, her knees pointing up. I nervously pull one of her knees, and I see the bottom half of her bright yellow swimsuit stained a rusty orange, blood diluted by lake water throughout the fabric.

"Do you need an ambulance?" I ask, struggling not to yell frantically.

"No," she croaks, and begins to sob softly.

"Is it …?" I can't finish. The wind partially covers the sound of Rena's sobbing.

"No more baby," she says.

I turn to look up at Todd, whose somber face says nothing.

With Rena's lower half wrapped in every towel we brought, Todd drives us back to the boat launch. I wait with her in the boat while Todd goes to retrieve his pickup truck.

"I'm sorry," I say. "I really am."

"Yeah," she says.

"I am," I say. "I'm really sorry. I don't want you to go through this. I—"

Her eyes become wet bubbles again, and the bubbles unceremoniously pop and dribble down her cheeks. She stares beyond me.

"I do love you, Rena. I have a problem … being an adult." I clear my throat. "I mean, I am, still, I guess. It's difficult for me."

Her lower lip pulls over the upper. Her brow creases, and then she dares to glance at me.

"Can you forgive me?" I ask. I hear the sound of crunching gravel and peek past the tip of the boat to see the pickup truck backing up with the boat trailer.

"What are you asking me to forgive you for?" He voice sounds broken and weak.

"For—" I squint. "For being me?"

"Try again," she says, shivering.

I try to think. I say, "For trying to sabotage everything?"

"Hmm," she says, still croaking. "Why do you think you do that?"

"Because I'm an asshole?"

"Too simple," she says.

"Because I let the past dictate my future?"

"Where did you read that line?" she asks, nearly smiling.

"Because I'm afraid that I'll become my parents, but I don't know what to be otherwise?"

"Interesting," she says. "But why would I have to forgive you for that?"

"OK," I say. "Will you forgive me for forgetting?"

"Forgetting what?"

The engine shuts off and Todd climbs out of the truck. Rena and I exchange meaningful eye contact, and I know that we can continue this conversation later, that she won't think I'm trying to get out of answering. Todd scampers down the dock and jumps back in the boat and yells, "Hold on, Plumps and the pretty one." He activates the boat's motor once more and eases us up into the trailer.

The next day, as I'm parking my car, I see a woman on the street corner take a sledgehammer out of a large purse, lower its head between her knees and bring it up to crack herself on the forehead. The spray of blood that emerges looks like a festive bunch of streamers. For a moment, I can't breathe. Then my phone buzzes, taking me out of the moment. Flipping it open, the display shows a number I don't recognize, so I don't push SEND to answer it.

When Ollie opens the front door of his apartment—holding a piece of bread with peanut butter slathered all over it and not a single bite taken from it—he's greeted by a smiling face not unlike the clown decorations littering the place.

"Hi, pal," I say, sweetly. Or sickly sweet.

"Hey," he says. His face is neither pro nor con.

"I'm coming in," I say, walking past him into the clutter and sour smell.

"All right," he says, shutting the door.

"Forty's the new twenty, right?" I ask this as if he would have a reasonable response. I shove some clothes over on the couch and sit in the gap. Something pokes my right thigh, and I slide my hand under my thigh, latch onto something pointy, and pull out what looks like a decorative pin.

"That's from that show you won't watch anymore," he says.

"What does it mean?" I ask, looking at the octagon.

"It was just a symbol," he says, and I guess that this is as thorough an answer as I will get, not that that stops me from pressing on.

"So it was representative of something, or it crashed loud or what?"

"Har dee har har," he actually says.

"Just tell me the ending," I whine. "Do they get off the island or not?"

"That ends up not being the point," he says.

"That's stupid," I say. "So, uh, I guess you know I got the shit kicked out of me at your stupid show."

He shrugs, literally upending both palms.

"So, what, you hate me now or what? What's the fuckin' deal? I thought you were my friend."

"I've been your friend. And sometimes you've been my friend."

"What does that mean?"

"I mean that sometimes you don't act like you're my friend." This is Ollie at a harrowing level of frankness. I feel chills on my elbows.

"A lady whacked herself with a big hammer outside," I say, changing the subject. "We should probably call 911." A tiny part of my subconscious surfaces and I realize that I have a horrible fear of being a tattletale because of a story my mother told me about a boy who told the police about his thieving father and his father was subsequently put to death by a king.

"I think I heard a siren," says Ollie.

"So, like, what?" I ask, turning the conversation back, keeping one step ahead of him. "What's up with your total apathy about me getting hurt?"

"Were you flirting with Sesha?" Ollie asks with a flat mouth.

"Yeah, right," I say.

"At the Tu$h gig, were you?"

"What did she say?"

"She said that you were leaning over and breathing on her, and that when her friend Lauren came by, you were saying sex things to them." He says this flatly, like he memorized it.

"'Sex things,'" I retort. "Me? And it was a thousand decibels in there—there's no way they could hear … whatever I was saying."

"What were you saying?"

"Yeah, I was saying sex things, but I was joking and didn't think they could hear me."

He looks at me skeptically.

"So what if they heard my joke and didn't get it?"

"I thought you didn't even like her," he says. "You never want to hang out with the two of us."

"What, am I going to hold her barf bucket while you feel her up?"

His skeptical face further distorts.

"Sorry," I say. "I just don't click with her. I don't really click with anybody. And I'm not feeling sorry for myself."

"Well, I don't feel sorry for you," he says.

"Good. I don't want your sorry feelings."

"Are you and Nestor and Rena still going to DC?"

"Yeah," I say. "Except Rena."

"Why's she staying?"

"Because you're going to be an uncle."

"Really?"

"No."

He sighs, looking bored, looking around.

"You're still coming," I say, not asking, but not too rudely.

"OK," he says, still sounding bored.

"OK?" I ask.

"OK," he says, sighing again. "If I get one quarter of the money and it's as much as Nestor is guessing, it's worth three days."

"That's pretty materialistic," I say.

"You don't care about the money?" he asks.

"I care about helping the new President communicate to his constituents so he can lead America to a brighter—" I can't keep a straight face and bust up laughing.

"So why are you going?" he asks.

"To find myself and kick his ass."

Ollie stares blankly. I can't help rolling my eyes before I clarify.

"Future Me."

The next day brings a scene that begins wordlessly. Rena and I communicate otherwise. At some point, I begin packing a suitcase.

Later, because I can't let it rest, I have to try to shoehorn what I'm thinking into words.

"Things will be different when I'm back."

She looks at me sympathetically.

"I promise."

"I know," she says. "They'll have to be."

11 CONFESSION

The stewardess or flight attendant or plane slave or whoever sets a tiny liquor bottle on my tiny tray, and I offer a correspondingly proportioned smile. A clear plastic cup with three ice cubes sits on a napkin. She places an opened can of Canker next to these other things, and now it's up to me to play bartender for myself. She moves on as I unscrew the plastic cap and tip the whiskey into the ice and consider lines that I should scrawl on the stall wall in the bathroom at Skizzers the next time I'm there. As I think of things, I feed my list in a half-whisper to Ollie, who sits to my right, wearing white earbuds in his big ears.

"'Old Fuck,'" I say. "More like 'Dead Fuck.'"

Ollie nods to some song I can't hear, his eyes mostly closed in a way where I can creepily see more of the whites of his eyes than I'm comfortable with.

"Never make out in a jewelry store," I say.

The male captain of the plane says something incomprehensibly distorted over the PA.

"You can get away with anything until you go on the offensive."

Ollie turns, opening his eyes, pulling the bud from his left ear. "Huh?"

"Black boxes aren't just for planes anymore."

In a seat across the aisle beyond Ollie, I see some gray-haired black woman turn and glare at me. Ollie continues staring at me expectantly, as if I've missed my half of a conversation. When he gives up and stuffs the bud back in his ear, I continue.

"There's no such thing as a first-class toilet."

On the small video display hung in the back of the seat in front of me, I watch a hieroglyphic representation of our plane following a dotted line, like this is a travel montage in an adventure movie.

"Not everyone gets the privilege of a deathbed."

I hear someone make a shushing sound, and I wonder if it's directed at me.

"Aphorisms are for assholes," I say, shutting up.

Later, Nestor wanders up the aisle.

"Whazzup?" I say.

"What's up?" he asks.

"Too bad they made you sit in the back," I say. "I thought, you know, because of Rosa Parks and all ..."

"The last row in first class is still first class," he says dryly.

"You should write that on a bathroom wall," I say.

"He been out the whole time?" Nestor nods his head at snoozing Ollie.

"You can never tell with him," I say. "That brainwave always seems pretty flat to me."

"I hope we can trust your friend," he says. "Or we're screwed."

"Todd? He's the real deal. He's a real man, you know. He like, does stuff with his hands, on purpose."

Nestor is referring to the fact that we have entrusted the duffel bag of black boxes to Todd Crabs, who is somewhere several miles below us, bringing them to New DC in his truck. When Todd asked if they were weapons, I said, "Not any more than the harmful words of relatives you don't see any longer are weapons." To which he stared at me and then said, "You said a mouthful, Plumps."

"Besides," I say to Nestor, "it's still way better odds that they'll make it there than if we tried to get them on the plane."

"I would not have wanted to answer those questions," Nestor says, glancing around.

Later, as the pilot begins circling outside DC, I look out the window and see a giant white shape burnt into the ground. What I remember from incessant post-7/11 footage as black terrain smoldering endlessly has been replaced by pale ash. Something about the shape makes me think of a big, unkempt fingernail.

Ollie, rubbing his eyes with fists, leans over my lap, stinking of cheese snacks, looking out the window. "It's a scab."

"Takes one to know one," I say.

"No one to take one," Ollie says, more cryptically.

We land at the airport in Virginia. When we get off the plane, the terminal is filled with people wearing suits and walking around with stern looks. I see security personnel pointing with great certainty, parents leading children with authority. I witness someone saying, "Hold on; I think I have exact change." There's an air of bureaucracy, and I feel a cold panic because it occurs to me that maybe nothing has actually changed. After picking up luggage and exiting the terminal, just at dusk, I look out and see what looks like the jagged skin of some hibernating behemoth. The display of normalcy inside the terminal, I realize, is an overcompensation for utter horror. The earth before me, stretching into the darkening East, seems alien and forgotten. This, in a way, seems to be the world's end, what Ollie called "the scab." Somehow, the story continues, like the director forgot to call "cut," and we're moving into an epilogue of questionable necessity. The vast sea of ash is flatter than versions of the wasteland I'd only seen approximated in pre-7/11 video games.

Somehow, my friend Seth, who dove to his death at the end of our teens, dove to avoid this. He foresaw the bizarro future that lay ahead—not only for himself, for his peers, but our country—and he opted out. At the same time, this feels like revisionist history, because for years I have lived with an understanding that there were deeply personal motivations for his suicide, nothing socially conscious in the subtext. My life became divided into what I would regard (never so consciously) into the time after Seth, and the time before Seth: B.S.

I explain all of this to our cab driver, who responds with a Southern accent, "Which hotel?"

Only a few miles outside of the radius of the blasts that decapitated the government, our hotel has a warmly lit interior and large-format prints of paintings of flowers in full bloom. The orange, rotund woman at the desk begins talking, and I realize that it's a clone of Cindy from the office of my ex-job, and I can barely tolerate the brief exchange that takes place across a slab of marble.

"Four forty-one," she says, handing me a key card.

I try not to swear at her, reminding myself that she can't help but resemble a woman I thought I was done with. "Thanks," I say, but I can tell she thinks I don't mean it.

Nestor and Ollie have their own separate rooms, but because Todd didn't have his own room booked, I've offered to share mine with him. The Provisional Government had offered to put us up in four rooms, but we said three would be OK because I was expecting to share one with Rena. And given that we felt awkward about calling the government back to see if they could tack on a fourth room after we learned that Rena was out and Todd was in, it became a matter that we had to deal with ourselves.

I had said to Todd: "Hey Todd, why don't you just book your own room? We'll chip in to pay for it since you're bringing our merch. Or you could pay for it, since you're a damn millionaire."

"That's arright, Harland," he had replied, strangely using my real name, "I don't mind crashin' in your room."

I throw my bag on the bed, looking over to observe a short couch that I have a hunch hides a bed in its guts.

"Enjoy the futon, rich guy," I say to the empty room.

Taking the time to put away three days' worth of clothes in the drawers below the television, it occurs to me that something blah blah blah and I can't complete the thought.

We meet in the hotel's restaurant at 5:30 p.m, even though I show up closer to 6.

"You should have called our rooms or texted or something if you knew you were gonna be this late," says Nestor. "It's rude."

"Believe me, you'll like me better now that I've cleaned the pipes," I say.

"Gross," Ollie giggles. "Gay."

"How is jerking off gay?" Nestor asks indignantly.

"Your hands are all over a wiener," says Ollie.

When I notice the hostess, I wonder how long she's been there.

"Three?" she says, gum in her mouth.

"Maybe the black boxes don't really mean anything," I posit, chewing a big bite of a Caesar salad with real strips of anchovy. "Maybe the concept of a black box is just a MacGuffin."

"What's a MacGuffin?" Ollie asks.

"It's like, just a plot device," I say, chewing what feels and tastes like liquid salt. "Something to move the story forward, but that never really materializes. Like retirement, or Heaven."

"They're real," says Nestor, not humoring me. "We tested them, remember?"

"You tested them," I say. "We just gave you the Heimlich."

"What are you implying?" he says.

"You told us about the things, you brought us one box pre-recorded, and the only other one we heard was you. Maybe they're just some kind of regular digital recording devices and you recorded that stuff as part of an elaborate practical joke. For all I know, you could have just made all of this up to freak us out."

"You think I recorded that poor woman as a joke?"

"That *poor woman* could have been a B-grade voiceover actor who unwittingly participated in your convoluted plot to trick the cabinet into paying you great sums of money by convincing them you can read Ruder-the-raisin-head's mind."

Nestor thankfully morphs his disgusted expression into something smirkingly dismissive. "Well, Harland, how about the fact that I started this 'con' before Ruder even went to that paintball place?"

"You did? I thought it was after. I can't remember details like that. Anyway, just teasing, anyway."

"We're all part of Lightvox," Ollie says.

"That's right," says Nestor. I study him to see if he's pissed at me. After a brief moment, I decide to test the theory.

"So you promise you didn't pre-record all that stuff? And that you don't have something pre-recorded for the President to say tomorrow? Or at least, if you do, you got a radio pro who sounds like him to do it?"

The moment hangs uncomfortably. "Did you smoke too?" Nestor finally asks.

"Not yet," I say. "Sounds like dessert."

We get our meals, ordering bottle after bottle of a red wine called "Sanguich."

The waitress asks if we want dessert, the three of us slumped back in our chairs in gluttonous afterglow.

"Sure," Nestor pants. "It's on the government."

"I'll be right back," the young black waitress says, smiling as she heads away.

"I think she has a crush on you," I say.

"Gay, remember?"

"Not that gay," I say. "That chick is one of the hottest black girls I've ever seen."

"Unfortunately," he says, "none of us are in a position to attempt it."

"I'll bet Todd would bang her," I say.

"When's he getting here?" asks Ollie, giggling with his mouth full of noodles.

"Speak of the devil," says Nestor.

Todd walks into the restaurant with his arms spread wide, one hand grasping a stuffed-to-capacity backpack and the other a large purple duffel bag.

"'sup, tards?" Todd swings into the fourth beige, padded chair. "I'm starving. What's good here?"

"We're ordering dessert for some reason," I say. "The meatloaf is pretty damn delicious. The gravy alone: fuck."

The waitress returns with three dessert menus. Seeing Todd, she asks, "Are you also getting dessert, sir?"

"Yeah," he says, and I know where he's headed when he adds, "for starters."

"I'll be back in a moment." She smiles, once again mostly at Nestor.

"Arright ..." Todd leans in, squinting at her nametag, "Gurl."

When she's out of sight, Todd pushes up a sleeve to reveal the tattoo of his own likeness and says, "I'm gettin' some sex on that one."

Todd makes us wait for him to finish his dinner, which I think is sort of rude but don't say so. Nestor reads from a note in his phone the private credit account number and password that the Provisional Government has provided for meals and incidentals. Todd and I insist that Nestor leave Gurl a twenty-five percent tip, despite Nestor reminding us that the Government only agreed to cover twenty percent gratuities.

Then we go out to the hotel parking lot where the great white absence of DC sprawls into a deadly bleak and dim horizon. Somewhere near its center lies the nucleus of New DC. We wander around to the other side of the hotel, finding a waist-high red-painted wooden log railing to lean against and watch the sunset. I smell burning wood, the scent carried by a light breeze from somewhere far away. We squint into the remaining orange sun beaming against purple-shaded clouds, the last light of day passing before our eyes. I can tell we're all trying to think of something profound to say in this moment. Unfortunately, I get so fixated on needing to come up with the most profound sentiment that I just sort of zone out.

Ollie loses a vote and his room becomes the designated smoking room. I extract the baggie of joints that Todd had smuggled in the purple duffel bag along with the black boxes. Ollie hits one first and passes to Nestor, who passes to me. I take a big hit, blowing out a smoke sculpture that looks like a globe with a mushroom cloud shooting out of it.

"Red herring, right?" I cough.

I pass to Todd, and Todd says, "Naw, man."

We, the high three, get on the offensive right away.

"Come on, buzzkill," says Nestor.

"You traitor," I whine.

"You should smoke pot with us," says Ollie, Captain Exposition.

It's all very junior-high-grade peer pressure we're throwing his way; we're not yet at our most eloquent.

Todd says, "I don't do that no more."

"This should be good," I say.

"It ain't a rehab story, Plumps. I just don't do it. Gives me acne."

"What?" I'm yelling, unable to not yell. "That's an old wives' tale they cooked up to dissuade kids."

"Maybe," says Todd, cracking his knuckles and shrugging.

"So you're OK with your excuse being bullshit?" I yell.

"Harland, settle down," says Black Me, then turning to Todd. "So there's a story?"

"More like a anecdote," says Todd, rolling his tongue within sealed lips in what I interpret as a defensive gesture.

"Sounds just like my attention span," I say, finally getting a handle on my volume.

"What's your anecdote?" Ollie asks.

"Arright," Todd says. "Remember Tighty Nighties?"

"You mean that thing where teenagers wore skin-tight, flesh-colored body suits to make it look like they were streaking even though they weren't?" I try to pronounce this with scientific detachment, but I can't tell if I'm pulling it off.

"So you did it?" asks Todd.

"Go on," I say.

Nestor mutters something that sounds a lot like, "Fucking crazy white people."

"Anyway," says Todd, "I'm suitin' up, and my brother Derek says, 'High Surprise,' and I'm all, 'What's High Surprise?' And he whips out a joint and blazes it up, then blows the smoke up my sleeve. And it's all elastic, you know, so it snaps back and the smoke is hangin' in the sleeve, sorta puffy. Then Derek passes it to whatever blond he was tryin' to bang, and she takes a hit and blows the smoke in my other sleeve. Then it's passed to Duffy, the towel boy, and he gets down on his knees in the dirt and blows his smoke up one o' my pant legs. Then this ugly girl, Mandy or Mindy or something, she takes a hit and blows it in my other pant leg. And I'm gettin' all puffy, filled up with pot smoke, and I'm gettin' a good contact buzz off all the stuff that's slippin' up through the neck hole. I'm super puffy-looking, which kind of defeats the whole lookin'-like-you're-naked thing, but I'm feelin' pretty good about everything, so I run out from under the bleachers and run across the football field just as the marching band's about to come on for their halftime show."

Ollie, wide-eyed, says, " ... And?"

"And ... I got a rash all over my body." Todd shrugs.

"From the pot or the bodysuit or what?"

"I dunno," says Todd. "But I ain't worn a bodysuit or smoked since then."

"That's stupid as shit," I say.

Todd, defensive or reasonable, says, "Everybody got somethin' they won't do anymore."

I wake up with what I hope isn't feces on my fingers. Seeing pieces of a shredded brown candy bar wrapper, I gladly recalibrate my assumption. Scanning the room from the queen-sized bed, my first glimpse of the futon reveals that half of Todd's pale body has been roasted to a smooth, sexy brown. This is when I realize that, after I had passed out, Todd had an independent adventure that ended up with Gurl the waitress naked in his futon. My rustling causes them to rouse.

"Hey," I croak-whisper.

Todd pushes his chest toward the ceiling, palms against his bedding, yawning wide and loud, looking over at me and winking with a smirk. Gurl makes cute young-woman-waking-up noises, achieving consciousness in time to pull the sheet more tightly against her torso before I can catch a glimpse of her breasts.

"Morning," she says quietly.

"Morning," I croak, feeling at once jealous and proud of Todd. "Well, since I'm still wearing clothes, I guess I'll get out of here and let you two …"

"Thanks," says Todd. "We'll see you down at the breakfast buffet."

"Is that what you're wearing?" I ask, gawking at the faded jeans—one knee ripped—and powder blue bowling shirt that covers the skinny frame of Todd Crabs.

"You said it was business or casual."

"Business casual," I say. "I mean, your shirt has a collar, but … Anyway. Hi, Gurl."

"Hey," she says.

"Is it weird to eat here because you work here?" Ollie asks, maybe on behalf of the other males.

"I like the pancakes," she says.

"So, you two got acquainted last night," says Nestor.

"You could say that," says Todd, raising and lowering his eyebrows so quickly that I almost miss it. "We're getting along pretty good."

"We got a lot of sim'lar interests," says Gurl. "We both divorced. We both been through unemployment before. We both want kids. And we like havin' sex. I mean, with each other. We almost woke up Harlan' there, but he would always just start snorin' again. It was kinda funny at first—I kept gigglin', an' I thought my gigglin' was gonna wake him up. It was like a crazy cycle."

"Sounds like you guys had a dense night of sex and getting to know each other," I say, summarizing so we can move on to actually eating. "Congratulations on hitting it off."

"Todd said your wife lost her baby," says Gurl.

"Pre-wife. But yeah," I say, looking at Todd. "Nice discretion."

"Come on, Harland," says Todd, slipping a small, burnt piece of bacon into his mouth.

◎

The limo rumbles over the black highway subdividing the white ash that spills infinitely in every direction, kicking up clouds that I have to assume are carcinogenic. The driver, up in the front seat beyond a tinted divider window, has shaggy gray hair spilling out from under a dark cap. His head tilts back and forth, either helplessly jostling due to the bumpy ride, or keeping time with some song I can't hear. Further ahead, through the tinted window and the windshield, a blurry polygon of shadow creeps toward us from the horizon of the makeshift desert.

"So that's New DC?" Ollie says this in a forced rhetorical manner, as if he's prompting an expert in a staged interview.

"Yes, Ollie," I say, lighting a joint.

Nestor turns into the annoying straight man and whines, "Are you really going to do that before we meet the President?"

"What?" I say, smirking and inhaling. Blowing a cloud directly in Nestor's face, I cough out, "None of it's real anyway."

"What are you talking about?" asks Nestor.

"None of this is real."

"What do you mean it's not real?" he asks.

Inhaling again, I look around at the other guys, hoping for empathy and reassurance. I want them to show me that they also think Nestor is being uptight. Instead, I see disaffected, maybe tired, faces.

"Do what you gotta do, I guess," Todd Crabs says.

"When did you become such a moralist?" I ask.

"What'd I say?" Todd does not become hostile, even though I fear that he will. "I'm just surprised you wouldn't want to remember this."

"I'll remember it," I say.

"Whatever you say, Plumps," he says.

I turn to Ollie, the holdout, expecting him to be the one on my side. I hike my eyebrows expectantly.

"I don't think you should be high for the White House," he says.

"There is no White House," I say.

"Well, whatever the new one is," he says.

"It's just a temporary structure," I say. "New DC is just a ghost town. But, like, a ghost town in reverse."

I glance back to Nestor, who has already moved on and is reading something on his phone.

"Fine," I say. "I didn't realize I was traveling with the three Hitlers."

The tinted window creaks as it lowers a few inches.

"Hey, buddy," says the craggy voice of the limo driver.

"What?" I say defensively.

"Don't joke about Hitler," he says. "That ain't funny."

I look at the guy's squinty eyes in the rearview mirror and say, "How would you know?"

We all jerk in our seats as the driver slams on the breaks.

"You wanna walk the rest of the way?" the driver asks, low and violent.

"Jesus, I'm joking," I say.

"You're done joking," he says. For a long moment he lets us think he's going to kill us. Then the limo starts moving again and the tinted window rises.

Making as conscious a decision as possible, I shut off my fury at the limo driver. Instead, as the limo veers at an angle, following some path in the white ash that may or may not technically be a road, I become transfixed by the approaching cluster of silhouettes. The structures seem impossibly tall, given the short timeframe since everything functional was decimated. It hurts my brain to consider the logistical analysis and manpower that must have been devoted to creating this oasis. The details of each stark tower and humanoid monument resolve as our vehicle approaches. Through all of this, I hear a low, growing hum, something almost subsonic in the soundtrack. The lower extremity of my spine begins to ache, and I worry that a primitive tail might burst through the back of my khakis. Through the windshield, a gray archway with deliberate art deco angles bears embossed letters reading:

NEW DC

Then there's a time lapse, or I faint, and then I'm being ushered down a dimly lit hallway, and a hand is snapping in my face.

"Jesus, Harland. What the fuck?"

"Wha?"

"Keep it together, Plumps," says a shape that must be Todd.

"I've got a good mind to make you wait in the lobby." This is Nestor: blurry, but obviously pissed off.

" ... I do?" I ask, realizing it's only half of a question.

"I now pronounce you barely a man," says Nestor.

"Shut up, Black," I slur, impressively following it up with the word, "Me," so it sounds less racist.

"I think you smoked too much," says Ollie.

"Thanks," I say. "Real detective."

"Suck it up, Chooch," says Todd.

"We're here," says Nestor, halting us in front of Suite 41.

There's a moment where we just stand without saying anything, barely making eye contact, and I begin to wonder if we're going to just turn around and go home, as if none of this has happened.

"It wouldn't be so bad," I say.

"What wouldn't?" Ollie asks.

"If it wasn't real," I say.

"Can you do me a favor?" asks Nestor.

"What?" I wipe my eye with the heel of my palm.

"Don't talk in there. Let me talk."

"Whatever," I say.

Then the door cracks open, a chain pulling tight across the width of the opening, and a white guy with a shaved head and a black suit and black sunglasses stands in the slit. The chain is exactly at the level of his mouth, and for a split second I become very concerned that he has a metal mouth. After a quiet beat, Nestor speaks softly.

"Sleeping Beauty."

Everything in the suite is one shade of gray or another. Picture frames that I at first mistake for a series of flat screen televisions hang on multiple walls containing actual canvases with grayscale paintings depicting, I guess, pivotal moments in history. A white wigged white man in dandy clothing stands with one knee bent at the front of a small boat. A guy with a mole, a top hat, and an Amish beard holds a crumbling parchment atop a wooden platform. A dark-skinned guy with a thin mustache, wearing a more modern suit, wags a finger at some onlookers while a white steeple creeps into the sky in the distance behind him. A crowd of peasant-looking gawkers gathered around a towering crucifix bearing some skeletal beatnik seems to be waiting for something. Three flying saucers hover over what I guess must be the Grand Canyon. All of this seems simultaneously legitimate and fictional.

"Welcome," says a heavyset white guy whom I recognize from TV.

"Thanks for having us, Mr. Vice President," Nestor says, extending his hand.

"Vice President Elect," says the guy, winking. "Until tomorrow, anyway." They shake hands, and it's cordial, and it seems to be going really well, and I sort of have to urinate.

"Nestor Little," says Black Me.

As the Vice President guy makes his way down our short line, exchanging greetings, I realize that the guard dudes lingering around the perimeter of the suite, five or six of them, are all wearing sunglasses like it's a sci-fi movie.

"Todd Crabs," says Todd, "tax-paying lottery winner."

"We appreciate your participation in the republic," says the guy, whose name I can't remember, so I just start thinking of him as *Coach*.

"Oliver Pilgrim," says Ollie, "musician, performance artist."

"Fine, very fine," says Coach. He seems to try to think of something clever, and instead adds, "The world needs artists, too."

As Coach, the VP guy, sidesteps once more, halting mere inches from my belly, a realization materializes—that I am stoned out of my mind—and I begin to hyperventilate in reaction to a supremely profound paranoia. The extended hand—too puffy, too white, the hairs sprouting from its rear too curly—can only be interpreted as a threat. In a flash, I see a flip-book depicting a rabid onslaught of red markers sullying the top margin of every test I ever failed. I hear my mother make a snide remark, and I watch my dad, who is too self-involved to notice. A pang of guilt punctures me; this pang comes in response to the realization that even if I had all of the time in the world to do what I would want to do, I still might not produce anything of worth. Worse yet is that this acknowledgement of my own laziness does not stop me from resenting my parents' inability to provide a situation where for the remainder of my life I could behave as the idle rich. Then the guy just crushes my hand—the most unnecessarily firm handshake I've ever felt in my whole goddamn life—bones seeming to not so much fracture as turn directly into powder, and the actual physical pain successfully extracts me from my psychic spiraling out of control. Somehow, I don't scream, and, forcing myself to lift the corners of my lips in what I hope looks more like a smile than a fart face, I miraculously remember how words are formed, and sound comes from my throat in what seems to be a civilized, even friendly, tone.

"Harland Ulysses Grant," I say, "niggard."

The Coach-VP—Garnder, I suddenly recall—does a double-take. If he had a drink, he would be spitting it. Then something seems to trip his subconscious and he does a quick glance to both sides to remind himself of who is here. His glance hangs a moment longer on Nestor, then snaps back to meet my eyes. He makes a confused expression, feigning that he didn't hear me correctly.

"Analogous to miser or curmudgeon." I say this proudly, my vocabulary on fire.

"Yes," he says, his grip mercifully subsiding, my hand healing. "Sure."

"This is a lovely suite," says Nestor, covering, an unsubtle glare directed at me.

"So," says Vice President-Elect Thom Garnder, Coach, his cheeks rosier than usual for his embarrassment about what I refuse to believe has been anything but a frank and pleasant exchange. "Before we proceed, can you tell me again how this is supposed to work?"

"Well, sir, the black box is activated by contact with a significant quantity of a hormone called Thanatopside, which is only produced when a person dies or enters a deathlike state."

"'Deathlike?'" Garnder asks, all kinds of skepticism.

"Comatose," says Nestor.

"Right near the edge," says Todd Crabs, helpfully.

"But not necessarily teetering," Nestor adds, in a tone that he must intend to sound comforting, but which I find condescending.

"And he's gotta swallow it?" the VP asks.

"Well," Nestor says, somehow not stumbling, "it has to be in his stomach. How it gets there is optional."

"What?"

"Sir, I discussed with your medical team the possibility of surgically implanting it."

"Yeah, OK, they told me that. No good. We're just gonna push it down his throat."

"Whatever pleases the Administration," Nestor says in this horribly stilted way that makes me want to hit him.

"So then, you get it out, and it tells you what he's thinking?"

"Well, Mr. Vice President-Elect," says Nestor, "your medical team and I are hoping that we won't need to extract it."

"Why's that?"

"So it can be read continually."

"Uh-huh."

Nestor raises his eyebrows in a gesture that dares another question to be asked. It becomes obvious that he has burned through all of the bullet points he had prepared and is not looking to improvise.

"OK, young men, follow me." Coach throws open a set of double doors that I guess I hadn't realized were doors. The doors swing open into a deep, windowless room with unnaturally tall walls, red like a Santa suit, and a shiny dark wooden floor. As I glance up, the ceiling seems too far away, and I wonder what happened to the levels of the hotel above this one. A dozen floor lamps line the edges of the room in a moody, mysterious lighting choice and surreal overall effect that perversely contrasts with the benign remainder of the suite. Golden scrolls, unfurled, hang tacked to the walls of the red room. I recognize one as a map of Pangea. Another seems to be the original Declaration of Independence. Yet another appears to be an ancient version of the boardgame Risk, or something post-Pangea. All of this frames the centerpiece of the room, a king-sized medical bed with four hundred beeping gadgets attached to it. Lying prone in the center of the bed is the living ghost President-Elect John Ruder. A gold-colored comforter pulled over his chest rises and falls almost imperceptibly. Pale blue pajamas cover his shoulders and arms, his hands resting, neatly folded. It occurs to me that someone folded his hands that way, like an undertaker would.

We approach the bed, a quiet cacophony of electronic gadget sounds creating a techno-ish white noise. I look forward to the harmonies from the QBBR231 when that gets overlaid in the mix. Through blips and a wavering hum, a sluggish rhythm is defined by the pump that continually forces oxygen into Ruder's nostrils. I notice that Ruder's head has been buzz-cut—the wavy gray movie star locks have been reduced to a simple bristly texture. His mouth hangs open just enough for some dental work to glimmer. The scene is unsettling in its quirky specificity, as if designed to be experienced while high, a notion that takes a great deal of restraint not to share aloud with everyone in the room. I half expect to turn around to find a black monolith hovering ominously.

Nestor sets the purple duffel bag on the glossy floor. Two men in white lab coats wearing surgical masks, whom I had at first glance mistaken for a pair of floor lamps, begin to move toward the bag. I try to quash my panic.

"Doctors," says Garnder.

They nod with a creepy twin-like synchronicity as they take steps toward Nestor. As they halt, the bag sits on the floor between them. They both reach down for it, each grabbing a strap. I see that they are already wearing latex or nitrile gloves. I entertain a final moment of cruel suspicion that Nestor has duped us all and loaded the bag with bombs. But the doctors lift the bag between them like it's a child they're taking on a walk, and they pivot, precisely, as if in a marching band routine.

They take the bag to a rear corner of the room and place it on a clear glass counter. One of them lets go and watches as the other one peels back the zipper. The active one removes the gallon-sized Ziploc bags containing the black boxes, one by one, and carefully sets them on the counter beside the bag. There's a bothersome theatricality to his deliberateness. Once all five of them are on the counter, I see the guy, in profile, scowling.

"Why do these two have shit in them?" The doctor sounds southern.

"Those are the ... test subjects," says Nestor. "I brought them for demonstration purposes, if you're interested in listening to the output before we proceed."

At this point, I notice that to my right, Ollie is knuckle-deep in his own nostril, wrestling out a good one.

"Hey," I whisper sort of loudly, "quit it."

"The others are sterile?" asks the southern doctor.

"Yeah," says Nestor. "Of course."

"OK," says the southern doctor, turning back to the duffel bag and reaching in for the final item. With two hands, he pulls out the receiver and sets it next to the other items, taking up most of the remaining space on the counter. Then he extracts the three daisy chain devices.

"Let's get this going," says Garnder, tapping his toes. "We've got a photo shoot in an hour."

The southern doctor removes one of the clean black boxes from its bag while the other doctor walks to the head of Ruder's bed. The doctor near the bed places one gloved hand on Ruder's chin and the other on Ruder's forehead.

"OK," says the face-holding doctor, sounding Canadian.

Southern Doctor produces a silver squeeze tube from his lab coat pocket, unscrews the cap, and squirts a large dollop of clear gel on the black box he has selected. He works the gel over the surface of the black box, and then produces what looks like a big orange dildo seemingly from nowhere. Southern Doctor walks with both objects to join Canadian Doctor at Ruder's head.

I glance over and see Ollie with one finger in his mouth.

Southern Doctor places the black box well into Ruder's open mouth, then positions the dildo thing with its tip to the exposed end of the black box. I suddenly wish I had a camera handy.

"Ready?" asks Canadian Doctor.

"Ready," replies Southern Doctor. Southern Doctor then holds the big orange dildo thing with two hands like he's playing tug o' war and proceeds to push it, shoving its tip against the black box until it is forced into Ruder's throat, ramming it all the way down the presidential esophagus. I expect Ruder to react to this, somehow, as if this were the precise stimulus that would bring him out of his coma. Instead, Southern Doctor keeps pushing the thing deeper into the unconscious gullet until it must be either in his stomach or already passed through it. When this realization seems to have set in, the Southern Doctor then swiftly removes the floppy orange tool, and a weird part of me is disappointed that he doesn't bother to lick it off like this was all part of a niche porno.

"It's in," says Southern Doctor.

Canadian Doctor lets go of Ruder's head, which slumps to one side.

"Now," says Nestor to the doctors, "it's time for the impossible." This strikes me as a line that a bad magician would say, and I have to restrain myself from leaning over to slap him.

A short while later, I'm trying to count the lamps in the room, but I keep losing track and having to start over.

"OK, let's try it," says Nestor.

The two doctors press the QBBR231 against Ruder's pale abdomen, the black plastic pressing down a turf of frizzy white belly hair. The chain of auxiliary devices form a train nested in the folds of the golden comforter. One of them turns a dial, and a warm tone fades in as a musical pad over the blips and bleeps of the life-support equipment. The tone blossoms into a full chord, barely discernible harmonics coming and going in subtle waves. For a moment, I become convinced that the high, shadowy ceiling will lift from the room to reveal a massive saucer speckled with blinding blue lights. The idea that this—this room, this trip, my life to this point—amounts to a convoluted practical joke becomes a front-runner for the most likely scenario.

The harmony swells, signifying something forthcoming. A cowardly part of me hopes that what follows will be nothing but gibberish, ones and zeroes, static, anything beyond human comprehension. I want this all to be a bust, so we can be excused, having only wasted a small amount of federal time. I can't shake the feeling that the safest bet would be for us to come off as hapless fools, amateurs who brought an invisible cloak for an unconscious emperor.

Then—and this is the painful part—I recognize that this is my *modus operandi*. I have paved a half-assed trail of self-sabotage. I've never fully dealt with my demons or fostered my fledgling talents. I've coasted, not really tried, and have resented a lot of people while denying culpability. Watching the doctors perform this experiment on the vacant chief executive, it becomes clear that I have never even earned the right to be a failure because I have never tried. Then my stream of shame is dammed as the ghastly electronic voice begins blaring in an impolite monotone.

What do you think you're doing you have no right.

This aliased stream of audio pours from the receiver, pops and hisses between syllables, the words nevertheless horrifyingly coherent.

This is an invasion of privacy I do not authorize this. You are supposed to wait until I am revived this is a rotten betrayal. This is outside of your authority you sons of bitches you must stop this right away.

Garnder frowns, looking down. Then he looks up pointedly at the doctors, reasserting control. "Keep it going. We have to see what else he says."

Canadian Doctor glances at the Southern Doctor for reassurance, gets nothing in return, and looks back down at the device they both continue to press against Ruder's abdomen. I notice that Nestor is barely containing a grin. Meanwhile, Todd's mouth hangs open and his brow has creased in extremity. Ollie seems to have half of his hand lodged in his nose.

This is a grievous trespass. These thoughts are private. Though I realize this I am unable to prevent communicating them. I do not believe I have a soul. I have cheated on my wife seventy times. I have paid to have two men killed. I never passed the bar exam. I only want the presidency to quench my bottomless thirst for power. My ego is the only thing that matters to me. I have paid for five abortions. I had a homosexual affair in college which ended when he professed love for me and I threatened to kill Jeremy if he ever told anyone. I cannot remember my children's birthdays. I pretend to be afraid of clowns but I secretly wish I were a clown. I will never care about tax reform and I do not fully understand the policy that my financial team has prepared. I believe that most of the world is worthless and that the United States of America should not stop until it is the only remaining nation on Earth. I was elected as a moderate Independent but I have no idea what that means. My penis is four and half inches long when erect. I have not spoken the full truth in thirty years. It is very difficult for me to maintain an erection unless I think about my Aunt Vicki. When Vicki died every hope I ever had died with her. There is no afterlife and I will never be judged for my actions. No one should listen to this because it is none of your business and it is part of my subconscious. Invoking the idea of God is the best way to make people do your bidding as if it is their idea. I wept miserably after I first cheated on Rose and then I quickly compartmentalized my feelings and have not looked back even though it is surely causing cancer in my stomach. I refused to go to couples counseling once Rose saw through me and that was the final straw even though we have remained legally married. I have never donated blood. I have spent over twenty million dollars on bribes. My son Will is gay and I hate him because I cannot accept that part of me even though I have never told him directly and instead choose to regard him distantly which I am sure is more hurtful. This limbo is the closest I will come to Hell and if someone is hearing this it was Garnder who tried to have me taken out so it would look like an accident. I picked Garnder as my running mate because I owed him a favor it was he who had covered up—

"OK," Garnder yells, "enough. Turn that fucking thing off."

The doctors yank the QBBR231 from Ruder's abdomen and the final few words, *"the babysitter incident …"* morph into a static sound pattern that quickly fades to quiet.

Garnder nervously glances between Nestor, Todd, Ollie, and myself. A loaded moment of silence follows, and then the floorboards creak.

"Well," I say, breaking the silence and rubbing my eyes with my palms. "You're politicians. So what?"

Another silence follows, and this time I hear crickets. Then the only sound is the demonic wheezing from Thom Garnder, his face red like it has been stripped of skin. The resonant timbre from the guy's corroded septum reminds me of a horror movie monster limping through the black woods.

"A million apiece," Garnder says. "Any word about anything you've heard, or that this ever happened—that we've met or anything of that sort—and I think you can figure out how that would work."

"Five million," Nestor says.

Garnder twists his head, preparing to balk.

"Total, I mean. Our fifth couldn't make it."

"Nice," I say quietly, nodding at Nestor, so thankful that I'm not sober for this.

Coach's wheezing plays for another moment, and then he shakily inhales before responding.

"Five. Fine, whatever."

"Excuse me." Todd Crabs speaks with uncharacteristic caution. "Will there be, you know, taxes taken out of that?"

That night, which in a way feels like the last night before the end of the world, the four of us lean against the red log fence again, looking up at a clear, dark sky filled with holes poked into other, brighter, dimensions.

"It was always going to go one of two ways," Nestor posits, maybe just realizing it.

"We could have disappeared forever with no explanation," I say, finally free of the short-term effects of delta-9-tetrahydrocannabinol.

"*That was the other way.*" Nestor looks up just like the rest of us. It is evident that his words are italicized.

"They could still lie and not give us the money." Ollie speaks with an adorable earnestness, the same tone he had used to call out the molester priest.

"Because they let us live," Nestor says, "they are keeping their end of the bargain. And we signed the non-disclosure form. So we're bound, or we're dead."

"Don't you think they'll just come back and find us later and make it look like an accident or some bullshit?" Following his question, a series of small bursts come from Todd's lips. He seems to be trying to spit out a speck of something he's discovered in his mouth.

"That's always been a possibility." I spit in solidarity. "The constant threat of murder at the hands of an infinitely wealthy oligarchy is just part of the trade-off that comes with the privilege of not living in the Third World."

"You mean they could have killed us anytime?" Ollie asks.

"Yes," I say. "Of course. But don't let this newfound realization spoil the rest of it for you. And for the record, I get that the fifth million is for Rena, but since Rena and I are a couple, I think we should split it four ways so that no one is resentful and tries to kill me. Because otherwise, I'm much more likely to be murdered by one of you than by the government."

"Why would we kill you?" Ollie asks.

"Because getting money only makes people more greedy, Ollie." I long for an actual cigarette for some reason. "Haven't you ever seen a movie?"

"We have to get up at seven," Nestor says, totally changing the subject in a way I'm getting sick of. "We don't want to be late for that asshole's inauguration."

The nightmare goes like this:

Everything I ever failed to attempt shoots up, blowing past my face as physical debris. Artifacts—film cameras, basketballs, military fatigues, silver condenser microphones, gourmet meals, vast canvases covered in dried oil paint masterfully pulled into finely detailed depictions of important moments in history, babies cured of illness, syringes filled with heroin, those sorts of things—appear as specks and disappear in streaks above me. The inherent implication is that I am plummeting. Things aren't going up; I'm going down. Falling, rocketing downward, I remember—in the dream—that my name is Seth, and my mother is crazy, and I've been dealt a rough hand, and I've become a lot of things despite that, and my punishment for not meeting the impossibly short timeline I had set myself to succeed (whatever that means) is to erase everything I've ever been. It sounds melodramatic, I, as Seth, think within the dream—conceding a certain degree of overstatement to some presumed audience. It must come off as cartoon, exaggeration. But anyone who's ever told a story knows that to get anyone to listen, you need to embellish the major features. This is, again, admitted to some apparent consumers of the inner monologue, transmitted either psychically or by stranger medium, perhaps by the misappropriated application of an electronic device of such a dubious origin that the dubiousness itself should be considered a grotesquery. Fostering this pet theory—that anyone is listening to this story—only serves to delay the inevitable. The fact—in the dream, you know—is that I am falling to my death. There will be no real explanation, and not even a million and a quarter could save me. And the sparseness of this template might allow people like my friend Harland to papier-mâché some pity story of their own onto it, using my death as the dividing point in their life's history or something equally trite. All of this leads to a trilogy of questions: Does it reflect poorly upon me to imagine my legacy as something perversely Christlike, as if I willed to sacrifice my own spirit for the sinful rationalization of my apostles? Am I now more of a story than I ever was a person? More to the point—and this is the last thing *Seth The Dream Consciousness* seems to formulate: Are such theories so tired and recycled that criticizing them would seem masturbatory?

I wake up on April Fools' Day.

12 FOOLS

The breakfast buffet is OK, but the biscuits are dry and the coffee from the large silver canister is lukewarm. Gurl, who is already acting like she's engaged to Todd Crabs thirty-odd hours after their first meeting, is starting to get on my nerves. A pale blue fuzz seems to pull across the scene, muting the deep yellows and beige of the buffet room. My first day waking up as a supposed millionaire: it feels the same.

Todd kisses Gurl goodbye. She's not coming to the inauguration because she has to work. I note, only internally, that if Gurl ends up with Todd, neither of them will have to work. Not for a while, anyway.

This time we have to call a cab, because the limo service stopped when we were dropped off after the meeting yesterday by the limo driver whose stern eyes I could tell were memorizing every detail of my face so he can someday hunt me down and who looked more than offended and drove off empty-handed when I offered him a cash tip of ten USD. The cab drives us for a half hour across more or less the same stretch of white ash, and then we're deeper into the center of the recently fabricated mecca than we had been yesterday. Angular towers and spires climb toward a vertical vanishing point. Considering the complexity and density of the surrounding structures, it seems impossible that all of this has existed for fewer than two years. Regardless, I find my attention drawn to the tonal difference between the dry, ashen earth saturated by direct sunlight and the parallelogram shadows cast by these new buildings. Shades of gray be damned; everything here lies in stark contrast.

We're let out at some point near the outskirts of a cluster of oddly proportioned buildings. Ollie mans up for once—now that money is no object—and forks over eighty dollars. Despite the existence of the post-post-anything structures encroaching the horizon in any direction, I note that I cannot see any humans other than the ones with whom I have just arrived. Once again, *ghost town* is the phrase that comes to mind.

"Feels more like a meteor is going to strike than we're gettin' a new President," is how Todd Crabs chooses to phrase what we're all feeling.

Then a drone seeps into the minimalist soundscape, and a crowd appears in the distance from behind a pale cloud of ash that disperses into transparency. The general sense of horror that I carry with me morphs into a precise dread. I'm thinking like this friend of mine who killed himself when I think, *This is what I get for not taking the easy way.* The light changes, and a shadow covers my toes. The way all of this is unfolding, the reaching of some revelation, suddenly seems unnecessarily tedious and overwrought. The details—the devil, whatever—seem more and more like padding to delay the release of whatever grand moment must be forthcoming.

Stubborn as anyone, I choose to focus on the minutia, maybe for a minute. The group huddles before a black iron gate delimiting the property of some official-looking building. It becomes clear that this is the new Capitol or equivalent. The crowd seems to be equal parts supporters and protesters, not split into two camps like checkers at the beginning of the game, but well integrated like checkers in the middle of a game. I see what I take to be a pro-Ruder sign reading, "Awaken." Then I see, right next to it, what I guess is an anti-Ruder sign reading, "President?! More Like The Executive Tater-Tard."

We get four gouge-priced Cankers from a nearby snack booth. I pay for the round of soft drinks with the last of my cash. I'm forced to remember an image of the fair where Ollie had jumped on the moonwalk. We're back at a fair, and its purpose seems nebulous. Drinking, slurping around the ice, I squint to make out a somber parade in progress beyond the gate. A stream of uniformed individuals flow into the pavement patio beyond the black iron gate. Now there are two uncountable masses of people, one on either side of the gate. The situation feels at its maximum capacity.

The black gates slowly open outward, creaking. Well beyond the gates, a gigantic pulley system hoists an enormous American flag vertically. When the flag has fully lifted and unfurled, it hangs from four stories high, its white and red stripes fluttering knee-high off the ground. My first impulse is to dismiss the flag as a mere symbol, but then the enormity of the thing reminds me of the importance of symbolism. Then I notice a black star in the middle of the starfield on the flag. The black star is the same size and shape as the white stars, and it's sort of subtle against the dark blue background. I am forced to assume that it's a tribute to the old DC, but I don't remember hearing any announcement about this change, and the fact that it seems to just exist without any apparent grumbling from the masses leads me to believe that this is indeed a parallel universe branched from a time before 7/11. In some neighbor dimension, there must be a regular flag, regular-sized, waving above the old White House.

"They're going to keep it in him," Nestor suddenly says. "They'll keep it in, but it will never be public."

I nod.

"Now they'll use it against him if he wakes up, and he'll protest that it's a breach of his privacy, but it won't matter, because they'll leverage his own thoughts against him. Garnder is the President now. Even if Ruder wakes up, Garnder is going to be running things."

"It doesn't matter," I say. "They're all the same. We're all the same. We've all got dirt. It's just a matter of whose gets dug up first."

The sound of distant snare drums echoes, a sharp and simple rhythm. The pattern becomes more complex, building to a crazy fill that then bursts into a full marching band rendition of a song I remember hearing years ago. A tom section plays a repeating syncopation. Tubas and baritones follow suit, matching the rhythmic pattern, establishing a bass line. Trumpets wail like dying animals. Clarinets and flutes create a pad not unlike the harmonies from the QBBR231. Trombones start spurting out sforzando offbeats like shrapnel. Piccolos riff on a single pitch, alternating with indeterminate frequency between full notes and aborted, staccato ones in a sequence that probably spells something in Morse code. Saxophones drone and squeal over the top. It's some song from around the turn of the millennium. It's familiar, and I'm waiting for the entrance of a vocal line that's not coming.

"Everyone," Ollie talks over the echoey racket, "everyone around here is going to see the beginning of something."

"Or the end," says Todd Crabs.

And of course it's both, I don't bother saying, figuring it's too trite.

The parade shuffles to a rest, the blaring brass and drums retreating into a subdued variation on the song. A swarm of red and blue balloons appears from the periphery of the gathering, the rubber bulbs rising and wiggling into the pale blue-gray sky. This release seems premature. The marching band's yellow horn bells glimmer between round white caps and dark blue plumage. The song stutters into a jarring coda and then, following a quick double-beat, ceases abruptly. Reverberated iterations of the doublet become infinitesimally quiet. The applause fades to a murmur. High warbling frequencies signal the activation of a microphone. Distantly, perched atop a platform near the rear of the crowd beyond the gate, Thom Garnder, wearing a black suit and purple tie, stands next to the space-age life-support bed containing what must be the recumbent John Ruder. A few feet from them, a small man with bright red hair, also wearing a black suit and purple tie, holds a silver microphone stand. The amplified sound of the little guy clearing his throat echoes awkwardly and then he begins to speak.

"Ladies and gentlemen—"

The explosion occurs beyond the gate, a deep boom paired with a white flash. The flash morphs into a black cloud, seething orange spilling through. Those within the blast radius scream and either fall to the ground or are disintegrated. The center of the flash is far enough from the new President(s) that I think, *Oh, it was botched.*

I get the uneasy feeling that someone is watching me.

The next explosion occurs within seconds, and this second one is what really sets off the madness. This one occurs just outside the gate, much closer, and the sound is more of a crack than a boom, sharper. The explosion is bright and piercing, close enough that I feel heat.

The fingers gripping my arm hurt me, but the pain is enough to shake me from an inability to react. I follow the fingers to the veiny hand, pale arm, and freaked-out expression of Todd Crabs.

"Come on," he yells, turning, to lead me.

Nestor and Ollie are already running, and then I'm following them, Todd to my left. A third burst occurs behind me, then a fourth. I feel tiny hairs on my ears being singed, as if I were sunburned instantly, instead of over the course of a drunken afternoon. The number of bursts becomes uncountable. Then we seem to be running from giant popcorn. I feel holes burning into my coat. Tears from the wailing heads of my friends pour into my face. My legs seem to be on fire, but only because this is the hardest I have run as an adult.

"USA!" someone androgynous screams, far to my right. While running, I turn my head just enough to see the person using his or her thumb to press a button on a handheld device. He explodes into light, and in my shaky periphery I see others spattered in blood and black from being scorched.

Further behind me and to my left, a woman yells, "Freedom Infinity!" She goes up in a fireball, taking three or four neighbors with her.

Oddly, it seems that the marching band has resumed playing. Or, it occurs to me in a horrifying moment, it may be that the marching band is instead being blown up in a way that sounds vaguely musical. Whatever the case, I continue to bolt away, toward the big shadow of a building with the unlikely shape of—and it takes me a moment of de-archiving rarely used nomenclature to conjure the term—a *gallows*. I continue checking both sides ahead of me to make sure that all of my friends are accounted for. I hear someone scream what sounds like, "You terror dot org," which is followed by the heat and deafening white noise of an explosion. We're all blown to one side, stumbling into one another. I see Ollie fall to the ground, but Nestor and I each instinctively grab his upper arms and hoist him back upright. The explosions continue around us as we scramble, and then a croaking voice calls out.

"Harland!"

My friends don't seem to hear the distant cry. They continue scrambling forward, and I'm veering at an angle toward what I am convinced is the source of the name called, a figure in shadow beneath the supports holding up the gallows building. The pudgy silhouette stands framed perfectly between the elevated platform floor of the gallows and the black shadow cast directly beneath it. Beyond these shapes the white of the ash desert seems to glow. As I run, my body feeling twice its age, the human figure remains monochrome, without definition, offset severely by the white background. I curse myself for not having gotten high for this. Soon, I am under the large structure, the explosions behind me seeming to taper off in both intensity and frequency. As I run, my eyes adjust beneath the structure, and the human form finally begins to gain features. I see the familiar stumpy legs; the plump, elongated torso. A forgotten fear emerges and blooms. The sad eyes, the poor posture, the hairline thinned to irrelevance. The summation of twice my mistakes looms there, and I skid to a halt, my skin virtually detaching from the muscles and threatening to sublimate. The sounds from whatever diversion was going on beyond this rectangle of shadow mute almost entirely, leaving an ambiance that sounds underwater. Time stops working properly again. A scary sound breaks the relative silence, and then I realize that I have whimpered. The sound is drawn long, lasting beyond when I feel I have emitted it. I blink and it seems to take a long time for the heavy lids to reopen.

The understanding that Future Me is standing before me is soon revealed to be a joke. But in the instant before I realize the bait-and-switch, I worry that my future self is going to do nothing but blame me for everything he's become. Future Me will see in me every shred of capability that I have yet to—but will—squander. He will look at me, unable to change anything due to the otherwise stable time-space continuum, and just shake his head. As soon as my resentment for this anticipated scenario reaches an unhealthy crescendo, the realization hits. My throat thickens, and my blood becomes solid. I realize that the situation is reversed. For what seems like a long moment, some horrible mental block stops me from saying what I need to say. Some truly defensive apathy then kicks in, and my voice cracks like I'm a teenager when I speak.

"Dad?"

When my mother died, I played happy. I told anyone who would ask that I was glad that she was gone, good riddance. I found it so easy to convince myself that my bitterness (at what, exactly?) was justifiable to the point of defaming the woman who had given birth to me and done her best. I talked smack. I postured. This mother of mine, the human being I had once called a "cunt" to her face, in a fit of selfish anger, as she lay there wasting away. One might wager that such actions would eventually be deeply regretted. And at some point I would realize I had gained a perspective. And I would realize that the impetus for this rage was probably mostly self-made and not really worth fussing about. Yet my caprice has haunted me as well as any real ghost.

Just as I cannot point to any specific injustice that would have formed a reasonable basis for my behavior, my dad never offered a clear defense for his choice to pursue a fruitless series of whims even at the sacrifice of his family's best interests. But what if the dream my father pursued (pursues?) was more beautiful than anything I've ever known? Would that have swayed me?

My father looks thinner than I remember him. There's still a paunch, but no excessive gut. His eyes glisten, and he's already on the verge of tears.

"Harland?" he says.

I whimper again. I feel like a pussy.

"Harland," he says. "I'm so glad to see you." He chokes, and he's rubbing his hands together in an unconscious nervous gesture. He's starting to sob. "I'm so sorry."

I watch my father break down in tears, and I'm following suit and hating myself, my cheeks and ears flushing with blood. I don't want to be like this. I keep struggling to be something that I'm not. Even now I can't let myself just feel something. I find myself trying to recall movies that contain moments like this. Then I remember that this is happening. To me. Right now. It's for real. I gulp, gasping, and I finally locate my ability to speak again.

"Dad, what the hell ..." I'm sure I grimace at him. "... the hell happened to you?"

"I'm sorry, son," he says.

Another echo from a bomb absently wavers through the space.

"This isn't a good time to talk," my father points out.

"I know," I say. "Let's talk anyway."

He looks sideways, then directly at me. "I only wanted the best for you and your mother," he says. His voice wavers so much that it sickens me.

"I've heard that somewhere before," I say, shivering, my vision blurred. My words seem recycled and predictable. I have to force myself not to deconstruct this ironically, as if it were a joke and not my life.

"I know," he says.

Echoes of things happening far away give the impression that they are outside a fishbowl, beyond the sphere containing all that can affect me. This, combined with the ongoing state of molasses-time, means that my perception is both well out of whack and providing an opportunity to attempt meaningful communication.

"The bottom line," Dad says. Then something clicks and I realize that what Dad has said is, "The Bottom Line," capitalized, a proper noun.

"What did you do?"

"They had a business opportunity. They ... gave a lot of people like me a chance."

"What do you mean people like you? Scammers? Deadbeats?"

"I paid my bills," Dad says. His expression is steady, not defensive. "I paid my bills."

"Maybe," I say. "So anyway ..."

"Anyway, I worked for them. They gave me room and board. They had an amazing pitch. I believed that they really would make a difference in people's lives. I helped to organize events—they called it *guerrilla* or *viral* or *reality*. Advertisements, you know. I made a lot of good friends, and I felt like I was really doing something. We were raising a lot of money, and we were each going to share in the profits. It was only later that I found out that we funded the USA. And I didn't know until much later what the USA really was. How could I have known that the deaths we kept hearing about were the advertisements? *Guerrilla* or *viral* or *reality*?"

"You planned other people's suicide bombings?"

"I didn't know what I was planning. I just knew that I had to arrange for one of our boxes to be sent to a certain drop point."

"Boxes," I say. "I'm no longer sniffling.

"The recorders," he says. "The Bottom Line had them produced."

"TBL," I say, a bell ringing.

His head falls. When it rises, his eyes are soaked and red.

"I never knew how to be a success," he says.

"You weren't the first," I say. "Or the last."

He looks up, away from me. He sucks air in through gritted teeth, and I see the veins in his neck. This is my dad when he's not selling. He's a broken thing. He exhales and shrinks, his chin sinking back into his chest.

"I'm so sor—sorry," he blubbers.

"Dad," I say, croaking again, following suit again, my eye sockets flooding almost instantly. "Why didn't you … I never heard from you."

"Y-yes," he stutters. "You did."

Now I'm looking up, some look of agony surely painted across my chubby face as I realize what he means.

"How did you know about Ruder?"

His face goes straight again. He lifts his head.

"What, The Bottom Line fixed the election too?"

His head lowers again.

"What the fuck have you done?"

"I had to prove to you … even if it was too late to prove to your mother …"

"Prove what?"

"OK, Frank," says a congested-sounding voice from nearby. "You've had your time."

When the tall person steps out from behind the nearby structural beam, my anus opens and by some miracle a load of shit does not explode into my pants. Thin—gaunt, really, like vegan-gaunt—and dark-haired, he wears a dark purple sweater-vest over a bleached white dress shirt. Dark black bangs hang in front of his eyes, and a contemptuous bile finds its way into my esophagus. I have to burp before I am able to speak again:

"Julius fucking Zorro?" I scoff.

"What's up, Harland?" He sounds like someone is pinching his nose. I already want to punch him.

"I hated you from the minute you emailed me," I say, cringing as I recall having once heard this line in a soap opera.

"Maybe," he says. "But you had no idea who I was. You're just a dick."

"So what the fuck?" I ask.

"Julie died on Valentine's Day," he says.

"I heard."

"From whom?" Julius Zorro asks. "Terry? That vulture?"

"I get the sense that you're the one waiting for people to die."

"Not waiting," he says. "Not anymore."

Another muddy-sounding explosion occurs from a long way off.

"So what?" I ask. "You, what? Found out that my dad worked for the company that funded the terrorist organization that brainwashed your girlfriend?"

Julius Zorro's face is a blank sheet of paper. I think I see a small red light blink through his purple vest.

"Please, Julius, please don't do this." This comes from my father, who shakes as if from hypothermia.

"Dad," I say, "let's get out of here. Forget this asshole."

"No," says Julius, revealing the device in his hand. His thumb hovers over a black button. The red light flashes again, and I notice the bulk beneath the purple sweater-vest. "The problem is that forgetting isn't an option. I certainly can't."

I realize that I can't drag out the conversation, but a certain horrible logic seems to fall into place. I picture Julius coaching my father, instructing him on how to lure me here, under the threat that people would die— maybe that I would die—if he didn't. I see Julius tracking me, noting what I'm up to, who I'm meeting. This is the only way *Future Me* could have known about what I was doing, that I met Nestor, that I got engaged. I strain my memory to recreate pictures of Skizzers filled with drunks, just to see if Julius Zorro may be lingering in the periphery, taking notes, biding time. And even though I can't substantiate it, I picture Julius pulling the trigger on a paintball gun. Understanding that I have been a patsy in a conspiracy makes me feel a little better about myself, like it's an anachronistic excuse for my behavior.

"Julius," I say, my voice steady now, no longer cracking, "he didn't know what he was doing. He was looking for a quick buck, or glory, or whatever. But he was convinced that he was doing the right thing. Right, Dad? You didn't know that people were getting hurt. Right?"

Dad, tears wet on his cheeks, "Not for a long time."

I wonder for a moment if we're having two different conversations.

"Well," I sigh, "are you going to kill us or what?"

"He's going to kill me," my father says, his voice also no longer wavering. "He wanted you to see it. He promised not to hurt you or Rena if it happened this way."

"No," says Julius, his dark eyes seeming dead. "I changed my mind."

"No!" barks my father, stern in a way I haven't heard him since I was a child. "I agreed to that. You cannot change the arrangement. We had a business understanding. I shook your hand. This cannot be a scam. You cannot do this."

"No." Julius Zorro stares through me.

I stare back, glancing over at my father. He and Julius form the short side of an isosceles triangle, with me at the point. The vast black structure of the gallows hovers over us. I wait for the whistle of a western movie soundtrack, but I can't hear anything besides the reverberations of distant destruction.

"I never got to hear her box," Julius says.

There's no response to this.

"I got a fax the day before it happened. It said, 'Please forgive me. Listen to the box and you'll understand.' The police said they didn't have a box. I didn't know what she meant. Then it leaked that they had those things. Their electronic suicide notes."

I think of my friend Seth, the missing explanation of his death, the sickening wealth of resulting speculation.

"What explanation could have helped?" I ask this having moved past fear into a strange calm. Logic is now the only comfort.

Julius Zorro dead-eyes me again.

"Harland," my dad says, not forcing a smile but actually allowing it, "I love you, and your mother loved you, and we both always knew you loved us. I'm sorry it happened this way."

As I strain to interpret Dad's side of the conversation, Julius Zorro lunges in my direction. My father is just as quickly at Zorro's ankles, pulling him to the ground. An odd clash of instincts forces me forward, toward my dad and the psychopath he has tackled. I register the sudden rush of heat before I can interpret the deafening sound. Then the only safe assumption is that I have just been killed.

13 BATHOS

Wiping the bar with a bleach-soaked rag, both my hands covered by lemon-yellow rubber gloves, I gaze out through the wall of windows into a street scene capped by an orange summer dusk. The aroma of deep-fried onion rings hangs in the air. There's a light crowd, an average Tuesday. The jukebox is turned down pretty low—that's one of the rules when I'm managing—and I can make out the guitar riff from the new hit song, "Everything That Got Me Here Is Stupid." I've actually sort of learned this riff, even though I haven't really built up callouses, even though building up callouses isn't something I need to worry about anymore.

Near a far wall, under a framed painting depicting friendly-looking raccoons and antelope, Nestor and Ollie sit opposite one another, a large clear bubble enclosing a dozen little hockey players between them. Ollie twists blue handles, and Nestor twists red ones. A puck the size of one of the little guys' heads shoots across the white plastic ice. Nestor's head drops, and Ollie shouts something and raises his fists joyously. The red digits are too far away for me to read, but I assume they have just changed.

Some big guy takes the stool down at the end of the bar. He's got shaggy salt-and-pepper hair and a few days of white beard growth. Slumped over, he glances my way and makes a quick, rude beckoning gesture. The guy looks like trash, stuffed into a sweat-stained business shirt that probably hasn't left this guy's frame in a week. Not willing to jump for this guy's whim, I make sure the labels of all of my liquor bottles are facing front. I carefully stack some tumblers on a foam pad. I slice up a lime and cover the wedges with plastic wrap. Then I wander down, and I realize where I've seen him before.

"Whiskey," he says.

"Paul," I say.

He looks up at me, not recognizing.

"Paul Jabber, right?"

"Who's asking?"

"I used to work over there—under Roy."

He sighs longer than I have ever heard anyone sigh. I wish I had timed it.

"You still there, slavin' away?" I wink.

He takes a rather deliberate pause, and then says, shortly, "No."

"Oh, really?" I say this as if it's conversational. Inside, I am insanely giddy.

"Whiskey," he repeats, trying to control the conversation.

"I heard you," I say, smiling. "Just one question: Who did you think you were?"

His disheveled, pasty face wrinkles.

"What I mean, is, did you really think that you were better than other people, and that you could just use and abuse them without consequence?"

He really looks at me for the first time. His head tilts, and his grimace intensifies. "I remember you. You were that lazy prick who never showed up on time."

"Victimless crime," I say. "I guess that's the difference between us."

"Get me a whiskey," he says. "And don't spit in it. I'm eyeing you."

"Don't worry about that," I smile. "This just made my day. First one's on me. But then it's cash only. I have a hunch that your credit is no good."

I turn to grab a bottle, and I'm sure that he mutters something. I can't stifle a laugh, and I almost spill the shotglass as I turn back around.

"Enjoy, you old fuck," I say.

"What did you call me?" he says.

"Sorry," I say. "It's just—you're sitting in his stool."

While he tries to figure out what I just said, I'm walking away, humming, picking up a few singles that someone has left.

A bell jangles, and Gurl walks in, smiling and waving. Todd Crabs, who has held the door open for her, follows.

"What's up, Plumps?"

"Hi, Harlan'," says Gurl.

"Hey kids," I say. "How you doin'?"

"Be better if the motherfuckers who promised us five mill' didn't get their asses blowed up before they could mail the checks. But I can't complain." He snorts, smiles and pulls Gurl close to him, kissing her temple.

"Good to see you, Gurl," I say. "How do you like Middle America?"

"It's real flat," she says.

"Least you ain't," Todd says. Gurl smirks and playfully smacks his arm.

"You guys want anything?"

"Whatchoo drinkin', Brub?"

"Water," I say. "And lots of it."

"Pretty weird that you took this job after you quit guzzlin'," Todd says.

"I suppose," I say. Not knowing what to add, I ask, "Margaritas?"

"Only if you make 'em, Chooch."

They wander over to join Nestor and Ollie at the table next to the hockey game. I watch the four of them and begin to wonder if they'll realize the characters in the movie I'm writing are based on them (if they were aliens who blended in with humans as part of an ongoing galactic search for brutal honesty).

"Kyle," I say, "keep an eye on things. I gotta hit the john."

Kyle, the young punk with dark bangs and pale skin, looking too much like Julius Zorro—about which I have totally justified mixed feelings—says, "OK."

As I finish pissing, zipping up absently, I look to my right at the list of nonsense. The last three entries are:

- *Sorry bout the mess —OF*

- *when I say I want to put junk in the trunk she asks KY?*

- *you x 2 = my dick*

Something comes to mind, and I pull the Sharpie from my apron.

- *Nothing happens all the time.*

I look at it and don't like it. I scribble it out completely, a complete OCD scribble that turns into a proper black censorship rectangle. Below the rectangle, I scribble:

    • *That thing you don't like to think about is still happening.*

I push the urinal lever with the heel of my palm, and I instinctively go to the sink to wash my hands, looking up through the smudges on the mirror at a face that doesn't look quite as old as I remembered. But I don't wash my hands; I wash the yellow rubber gloves I'm wearing.

I step into the dark hallway leading back into the bar. It becomes a long moment. I think about my father, how he died like so many questionably innocent people at the bottom of a gallows. I think about my mother, a virtual mummy when she finally let go of life in a non-cinematic exit. I think about my late friend Seth, the ghost teenager, his decidedly flamboyant daredevil act and the mess it must have made, which someone else had to clean up. I think about the country (if we can even call it that anymore), once again running headless into uncertainty. Today is 7/11, the two-year anniversary of when my dad died the first time, presumed taken out along with the old government. Now, three-odd months since they were actually claimed, only my perception has changed. For a long time, I have felt a responsibility to internalize these kinds of things, to make sense of them. At times, I struggle with the feeling that it's inappropriate to invest so heavily in things that didn't happen directly to me. But sometimes the fallout seems to cascade into my path, meandering as it is, whether I like it or not. So, I surmise, deal with it or be dealt with.

On a shelf over my TV at home are two objects which seem more and more like God and The Devil.

I bring my hands up to rub my temples. The rubber against my forehead feels itchy.

On April Fools' Day, Ollie had shaken me awake and I looked up at a hazy *Wizard of Oz* tableaux of three friends hovered around me. The only sound now was a distant mass wailing. The explosions had ceased. Lying on gravel in the shade beneath the gallows structure, a collection of withered sausages seemed to be hovering at the forefront of my field of vision.

"Are you OK?" Ollie asked, real tears on his face.

"Relative to what?" I croaked.

"Your fuckin' hands are wasted," Todd Crabs had helpfully added.

I squinted to focus my vision. I groaned when I saw what he meant.

"They probably saved your life," Nestor said, spinning a silver lining.

All the digits were there, I could see, but they looked like smoky links that had been microwaved to oblivion. At the time, I couldn't really feel anything.

"Who were they?" Ollie asked, gesturing with his chin over his shoulder.

It took me a moment to realize what he meant. I swallowed, tasting dust.

"My dad and some dick I worked with," I said, coughing.

After a moment, Nestor said, "We should get you to an ambulance, if there are any left."

I shrugged.

"So," Nestor glanced at the other two before looking back down at me, "I'm going to get them, just in case."

I remember sounding cranky. "Get what?"

Two black boxes sit on the shelf over my television at home. One from Julius Zorro, and one from Frank Grant, my dad. They sit there, clean, shiny. They get dusted as much as anything else at the house. They might have something recorded, ramblings of madmen, secrets of the universe, or somewhere in between.

Nestor had gathered them from the bloody pulp that remained, those crude, indestructible tokens. He had stowed them in the duffel. We had ended up finding an ambulance, which had returned from the nearest hospital for its third pickup of the day.

I remember Todd saying something like, "Good thing we were late to the ceremony or we woulda been right in the shit when it all started goin' to fuck."

I don't remember exactly what Todd said because my focus had been on the swaying duffel hanging from Black Me's shoulder.

Now the boxes are just clutter at the house. They sit on the shelf. And even if the QBBR231 hadn't been blown up along with Ruder, Garnder, and the others, even if Courtney the witch from the pawnshop had denied ever having handled the first one, let alone having another when Nestor had gone back a few weeks after April Fools'; even if a receiver was delivered to my doorstep and a gun was placed to my temple, I would never listen to the contents of either box.

Zorro was a selfish manipulator, and no rambling justification could redeem him. I've even had to apologize to Terry that I refuse to listen to the Culture Vulturz album.

I realize that I received something that few people probably get: My father gave me the thesis of what he needed to say to me. Maybe there are details that would be interesting. And maybe the true allure of his dreams would be revealed. Maybe the years of possibly misunderstood pursuits would be explicated, painting a redemptive portrait. The possibilities are pointless. I don't want playback from a box. I don't want anything to corrupt what I got from the man.

When Rena enters the bar, she's laughing, her cell phone held to one ear. Her cheeks are flushed from the heat of an evening which has yet to cool.

"How could they confuse Brad with 'Bard'? Did they really think he was Shakespeare?"

I hear the garbled laughter from Janet through the phone from across the bar, and I'm surprised Rena doesn't grasp her ear in pain.

"Later, lady," Rena says, giggling, thumbing the touchscreen to end the call. She waves in the general direction of our friends at the far table.

"Hi," I say.

"Hi," she says, taking a seat at the opposite end of the bar from Jabber.

"Wanna go upstairs?"

"Sure."

"Kyle," I snap, realizing I snapped and quickly trying to shift to a casual tone. "Hey, man, uh, would you mind watching things again for a bit?"

Kyle rolls his eyes, the little punk.

I open the "Staff Only" closet door with my skeleton key. We climb a steep, musty staircase, pivot once, climb a few more steps, and then I open a hatch in the ceiling.

We climb onto the roof, gravel over tar, and step gingerly toward the two lawn chairs facing west. Rena sits. I sit to her right. Between us is a white Styrofoam cooler with a worn hardcover book weighing it down. The book is called *Monolith*.

A breeze blows, rippling my polo shirt and Rena's blouse. The lingering light from the horizon makes Rena's face glow in soft orange, contrasting the dark blues and grays of the rooftops and sky behind her. I pull her glasses from her face and kiss her on the cheek. I replace her glasses, and she looks at me skeptically before chuckling.

"Did you ever even consider quitting your jobs after we both agreed to quit our jobs?"

"Harland, I love you. But I'll stand by my decision to renege."

I look out at the remnants of the sun.

"Someone's got to hedge your bets. For a while, anyway."

"I know," I say. I look over at her. She looks at me. We make eye contact, and we hold it for a moment.

A dog barks. A car horn honks. Somewhere further, a train chugs, blowing steam. A flock of bird silhouettes glides by.

I lean down to my left and lift the book from the cooler. I remove the Styrofoam lid and reach in to grab the kangaroo dick.

When Rena sees it, she says, "Do you really think that's a good idea?"

"Rena," I say, "I'm an alcoholic, not a robot."

Her skeptical expression returns, but after a moment of me not flinching, she relents. I light it for her, cupping around it to block the wind. She takes the first hit, and then I bring it to my mouth, puffing the bowl while the weed is still glowing. I don't inhale too deeply, or too long, and I let it go, rationalizing but feeling better and better.

I swear I hear an owl. "You hear that owl?" I ask.

Rena nods condescendingly, and I laugh.

"What would a million dollars have done?" I say, forming and explaining a theory in real time. "Given us the illusion of success for a few years?"

"It would be nice not to have to work with that goddamn hormone factory Danielle, or to stink like Egg Foo Yung for half my life."

"Yeah," I say, "but don't you think it keeps us humble?"

"Is that something you really worry about?"

"Touché," I say. The light on the horizon seems to twinkle like a candle hanging on against the odds.

I carefully pull the fingertips of the left glove until it slides off, revealing a mass of scar tissue. I reach and take her right hand with my withered left hand. Despite its appearance, most of the sensation has returned. I feel a lump in my throat.

"Should we go back downstairs?"

"I never apologized," I say.

"For what?" I can't tell if she really does not remember, or if she's baiting me. It doesn't matter.

"You are more than I deserve," I say. "I love you."

"I love you, too," she says. "Are you apologizing for something?"

"Give me a minute," I say. I squeeze her hand.

"OK," she says. I glance over and see her sort of smiling, waiting patiently.

The breeze comes again, cooler than before. Rena's hand feels comparatively warmer.

Looking into the slit of the horizon, I say, "I forgot to focus on what was real."

"What do you mean?"

"My dad was always looking forward to the next Big Bang. My mom was so bitter about the past. I don't want to get so caught up with what has happened, or what might happen, that I'm forsaking now."

In my periphery, Rena nods.

"But, you know, life gets in the way, or that's how it seems. Like—and I totally realize this sounds like a high person talking now—but, like it's as if life is the distraction from what really matters. But that's not life. Life is not the distraction. Distractions are distractions. Life is the ..."

"I know what you mean," she says.

"Yeah," I say. "I just mean, I want to focus on life, on now, on the most important thing, the thing that means everything to me, that makes me want to be better and get up and go to work and do all the shit I have to do so I can keep enjoying that most important thing."

I look over at Rena, knowing it's going to seem corny, and not caring.

"You."

ACKNOWLEDGMENT

Thanks to my early readers, proofreaders, my editor, and those who would listen, especially Carrie.

ABOUT THE AUTHOR

Ryan Parmenter is:

- The author of the novel "Hyperbole" and the older but yet-unpublished "Hole Filler."
- One-third of the musical trio JRS.
- The singer/keyboardist of the defunct band Eyestrings.
- A solo musician who has produced several alt-rock albums and indie movie scores.
- Creator of YouTube hijinks under the username Zuccer.
- A comic improviser who wrote and starred in the one-man stage show "Jerks" and co-created the characters "Shim & D'rothy."
- A huge fan of lists.

He lives in Michigan with his wife Carrie and their pets: Izzy, Chester, Pickles, and Bonkers.

"Hyperbole" was written between May 2010 and September 2012.

www.ingramcontent.com/pod-product-compliance
Lightning Source LLC
Chambersburg PA
CBHW071824020726
47502CB00004B/1232